AFGHANI

BRENDON PATRICK

BULLDOG PUBLISHING

Printed in Australia

Published by Bulldog Publishing

Cover and internal design by Coven Press

www.covenpress.com.au

First printing: August 2025

Paperback ISBN 978-1-7637-9213-5

Hardback ISBN 978-1-7637-9212-8

eBook ISBN 978-1-7637-9214-2

www.alifeofprose.com.au

A catalogue record for this work is available from the National Library of Australia

Distributed by Lightning Source Global and Kindle Direct Publishing

I want to be there when everyone suddenly
understands what it has all been for.

—*Fyodor Dostoyevsky*

CHAPTERS

Introduction

Afghanistan still looms large as Australia's longest ever running war. The very cost of the war plagues many, not least the Afghan population. Yet in 2001, the then Prime Minister John Howard wasted no time invoking the ANZUS Treaty and sent us off to battle.

It was the treaty's first use in its fifty-year history and Howard's decision faced only meagre opposition in the upper echelons of government. Australian citizens—for the greater part—remained unfazed. Then, before the nation could read the fine print, we were marched headlong into a country we knew little about.

Operation Slipper had begun in earnest, and the Australian Special Forces introduced the Taliban to the full spectrum of their capabilities—proving pivotal as the oppressive stranglehold crumpled. The beer flowed and pats on the back were abundant.

Many will say the war could have ended there—

But Operation Slipper soon snowballed into war with no clear goalpost and no end in sight and, over the next two decades, with conflicts stretching beyond Afghan borders, into Iraq, we had become entrenched in warfare. Australia committed to 41 rotations involving 26000 soldiers. 41 soldiers were KIA.

By 2005, with the war in full swing, the Australian Regular Army turned its operational focus to reconstruction efforts. A Mentoring Task Force (MTF) was—with pure intentions—created, and Australian soldiers soon began working alongside Afghan forces.

The goal was to build the Afghan National Army's fighting capabilities. Meanwhile, reconstruction teams made an attempt at developing the country's more remote regions. Despite the many successes in these missions, any strategic goals remained elusive.

Many soldiers returned home feeling the long-lasting effects of combat. Afghan civilians—through their own discontent—ignored these reconstruction efforts, too. Schools went unattended. The mosques remained empty, and the reconstruction efforts amounted to little, but long after Bin Laden's dismissal, the works continued.

It's a bloody and somber tale of war. Yet, Australia's relationship with Afghanistan does not begin here. It begins more than a century earlier.

In writing 'Afghani', I explore this relationship with the Afghans via the legacies of war. I also pay due attention to the influence the early Afghani Cameleers had in Australia. To achieve this, I ventured down two parallel narratives. The contemporary, and the historical.

The contemporary storyline follows Patterson. He is a naïve soldier who transforms—via the war—from an idealistic recruit into a broken veteran.

In the realms of soldier's careers, particularly in times of war, it's not an unfamiliar story. But it's through the moral ambiguities of war, and Patterson's lived experience that war's true purpose is postulated.

The historical narrative traces George Sher Gul, an Afghani Cameleer. Like many of his countrymen, he's seeking new horizons in the 19th century, outback Australia. But it is here where George meets with fierce opposition. His presence in the country is unwelcome. Yet, he still delivers insight into the cultural challenges seen in the present day.

Each protagonist grapples with questions abounding in purpose and belonging. Navigating through environments hostile to their presence also poses many challenges. Ultimately, their parallel journeys illuminate Australia's engagement with Afghanistan.

'Afghani' is more than a modern-day military tale. It seeks to highlight complex intersections in history. How culture, identity and war continue to shape national stories. And more to a point, how global conflicts arise.

This story offers no simple answers. I have no solutions to war; nor do I offer an alternative. Instead, I seek to examine man's resilience in the most austere conditions. And finally, I dare to ask what 'war' is about.

For Queen and Country

They always caught us young—

It was the end of the century. The birth of a new millennium. A dawning of a new era. The year I'd finally become a man—

What a trip.

I grabbed my textbooks and was headed in for the last day of school when my friend Tony grabbed me by the arm and told me his brother had recently enlisted.

Hey, Patterson, he said. It ain't nothing like those old days, you know. Nuh-ah, it's all sunshine and rainbows now.

I was suspicious. After all, I'd never heard such a preposterous thing.

They'd never let me join.

Tell me more, I said.

Good pay, he said. Better than pushing shopping trolleys or digging holes for the council. The chicks love the uniform. Plus, you get paid to travel the world.

Tony! TELL ME MORE!

Tony stood motionless, then smiled through the corner of his left eye. It was crooked and lazy but incapable of telling a lie.

The best thing? he said. They'll let almost anybody join.

Well, the hooks were in. I packed a brown suitcase and shut the lid. Its buckles were rusted and broke, so I tried strapping it shut with silver duct tape. That did the trick, and before you knew it, I was standing inside Defence Force Recruiting. A portrait of the Queen hung, dead level on the wall, with Old Lizzy's face shining down through a thin glass pane. The picture frame was painted gold, and the vibe in the room was rigid and formal. I began to sweat.

Had I made a poor choice? I couldn't be sure, but as I looked back through the exit door all I could imagine was abandoned shopping trolleys. Fuck that, I said, then tucked in my shirt and walked to the reception desk.

A female Officer in a khaki uniform smiled at me tightly, then handed me a Bible.

Hold it in your left hand, she said.

I did, then looked down at her chest. The buttons on her uniform top stretched tight. I smiled and waited for the top to burst wide open. They didn't. Still, I continued smiling at her chest.

She crossed her arms. How old are you?

Seventeen.

Seventeen, Ma'am! Where's your father?

Beats me, Ma'am.

Mother?

Haven't seen her in years, Ma'am.

And your shoes… do you own a cleaner pair of shoes, or pants that aren't ripped?

I looked down at my shoes.

No, Ma'am, this is all I own.

Filthy, she said, then continued handing out Bibles to the other recruits.

I peeked through the ranks. We were all kids, but I was the youngest—if you wanted to know. Standing among those would-be soldiers wearing tight-pressed suits. All puffing their chests out like cocky red sparrows. All except me, of course, looking like a dog's breakfast in my torn pants and tired old shoes.

Hold the Bible high with your left hand, said the Officer as she walked to the centre of the room. I looked above her head, to where Her Majesty's portrait hung on the wall.

You are now going to pledge your Oath and Allegiance to Queen and Country. Repeat after me…

Sweat split my butt-cheeks, and trickled down the backs of my legs and the book became so heavy I had to close my eyes.

SO HELP ME GOD.

I lowered the book and thought about the Queen. Then I prayed (even though I wasn't a praying man): so help me God.

Corporal Baker

Things began to move fast from there.

My head was spinning and it was hard to keep up.

First, they stowed us on a bus, swearing, yelling and calling us lazy slugs and useless fuck-bags—it was a crude introduction. Next, they were telling us to hurry the hell up. Which we did, but it never seemed fast enough. Then they shut the bus doors.

It was too late to exit, I thought. My arse now belonged to the Queen and God. Damn… all the praying in the world wouldn't save me now.

Before I could even take a seat, the bastards had hit top gear. The bus was now moving at full pelt, south along the Pacific Motorway with the engine screaming so loud I thought the pistons were about to punch clean through the roof.

That was the first red flag.

Fuck me, I said to the recruit sitting next to me. I don't understand the rush; they're going to get us all killed, or injured and maimed, at the very least. What have we gotten ourselves into?

The recruit didn't respond and slowly rocked back and forth in his seat.

That was the second red flag. I didn't see it coming. No one did—at the speed we were travelling—there wasn't a chance. We all missed it, that's for sure. But ho-hum, it's off on an adventure we go.

At midnight, the bus rolled through the barrack gates. The

driver swung into a large parking lot. It looked like Changi,[1] at night, and we were its new POWs—fresh meat for Tojo's bloodthirsty sojourn into the South Pacific. Then the driver cut out the lights. I bounced in my seat and whispered, screw these bastards, I don't trust the smell of this place, gentlemen.

I was acting brave in front of the other recruits, but in truth, I was shitting my pants.

The bus door opened with a relieving hiss. Though it didn't help my situation at all.

A soldier in camouflage fatigues climbed the stairwell. His shoulders were wide, and his neck was thicker than a pylon.

I bet that man eats concrete and marble for breakfast, I said to the recruit next to me.

He didn't answer, but for now at least his rocking had stopped.

The soldier shone a Maglite up and down the aisle until the beam hit every recruit in the face.

Fuck me, I said. Is he tryin' ta make us blind or what?

Quiet, said a recruit from behind, you don't wanna piss that man off.

The recruit had a point, so I kept my mouth shut.

LISTEN UP, said the soldier. My name's Corporal Baker. You will address me as Corporal. Not corps, or mate, and never Sir.

Baker beamed the Maglite[2] across our faces once more.

Understood?

Yes, Corporal.

One other thing: once you step off this bus, it means little where you came from. Or even who you pray to. You'll become the welcome property of the Army. From here on, nothing else matters.

Baker switched off his Maglite and walked along the aisle.

---

1   World War 2 reference to Changi Prison Camp. Located in Singapore and guarded by the Japanese Imperial Army from 1942, the prison held up to 50,000 British and Australian Prisoners of War.

2   A large aluminium torch, approximately 14 inches long, with an effective range of 400 meters.

Is there anybody no longer wishing to be here?

The bus was silent.

Good-oh, said Baker, and returned to the front of the bus. The Maglite's beam also returned, and once again it swathed its way across every face on the bus.

Now, I have only one rule. It's the Corporals who run this Army. Not the Sergeants. And not the Generals jerking one another off in Canberra. FUCK THEM. It's the Corporals who're in charge. We're the Almighty and, to you, we're God. Follow our orders without question and you might just survive training. Got it?

Yes, Corporal.

Great. Now, grab your cocks and socks and get the fuck off my bus.

The bus driver opened the stowage compartment doors. All the recruits rushed in, like vultures to dead flesh. Pillows and suitcases and doonas soon flew out across the carpark, and it became impossible to tell who owned what. There was even a stuffed teddy that nobody was brave enough to claim.

Hurry the fuck up, said Baker, shining his Maglite into the recruits' faces.

Argh, said a recruit and fell to the pavement, cupping his face. My eyes … I can't see!

What the fuck, I said to another recruit. He could take out the entire Soviet Army with that torch.

The Soviet State's disbanded, he said.

Are you sure?

One hundred percent.

I pulled out my brown suitcase from the stowage and stacked it by my feet. Disbanded, my arse!

Baker shone the torch along a white painted line. It stretched across the carpark, into the dark of night.

I want everyone standing on this line. Then open your suitcases in front of you.

Another soldier, wearing a red beret, walked in front of us. He too held out a Maglite and panned the beam across our faces, like it was a weapon. The recruits began dropping to the pavement—one by one—screaming as the bright light burned into their retinas like warm piss through snow. Very few of us remained standing; and those of us who could were temporarily blinded for our efforts and left standing in a wild state of purgation, completely disoriented and a long way from home.

The soldiers had us right where they wanted.

Baker approached. I'd flattened out my towel and laid out what was in my suitcase. Toothbrush and paste. One razor blade. Two changes of underwear and socks. A book: *The History of the Great War (Volume 1)*. A small pocketknife.

Where's all the rest of your belongings, recruit?

Here's all I own, Corporal.

You were given a list of items to bring—

Baker knelt, then took my pocketknife.

These are contraband at Kapooka, recruit, but you look so poor I almost feel bad taking it from you.

He slipped the knife inside his trouser pocket. Why do you want to join my army, recruit?

To fight for my country, Corporal.

Argh, hot cock, recruit. Everybody here will say that same thing… but not a single one of them truly believes it.

Because I'm a proud Australian, Corporal.

Pig's arse, recruit… pride's the kinda thing that'll get a soldier's nuts blown clean off. Then what's he left with… NOTHING!

Baker kicked my suitcase shut. I want a better explanation, before you leave here, he said, then moved to the next recruit.

I got stationed in a room with five other male recruits.

Davis was the first roommate to come and say hello. We split a bunk and played 'rock, paper, scissors' for who got top. It went to best of three, and I took the bottom.

Davis was, by far, the oldest of the recruits, and had long blonde hair, which he'd tied neat into a ponytail.

What do you prefer to be called? he said, standing before a wall mirror where he released his ponytail and began combing his hair. First on the right side, then the left.

Patterson.

Everyone usually calls me Davo. I hate that name, if I'm being honest.

Okay, I said, and slipped into my Army-issued pyjamas. They were blue flannel, with button up fronts—the kind my grandfather used to wear.

I looked into the mirror. It was nearing then end of my first night, and the closest thing I'd seen to a weapon was a torchlight that rendered me part blind.

LIGHTS OUT, came the call from the hallway. I pulled my trousers high, past my belly button and tightened the chord.

Haha, said Davis, you're really in the Army now.

I smiled and flicked the light switch, then peeled back my blanket. It was a thick, harsh wool job that smelt like mothballs and caused my skin to itch.

Hey, Davis! I said. I sure hope you don't piss the bed.

It's my first night here… stranger things have happened.

The mattresses were narrow and hard, and the pillows were soft and lifeless. I rolled to one side but couldn't get comfortable. So, I beat the pillow, folded it, tossed my head once, then turned again—

Hey, Davis?

What?

That Baker … did he scare you?

A little—

I bashed my pillow with my forearm, then flipped onto my back.

Hey, Davis

YES.

Do you think we'll get our own Maglite?

Sure … I guess.

Another recruit let one rip. The windows were open, but the smell hung in the air. We all covered our faces and chuckled through our bedsheets. Then the room fell silent, and the night was dark.

The bugle sounded out reveille. It hit like a slab of concrete to the side of your face. I sprang out of bed and looked at my watch—it was five-thirty in the morning.

The sun wasn't barely up yet, and those Corporal bastards were already marching up and down the corridor, stomping their jackboots on the tiles and bashing on the doors. There was yelling and Corporals screaming, hurry up and get out of bed, you lazy thumbsuckers. This isn't school camp! This is no holiday, and it sure as shit ain't grandma's house. So, get out into the hallway. NOW.

I rolled over in the bed and buried my face into the pillow. Just give me five more minutes, Corporal—

OUT IN THE HALLWAY, RECRUIT, barked Baker.

I buttoned up my pyjama shirt. It went on crooked, and the buttons had slid into all the wrong holes. But it was too late to fix and, with the job half done, I ran into the hallway.

STAND UP STRAIGHT, WITH YOUR BACKS TO THE WALL.

Christ, I muttered, what small thing's crawled up this man's hole?

There was a chuckling among the recruits. I rubbed my eyes and, when my vision cleared, I looked across the hall to see a pimple-faced recruit smirking at me.

Hey, what gives, shit-lips? I said and clenched my fist. I'll wipe that smirk clean off your face if you're not careful.

The recruit ignored my warning, and the smirk remained, and I got mad, until Baker stepped in between us to quell the situation.

Holster your cock, recruit, he said, glancing down at my open fly.

I quickly covered it, with my hands, but not before the entire hallway noticed. All the recruits were laughing. I looked down at the floor tiles—suddenly feeling small—and buttoned up my pants. Baker shook his head with a beaming smile.

Baker marched back to the far end of the hallway where he dragged a large green trunk across the floor and into the middle of the hallway. He climbed on top, then stomped his boots on the plastic lid.

LISTEN UP, RECRUITS. From here on, Hallway One is how I'll address you. So, whenever you hear Hallway One, you all jump. Understand?

YES CORPORAL.

Ok, Hallway One. I have only the two rules.

Rule number one: Real men don't squat to piss.

Rule number two: In this hallway, I am God and when I say GO, you move faster than you've ever done in your life. Got it?

YES CORPORAL.

Good, said Baker. Now, you have exactly two minutes to grab your shit, brush your teeth and shave. Every second over, and you're cutting into your breakfast time. Got it?

YES CORPORAL.

Good. *GO.*

All the recruits vanished into their rooms. Within seconds, half of Hallway One was running towards the latrines.

RULE THREE: NO RUNNING IN HALLWAY ONE.

No running, muttered Davis. He grabbed his shaving bag and slung a bath towel across his shoulder. It's fifty meters to the dunny and fifty in return. That's not enough time to brush and shave.

There's barely a single hair on my chin, I said.

It's the Army, Patterson. They'll make you shave anyway.

But razors give me a rash.

Tough luck, Buttercup, said Davis. Then he left for the latrine.

I laid back down in bed and stared at the base springs of the top bunk. The blankets were still itchy, and the mattress was still hard. I couldn't get comfortable, so I grabbed my razor and followed Davis to the latrine.

BY THE LEFT, RIGHT LEFT

By mid-afternoon, the Corporals were still at it. They never slowed up and never quit screaming at us. It lasted the entire day and was all stand up; stand down. Don't lean against the wall. Straighten your hat. Blouse those trousers. Shine those boots until you can see your own reflection.

Fuck me, it never stopped. We couldn't move, let alone breath in this place, unless it was under the Corporals' orders.

But the recruits were catching on. Nothing we did would ever satisfy those Corporal bastards. We were being set up to fail—indefinitely. This was the Corporals' way of ensuring they squeezed every last drop of juice out from our day—by setting the bar impossibly high. The only way to combat it was to smile and wave. Or laugh hysterically when the moment arose. Because humour—not routine, or discipline—was the bedrock of any soldier's career and, by lunch, we'd gone a long way to figuring that out.

Baker was old hat, though. He'd seen it all and always remained one step ahead.

An hour before dinner, he marched the platoon to the parade square.[3] It was hot, and it was humid. Recruits were drinking water at a bullish rate. Those who didn't slowly went pale and began to sway.

---

3   Typically, a paved and guttered surface, with no officially set dimensions, the parade ground—or drill square—is constructed for the purposes of practising and executing military drills.

In historical times of war, the parade ground was also used for the purposes of the secured collocation of deceased soldiers prior to identification and repatriation or burial. Therefore, the space maintains a sacred symbology, and soldiers are prohibited from crossing the area as a means of thoroughfare or recreation.

Baker started our first drill lesson before they had a chance to fall.

First, he explained, there was *The Left*. Which was also *Your Right*. And that *Your Left* was *The Right*. In the end, we all turned right, when we should have turned left. And left when should have turned right.

Sometimes I failed to turn at all; and that really pissed Baker off.

You're a clusterfuck, Patterson, quit jerking off on my parade ground!

Next, we learned the salute. It was always performed with the right hand. A salute could be to *The Left*, to *The Right*, and even straight ahead.

Whatever the direction, the gesture seemed more important than any other drill movement. Because, when an officer walked by, it was essential to pay your respect. In fact, if a soldier failed to salute, the entire Australian Defence Force could come crashing down. Global markets would crumble. Billions would be out of work. The earth's rotation would churn to a halt and human life—as we know it—would cease to exist.

Even Baker was scared to cock this business up. Saluting was that serious.

H. Miller and the Beats

It was a nice summer morning, and I thought about the beach.

The closest beach was still a day's drive away and, instead of the coast, the platoon found itself in a warehouse, with Baker and a soldier we'd soon learn was 'The Quartermaster'. It was a commanding title that wreaked of authority and demanded the highest levels of respect.

The Quartermaster raised a mesh roller screen then slumped behind a stainless-steel bench. He was old, well overweight, smelt like cigarette and had a rum nose that glowed brighter than a red stop sign. The man did not look happy. He grimaced, then proclaimed, the Quartermaster is the backbone of the Army; without me, all war would stop, because you cannot have a battle without supplies.

Nobody argued with the Quartermaster and eventually each recruit was issued a large field-pack. It was capable of carrying twenty litres of water, two-days rations, a sleeping bag, a hoochie shelter and a spare change of socks. Next were our webbing belts, which carried ammunition, and more water. A soldier could never carry too much water, or ammunition. That was his life source, and without it, he was a static target and as good as dead.

Finally, we were issued a pair of dog tags. These were two brass discs that hung on a silver chain. In the event, one disc was placed beneath the tongue. The other hung around the big toe. That was for when we fell on the battlefield and pronounced dead.

I stuffed the tags inside my shirt pocket, then tried on the webbing belt.

The belt was loose, and the ammunition pouches slung low, beneath my hips and blocked my thighs when I attempted to walk.

Hey, what gives? I said. This belt's way too large.

Nonsense, said the Quartermaster. The Army doesn't make such mistakes.

I stuffed both arms between the belt and my hip, then drew large circles with my fists.

Bullshit, I said, you could fit two of me in here.

You'll grow into them, said the Quartermaster. And that was the end of that.

Baker helped me adjust the shoulder straps on my field pack. The straps eventually fit snug, but with any weight applied, they dug into my shoulders and sent sharp, stabbing sensations into my neck.

Harden up, said Baker, you'll get used to it.

Sure, I said and removed the pack.

Do you read, recruit?

Only if the sports pages and the classifieds count, Corporal?

Shit no, Recruit. I'm talking about literature. Actual books—Tolstoy, Dostoyevsky, Celine. Hemingway, H. Miller and The Beats!

Never heard of them, Corporal. Why?

They're writers who changed the global landscape. Their words were mind-altering in terms of how we view the world.

Really? I said, then sat on a timber bench, and adjusted my webbing belt.

Absolutely, said Baker. Without sharp literature and art, civilisation would be rendered brain dead—it's that important.

Okay, Corporal.

Baker moved on, to help the next recruit. I kept adjusting my belt and, for the moment, the world was slow and quiet, and Baker seemed alright.

Maintaining the Upper Hand

Hallway One.

I was in my room sleeping when Baker called it out.

We all had clean-shaven heads.[4] That way, each recruit looked the same and each recruit conformed. In the Army, there was no other way.

Davis stood forlorn in front of his mirror. He was running both hands across his clean-shaven head.

That ain't ever growing back.

He turned from the mirror. Oh yeah? he said. You'll see Patterson. One day you won't have any hair left at all.

I prefer mine short. It makes me look tough—you know, indestructible.

Patterson, you'd cork up in a proper battle.

I'll show you, I said and balled up my fist. I come from a long line of Afghan warriors, and I fear nothing.

I jammed my fist beneath Davis' nose.

You look nothing like an Afghan, Patterson. Quit dicking around, and let's go see what Baker wants.

Baker stood behind an ironing board. He looked proud to be up there for reasons that were lost on us. A tightly pressed shirt hung stiff, like sheet steel, from a wooden coat hanger. A name tag

---

4   The shaved head is an integral part of military induction, in terms of both maintaining tradition and providing a form of soldier standardisation.

that read BAKER was neatly stitched, level above the right breast pocket. Each time he looked at the shirt, his eyes glowed, proud. I couldn't understand why. Where I'd come from, no man dared to wield an iron. That was the female domain.

Baker did not care for old fashioned sensibilities. Man or woman, a well pressed shirt was something everybody should aspire to, he said as the iron pushed hissing steam across the ironing board.

For many of you, this is going to be a tough love kind of day. Your mothers are no longer here to cook and to clean or slave over a hot iron for you. That was yesterday. Today you'll each become men, because today, you'll learn to iron for yourself.

He squeezed a button on top of the iron, and a spurt of water streamed out its jets.

Now, I know what some of you might be thinking… that Baker's gone insane. That ironing is not a man's job. Well, I'm here to show you all that a real soldier knows how to iron. And nothing boosts a soldier's confidence and pride like a well-pressed shirt. Especially one that he's ironed himself.

I slumped down into a seat. I'd never heard a thing so absurd in my life.

I poked Davis in the arm. I thought we came here to learn how to be soldiers. When are they gonna give us our rifles?

Shhh, said Davis, gawking up at the ironing board.

First, begin with the sleeves, said Baker.

He laid the sleeve across the ironing board. Flattened it with his palm, then sprayed it with a water bottle.

Baker held up a shirt sleeve. There was a crease, running hard and sharp down its outer edge. He extended it out, horizontally, from the shoulder to the cuffs. Then he smiled.

Fuck me. I don't know how much more of this I can take. No one mentioned this in the recruiting brochure.

Baker ironed the rest of the shirt, then held it up high.

Now, is that not a thing of beauty? he said.

I smirked and looked around, expecting all the recruits to be doing the same. Except they weren't. They all stared at Baker, goggle-eyed, then began to clap their hands.

Any questions? said Baker.

Yeah me, I said.

What do you want, Patterson.

Corporal, I don't get it. What good's an ironed shirt when you're going into battle? No matter how sharp you iron those sleeves, it's not defending you against the enemy?

It's called discipline, Recruit Patterson, and discipline fosters self-esteem and confidence. Therefore, a confident soldier is a competent and effective soldier. Understood?

I've never ironed a thing in my life, Corporal. All I want to do is fire some guns.

Baker leaned over, grabbed my wrist and squeezed it tight.

Well, Recruit, he said, and smiled. If you can't handle a simple iron, then how are we ever going to trust you with a rifle?

I had no answer. Even from behind an ironing board, Baker was always one step ahead.

FAREWELL RECRUIT JONES

At 5:30am, the reveille bugle sounded.

Hallway One, a recruit shouted.

The building echoed with repeated cries of Hallway One.

FUCK THIS, said recruit Jones from the bunk next to ours.

He leapt out of bed, then threw himself out the window.[5]

Davis and I poked our heads out over the ledge and looked down at him. It was a two-storey drop, straight down into a courtyard where the recruits hung their washing.

Jones' body lay twisted on the ground. He had a pained look on his face and grasped at his shoulder.

You are a mad motherfucker—with white hot balls of steel—doing a thing like that, I said.

Jones didn't answer.

I think he's hurt… real bad, said Davis

Who cares? That was the coolest thing I've ever seen.

I turned around when Baker stormed into the room.

---

5   Military recruit training is an intense and confined period of residential programming that aims to condition soldiers for the demands of military life.

Each recruit is faced with an indeterminate amount of stress and punishment in order to foster conformity. This conformity, applied through Military Drills, Physical Training (PT) and Armed, or Unarmed combat conditions the soldier to apply the skills learnt during recruit training in high stress situations, such as combat, war and peace-keeping operations, to a point where it becomes a reflex.

Throughout the training period, recruits will form a bond with other recruits, and in best case scenario, develop self-esteem.

Many recruits do not adapt and quickly drop out during this process, either via request, or in extreme circumstances via self-harm and suicide.

What the fuck's going on in here, recruits.

It's recruit Jones, Corporal; he's gone and spudded on out the window, said Davis.

Ahh, Christ, not another one.

He stuck his head out into the hallway.

SOMEONE CALL THE MEDIC.

Baker approached the window. He was steady putting his head out over the ledge.

Don't move, recruit. Help will be there real soon.

Go to hell, ya bastard, said Jones.

Are you hurt bad, recruit?

Eat shit and die, Nazi. Hey, Corporal! I said. Why'd Jones go and do a thing like this? Then he calls you a Nazi?

Baker moved back from the window then pulled it closed.

I ain't got the faintest clue, Patterson. But the Army loves to open its door to all these messed up kids. And, by some sheer act of God, they always end up on my bloody doorstep.

Baker put on his slouch hat and adjusted the chin strap.

They think they're gonna turn their lives around by God damn enlisting, he said. But they always end up like Jones—in some form or another.

And the Army takes no responsibility for that? said Davis.

Absolutely not, recruit. Some kids ain't cut out for this business. They lack the heart, and we can't go blaming the Army for that.

Heart? said Davis. That's real cold-blooded—if you know what I mean.

I pressed my nose against the windowpane. Two soldiers were rolling Jones onto a green canvas stretcher.

What'll happen to him? I said.

Eh, they'll find him a bed down at Diggers James.[6] Then, when he's better, it'll be farewell Recruit Jones.

6　　Digger James is a rehabilitation centre for recruits who're injured during the training process. The centre is named in honour of Maj. Gen. William Brian 'Digger' James AC, AO, MBE. James was an Australian soldier and military physician who served in the Australian Army during the Korean and Vietnam Wars.

Then what? said Davis.

Then what? The Army has no use for a soldier with a busted shoulder.

Baker turned and walked out the door.

Something tells me that's the last we'll hear about this, said Davis.

Then he grabbed his towel and shaving bag and walked on down the hall.

THOU SHALT NOT KILL

The entire platoon was sitting inside the Barracks Chapel.

All the Baptists sat next to the Catholics. The Catholics sat next to the Atheists, who sat next to the Jehovah's. And the Jehovah's sat next to nobody.

The Padre[7] invited the platoon's Agnostics to remain inside. But they all stood up and left.

If you guys change your mind, all you have to do is knock on the door, said the Padre.

The Padre moved to the front of room.

Thou Shalt Not Kill, he said.

Then he picked up a Bible and held it above his head.

Race. Religion. Money. Sex. Power. All are contributing factors to war.

He lowered the Bible to his chest.

But what makes one man wish to kill another he's not even met?

I can answer that, I said. I stood up and took that Bible straight from his hands.

Listen… I know it's written somewhere in here.

---

7   The Padre is a well-respected figure within any military who is welcomed by soldiers, religious or not. His standing within the military carries with-it long-standing traditions and history. Typically a male figure, the Padre holds an official rank of a commissioned officer but is simply addressed as 'Padre'.

I opened the bible and waved it in front of me. The pages flipped.

War, I reckon, is nothing but a dog-eat-dog affair, Padre. Eye for an eye. Tooth for a tooth—it's written all throughout your bible. That's why men kill: Because your good book tells them to kill all the sinners and non-believers. Isn't that what it says, Padre?

Padre paced around the room, the look on his face giving no insight into his thoughts.

I feel you're missing the point, Recruit. Because, you see, all murder is a sin; but when God commanded the Israelites to possess the promised land, they were only following God's orders. And when King David led the defeat of the Philistines, he did so by following God's great plans. God did not order these men to commit a sin; therefore, killing in war (when ordered) is not the same as murdering a man over a petty dispute.

That all sounds like the same bag of fruit to me, Padre, because once a man is dead, that's that… it's game over, and not even God can bring him back.

I handed him the bible and returned to my seat.

That may be so, Recruit, but you see… God forgives, and God forgets, but man will have to live with his actions for the remainder of his mortal life; then, perhaps beyond.

The Padre turned and left the room.

Are you insane, Patterson? said Davis. You don't know the first thing about killing … or God, for that matter.

WHAT? I said.

Davis didn't say another thing.

The Padre returned and wheeled in a TV.

We're going to watch a movie, he said. It's called Platoon.

I lay down on my belly and kicked up my feet.

I turned to Davis. Now this is my kind of flick, but Davis just turned and looked away.

A Soldier and his Rifle

I held my uniform up to the morning light.

The lapels were now ironed back flat, sharper than a razor's edge. My epaulettes were immaculate, and I'd eliminated every wrinkle or crease I could find.

Baker would be proud.

It's ok, said Davis, after I demanded he appreciate my uniform.

That's a pretty darn good job, said Baker as he entered the room. A couple of loose threads here, a little food stain there, but otherwise, Patterson, a job well done.

Davis handed over his shirt to Baker.

God damn it, Davis. This shirt's about as close to military precision as it gets.

Baker handed the shirt back.

I bet you've done this shit before.

I used to be a seamstress, Corporal.

A seamstress. How in hell's a seamstress come to join my Army?

Bad luck, I guess, said Davis.

The response made Baker's eyes freeze and, for a moment, he chewed on his thumb nail.

Say, boys, how 'bout after breakfast, we head down to the weapons range and shoot everything that moves.

I'd never believed in monsters or ghosts, or life after death.

But hearing those words felt like being in the presence of a Holy Divinity.

My spine immediately tingled, and I had to fight myself from falling to my knees.

But I stopped and turned. I tossed my shirt onto the bed.

Swear on your mother's grave this isn't a lie.

Recruit Patterson, he said. Why the hell you'd decide to join my Army?

I held the rifle to my shoulder. It was a green composite of plastic at one end.[8] But the opposite end was all business.

I put my eye up to the rifle scope.

I was born for this, I said to Davis.

There was a sideward grin on his face that not even a slap from a wet trout could remove.

I'm more concerned that you might shoot yourself in the foot, he said.

Baker split One Platoon into three sections.

He ordered the first section to the firing mounds.

The second section walked 300 metres to the firing butts.[9] I didn't like that name much, but it's where I found myself.

The third section counted bullets, loaded magazines, and conducted weapons drills.

Weapons drills are futile, I said to Davis. Much like having sex. Alone. And in the dark.

---

8   The F88 Austeyer. Manufactured in Australia, the F88 is the standard issue rifle for the regular Australian forces. Designed in 1960, it fires a 5.56mm round, and can carry up to 30 rounds in a standard magazine.

9   An earthen bank used to support a target on a firing range.

That's hard to picture, said Davis.

Exactly, I said. But a rifle should become an extension of a soldier's arm. It should all be instinctual.

What?

A soldier without arms is useless, God damn it!

Christ, Patterson.

Davis sat on a concrete bench as Baker began instructing the section on how to raise and lower the targets, with the single push and pull of a lever. The section marvelled at how simple the operation was.

Then, he led the section into a corner and pointed to a hole in the concrete ceiling.

A recruit shot himself right there in that seat.[10]

I moved beneath the hole and looked deep inside.

Now the Army won't allow soldiers to carry rifles down here.

But, Corporal, I said, what good's a soldier without his rifle?

My point exactly, Patterson.

Baker moved away from the hole. All eyes followed him.

Team, he said, don't be that selfish bastard who gets rifles taken away from his section. Nobody likes that man. AGREED?

Yes, Corporal.

The section returned to the targets.

Targets up, said Baker.

The targets went up and were soon filled with tiny bullet holes.

Beautiful, said Baker. That's where bullets should go… straight through your enemy's chest.

Why the chest, and not the head? I asked.

Because, Patterson, the head is too small a target, and that means wasting bullets. Plus, a torso shot might not kill a man—

---

10   From the author: this was my introduction to the topic of suicide in the Australian Army. It was the first of many confrontations with the realities of military life.

instantly—but it will disable him. Then he becomes a liability to the rest of his team. It's more combat effective. Understand?

Yes, Corporal.

After the weapon lessons concluded, Baker nodded, satisfied with our efforts.

It's always a good day when nobody dies. Remember that as you transform into the soldiers you were born to be, because not every man gets to make it home. Understand?

The platoon all grunted in agreement, and I imagined life after graduation as we marched back to the barracks.

March-out was in two days.

Straight Up the Guts with Heaps of Smoke

A prospective soldier learns many things whilst enduring military training. And they'll continue learning a variety of lessons throughout their military career, irrespective of how long, or short, that may be.

On a technical level, he'll learn how to survive for months out in the field. Master the art of bushcraft and combat skills. Hunt and evade any enemy. Turn water into wine and maintain his ecological environment. All while sustaining himself on Jack rats, ration packs and recycled porno mags.

The soldier will develop a level of vocational skills. Skills you won't learn anywhere else. Skills that any future employer—in their post-military career—will struggle to recognise. And, as the soldier will eventually come to attest, skills that'll cause him to no longer recognise the civilian world or his place in it.

He'll adapt with new behavioural and psychological patterns and techniques. An invaluable set of tools to encourage or motivate himself. All in order to advance his military career.

Consequentially, this all renders him completely and permanently dysfunctional. Totally incapable of operating in any other professional or social system which exists outside of military realms.

Nobody said his life would be simple!

Discipline and routine will be chief among the vices a soldier uses to keep his head above water. All this and cold cans of VB. Wild Turkey and cheap cigars. Or, in more dire circumstances, narcotics and inappropriate jokes.

Yes, oh yes, ladies and gentlemen, our soldier swims in that deep sea of dark humour. A sea so dark that his every breath's likely rendered criminal, in the civilian world.

It all begs the question: Where's his next illogical stop from here?

It's what looks to be an insane asylum; but alas, that's just a promotion.

Yee-haw, you've passed. Your development is almost complete.

So, steady yourself as we advance: straight up the guts, with heaps of smoke.

THE GREAT GAME

There were three parties vying to get it on in early-nineteenth century Afghanistan.

The British, French, and the chess-masters of Mother Russia.

No, no, no—this wasn't some *ménage a trois* in the making. It was a serious and deadly affair.

Napoleon was already moving his chess pieces around the board when he invaded Egypt. A move he considered as vital in cutting off lifelines to the British in India. And thus, Old Blighty would become a hanging piece.[11]

British invasion was, of course, the longer-term plan, and Egypt was the *en passant* move that bookended the entire strategy. The Egyptian people were crucial pieces in the game—as Napoléon pinky-promised to liberate their country from the Ottoman's—but they turned their backs on him and sided with the British.

This is the worst day of my life, said Napoleon.

But he was still a long way from Waterloo.

South, in India, the British were blind to any moves the French and Russians had made and were growing paranoid.

---

11   Chess: A piece that is unprotected and can be captured.

But, in time, they grew bold enough to make a few moves of their own and dispatched an emissary into Afghanistan.

He was an officer of the crown named Alexander Burnes, and his role was to report on Russian objectives in Afghanistan.

As chance would have it, the Russians were also blind to the moves occurring across the board. Then they grew paranoid and sent out an emissary: Jan Witkiewicz. His role was to report on British objectives in Afghanistan.

Jan arrived in Kabul with vigour, only to discover the British had beaten him to the punch.

But Jan was Russian, and a sneaky Russian at that. And what he did next was not only industrious, but a daring rook move as he set to form an Afghan-Russia alliance with Dost Mohamed. Queen takes King: in what was looking like a clear checkmate.

Russia one; Britain nil.

Yet, the Tsarists didn't see it this way, and ordered Jan withdraw all pieces from the board and start again. Jan went home and promptly committed suicide. Such was his disappointment.

Burnes opted for a different tactic—as he wished to remain alive. Upon his return to Britain (where he was received with much acclaim), he declared Russia was nothing more than an imaginary monster hiding in the closet.

There's nothing in there, he said. Trust me, I checked.

If only his bosses weren't all deaf, dumb and stupid: they otherwise might've listened.

Instead, they returned Burnes to Afghanistan to gather further intelligence. He wouldn't have minded, only he was killed by Afghan rebels in 1841. It was a right cock-up, indeed.

Napoleon had since thrown his chess board out, along with the bath water, after his whooping at Waterloo, he was stricken from the game. Afghanistan became a two-horse race and gave Britain the perfect chance to advance north from India.

By 1839, the British were knee-deep in Afghan dust and began sporting for a battle. They scored one, of course, but got fed with more than what they'd bargained for and retreated from Kabul back to India, losing thousands of good men along the way.

Hey, nobody said Western Imperialism in Central Asia would be easy.

Treachery, bribery, lies and deceit were how the game was now played in Afghanistan. And—interlaced with a sprinkling of diplomacy—victory often landed with the highest bidder. The Russians knew this; and, in their own quaint battles, Britain's generals knew it as well. So, after some success in Kabul in 1878 the Dost Mohamed[12] government of the day was overthrown, and Britain looked to install a leader they could openly bargain with.

But not everything in war goes according to plan. And, in the spoils of Kabul, and after a disaster in Maiwand, the British stumbled upon the realisation: Afghanistan could never be theirs. There was a weakening in their castling—a fact they were discovering the hard way.

We couldn't maintain the rage in the treacherous mountain passes. Or in the austere Asian deserts. And the Afghans won't allow us to see it any other way, said an unnamed British soldier.

Despite such harsh realities, the British kept calm and soldiered on. They installed Abdur Rahman as their leader and

---

12   Founder of the Barakzai dynasty and one of the most prominent rulers in Afghanistan history.

attempted a treaty with the Afghan peoples. It also failed but they'd done enough to keep the country out of Russia's prickly hands. For the moment.

Britain designed The Durand line in 1893. It split the Pashtun Heartland straight down the guts and shielded economic policy from their Russian adversaries.

Later, in Europe, another threat was rising as the century came to a close. British and Russia soon turned their attention away from Afghanistan. There was bigger fish to fry, and all the blood and sweat spilt on Afghan soil was swept away and buried in the dust.

Britain gave up any remaining control of Afghanistan in 1921 and dumped all economic interest in the country which soon faded from their consciousness.

Then, lickety-split, the Russians slipped through Afghan's back door. They fostered alliances and brokered deals for happier days. Meanwhile, the cut-throat Soviets were revamping things in the old motherland.

MISS MALALAI OF MAIWAND

When you're wounded and left on Afghanistan's plains,
And the women come to cut up what remains
Just roll to your rifle and blow out your brains
An' go to your Gawd like a soldier

—RUDYARD KIPLING. The Young British Soldier.

The Artillery Officer stood in the ravine and masked by the terrain, he barked his orders.

If you see an Afghan, shoot him, and watch the rest scatter like flies.[13]

The AO's band of men stood, then began their advance toward the ancient city of Maiwand.

Steady as she goes, said the Troop Sergeant Major. 25,000 is the strength of these Afghan forces. All standing, ready to cut us up like sheep.

Splendid, said the Officer. Should I give the whistle blast?

The initial sound of musket rounds cut through the morning air. Cries of death, hatred, and bloodlust spread across the Dasht. The cacophony of war.

---

13   'From villains, to flies, to niggers, in the space of 100 pages', was the remark made by Robert Fisk, war correspondent, upon reading his grandfather's account of the Second Afghan War, in the book titled 'Tom Graham, V.C: A Tale of the Afghan War'.

Both armies lodged themselves deep into battle.

There's no going back now, said the Troop Sergeant Major.

Heavens no, said the Officer as he tracked behind his men.

The flow of bullets continued to flourish. A lead cloud floated over and between both armies.

It's hotter than a boiler room out here— said the Officer. He immediately stopped speaking, sighted a clearing, lined up his iron sights and pulled the trigger.

—but a jolly good morning, isn't it? he finished. It was a direct hit.

The way was now clear. So, he bound up the nearby escarpment… only to catch one in the gut for his efforts. Thus, finding himself lying face down in the dirt.

Help me, he said. I can't see a darn thing from down here.

When the medic arrived, he had forgotten to pack his bedside manners. He was Old-Irish and, after inspecting the wound, jammed his fingers deep inside the hole.

Is it bad?

The doctor retrieved his hand. He was now covered up to his elbows in blood.

Aye, he said, and shook his fist. Lawd-blast those murtherin' villains.

And it was aye indeed. The Afghans hadn't scattered at all. And the battle risked cascading into a deadly stalemate.

Don't hold back, men, said the Troop Sergeant Major. We're not going home until we've killed every one of those bloody Niggers.

A young Pashtun woman knelt on the field of battle, where wounded warriors laid all around. They were all bloodied, beaten and torn to pieces by rampant bullets and shrapnel.

What do I do? she said and looked towards the sky.

Praying won't stop the bleeding, said a boy warrior, but if we stay any longer, we're all going to die.

Allah would never forgive us, she said.

To hell with Allah! He's abandoned us, Malalai, and it's time we retreat.

Warriors—all fresher than daisies, and without a mark upon them—stood and agreed.

Send those colonial bastards to hell, said one. I'm going home, while there's still time left for tea.

Malalai[14] threw her musket to the ground, then leapt on top of a boulder.

There will be no more dinners if we don't stand and fight.

Get down from there, Miss Malalai, all the warriors screamed.

No, she said, as a viscous musket-fire screamed past her head. And, facing her foe, she cleared her throat and sang:

Young Love
If you do not fall, in the battle of Maiwand
By God
Someone is saving you as a symbol of shame
With a drop of my sweetheart's blood,
Shed in defence of the motherland
Will I put a beauty spot on my forehead
Such as would put to shame the rose in the garden[15]

The warriors stood in awe. Malalai had more stones than all the men combined.

They all fought on. Some for honour; others for personal

---

14   Malalai of Maiwand carved her name into history when, upon seeing the Afghani soldiers fleeing, tore off her veil then led a charge against the British Forces. She was cut down by British bullets and died of wounds inflicted on the battlefield. However, it was her courage which turned the fight in the Afghan's favour. She is a symbol of national pride and heroism.

15   The Landay/Poem sung by Malalai as she waved her veil in the fashion of a flag in order to inspire her countrymen.

pride. But, as the British efforts waned and the bullets quelled, Malalai stood the tallest. Falling short, only as the British turned—beaten—then retreated.

CALL ME GEORGE

There isn't a thing I don't know about camels.

I've marched these ancient desert beasts from city to city. From Peshawar to Tehran, and from Kabul to Beijing.

I've carried loads that'll make a Mullah blush and charged the bullets in Maiwand.

I've met warlords and warriors in seven different countries. And learnt English and traded with the Poms. I didn't shed a tear while my fellow man lay dying—beneath the bullets and the bombs—but wept when they cheered. Good heavens, the Afghan's won.

So, I'll tell you now, as I would have told you then, there ain't a thing I don't know about camels.

People here call me George.

Searching For Amooz

Penny spat at the sky, then kicked her heels.

Her load lurched to the left, then back to the right.

Settle down, you bitch, I said and clouted her across the nose with my cane.

The beast straightened. I checked my compass, and we continued on our path.

The day was coming on dusk. Smoke rose out from the Quoras below, and sounds of the Quran filled the air. The stars began to glow, and one by one they punched tiny holes into the night sky.

The brightest star shone from the North.

What do you say, Penny? We'll call that one Amooz, then make a wish.

Penny swished her stumpy tail. Groaned—in her own indignant way—then pissed on the middle of the trail.

I wish for something nice to eat.

I rummaged through my trouser pockets and in my saddle bags. They were all empty.

Come to think of it, Penny, anything now would be a treat.

A shining white light in the distance grew brighter. It moved about, much lower than all the stars in the sky. It floated up, then floated down. It floated left, then floated right. It slowed. And it sped. Then it began making a god-awful whirring sound.

It was a helluva frightening sound, indeed; much like the sound of cats scuffling in the street.

This led me to believe it wasn't cats at all. It was some devilish creature sent straight from the gates of hell.

I panicked and swore out loud: Damn you, Allah! Then fell off my camel and split my trousers.

In heaven's name, George, I said, pull yourself together.

The sound grew louder. Much louder. I forgot about my trousers and dove to the side of the trail and buried myself beneath a whittling brush.

The shining white light began floating my way.

Oh, dear God, the devil has eyes, I thought. My efforts to hide were well and truly buried.

Penny groaned. She gave me all the excuses I needed, so I blamed her for giving up the ghost.

To hell with you, I said, I shall leave you here to rot, you muddled beast.

Penny became upset. I could see it in her watery eyes as her head lowered to the ground.

Words can cut to the bone faster than any bullet or blade on a man, a horse, or a beast.

Ahh, Christ, old girl—what's said is said. It was in the heat of the moment. .I was shitting bricks, and now regret every single word.

I thought long and hard, and even twice, about the matter. But had to let my affront slide. Because the demon creature finally came to a halt. Then, the noise ceased—right before my eyes.

Tis finally the end, I said and prayed.

Is that you, George Sher Gul? said the man.

Depends who's asking, I said, burying my head between my shoulders.

The Khan is asking about his package.

The Khan?

I stood and brushed off my ripped-up trousers.

Mahmout?

As I live and breathe.

What's that devilish contraption?

This? said Mahmout. He wrapped his knuckles across the fuel tank. This's called a motorcycle—

I take Penny by the harness and pull her body in tight.

What does it do?

Transports things, George. Khan says one day it'll replace the camel.

Heresy, I said. I walked around Penny, pretending to tighten her load.

I returned to her head. She was gnawing away at her harness strap.

Quit that, you thoughtless cow, I said, and reefed the strap from between her molars.

How about that package? said Mahmout.

I ducked my head beneath Penny's neck and poked it out the other side.

Tell the Khan I'll bloody deliver it myself.

Bashir Khan's palace resembled a medieval castle.

Its high walls dwarfed the outer Quoras. The villagers believed the walls only kept the evil guys in rather than the bad guys out.

I do not think those walls bother me, Penny, I said. Not at all.

Penny swished her tail and let out a bellowing groan.

I completely understand, I said, and approached the entrance.

Khan's guards stood at the front gates. They all wore white shirts, black sheepskin vests, with black Pakol caps[16] on their heads.

What's the purpose of your visit? said a guard.

I've a package for the Khan.

You're late, Pashtun.

Blame this devilish weather, I said.

The sky was black and filled with dense rainclouds. A guard unsheathed his sword. It was long, silver, curved and sharp, and would have sliced a stone in half.

Steady, I said, backing away.

I'll cut your head off if you speak another word, said the guard.

The four guards pushed the gate open, then pointed me towards a wooden door.

I walked along a stone path towards the main homestead. Cooling rain droplets fell at my feet and glistened beneath the garden's lamplights.

Thousands of pink roses filled the garden beds, and the smell of fresh cut grass filled the dampening air. I knelt down and buried my nose deep into the lawn—I hadn't seen green grass in a long, long while.

The door opened.

George, what are you doing down there? Mahmout said.

This place is beautiful.

You're still in Afghanistan, cameleer.

The sound of a lone violin filled the inner halls.

What is that tune, Mahmout? I've never heard it played before.

---

16   A soft, flat, rolled up and round-topped cap worn by men in Afghanistan and Pakistan. Such hats are culturally significant in Mid-Eastern cultures.

That would be the Khan's guests. Officers of the British 66th Regiment; they're playing Wings of Song.

British? Didn't we rout their forces all the way from Herat to Kandahar, and back to Blighty?

The war may be over, George, but some ghosts were bound to remain.

I walked along the hallway. I amused myself with many of the paintings. Most were portraits of Persian royalty, all the past Princes of Afghanistan propped-up level on the walls.

A bowl of pistachios was on a table, which nested against a pink marble wall.

I dished out a nut, then split the shell.

I suppose that it's true what you say about the ghosts, I said and dropped the empty shell on the floor. At least until the next war.

A British Officer entered the hall. He was carrying a brass cane and moved with a limp.

Is that the package for Master Khan? he said and smiled.

Yes.

Oh, be a sport and hand it over, old chap. We've been waiting here for hours.

I looked at the Officer's cane. Then I looked at his leg.

What happened? I said.

This? said the officer, as he tapped his leg with the cane. Well, that is nothing more than a tired old remnant of war.

I smiled at Mahmout. Not all ghosts are bad.

The package? said the Officer.

Two shillings was the agreed fee, I said.

The officer retrieved a small felt pouch and produced two gold coins.

Two shillings, said the Officer.

I held out my hand.

One for you, and one for the King's taxes.

The King's taxes? Why, you smelly infidel—I should squash you like a prune.

No, George, no, said Mahmout, and he moved to intervene.

He took the package from me and passed it to the Officer.

Tut, tut, said the Officer. His top lip stiffened, then furled. Be careful not to bite the hand that feeds. He turned on his heel and left the room.

WHAT THE HELL DOES HE MEAN, MAHMOUT?

He means mind your manners, George.

Oh, to buggery with manners.

I lifted the bowl of pistachios and poured the nuts into each of my coat pockets.

If the Khan comes looking for his nuts, tell him the serfs haven't eaten in days and could chew the hoof off a live boar's trotters, I said, then walked out the door.

I sat on the palace steps. The rain was drying up, and the clouds were clearing.

I looked towards the sky and began searching for Amooz.

The world is changing, said Mahmout. What was old is now new again, but things around here will never be the same.

I walked to the garden and knelt to smell the roses.

It no longer feels like home anymore, I said, and snapped a rosebud from its stem.

It's still the same old Afghanistan, George.

If you say it is, then it is, I said, looking at the pink rose. Only, I don't recognise her anymore.

HALT! Someone stop that thieving A-Rab, said the Officer.

He flung open the palace door and came skating across the wet tiles stopping dead at the top of the stairs.

The four guards turned at the front gate and drew their swords.

He's pilfered the King's gold, and now he's taken to the Khan's prized rose garden—guards, arrest him at once.

HUZZAH! said the guards and—at once—they bound up the garden path.

I stood in the middle of the stairs and dropped the rosebud at my feet. It rolled down the stairs, then its pink petals sank into a puddle. The stem remained above the waterline, and its clipped end pointed towards the sky like a compass arrow.

Three of the guards mounted the stairs. A fourth guard steadied behind. His right boot-heel drifted over the puddle. Then it came down, crushing the rose, like a tempestuous pestle.

I told you, camel man, I'd cut off your fucking head.

The guard lifted his boot-heel, then scaled the first step. The rose was now pulp.

But hand over the gold coin, and Allah might spare you yet.

I dug my hands deep inside my pockets and yanked out the coin.

This coin? I said. This gold shilling I earned fair and square.

It's property of the King, said the Officer. His Royal Highness's benevolent head resides on the back of that very coin.

That's not my King.

The rose pulp drifted to the edge of the puddle. A soft scent strayed through the air. Was it life or death that I could smell. Happenstance. Or a simple tout of indifference?

Whatever it was, I wasn't afraid. Either way, it smelt.

You want the damned coin? I said and held it overhead.

I tipped my head back, and dropped my bottom jaw wide open, then released the coin to the back of my throat and swallowed.

Come and get it.

That's it, camel man… say your last words.

Go to hell, I said. The whole stinking lot of you.

The guard raised his sword.

I hope wild dogs piss on your corpse, I said to the Officer.

The Officer huffed, and the guards laughed.

Stop this nonsense, said a man.

He was wearing a white robe and stood at the peak of the stairs.

I wish to keep this man alive, to be trialled by his peers.

The guard lowered his sword and frowned.

Take him to the pits, he said.

Yes, Master Khan.

The guards bound my hands with thin chord. Then they draped a black leather sack over my head and shoved me down the stairs.

I landed face down in the puddle. Cold water trickled inside the sack. The smell of dying rose crept in after, and I closed my eyes. All the stars were back. The sky was clear and, to the North, was Amooz.

THE MILLENNIUM BABIES

They dubbed us the Millennium Babies; I guess it's obvious why.

Being the first Platoon to graduate Kapooka—in January 2001— was a real big deal.

But you will have never read about it in the papers. No, it was all Y2K, and some other bullshit I can't, for the life of me, recall.

And this so-called bug was somehow posited as the single greatest threat our society had ever faced. What a laugh.

Now, if you ask me, I failed to see what all the fuss was about. Besides, what's a soldier to do. Our business was making beds. Ironing collars and firing rifles, and all this other AJ[17] crap. Crap the recruiting ads always failed to tell you about.

In the end, the little bug never amounted to anything. So, we went on about our business. Keeping one eye open for whatever threat would show up next. We'd no idea what that might be. Nobody did. But that was the Millennium Babies' first big role.

The Regimental Quartermaster threw a colour patch[18] at my chest.

---

17   Army Jerk.
18   A traditional and embroidered patch used to denote which Corps and Regiment a soldier belongs too. One patch is often ironed or glued to the right side of a slouch hat's puggaree, opposite the curled side of the hat-brim. A second patch is worn on the right shoulder sleeve of the uniform.

It was a small, purple embroidered square. And inside the purple square was another, smaller red square.

What does it mean, Sir?

It means you belong to this regiment, he said, then threw an iron at me. Stick it to the side of your slouch hat.

I have never belonged to anything before now.

I plugged in the iron, and centred the patch on the side of my puggaree when Davis walked in.

What's that? he said.

It means we're part of a regiment now. One hundred percent.

I'd like to think I'm more than a mere soldier, Pat.

I put on the slouch hat, then stretched the chinstrap beneath my jaw.

Think what you like, but, to me, nothing else matters, I said.

Then we marched over to the Regiment Headquarters.

Corporal Baker stood in the centre of the Orderly Room. His back was facing the reception, and he was shuffling papers from one table to the next. I knocked on the counter.

Morning, Corporal Baker, I said. A pleasure seeing you here!

Baker turned.

It's Sergeant now, he said, with a furrowed brow, and pointed to the three chevrons[19] stitched firm to his sleeve.

Well, I said. Now isn't that a pearler!

Baker looked at Davis and me.

What are you two numb nuts doing in my Regiment anyhow?

New march-ins,[20] said Davis. We arrived only yesterday.

Baker sighed, then rolled his eyes.

---

19   V-shaped insignia, used to denote rank. A Lance Corporal has one chevron, a Corporal two, a Sergeant three.
20   To march-in, to march-out; an induction process at a new Unit/Regiment, and the consequential departure.

I guess that makes me your new Troop Sergeant then.

He picked up two thick stacks of A4 from the desk, then slapped them on the counter in front of us.

Sign these bad boys, then dump them on Corporal White's desk when you're done.

Davis flicked through the pile. Every sheet looks empty except for the signature box, Sergeant.

Nobody gives a flying fuck, Davis. Name, rank and regimental number, on every page. Just get it done.

I didn't bother myself with scanning the forms and only looked for the spaces where my details went.

Patterson. 1814636. Private. DOB: 31 Aug 1982. Signed, done, and onto the next one.

Hey, Pat, said Davis. How'd you remember all that?

Remember it? I'd forget my mother's name before I forgot my regimental number.

I pulled out my dog tags and flashed my number at Davis.

Far as I'm concerned, Davis, it's the only thing I've got.

One more thing before you finish up, boys, said Baker. This isn't Kapooka. It's the real Army now, and I've only got three rules: Do your jobs, without bitchin' or moaning. Never let me catch you falling last on a PT run. And whenever you step on your dicks—and you will—the last person you want finding out is me. Understand?

YES, SERGEANT, I said, then flipped over to the next blank sheet of A4 . *Signing* my life away.[21]

Corporal White was asleep behind the desk. His stomach plunged out from beneath his undershirt. It was pink and covered in stretch marks. There was a half-eaten Mars bar melting in his left hand.

---

21   A metaphorical statement. Signing your life away is akin to a soldier handing over a blank cheque to the Army for any unspecified purpose or role that may otherwise be innocuous or career altering.

Davis dropped his stack of A4 on White's desk.

White jerked from his sleep. Nudged the desk with his stomach and let the chocolate slide from his hands and onto the floor.

Hope we're not interrupting smoko, said Davis.

Who are you two? said White.

Sergeant Baker said we're to hand you our new march-in paperwork.

Great. More fucken lids, said White.

He stood and walked to a bar fridge at the corner of the room; hiked up his trousers, then tucked in his shirt.

Signed your lives away?

Sure have, Corporal, I said. Name, Rank and Serial number in every box.

White opened the fridge door. He got out a can of Coke and a fresh Mars bar.

Good drills, he said. Leave it on my desk, and, after I finished my fang, I'll show you boys around the Regiment.

White sucked in his belly, then buttoned his trousers.

First, I'll show you the transport yard, then the workshop, he said.

Davis and I followed him down a long, tiled corridor and out into an open yard.

This is it. This is where it all happens.

Ha, said White. If we're being frank—not much happens here at all.

We stopped and looked around. The bitumen surface stretched its way across the compound, and an old split cricket ball sat on the edge of a drain.

Where the hell is everybody? said Davis.

HQ deployed majority of the Regiment to East Timor, said White.

He unbuttoned his coat pocket and whipped out a packet of cigarettes.

Smoke?

Smoking's for losers, I said. Nothing short of cancer in a stick. A man might as well go suck on an exhaust pipe for all a cigarette's worth.

Bull crap, said White. Everyone in the Army smokes. And those who don't, just get durked on.

White led us to a Coke machine. He put in a dollar coin and waited for a red can roll out.

What does everyone do around here? said Davis.

White popped open the red can and took a large gulp.

Fucked if anyone knows, he said. But I guess that's why we all smoke.

White unlocked the door to a small brick hut.

Inside was an empty desk, and two rows of empty shelves.

Congratulations, said White. This here's your new office.

He flicked the light switch, then tried powering on the air conditioner.

I guess we'll have to open the windows, he said, then hung his slouch hat on a wooden coat rack.

Davis walked around the barren room.

Where's all our stores and equipment? he said.

White unbuttoned his pants. Sat in an office chair, then took a gulp of Coke.

Your guess is as good as mine, he said, although she's a good little hide-out, right? But, whatever you do, don't let Baker catch you zonking beneath the desk, he'll trim your cherry tree as quick as a flash.

Get out of town, I said. That Baker's nothing but a big ol' teddy bear.

Yeah, said White, but even teddy bears have sharp claws.

He slid out of his seat and walked to the window.

Over there's the transport yard, he said, and he pointed out the window.

There was a long row of trucks, painted in Army camouflage.

We get to drive them?

Sure thing… if any of 'em start.

Davis removed his slouch hat and rested it on the desk.

They're all broken? he said.

There's not much around here that isn't, said White.

He crushed the red can with his boot, then hurled it into a dustbin.

C'mon, he said. We'll head over to the workshop.

Behind the workshop, a wild green vine cascaded its way down the chain-link fence, and purple flowers spotted their way along the vertical facade, while several bees zipped their way in and out through the spaces in the creeping verdure.

I fucking hate bees, said White.

Why? said Davis. They're an integral part of the ecosystem. Society would crumble without them.

White steered his way clear of the fence and walked toward a mangled Land Rover.

Whatever, he said. I still don't like them.

He removed his hat. Rested it on the Land Rover bonnet, and cracked open another can of Coke.

Anyway, he said. Come check this out.

He pointed inside the cabin.

That's pieces of someone's skull.

That's insane, I said, and jammed my nose inside the cabin.

How'd it happen? said Davis.

White took a deep gulp of Coke, then wiped his top lip.

Vehicle roll-over. Bosses made the driver hook it all the way from Shoal Water, and back to Vegas without a single break.

Davis walked around the Land Rover. He poked his head inside the cargo tray. Beneath the wheel arches, and even underneath the engine bay. The entire vehicle was a mess.

What was the rush?

Boss wanted to watch the Wallabies play the All-Blacks, but the driver only made it half the way.

Those bastards, I thought, and opened the passenger driver side door. I wiped the dust and dead vines leaves from the seat, then climbed in behind the wheel.

If you look at the roll-cage, said White, you can still see strands of the driver's hair.

That's a helluva way to die, said Davis.

White rest his Coke on the bonnet of the Land Rover. A small bee circled around his head. He swiped at it with his hat.

Scram, you hairy buzzard, he said.

But the bee continued circling around, then landed on the brim of the Coke can. White flicked at the bee with his finger until it flew away.

Well, said White, Army isn't like other jobs. Every day we put our lives at risk. It's a sacrifice we all signed up to make.

Bullshit, said Davis. I didn't sign up so the brass could watch a football game.

I climbed out of the cabin and slammed the door behind me.

Damn straight, Davis, I said. But ya preaching to the choir, I reckon.

Shut-up, Patterson.

White took a last gulp from his Coke, then crushed the can with his boot.

Why did you sign up, then, Davis?

Because I thought I could make a difference—

Ha! Good luck, said White. He put on his hat, then looked at his watch.

Looks like it's boozer-o'clock, hey lads. I could murder a cold one.

I looked at my watch. It was a half hour till twelve.

Been Caught Stealing

The pit was dark and cold. And, from all I could I tell, I'd been in here, alone, for several days.

Oh, George, I thought. Will I ever see an open road, or witness golden sunsets, ever again?

I couldn't tell if my eyes had glued closed or peeled wide open.

It was a kind of sensation that made you wonder: was the body now separated from the mind?

I flipped open my old brass compass. The degree markings glowed green and bold. I moved the light around the pit. It was cold. It was damp. And it was deafeningly hollow.

I dropped to my knees and prayed.

A hatch opened, and harsh light poured in through the gap in the wall. Some unknown pair of starving eyes followed—straight after. They had bloodlust written all over them. It was a daunting sight.

My feet were itching to move.

Let me out of here, I said. I demand you set me free: right here and now, you cowards.

There was no response.

I rose from my knees and banged my fists about the opening.

Wooden panels surrounded the hatch. I ran my hands around its surface. Huzzah, I thought. There's the goddamned door.

Open her up, right now!

I stepped back. About a foot or two, then kicked the door—right in the guts. The damned thing wouldn't budge.

How long are you planning to keep me in here?

The hatch swung shut.

A few days had passed. Then more. I kept my eyes locked on where the hatch sat in the middle of the door.

Some days, I got in real close and pressed my face against the wooden boards. I'd close one eye, then squint with the other, until a needle of light would appear. It was like striking gold. Soft and precious and visceral to the eye.

One day, the door opened. The pit filled with light. I looked at my arms and the skin on the back of my hands. They'd grown pale from the dark.

How long have I been in here?

There was no response.

A man in black stepped through the opening. He dropped his trousers.

Get that thing away from me, you hound.

The man laughed and pissed on the dirt. Then he fixed his trousers, and turned and grabbed a bucket.

Eat up, said the man.

He lifted the bucket and poured water-soaked bread where he'd pissed, then laughed.

I wasn't feeling too hungry and sat back on my heels.

The man continued to laugh and shut the door.

That evening, the door opened again.

Rats had been scouring around the bread, but disappeared when light entered the pit.

Get off your arse, Pashtun, said a guard wearing black.

He stepped inside the pit. The wet bread squished beneath his toes.

Go to hell, you ape, I said, then curled myself into a tight-fisted ball.

The Khan wants a word.

I lifted my head and looked at the guard.

Tell that mongrel I'm not moving.

Suit yourself, said the guard.

Two more men entered the pit. They bound my hands and bagged my head.

Take him to the Khan, said the guard.

Allah almighty will shit on your graves, I said and stiffened my legs.

The guards laughed, then dragged me out by the heels.

Bashir Khan walked around an old oak desk and wedged a cigar into my hand.

Tell me, Sher Gul, are you an idealist, or an Afghan?

I bit the cigar in half and spat out the end.

Neither, I said, then threw the other half of the cigar against the wall.

Neither, huh?

I am a goddamned cameleer, and there's nothing more to it.

Bashir Khan reached inside a box and took out another cigar. He split the end with a cutter and wedged it between his teeth.

This tobacco's grown on the banks of the Moskva. It's the most beautiful city.

Bashir stuck a match and lit the cigar. He drew in short bursts of smoke until the tip of the cigar glowed cherry red.

Perhaps, Sher Gul, you have been?

I slapped my hand on the oak desk. It brought a sparkle to the old Khan's eyes.

Of course, I've been. In fact, there isn't a city on this continent where I haven't visited. Traded in. Slept in. Danced with all kinds of women because I'm the best damned cameleer Afghan's ever seen.

Bashir Khan smiled and stubbed his cigar in a square emerald ashtray.

Good, good, good, he said. The country always needs men like you but you got caught stealing, George. And the penalty for that is death.

I kicked the table leg but failed to move it.

First, I said, it was from a British bastard. And second, I never stole a single thing.

Oh? said Khan.

Smoke billowed around his face. He walked around the table, then placed one hand on my shoulder.

Of course, there is some difference in the matter then.

Yeah?

Yes, always. The British will pay ten shilling—or maybe more—for a skilled worker like you, but only half that for a thief.

I spat on the floor and stomped my feet.

Why? They're filthy rotten scoundrel, I said. Besides, they know nothing about the Pashtun way!

He flicked a ball of ash at my feet.

Indeed they don't, said Khan. He rapped his knuckles across the table. The British believe we're unsophisticated. Barbaric and tribal savages. But we are men of honour, cameleer.

Khan smiled.

Yet even the British know every Afghan has his price.

Honour? What horseshit, I said. If you had any honour, you would set me free.

Bashir Khan laughed, then bit hard on the end of his cigar. It burned bright, and he filled the room with smoke. He clicked his fingers. Two guards entered the room and took me by my arms.

Careful with him, men. He's the property of the Empire, now.

When in Rome

My experience is, that if you have to deal with hornets only two courses are possible—one, not stir them up or aggregate them, the other to smoke them out and take their nest. To stir them up, put your hand into the nest and keep it there is not what a wise man would do; yet that is what I'm afraid of, if our present position is maintained.

—Sir George Campbell. The Lieutenant Governor of Bengal

'When in Rome', is a fine rule that has withstood the tests of time—for significant reasons—and for the smart traveller, it would pay to keep such a rule front and centre of mind.

Afghanistan is a stunning example of where such a rule would pay the worldly traveller's bountiful dividends.

Even for the not so keen observer, the country represents nothing less than brutality and relentless oppression. A place where a woman's seen as an object, or a tool for breeding. In their eyes, a woman is something that can be owned or sold for a cheap dowry. And that both men and boys were something to love, to cherish and even penetrate, when the mood is right.

But their rules stink, and they're disgusting, backward peoples, so why the fuck'd you want to travel there, anyway.

Ah-ah, old chum… judge not least he is prepared to front the man in the mirror. After all, it's their country. Why shouldn't they get to dictate the rules and way of life. And who are we—as foreigners—to question their law enforcement, as barbaric as that might be.

My word of advice; don't go poking inside any Afghan hornets' nests … unless you're sick in the head and enjoy getting bitten.

The hippies, in the sixties, understood this (while on their great, holy quest for opium, hashish and an inner sense of Dharma, during the country's 'Golden Age'.[22] The British Empire, in the early half of the nineteenth century, did not.

No, they weren't the least bit worried about the laws, customs, and traditions of the lands they'd be trampling on. They were too fucking paranoid about what the Russians were doing. Hence, they failed to grasp the complex, yet hospitable nature of the Afghans and their deep thirst for resistance.

Ah-hum, these primitive folk will happily scratch your back, and feed you, just don't expect them to do so from their hands and knees.

Still, in all their pomp and ignorance, the British marched confidently into Kabul, and opted not to integrate themselves into the village life. Instead, they set up their adjacent camps, completely shielding themselves from a rich civilisation with its own laws, governance and patronage that had been deeply grafted over the Millenia.

---

22   In the period between 1930 to 1970, Afghanistan was referred to as 'The Paris of Asia'. During these years, the nation's monarchy often worked with Afghan intellectuals and technocrats in order to advance the country—many of whom had earned their graduate degrees in American universities.

Food and hash were plentiful in the bazaars and tourists often remarked at the beauty of cities such as Kabul.

50 per cent of Kabul's teachers and government employees were women and often dressed in modern, Western attire. They were also free to come and go, as they please without male escorts—a practise prohibited in the modern, conservative Afghanistan.

International aid workers, teachers and developmental organisations spent considerable lengths of time in Afghanistan, and foreign women travelled the trough the cities with little fear for their security.

On the flip side, the Afghan men viewed these crude invaders with a hostile feeling of distrust. Yet, for a while, they allowed the British poor bedside manner to slide and sought to coexist. Through ill or goodwill, good were traded, gifts were exchanged, and peace was maintained.

For a time, this approach worked… until the young and virile British Officers decided they'd go interfere with the Afghan women. The Afghan tools. The Afghan possessions. The Afghan rights to breed and a promise of the next Afghan generation.

The devil they did?

The match was lit. A Jihad sparked. Blood spilled and the birth of a new Afghanistan nation was now in its infancy.

The British retreated, with their dead, and one simple lesson in their back pocket: When in Rome, leave their women alone.

Sylvia Dances

It was a Wednesday night. She was tall and blonde—with a Gold Coast tan—and had curves in all the right places.

I'd watched her all night, as she danced and drank. First, she danced the Booty Pop on table tops. Then she danced the Two-Step on the bar. She even sculled beer straight from the tap. She was a goddess with all the grace of Gaia.

I'm think I'm in love, I said to Davis.

He jabbed me in the arm with his elbow.

Well, how about you grow a pair, and ask for her name?

I reckon I will.

Davis laughed.

You wait and see.

You won't do nothing, Patterson. You're a little wuss.

The pub was emptying. I turned to the barmen and ordered.

One shot of tequila, and a rum and Coke, I said.

That's the spirit, said Davis.

I took the shot glass and held it to my lips. The tall blonde was back on solid ground and rummaging through her purse.

I downed the shot and walked over.

Everyone calls me Patterson, I said to the blonde.

Aren't you a little young to be drinking? she said.

I showed her my dog-tags. And, for the moment, she looked impressed.

Old enough to kill, and old enough to drink, I said.

Wow, she said, I don't think I care too much for that.

Okay, she's not into AJs and killing, and all that crap, I thought. Time to change plan.

How about we cut the small talk then, I said, and you let me buy the next round.

She snapped her purse closed and held it close to her chest.

Ooh, I can't, she said. I've got work and uni tomorrow.

I sipped at my rum and Coke. The blonde clung tight to her purse, as the music in the bar cut out.

LAST DRINKS, said the barman.

I turned to the bar. Davis was gone, but the blonde remained.

Listen, I said. I like your vibe. What's your name?

It's Sylvia.

Oh, like the song. 'Sylvia's Mother'?

Sure, she said. But she looked confused.

Listen, Sylvia—will I ever see you again?

Sylvia lowered her purse to her waist. Opened it, and pulled out a pencil and a TAB horse racing slip.

She wrote a small note, then handed me the slip.

Goodnight, soldier boy, she said. Turned, then she left the pub.

I flipped over the slip. She had a pineapple on *All a Lady* for a 9 to 1 win.

I caught the train south the following Tuesday.

Sylvia lived in a rented apartment along Annerley Road. I had to climb three damned flights of stairs, just to reach her front door.

C'mon in, she said. I wasn't sure if you were going to make it.

Are you kidding? I said. Cyclone Tracey wouldn't have stopped me.

I opened my wallet and took out the betting slip and laid it on the kitchen bench.

All a Lady, I said. Your nag got up.

Wow-wee, said Sylvia. I'd no idea about that.

She kicked off her slippers and danced. Then she opened the freezer door and pulled out a bottle of Grey Goose.

Let's celebrate, she said.

Vodka, I thought. It's only 5 o'clock.

It was too early for a booze-up, but it was always midnight somewhere in the world. Besides, Sylvia was beautiful with all that hair and all the curves. Just being in her presence had me at attention; I was ready to drink until the sun came up. And with a girl like Sylvia, it was impossible to say no.

A couple won't hurt, I said, but I've got PT in the morning, and my Serg's a real anal bastard. He'll rip me a new arsehole, if I'm late.

Take off your shoes and pants, she said. You're not getting in my bed like that.

Sylvia held the near empty Grey Goose in one hand and unbuttoned her pants with the other.

I got my pants unbuttoned too, but in all the pantomime, I'd forgotten to kick off my shoes. The result was an embarrassing mess.

Sylvia laughed. Your cheeks are bright red.

Really? I said, and with the bottle of vodka between us, we climbed beneath the sheets.

I like you, she said. You're both innocent and wild; with a naive freedom that'd terrify most people.

I smiled, thinking it was the booze doing the talking, but then she held my hand with hers. It was soft and warm, and I knew she wasn't lying.

I've an idea, she said, and pulled open her bedside draw.

She took out a small Polaroid.

Smile, she said, and the camera flashed.

I took the film and blew cold air on it, then waved it above the bed.

Only Sylvia's face appeared in the frame. Along with the corner of my shoulder.

You can keep it, she said. Then rolled over and fell asleep.

In the morning, the room was still dark save for a small bedside alarm clock with numbers that flashed a dull red.

Ahh Christ, it's only half-five, I said to Sylvia. I'm going back to sleep.

Nah-ah, said Sylvia. The six is always half dead.

What do you mean 'half dead'?

I mean it's actually half six.

Ah fuck… I have to go.

Sylvia sat up in bed. She reached beneath a pillow for the Grey Goose.

That stuff will make your skin turn yellow, drinking it this early.

Don't be a drip, Soldier boy. I can stop any time I like.

I gotta go, I said and climbed out of bed.

Why not call in sick?

Sick? I could call in dead, and the Army would demand I still get to work on time.

I walked into the bathroom and ran the shower. Sylvia stayed in bed with the bottle. She cuddled it like an old friend.

I scrubbed my face and my armpits, then grabbed the towel and wrapped it around my waist.

Back in the bedroom, Sylvia was reading a book. It was Hemingway: *For Whom the Bell Tolls.*

I can't stand that book, I said.

Sylvia put the book down.

Why'd you join the Army?

I stopped drying myself for the moment and thought.

It was that, or pushing trolleys, I said.

But don't soldiers die?

Well, yeah, that's one downside of the job.

Sylvia swung herself out of bed. The empty bottle of Grey Goose fell onto the floor.

Doesn't death frighten you, she said.

Well, yeah, but so does skydiving—

I dropped the towel to the floor and shook my hips. My cock swung from side to side and slapped against the top of my thighs. Sylvia pulled a pillow across her eyes.

That's disgusting, she said. Why the hell would you do such a thing?

I pulled on my pants, my shirt, then laced up my shoes.

Damn it, I thought, she's not into dick tricks, I'd better think up something, quick.

When can I see you again?

Sylvia took her book up and climbed back into bed.

Goodbye, soldier boy, she said.

I turned and left for the door.

Call me, she said.

September Eleven

I arrived without a moment to spare, only to find the joint was a complete fuck-fight.

Soldiers and officers were scrambling in and out of HQ to, well, God knows where.

There was screaming, and there was shouting. Sergeants blasting orders, and diggers running for distant cover.

I decided to slink in via a side gate and moved along the shadows cast by the HQ building.

The Regiment's Land Rovers lined up on the parade square. They looked ready to deploy at a moment's notice as diggers leant over the engine bays, checking the oil and topped up the fuel tanks with Army green Jerry-cans, then kicked the tyres.

Bugger me, I thought, have all these dumb fucks gone mental?

God damn it, said Davis. Where in the hell have you been?

Calm down, Sar-Major,[23] I said and held out my watch. I've still got two full minutes to spare.

Yeah, said Davis, smothering both hands over his face. Another two minutes and Baker would have hung you from a flagpole—you wouldn't have lived to see another day.

We walked to the smoko hut. Corporal White was sitting on a bench. He had a can of Coke in one hand, and a sausage roll in his mouth.

---

23   A soldier might condescend or mock their peer by addressing them via an incorrect rank if he or she is pushing the boundaries of their actual level of authority.

What the fuck are you doing, Patterson? said White. Why aren't you in uniform?

I watched as fresh pastry crumbs and tomato sauce rolled down his chin and crashed onto his gut. It was comical. But I had to avert my eyes and save myself from the big guffaw that was roiling inside my gut.

It's Wednesday morning, isn't it?

Yeah, said White.

Don't we have PT on Wednesday mornings?

White wiped a spot of tomato sauce from his chin, then washed down the last of his breakfast with a swift sip of Coke.

It's complete madness, Patterson. Pure psychotic madness. White belched, then held his hand to his chest. His face scrunched up; but in a short moment he looked relieved. Don't you watch the news?

I turned to Davis. He too had a sickened look on his face. For Christ's sake, I thought, I've gone and stepped into a god damned monkeys' cage.

I turned back to Corporal White, who was now having trouble breathing.

To be honest, Corporal, I don't even own a TV.

Are you serious? he said and took a gulp of Coke (this appeared to recharge his lungs). How on earth can anybody live without a TV?

White crushed the can between the palm of his hands, then his entire face turned to cherry red.

War, said White. Some primitive towel heads have gone and crashed their planes into the World Trade Centre—took both them suckers out. He took in a deep breath and the colour of his skin turned to pale grey.

Are you okay?

No, said White. Australia's going to war.

A Land Down Under

God. What a mess, I thought.

It was the closest thing to death the Devil had to offer. Nothing but soggy, piss-soaked bread and dirt to eat. Nothing but darkness to stare at, and nothing more to imagine than a destitute horror that would make a demon blush. But there wasn't a thing I could do; Bashir Khan had thrown me straight back in the pit.

That filthy heretic.

I laid on my back and begun drawing circles, in the air with the tips of my toes, praying for this nightmare to end.

That only made matters worse.

Then picture this if you will: I was perched on a hiding to nowhere, the British were coming to haul me away. For ten shillings—or less? SHIT. I was worth at least fifteen.

Still, I wasn't fixing to be no whipping boy. And my only shot at escaping with my brains intact would require nothing short of good old-fashioned skulduggery. I needed a plan. But the big problem was still glaring at me—I was trapped inside this nasty smelling pit. My chances were looking paper thin.

Let those dirty pigs come and take me.

Bugger it. Let's see them come and try.

I jumped to my feet. LET ME OUT, I said, then kicked the door.

It buoyed morale and provided me with added pluck, if only for a short while. Because—truth be told—nothing good ever lasts in hell. The only antidote to that, I said, would be sweet revenge.

There was a brief thought of escape; I could cut off the Khan's head, then flee.

I knew the plan could never work, but it beat curling up to die. That just wasn't the Pashtun way.

Some days I would sleep standing; while others I'd settle for lying down. I tried sleeping on my front, and often on my side. Then, when all the tossing and turning became too tiresome, I tried sleeping upside down. That was always the hardest, and often futile way—trying to get those angles just right so all the blood couldn't drain out from my skull.

And trust me when I say this: a man is not a fruit bat, and a blind one cannot fly.

One day the door opened at an unusual time. It was neither morning, noon nor night, which threw my pupils out of sync.

I damn near shit my trousers, and dove for the back corner of the pit.

Who in this hell is it? I said. And why are you fucking up my sleep?

A man stepped forward. He was wearing all black and had covered his face in a green shemagh.

Stay back, I said, or else I'll kick you in the balls.

Shhh, he said. You don't want to wake the guards.

Mahmout? I said and poked my head out from the pit. What are you doing here? Where is your motorcycle?

Mahmout cleared the shemagh from his face, then put both hands on my shoulders.

I sold it for two boat fares to Australia, George.

I stared at Mahmout square in the eyes, but couldn't decide if the man was serious or not.

Australia? I said. Where on earth is that?

It's wonderful country, George. Located somewhere down under.

I laughed. Because now I knew the cheeky Pashtun was having me on.

Mahmout opened his coat and pulled out a map.

It's right here, he said, and pointed to an island.

I laughed again.

Dear God, I said, it's surrounded by the ocean. No cameleer could ever cover that.

Mahmout pushed the matter further but, with all the stubbornness of a mule, I resisted.

No, Mahmout, I said. I cannot run like a coward; let the British swine take me, if it's all the same

The British swine, George? You poor fool, don't you know the Khan plans to hang you in the street.

I paused and chewed on this fresh information but could see no courage in Mahmout's sense of morality. Running was not for me.

No, I said, I have to remain here, Mahmout, I'll slice off the Khan's head, long before he can loop another rope around Sher Gul's neck.

Mahmout pulled the shemagh back across his face.

It's a fool's errand, George. You'll never make it past his guards.

I stumbled. The Pashtun had a point. But how'd I not see this in my plans. Then I scratched my forehead. Then dug my hands deep inside my trouser pockets and pulled out a single pistachio nut.

How far away is this Australia place? I said and split the shell.

Mahmout held out the map and ran finger across the Indian Ocean.

A short stone's throw, he said.

As the crow flies?

There may be a detour along the way. I can't be sure.

It forced me to take stock when considering it. When things like this sound too good, it's often because they are—too good.

When can we leave? I said.

Before first light, George. Your beast is waiting outside the city walls.

Huzzah, I said, and shut the pit door.

The Sykes & Picot Treaty[1]

Throughout the Great War, the control of oil became paramount.

It was imperative that we kept Arab oil out of the Hun's hands, said General Ironside.

Come 1916, British and French officers Sykes and Picot drafted some super secretive plans. Together, their grit and cunning would safeguard said regional oil for years to come.

The traditional borders of the Middle East are about to be redrawn, said Sykes.

The oil will be safe in French and British, monsieur, said Picot.

May that same year, the Sykes and Picot agreement became official.

Our boys were accurate with their plans. That oil wasn't going anywhere, but into allied tanks, warships and planes.

The old relics of an Ottoman Empire subsequently faded, and the region wouldn't be the same again.

After the Great War concluded, so did the Sykes and Picot agreement. But all cards were still in play, and the plans for Britain and France[24] to inherit the area were now coming up a royal flush.

---

24   Britain and France divided the region between their own administrative areas of control. Over the years, several borders and country names have not only changed, but morphed the region into the geopolitical hot bed it is today.

Leon Trotsky soon caught a whiff of this bogus deal. And the Soviet's—in their current infancy—well and truly cracked the shits.

This is the agreement of Colonial thieves, said Comrade Stalin.

True to form, nobody listened to Trotsky (whose fate was sealed) and as far as Old Blighty considered it, nobody heard a peep.

All wars must end—as they do—and it was time the Empire's soldiers packed up their troubles in their old kit bags[25] and headed on home. Now, either the British and French leaders didn't get the memo (that their time in the region was over), or flat out ignored it.

Non, said the Les Pays Des Droits De L'Homme. We must've have misunderstood.

Beirut and Damascus were next to be re-annexed and collectively formed the new State of Lebanon. All under a mandate called the San Remo Agreement. In 1932, Damascus was re-annexed within The State of Syria.

Iraq and Lebanon. Transjordan. Syria and Palestine. All were becoming colonised. Confrontations flourished throughout the region, as the new boundaries messed up the old ways and created a sort of Middle Eastern stew.

In this case, one too many cooks were spoiling the brew and the beef was burnt. That really pissed the locals off.

Where the British done yet? Oh, no Sir-ee Bob.

In 1948, they decidedly ended their mandate in Palestine.

---

25   A WW1 marching song, written by Felix Powell. The tune strongly typified the phlegmatic demeanour of the British Soldier, even in the shadows of a receding empire.

Then—almost immediately—they trans morphed it into a Jewish state.

Baruch-haba, they said. Come on in, you'll feel right at home.

The French and British stranglehold eventually dwindled in the region. And by 1970, they became ghosts from the past.

Did they bemoan missing out on 69's 'summer of love' occurring in the United States? Who knows? But the fun (in the Middle East region) was just getting started.

New parties were forming in the ashes of the Sykes and Picot agreement, and various other accords. The Israeli's, Palestinians, Syrians and the Lebanese remained. Fresh figureheads were sharpening their teeth. Old scabs were being peeled, and ancient battlefronts were—once again—preparing to taste the blood of everyday people like you and me.

WHEN THE CHICKENS COMES HOME TO ROOST

It took the Russian's two-hundred and fifty years to get into Afghanistan. The British started later, but got there much sooner.

—Rodric Braithwaite. AFGHANSTY.

The 60s and the 70s came and went in Afghanistan. The Golden Age was over, and the hippy trails were long gone.

Western Scholars. Foreign Diplomats. Bourgeoisie businesses, engineers, and tourists had all packed up their Shisha and vanished.

Even the once fabled Chicken Street Bazaar had got up and flown the coup. And bulk tourism hasn't been back since.

It was almost a tale of what could have been for Afghanistan. An age, and an era that would spell the end of feudalism. An era which provided women with a right to education and—for the first time in Afghan history—the chance to vote.

It wasn't to be.

The Soviet-built Polytechnic University opened its doors in 1967; and thus, enabled academia to flourish. But the growth unfolded way too fast, and the country's sluggish economy failed to keep pace.

This misalignment stifled the budding graduates and left them without gainful employment. So, they placed their anger within the rising communist movement.

Yes, the times they were *a*-changing. Many learned students were returning from overseas sojourns in Soviet and US universities. All were hitting the streets of Kabul to join their comrades with the future in their hearts, and reform on their minds.

In the cities, the more progressive ideals were a number one hit. While in the countryside, it was a different story. Villages were under the rule of Tribal Leaders, Mullahs and hard-line Islamic conservatives. And, out there, this new fan-dangled shit wouldn't flush.

Well, Nostradamus couldn't have predicted what'd happen next.

The only antidote to mental suffering is physical pain, said one K Marx.

The progressive Afghans took such words with far less than a grain of salt.

What worked for Stalin will work in Afghanistan too, said a Persian Comrade all the way from Moscow.

In 1978, a vicious Communist coup rose up. The old monarchy fell, and it was high-fives and fist pumping all-round. But, like the old hard heads in the villages suggested, such putrid crap would not flush.

The retaliation from the village Mullahs, leaders and hard-line conservatives was nothing short of brutal; and The Mujahideen was born.

Early in the fracas, the Soviet Government refused to provide aid. That was until the Afghanistan President caught one, short and stiff. So, they sent in the Spetsnaz to kick down The Mujahideen's front door.

We'll have these prehistoric rats rounded up within six months, said the Spetsnaz command. Then we'll train up your guys, so this will never happen again.[26]

Nothing in Afghanistan is ever that straightforward. Nor is it ever that simple. Alexander The Great knew this. Ghengis Khan knew this, and clearly the British were handed their own lessons in Afghan occupation. Now it was the Soviet's turn to take a seat, at the very front of the classroom.

The Royal Saudis took some umbrage with the non-Islamic, Soviet presence in Afghanistan. It wasn't the Wahhabi way.

We'll raise an Arab legion, said the Royal family. I'll send my son, the Prince, and we'll kick those Russkis out.

The American CIA encouraged this message. And even sold arms and munitions to Saudi Arabia for deployment in Afghanistan. Only the Prince refused to go.

A Saudi billionaire business owner, who counted his coins in the construction game, stood up. You're nothing but a Royal coward, he said to the Prince. Then he packed his kit and headed for the caves of Afghanistan.

Throughout the ensuing ten years, this business owner piously fought alongside the Mujahideen. But his generous contributions didn't stop there. With his money and skills, he built roads and vital infrastructure. Plus, some heavily fortified caves along the

---

26   A strategy later adopted by former Secretary of Defence, Donald Rumsfeld. Due to cultural differences, the strategy failed for the Soviets and the US.

ridgelines of Tora Bora[27]—an area the billionaire would become heavily familiar with.

The US media lauded him as a modern-day Laurence of Arabia. A new star was born and, in the young businessman, America had found themselves a powerful ally.

In short, and with a little help from Uncle Sam, the Soviets admitted defeat. Both in Afghanistan and, arguably, in the Cold War.

The USSR soon collapsed.

But the tensions didn't end there for the Afghans. Yes, the Soviets were gone, but a fresh struggle had begun in the aftermath of the war. First disharmony snared tribal leaders, mullahs, and warlords. Then things got out of hand. The billionaire business owner grabbed his tools and departed. Leaving behind him a brooding civil war.

I just couldn't stand sitting around why the old men bickered, he said. There's more work to be done.

So, off he went, with his billions, and many loyal followers. Off to Sudan, where he'd planned to construct a new highway and such.[28] Yet this cat wasn't naïve—he knew the world wasn't all rainbows and pretty white unicorns. And he knew exactly which way the wind blew.[ii] A bad scent was in the air which told him something fishy was going on.

In hindsight, he should have kept his nose clean. An honest

---

27   The battle of Tora Bora was both a physical and psychological defeat inflicted upon the US Military commanders in the early stages of the Global War on Terror. This was mainly due to poor military intelligence. The Mujahideen had not just inhabited these mountains during Soviet occupation, but heavily fortified the high ground. The Taliban used the same fortifications for their own geographical advantage. This meant they were equally guarded from air strikes, which could not penetrate the fortifications. The knowledge of the terrain enabled the Taliban to defeat a far superior force. And, to pour added salt onto the US wounds, the key target, Osama Bin Laden left the Tora Bora valley for safe haven in the neighbouring Pakistan. They'd have to wait a decade to catch up with him again.

28   International Correspondent, Robert Fisk, first met with Osama Bin Laden in Sudan (1990), shortly after Saddam invaded Kuwait. Fisk described Bin Laden as a shy man and noted that the people of Sudan had warmed to the 'Holy Warrior'. The last time Fisk interviewed Bin Laden, in a secluded cave, was days prior to the 9/11 attacks.

man cannot allow his better judgements go pissing in the wind. No, he should have been content, sitting alone in silence. Building roads with only himself and Allah counting tea leaves.

But that wasn't how this—soon to be—death dealer rolled. And, when George Double-ya overstepped the mark(s) in Kuwait,[29] he turned to him and said, Hey Yankee! Kiss my Saudi arse.

The cat was out of the bag, and the billionaire got painted public enemy number one. A bona fide outlaw with a target on his back. And now it seemed like everywhere he went, the suckers wanted him dead.

The once US-backed Gaddafi[30] was also realising his new title as *adversary.*[iii] And long before the US Government seized all Libyan assets,[iv] Gaddafi noted: Elvis has left the building.[31]

Saddam, too, was counting down the days, and by the time Bill Clinton arrived in office, the entire economical rug had been tugged out from beneath his feet.[32] Next to go was his military— causing a vacuum, of sorts which opened the door for more nefarious opponents.[v]

But was Clinton finished? No. Not before a blood-red sunset began fading over the Arab desert.[33][vi]

---

29   Saddam Hussein had initiated the invasion of Kuwait—sparking the first Gulf War—and although he'd once been backed by the US Government, he'd now fallen out of favour and the US sought to have him replaced. Initially, Osama Bin Laden had declared his militia would combat Saddam's forces; however, Bush Sr bypassed Bin Laden, thus igniting the feud between the two states.

30   In 2008, Diplomat David Welch first established diplomatic relations with Gaddafi, during the Bush administration. Welch was said to be supportive of Gaddafi and was heavily influential in providing guidance on propagandist strategies in the region.

31   Libyan assets frozen by U.S. exceeding $34billion.

32   As a result of UN sanctions, 500,000 children lost their lives.

33   During the Monica Lewinsky scandal, Clinton had bombed Afghanistan and Sudan. Facing impeachment, he turned his attention to Iraq.
Since 2003, figures estimate that more than 280,000 Iraqis were killed as a direct result of the US invasion. Many more had been killed indirectly.

One day the billionaire returned to Afghanistan, where he began whittling away at the next big plan. His next big move. And what that meant for US Government was that the chickens were now coming home to roost.

Something We'll Never Forget

I have no visibility into who the bad guys are.

—*Donald Rumsfeld, US Secretary of Defence*

People will always remember where they were on the day, said Sergeant Baker.

And I guess he was right.

About the terror at least. It was something we'll never forget. Because you can't forget. Not a thing like that.

Yet, if I could express my own opinions on the whole affair, it'd be to say we each watched it unfold in our unique way.

For now, that's all I'll say on the matter. Because, for me, the past had passed. The towers had crumbled and thousands paid the ultimate cost. Millions were left in shock and mourning. There was so much horror you could not erase; but it was a soldier's prerogative to always focus on the future. We had a job to do: finding and killing the fuckers who created this whole mess.

Baker stopped the Land Cruiser at a red traffic light. He lit up a cigarette. I watched the tip glow a cherry red. He exhaled and a dense cloud of smoke drifted into the rear of the cabin where Davis and I sat.

I wound the window down until all the smoke cleared.

Baker laughed.

It's about time you got into the game, he said. It'll harden up your lungs.

The traffic lights remained red. A small boy in a neighbouring car pressed his face against the glass. He made a pistol with his hands and pointed it right at me.

I smiled, and the traffic lights turned green and his car sped off. But I spotted a sticker on the rear windscreen, which read: Make Love, Not War.

Australia cannot ignore it, said Baker as he tabbed his cigarette on the ashtray.

There'll be the many who disagree, said Davis.

Fuck them, said Baker.

The Land Cruiser hooked a left towards the Barracks. Baker had a fresh cigarette lit before we completed the turn.

It's the sharp end of a stick here, gentlemen, said Baker as he blew out a fresh puff of smoke. You'll come to learn that all smart soldiers bury their dissent on war, and politics in some dark, old-fashioned way. We'll never question it, and we sure as hell don't go flapping our gums about in the streets.

Surely the powers that be wouldn't deprive a soldier of his own good conscience? said Davis.

Baker stubbed his cigarette on the thin edge of the windowpane.

He can keep it for as long as he pleases, said Baker, but he must follow orders, no questions asked, and keep that shit to himself.

What the fuck were they talking about?

Some faceless terrorists had just spudded into the World Trade Centre. The twin towers were a bloody rubble, and here Davis was gobbing off about some bleating conscience caper.

It was all bull crap, of course. Loose lips and morality all take a back seat when you're going to war.

Whatever the rate, the average soldier didn't know where the war was heading, let alone where it came from. But, for now, the terrorists were dust; pronounced dead on arrival, and anything clearly resembling an enemy had vanished in the fray. Whoosh. In one big puff of smoke. So long. Farewell, Allah Akbar, and good luck sleeping easy at night.

Howard's henchmen in Canberra hadn't the foggiest clue either of what the hell we were doing.

Would terror arrive on golden soil? Perhaps not.

They all put one foot in fire, just in case.

The cynics in the House—and throughout the cross-benches— argued until they were black and blue before they could decide: what no-one else could decide (on what to do) until it was finally agreed: we should support the US regardless.

Whenever I looked upstairs, the brass were clinging tight to such suppositions and superstitions. The readings between the tea leaves were floating thick and fast. It was short-sighted mysticism. I shit you not.

Millions of litres of Earl Grey were devoured in the dead of night, and truckloads of prawn sandwiches were shipped in throughout the entire malarkey—that was the days following 9/11. Officers and enlisted men alike quit; but thousands more enlisted to fight this cruel, but vanished foe. Then it was decided: Afghanistan is where this Global War on Terror would be fought and won.

Well, that really tore my guts up the middle.

Prior to the disaster, I was a happy little Vegemite. True blue, like backyard cricket in the melting Queensland summer.

Bundaberg Rum and XXXX Gold went waltzing through my veins in a river of green and gold malady.

But so did some wild Afghani ichor. Or so I was told.

Straight down the line, I was now at war with my own family history, and the situation was incurable.

Meanwhile, back in the public domain, it appeared like business as usual. People were driving to and from work, listening to B105 and 4KQ. All while their kids still went to school playing who's afraid of the big bad wolf.

But everyone was still double checking their deadbolts at night, because you never knew who, or where the wolf was, until he was deep inside your chicken coup. As a result, we became the most secure generation in history—almost overnight—and anything closely resembling a turban was viewed with suspicion.

Baker steered the Land Cruiser through the front gates of Gallipoli Barracks.

There was a 24/7 patrol navigating the Barracks perimeter, aiming to keep the bad guys out—whoever we imagined they were. Every patrol soldier carried a Maglite and clean pick handle as their only defence. Some also had pocketknives and multi-tools strapped to their utility belts. And most weren't afraid to use them.

Now that's not much, I hear ya thinking. However, it's still a menacing step-up from a torch. Under any circumstance, you'd be surprised what a soldier can do with a folding blade or a Phillip-head screwdriver. And even though that wouldn't have been enough to turn The Desert Fox[34] away from his dinner, it still kept the neighbours sleeping snug in their beds each night.

But regardless of their utility, the multi-tool could not defend our nation against the world's terrorist organisations. No matter how large, or small they were. And only a goose would choose to believe otherwise.

---

34   General Erwin Rommel in World War 2 is considered as the one of the greatest ever Field Marshalls.

That's right. What we needed were bigger weapons, and more munitions. Right now, pronto, and on the double. Yet would the Generals answer our prayers? Well, we'd all have to get on our hands and knees then wait and see.

We continued driving through the Barracks until we arrived at a red-brick auditorium.

It's named after Monash, said Baker. He was one of the best, fellas. Only they don't make them like that anymore.

Davis and I both agreed, even if we didn't know otherwise, then followed Baker through the front door.

The Commanding Officer ordered us to our seats. He was a short but thin man who wore thick, black-rimmed glasses and was running short of hair.

What we're up against, ladies and gentlemen, is nothing short of farmers in sandals. It's asymmetric warfare—they're an inferior force.

He turned and paced along the front of the room. He put his hands in his pockets, then he took them out again, and wiped his brow and stopped.

In sandals, can you believe it? We'll be in and out of there in no time, right after we deliver them a good old-fashioned Aussie kick in the arse. The deployments will come thick and fast. This war will make East Timor, Bougainville and even Rwanda seem like a walk in the park. No, we'll make the bastard terrorists think twice before they pull a stunt like that again.

He removed his glasses and wiped them clean with a small white cloth.

Questions or queries, ladies and gents?

Yes, Sir, said a soldier in the back row. How did a bunch of farmers man a plane all the way from Afghanistan to New York?

Now isn't that the trillion-dollar question?

I looked to the boss and waited for his response.

He folded the white cloth, then returned his glasses to the bridge of his nose.

Well, it's quite obvious, isn't it? Said the boss.

He mounted the steps of the auditorium and removed his glasses once again. His eyes tracked down the questioning soldier.

They hijacked the planes while they were mid-flight. They slashed up the pilots. And harboured no intentions of ever landing on solid ground.

The auditorium fell silent. Then the boss walked back to the front of the room.

Final questions? he said.

The audition remained silent.

These terrorists are the worst humans possible, ladies and gentlemen. International criminals of the highest order and we must crush them with both hands.

The front row of the auditorium began clapping.

The boss nodded. You're all dismissed from here, and I'll see you again at the boozer for 3 o'clock beers.

Baker climbed back inside the Land Cruiser and slammed the driver's door shut.

That bastard doesn't have the faintest clue, he said.

Well. We get to follow his orders?

Fuck him, said Baker. It's people like that who'll get a soldier killed.

The engine started, and all the windows went down as Baker lit a cigarette. Then we drove over to the boozer without a single word.

Some Mother's Son

I was nine beers deep at the boozer when Davis stood up and ordered his first can of lemonade.

First, he arched his knuckles back on the ring pull. The can let out a quiet hiss. Then he took a sip, and walked out the door.

Hold it, you bastard, I said. Where in the hell you think you're going?

Can't stand the smell of this place, he said.

Ahh, man, wait for me.

Davis kept walking and sipped at his lemonade. It wasn't apparent that he had anything considerable to say or that he wanted to speak at all. So, I thought I'd do the talking for the pair of us.

Hey, Davis, could you ever imagine being any of those farmers?

He took another sip, then lowered the can.

Can't imagine it's different to being an Australian, he said.

Sacrilegious bullshit, man. You telling me we're no different to them savages over there, living in dusty caves—plotting our deaths?

Patterson, you idiot—we're all born and then we die. Can't you see we're all part of the same human race. Everyone is living for something. Or don't you get that?

When we reached the living quarters, Davis mounted the top floor's steps. I started making my way along the bottom floor.

Say that's true, Davis. Say it's true: that we're all born and then we die, but isn't that where the similarities end? And what do suppose goes on in between birth and death. Doesn't that count for something?

I haven't got the faintest, he said, looking down from the second flight of steps. All I know is, we're all some mothers' son and you can take that to bed. Or not. I don't particularly care.

AND THE BEAR WENT OVER THE MOUNTAIN

Mahmout and I moved North, via Kabul, then headed East towards Jalalabad and into the Khyber Pass.

We had Penny, a second camel and a donkey we'd commandeered for the trip. It walked slow and lazy and trailed far behind its longer-legged travel companions.

Don't worry, George, it'll come in handy when the journey heads into Pakistan, said Mahmout.

The day had reached high noon when Mahmout froze on the crest of a dusty knoll.

What the devil is it? I said.

It's a bear.

A bear?

Yes, a Russian bear.[35]

The beast stumbled down through a ravine, then stopped, scratching its stomach in the centre of the track.

---

35   While the Khyber Pass stands as a major trade corridor between Afghanistan and Pakistan, along the old Silk Road, China also shares a boundary with Afghanistan. Former Soviet Union countries, such as Tajikistan, also shared a border with Afghanistan, enabling Soviet forces to cross the border during their decade-long occupation.

Today, the Wakhan Pass/corridor still offers a passage into Afghanistan. Regarded as a somewhat safe region, travellers often cross through on motorbike and 4-wheel drive. It's not uncommon to sight Asiatic Black Bears in either the Khyber or Wakhan Pass.

What's a Russian bear doing out here, Mahmout?

He didn't answer.

Then the bear squatted.

Whatever you do, George—don't move.

I don't intend on it.

The bear stood and sniffed the air. Then the bear went over the mountain,[36] and we continued our journey East.

Two guards jumped out from a wooden hut and stamped their boots on the track. They were wearing black vests and green Pakol hats.

Stop, you dogs, said one guard. You're now entering British India.[37]

Aww, poppycock, I said. It's all Pashtun heartland.

One guard unsheathed his sword and carved a straight line into the dirt. British India is on this side of the line. And that side is yours, Afghan dogs.

That's all hokum, I said. I scuffed the line with my heels. Our people have had free passage through here for a thousand years.

Well, if you wanna pass now, it'll cost you a thousand Afghani.[38]

I looked at Mahmout, and we both squat down on the path.

We have no food, no money, and nothing to trade, said Mahmout.

I stood and faced the guards.

Will you accept our donkey?

---

36   Soviet Forces were not trained in guerrilla warfare and had to adapt to the tactics throughout soviet occupation. The lessons were recorded, and counter tactics were developed and published in the military pamphlet: The Bear Went Over the Mountain: Soviet Tactics in Afghanistan. Lester W. Grau. 1996.

37   Now Pakistan. The border, as dictated by the British Government, splits the two countries, via the Durand Line which divides Pashtun heartland. The Pakistan side of this region became a safe haven for the Taliban during the war. It's also the region which gave birth to the Taliban, post Soviet withdrawal.

38   The national currency of Afghanistan.

The two guards walked around the donkey. One guard ran his palm across the donkey's dock and pushed the tail aside. The donkey didn't move.

Perfect, he said. Welcome to British India.

THREE SHEETS TO THE WIND

The days, weeks, and months quickly passed after 9/11, but I'd noticed something changing within Sylvia. It was this curious thing which drew her closer to me, with a warm, innocent touch. I couldn't put my finger on the cause of it. Was it the terror which now gripped our lives, or the fear of war, hovering over our heads with the prospects of dying? Whatever it was, the warmer she became, the colder I got as I struggled to keep the soldier separated from the boy.

I stood on her balcony—three sheets to the wind drunk—and emptied the last of my beer into the garden below. I began rapping on her door.

The living room light flickered on, and the door swung open. She was wearing a long t-shirt, which covered her hips. Her legs were bare.

Have you been drinking? she said

Have I been drinking? It's Friday night.

I walked in and sat on the couch, still wearing my camo pants from work, and a pair of blue thongs. I kicked them beneath the coffee table.

So, you're going out tonight? she said.

No.

Wanna take me out?

Nope.

She closed the door and folded her arms. Why don't you ever invite me out with your friends?

You wouldn't enjoy them, I said, and picked up a *Cosmo* magazine from the table.

Oh, and says who?

I threw the magazine back on the table. I don't understand how you can read these magazines, I said. Anyone reading them is living in fantasy land.

Sylvia walked into the bathroom. I followed her, but she shut the door behind her and locked me out.

I'm sorry, I said. Us soldiers, we don't understand these sensitive civilian things. We're all conditioned to war: life in the field, eating with our hands, shitting into dugout holes.

It's not our fault, I went on. Our compassion gets warped at an early stage. We bury our feelings where no one can ever find them. It's the only way a soldier can function. Christ, it's the only way a soldier can survive.

I knocked on the bathroom door. The toilet flushed, and water ran in the sink. Sylvia came back out, wiped her wet hands on her shirt, and sat on the couch.

There was a late news program on the tv.

What if we sit and watch a movie? I said.

Can't. I have to study.

The news switched to the Middle East.

This news just in: America has committed a further 1000 troops to Afghanistan. It's expected the US Government will deploy 10 000, to the country to fight the Global War on Terror.

Our own PM has also committed a contingent of Australian troops to the Middle East.

The news crossed to the vision of the Prime Minister standing before Parliament House.

Australia's contribution is significant. And important, said Prime Minister Howard. *And it should be vital to the security of the Australian people.*

Will you be going? said Sylvia.

Damn, I hope so. We need to stop those bastards in their tracks. God knows who they'll target next.

Sylvia poured herself a glass of vodka, then passed me the bottle.

If you love me, and you trust me, you won't go, she said.

Trust and love? I said. What's that got to do with war?

Sylvia ripped the bottle from my hands and topped up her glass.

We can only build relationships on trust, you know. Besides, why do you wanna go to war, anyway.

Fucking *women*.

What the fuck are you talking about?

I grabbed her purse off the coffee table. Reached deep inside and pulled out my credit card.

See? How's that for trust?

I waved the card in her face then she began crying.

Oh, please. That isn't the point, she said, and poured another glass of vodka. I want to meet your friends. I bet them boys are at least a bit scared. I snatched the bottle back from her and began sculling. It burned the back of my throat and my nostrils. I sneezed, and my nose started running. Scared? Sure, we're scared, I said, but we can't allow a few butterflies in the belly stand in our way. Those bastards need removing.

Well, why us? Why should Australians go fight America's war? The terrorists never harmed us—

Because it's our duty, and it always has been ever since Gallipoli. Australia refused to let bullies push our friends around.

I tried to put my arm around Sylvia—to calm her down, if nothing else.

Piss off, she said, and ran back inside the bathroom, locking the door behind her again.

That's twice in five minutes.

Sylvia. *JESUS.* Come out!

FUCK OFF. Go and play in your silly war. Get shot up and blown to pieces. Come back a cripple that can't wipe his own arsehole for Christ's sake. GO DIE, I don't care.

I sat outside the bathroom door and considered my next move.

Do you want me to leave?

Sylvia opened the door and stood in the hallway. Her face burned red with anger and her eyes stabbed through the night air.

Sylvia pounced forward and punched me square on the chest.

You bitch, I said. Why the hell'd you go and do that?

She held up her fist and shaped to punch me again. I moved to cover my face.

I'm gonna kill you, she said.

Okay, okay, okay, I'm going! and I scuttled my way out onto the balcony.

The door slammed behind me. The deadbolt clicked, followed by the door-chain. Finally, the lights went out.

Christ, I thought. All I wanted was to sit and watch a movie.

In the Grip of the Grape

It was a warm Monday morning, and I was in the grip of the grape and looking pale.

Christ, I thought I should've stayed in bed or the bar. Instead, here I am stooped outside and screaming at the sun.

Talk about burning it from both ends.

Form up, said Baker.

The troops made their way out onto the parade ground. I took my position within the ranks (on Davis's right) and clicked my heels together.

You stink like shit, he said.

Thank you.

You look like shit, too.

I cocked my elbow and handed Davis a solid jab to the ribs.

Enough with the flattery, already, I said and brushed the lint off my PT shirt, then straightened my hat.

Big weekend?

Sylvia jacked-up, big time, and now it looks like we're toast.

Baker halted, then came to attention right in front of us.

Three Squadron… ATTENTION.

Have you tried apologising? said Davis.

Fuck that, I said. I've done nothing wrong.

Apologise anyway, you fool.

AT EASE, said Baker. Answer your names, excusing rank:

ADAMS

Present

ANDERSON

Sir

DAVIS

Present

PATTERSON

Sir

WHITE—

WHITE—

Has anyone seen Corporal White?

Nobody answered, and Baker placed the roll book in his pocket.

Three Squadron. ATTENTION.

The morning's PT we'll be running up Mt Enoggera. After falling-out, wait by the gate for further directions.

Squadron. FALL-OUT.

I stood by the gate with Davis. Baker disappeared inside Headquarters. Then he returned, with a coffee mug and cigarette in his hand.

Davis looked at me, then raised his eyebrows.

Patterson. Davis, said Baker. Drop your cocks, pull up your socks, and get your arses over here.

We ran across to Baker and stamped our feet at attention.

Either of you hairless ball-sacks got plans for the rest of the year?

No, Serge!

Got wives, girlfriends or any whelps at home?

No.

Christ, a God does exist, he said, then pursed his lips over his coffee mug and took a sip. Now, surprise, surprise, fellas. Corporal White has gone and choked himself on a burrito.

Baker wedged the cigarette between his lips and took a drag.

Is he gonna be alright?

Ha, said Baker. Here's the funny part. His heart stopped for two whole minutes before kicking off again.

Shit, I said. I didn't know he had a heart.

Damn, that's cold, said Davis.

Fuck him, said Baker. This is the Army, not a fat camp.

The sun was now cooking with gas, and hot sweat crept between my butt cheeks.

Davis looked at me with his eyes widened then Baker pulled out a giant carrot and dangled it before the pair of us.

We need more bums on seats, he said, but the question is can you fairies handle Afghanistan?

My skin dried and went cold. My guts swirled and rumbled like a volcano. I looked at Baker and swayed. Bugger me.

I swayed a little more, then puked at Baker's feet.

It was a cool yellow—textured by small food chunks—that attracted a swarm of flies.

Christ, Patterson, he said. You stink like shit.

The troops lined up at the front gate. Baker dropped his cigarette on the bitumen and scrubbed it out with his heel. He flashed a wristwatch before mine and Davis' eyes. It was a black G-shock containing more buttons than a jet-airliner.

Fifty minutes, he said.

Fifty, Serge? said Davis.

To get to the top of Mt Enoggerra and back.

He pointed across the Barracks, and up towards the minor peak which shadowed the base, then smiled.

Because you guys are half my age, you're gonna do it in forty-five.

It'll be a piece of piss, said Davis.

I didn't mutter a word—either way I was up shit creek.

Neither of you two ball bags wanna finish behind me, he said. Else you can forget Afghanistan even exists.

Baker tossed the dregs of his coffee into the drain, then pressed the start button on his watch and shuffled out the gate.

I damn near gave birth to kittens when I saw Davis tucking-in, right beside him.

Like hell ya do, said Baker, and he switched up a gear.

Davis kicked his heels and kept on the pace. And, pretty soon, they left me, dragging my sorry knuckles, a good hundred meters behind.

It took me fifteen minutes to reach the foot of the hills and I was already knocking on heaven's door.

Our dearest Father, which art in heaven, I said. Spare me the indignity and forgive me for my sins. For ever and ever, dear God. Take me now. Amen.

My legs wobbled at the first sight of the incline. My chest burned, and my stomach continued to roil. I was in one helluva of a mess and paused beneath a tree then puked all over the scrub. It was still the same cool yellow.

Baker was marking time on the next plateau and turned to watch me as I wiped the drivel from my mouth.

C'mon, Patterson, he said. We're not here to fuck spiders. Now move your arse.

I looked further up the hill. Davis was nowhere in sight.

That sneaky bastard, I thought, and stumbled back onto the road.

I caught Baker at the next dip in the climb.

C'mon, he said, we're only five hundred meters from the peak. Pick up your feet.

My body hunched over into a sad little frump, and I couldn't breathe. The grape still had me by the throat.

I sighted the top of the climb.

Five hundred meters, my arse. This prick of a hill will never end.

Why'd you join my Army, if all you're gonna do is skulk about like a drunken bag of shit? said Baker.

Then he got in close and punched me in the arm. The knock tipped me off balance. My knees buckled and my entire arm throbbed.

Well? he said.

Sylvia, the bitch, Serg. She went and dumped me. All because of this fucken war.

I regretted ever opening my mouth but there was no turning away from it now.

Christ, I thought. What kinda soldier talk was that. Baker will take this news and run.

Hell, said Baker. All this over a girl?

She wasn't just any girl—

Ahh, bullshit. They're all the same. Besides, you'll have forgotten about her by the time we've reached the *Ghan*.

We reached the peak.

Sure is beautiful up here, said Baker.

I looked about. There was nothing but trees blocking my view.

We turned and ran back down the mountain.

The grape was slowly letting go.

Red Hair, Brown Hair, Blonde Hair, Pink Hair

Our blessed community is fast becoming a mixed bag. Yet, more of these shipments continue reaching our shores. You'd better believe it: the coloured race is increasing their numbers at an alarming pace. With all these yellow, pigtailed Chinese. The docile Malay. The cunning Japanese. And the petticoated Afghans; any business owners will soon feel a sense of saturation.

—1 July 1892 The Victorian Express.

Mahmout dragged his beast towards the water's edge.

Guess she's never seen the ocean before, he said, or ever sailed across one.

White water crashed against the breakwater and Mahmout's shemagh waved in the breeze as I looked towards him.

It's not too late to go home, I said.

And for you, Cameleer?

I fastened Penny's lead to a hitching post, then looked out over the bustling Karachi harbour.

My dear Mahmout, I said. I've already come this far. There's no turning back now.

At the entrance of a cattle yard, an Australian man stood in a buttoned flannel shirt and a rabbit skin hat.

How much you want for the beasts?

Forget about it, I said. They're not for sale.

Alright, alright, he said, there's no need to get yer knickers in a twist. I always thought they were a hideous-looking creatures—mongrels to handle, but a real asset in the desert. Wouldn't you agree?

I didn't answer, and watched Penny swishing her stumpy tail as the man circled around her rear. He looked at her knees, then her feet, and finally her hips.

Tell you what, Mohamed: I'll give you five shillings?

Like I said, she's not for sale.

Gawd bollocks, said the man, for the right price everything's for sale.

The man paused, and spat in the dirt, then circled around Penny one more time.

Tell me, Mahomed, what's your reason for travel?

Work, I said. I'm going to show Australia I'm the finest cameleer they've ever seen.

Is that right? he said. Well, I've heard you Mohamed blighters are nothing but trouble.

Oh yeah?

Yeah. When you're workin', you're really workin'. But when it's time punch-out, that's when all the fracas begins.

I stepped in front of the Australian. Your country... it's not like Britain, is it?

Crikey, no. They're a tight-arsed mob. But that's no excuse for a young Mohamed to take the piss or go buggering about.

He stepped aside, then took Penny and Mahmout's camel by their leads, and led them towards a small pen.

C'mon, he said. Let's get these bludgers on board.

The sun was high when I caught Mahmout skulking beneath a tree.

What are you doing?

He kept his eyes locked off into the distance and didn't move.

I sat next to Mahmout and took a long look across the harbour.

Are you scared? said Mahmout.

A little, I guess.

In the morning, the crew loaded the remainder of the cargo while Mahmout and I studied the operation from the gangway.

I looked up at the deck where the Australian man stood with his arms stretched across the ship's passenger entrance.

Tickets please, he said to a white man who'd since placed a foot on deck and waved a paper note in his hand.

Welcome aboard, said the Australian.

I walked up the gangway with my ticket, and Mahmout followed behind.

Tickets, please.

We held out our tickets.

The Australian nodded.

I mounted the promenade where the white man had earlier hauled his trunks, and headed towards the cabins.

No, no, Mohamed, not so fast, said the Australian. Your beds are down below on the cargo deck, with the livestock.

He pointed towards the aft of the ship. Several pigs were being loaded in via crane, and two Arab men split the shade beneath a timber awning.

We walked down. It was spacious and calm, and I spread a towel across a bale of feed that'd long since faded in the sunlight and I invited Mahmout to take a seat.

What do you know about Australia, Mahmout?

I heard it's surrounded by long sandy beaches, and is filled with rainforest and exotic birds, he said.

I stuck my finger in my ear, then scratched about inside there for a little while.

Well, I said, Afghanistan has lots of sand too in case you hadn't noticed?

It's nothing like Australian sand, let me tell you.

It was all quiet then the ship blasted the foghorn, and the mooring ropes unfurled. The tumult of the blaring pipes excited me, so I walked to the edge of the ship then piddled over the stern. Farewell, Afghanistan.

There are women in Australia? I said.

I'm absolutely certain there are, said Mahmout. There are women with red hair, brown hair, blonde hair—hell, there are even women with pink hair. There are women who drink and fight like mad butchers, and swear like sailors. Women who cook, and women who clean. And women who'll make you feel like never leaving home, Sher Gul.

The foghorn sounded, once again, and a small tugboat wedged its hull between the ship and mooring pylons. I leant on the railing as we slowly edged away.

Women with blonde hair, you say?

Long and flowing and free, Sher Gul. Just like an angel.

Steady as she goes, boomed a sailor from all the way up on the bridge, as we set sail into open waters. She was a big ship—perhaps the biggest ship in the yard. But, out in the wide blue yonder of the ocean, she soon felt insignificant and small.

I'm going to marry one of those angels, Mahmout.

Mahmout laughed and look down at the turbulent waters

splashing its way along the hull of the ship. Of course, George. I believe you will.[39]

---

39   Many of the Afghani cameleers who travelled to Australia were married; however, their wives were prohibited from the voyage, due to the vocational requirements of travel. In other words, unemployment rendered them *not welcome*.

Life's More Complicated Now

I was now living in a complicated mess. I'd be lying if I told you my life wasn't simpler before those deadly planes banged into the Twin Towers. A ratty, chain-link fence surrounded our Barracks. You'd have to see this to believe it, but the damned fence stood no higher than any common garden fence. Typical of any garden fence seen around Brisbane since the nineteen-bloody-fifties. It lacked any useful gate and, in some parts, there was no gate at all. Hell, in some places, vexatious weeds replaced it. And, in other places, there was no fence at all. Almost anybody could have gotten inside the perimeter and walked a half mile before the MPs jumped on them.

Anyway, our Barracks' accommodation neighboured this female couple who lived in a small flat. The only thing keeping us separated from them was that chain-link fence. But get this: the couple operated a homegrown bottle shop and they were the friendliest neighbours one could hope for. Their fridge was always full, and their front door always open—regardless of the time of day. People like that were a dying breed.

The Alderley Arms Hotel was within walking distance—a real AJ dive. It was a young Digger's playground. And a playground it was, because, whether it be a Monday, a Thursday, or any other day, the bouncers would kick up a real stink. Right at midnight and without fail.

Hey, you little green bastards are always too loud, they'd say. You're too violent. Too disorderly and always breaking the glasses. You'll all have to go, pronto, and on the double.

We'd argue back, saying that we were only young; we were the Millennium babies, and we were off to war. So, cut us some slack, because there were only so many Wednesdays and Thursdays remaining on the calendar, and our weekends are not finite.

I can't believe you're professional soldiers, a bouncer would reply, right before the hotel doors slammed into our face.

Well, that was it. Our gig was up for the night, and we'd all go home high and dry—if not for our friendly neighbours.

I'll never forget the sound of those doors being slammed… as if that could have stopped us drinking.

Now, the twin towers are gone, all returned to Ground Zero dust. American dust. And the small chain-link fence has gone too. A taller, and sturdier, fence replaced the old one, with security gates and CCTV marked all the way around. Our neighbours are gone too.

AFGHANSTI AND THE GRAVEYARD OF EMPIRES

*May God keep you away from the venom of the cobra, the teeth of
the tiger, and the revenge of the Afghans.*

—Alexander the Great

As far as countries with haunted battlefields go, Afghanistan is
peerless. You best believe it, sonny, because no country, in the past
three millennia, has seen more bloodshed and death.

In 330BC, Alexander the Great came and saw and somewhat
conquered, briefly.

In saying that, the war did not go well for the Crown King.
And, as they say, the wild mountains of the Hindu Kush move for
no man. And any man who thinks otherwise is futile or stupid. Or
both. And will come to find their mis-errands both costly and fatal.
Ooh, I love to go a wandering along the mountain track.

Yet topology and climate weren't the only thorns etching into
Alexander's side.

The Macedonians also found themselves curtailed by their own
rigid and conventional tactics. After several years of facing guerrilla
tactics (imparted to them by Afghan Bandits), their challenges widened.

This enabled the bloodthirsty warlords—who didn't fuck

about—to achieve the upper hand and the toll was brutal and horrific.

The Greeks stayed in Afghanistan[40] for another 150 years, but at what cost? Certainly not what Alexander wished to pay for it.

The year was 1221, and it was Genghis Khan's turn to invade.

During the siege of Bamiyan, he watched an arrow go piercing through his grandson's chest. Mutugen Khan's death drove the Mongolian warmonger toward the brink of insanity. And the retort was blood curdling, as he went on a one-man mission to rape, stab, bleed and kill every Afghan in sight. And he almost succeeded, even smashing down their cherished citadels.

In the end, there was nothing left. Genghis packed his bags and departed—leaving many of his sordid warriors behind.

The Afghans spotted this as a prime opportunity and took swift revenge. Thus ensuring the last of the Mongols were gone and would never return.

In fact, the Mongolian forces didn't even consider returning. But their legacy remains on the face of every Hazara,[41] still living in Bamiyan, to this day.

The Soviets vowed to show up in 1979 with the match-winning game-plan. Their intelligence was immense, and they arrived with enough firepower to knock the Mujahideen for six. But in dreaming so, they ignored every single red flag on the map.

---

40   Then known to Alexander as the region of Bactria.
Throughout the years of Greek residency, Kandahar was also known as 'Alexandria'.
41   As descendants of Ghengis Khan's soldiers, Hazara peoples bare a close resemblance to the people of Mongolia. They are subject to harsh prejudices from Pashtun and Tajik Afghans and other denominations.

Ignorance sure is bliss.

Don't bother pressing that eject button, soldier: just get out and run.

That's right. Run, you fool.

Pray the Afghansti don't blow you away.

Then, and only then can you say, Hooray for communism, and Hooray for Brezhnev's[42] men (who ultimately choked in the final innings which ended in an asymmetric stalemate.)

Benefit must go to the home-team, said Shah Masoud.[43]

Hold-up, said Gorbachev.[44] These men deployed guerrilla warfare tactics and that's just not cricket.

There wasn't a re-match but, with that said, the Soviets earned a lesson or two in fighting Afghans:

1 - Aiming conventional warfare against guerrilla tactics makes for a lopsided affair.

2 - The only way to succeed against the Afghans is to not fight them at all.

The war concluded with the Soviets' stating Afghanistan is no longer a graveyard of empires. Now, it's now just a graveyard.

Many Soviet Officers scribed their experiences in the war. The lessons they'd learned. And the tactics they'd deployed when confronted by guerrilla forces. Someone collated these scribes into a small military manual, titled *The Bear Went Over the Mountain*.

Most Talibs fled into exile during the Soviet occupation and sat out the war in Pakistan. Yet the second the Soviets withdrew, the Talibs crawled West across the Durand line. Their destination: Kabul.

---

42   Former Secretary of the Communist Party of the USSR who instigated the Afghanistan invasion.

43   The Afghan Napoleon, or the Lion of Panjshir, Ahmad Shah Masoud was an Afghan politician and guerrilla leader of the Mujahideen.

44   Former President of the USSR.

The removal, disavowing, and destruction of everything non-Islamic was priory. Then by, 1996, anything that the war hadn't destroyed was gone.

Female education—gone.

Female voting—gone.

Females in the workplace—gone.

Females outside—gone.

Art—gone.

Artefacts—gone.

Bin Laden—gone.

The Buddhist temples of Bamiyan—gone.[45]

The draconian oppressors didn't quit there. They smashed televisions and radios, then hung them in the street as a strict warning: fuck with the Taliban and this is where you end up. To ensure Afghans received their message loud and clear they set about cutting off Shias' heads and hands, and let the blood run through the streets.[46]

The Hazara peoples copped it worst; often finding themselves locked inside shipping containers—for days and days in the heat. It's hard to imagine a worse way to die.

The California-Asian Oil Pipeline project (UNOCAL) sighted an opportunity when the Soviets left.

Hopes were high, and negotiations with the Taliban began, post haste.

A pipeline was to be run between Turkmenistan and Pakistan. But because their plans ran through Afghanistan, UNOCAL had to secure rights before digging up the dirt.

Then they hit a snag.

---

45   Located Northwest of Kabul, these 6th century monumental Buddhist statues were carved alongside the Silk Road.
As a holy site, the Buddhist carvings stood at 130 and 180ft tall respectively.
Considered an insult to Allah, Mullah Oman, the then Taliban commander ordered their destruction.
The carving ruins are now a UNESCO World Heritage Site.
46   This was a hardline stance taken by the Sunni Taliban who'd blanket banned all art and media, to an extent where they destroyed libraries and radio stations.

It was like a bolt of lightning had crashed into the desert, they said as negotiations in Afghanistan collapsed. The pipeline fell through, so it goes.

Such was life with the Taliban.

Boys Will Come, and Boys Will Go

Sylvia moved back in with her mother, who lived in an old weatherboard hut located a long way from the city.

She sat at the kitchen table and looked out the window.

This hut's surrounded by nothing other than bush, she thought. Beyond that—more bush?

Nobody knew.

Sylvia found it easy to get depressed—being so far from the city, so far from her Pat, and with nothing to stare at but trees.

She stretched out in her seat, then poured herself a cold beer.

Where's this fella you've been telling me about? said Sylvia's mother.

Sylvia didn't answer. Instead, she leant back and blew the froth from the drink.

Over before it began, hey love?

I don't wanna think about, she said, let alone talk about him.

Sylvia's mother cracked a longneck and pressed it to her lips.

Don't worry, love, she said. Boys will come and boys will go.

She gulped at the beer, then burped.

Ahhh, she said, and wiped her lips with her forearm. Best you focus on your studies and let them do their own thing.

It's not like that, Mum, said Sylvia, as she topped her beer. He's going to Afghanistan, and I'm frightened I'll never see him again.

Afghanistan?

Yes, Afghanistan

Why the hell'd anybody wanna visit Afghanistan, love?

The war, Mum.

Ahhh, said she went, holding the longneck to her lips. Doris down the road says that whole thing's a sham. Says that old Binny-Laden fella is not even from Afghanistan. She says the country doesn't want war with the Yanks, just wants that Binny-Laden character gone.

Sylvia's mother tipped her head and finished the beer. A horrible thing he did… hope they bury his stinking guts in the ocean.

I don't believe it's that simple, Mum.

Nonsense, said Sylvia's mother. We go over there. Shoot him. Then come straight home. It shouldn't be too difficult.

She slammed her empty longneck on the table and ambled towards the fridge. Other than that, we've got no business in someone else's country.

Sylvia placed her cup in the sink. You have anything heavier than beer, Mum?

Check in the pantry, honey.

I've been thinking… now's a good time to defer my studies.

What on earth for?

I want to travel and to see the world. I want to swim in the South of France. See the art in Venice and run with the bulls in Pamplona. Christ, Mum… I've had God damn enough of XXXX Gold and want to taste the beer in Prague.

What's wrong with our beer? It beats any beer in the world… if you ask me.

I'm serious, Mum.

Sylvia opened the pantry door. There was a bag of flour on an otherwise empty shelf. She looked down at a basket full of potatoes sitting on the floor and began crying.

Mum, she said, I don't want to die trapped inside some fishbowl and watch as time passes me by.

Solid Rock

The elder Indigenous man stood upon a solid rock.

There wasn't room in his heart for the promise of the future or fears of the past.

Not in progress, either. Not in money. Not in power or in fancy homes. That was all material to him. It had no rhyme and held no meaning.

Instead, he preferred spending his days by the lake, listening to mother earth, and telling his grandchildren how the great hawk visited in his dreams. How he followed it into the desert and how it led him home to safety.

Four men approached on horseback looking to drink from the lake.

The elder hadn't seen these men before, and when one horseman sighted him, he jumped down from the rock.

One of the horsemen stretched his back, yawned, then faced the elder. He flattened his palm and held it high. The elder mirrored the gesture. He nodded, and all the men dismounted their horses then led them to the water's edge.

The elder sat at the base of the rock. The sky was clear blue, and a brown hawk flew high overhead.

Australia's Muslim Cameleers

In 1860, a couple of lads named Burke and Wills set off on a gruelling expedition to the Gulf of Carpentaria. They were going to be the first Europeans to traverse the continent from South to North.

That same year, cameleers from Iran, Pakistan, Afghanistan and India arrived in Australia. The Afghanis, as they were now known, were here to assist in the pioneering of the Australian outback.

Burke and Wills had other plans for them and purchased two dozen camels for their trip north.

The expedition was an utter and complete failure. Several of the camels died. One became camel stew, and others—it's said—was released into the wild, as the wheels fell off the historical venture and both Burke and Wills, and many others, died throughout the journey.

Still, the expedition pushed multiple boundaries, and mostly due to the camels and their handlers, gone farther than any expedition prior.

By now, the camels and their handlers had proved their worth and went on to seek other work in the country's interior. They helped establish The Ghan (railway line, which now stretches from Adelaide to Darwin). They carried supplies across the country to build the Overland Telegraph Line. Then opened up the outback to future transport and trade.

But, despite the cameleers' successes, Australians did not wholly accept them. Many faced discriminations for their troubles and several faced jail. By 1930, work dried up for the Afghani as trucks and trains took over. Most returned to their homelands, while others remained to set up businesses and start new families.

It's been 160 years since the Afghanis arrived and their legacy is still unknown to many Australians. That was never their goal. But still, the cameleers' history echoes throughout the belly of the continent.

MISFIRE

This is going to be a very expensive war, and Victory is not guaranteed—for anyone, and certainly not for anyone as baffled as George W. Bush. All he knows is his father started the war a long time ago, and that he, the goofy child-president, has been chosen by fate and the global oil industry to finish it. Now.

—Hunter S. Thompson

The Taliban's brutal regime had buckled and folded inside six weeks, and Australia's commitment to the campaign was ending.

Any remaining Taliban Commanders fled East beyond the Durand line and took shelter in neighbouring Pakistan.

Proud of his accomplishments, Bush spun his attention to Iraq and begun the tumultuous act of juggling multiple wars at once. A misjudgement that would prove to be severe.

Despite the Taliban waving their white flag, Bush ignored peace talks and the actual war was about to begin.

A plan to train Afghan nationals—ala Vietnam—was drafted, in order to enable the countries to defend themselves against their oppressive overlords. However, such plans were either ignorant, or failed to acknowledge the indigenous culture and its way of doing business.

The training was a big misfire,[vii] so the Pentagon continued firing spitballs at the wall.[47]

They moved to a Hearts and Minds approach. Reconstruction and aid, via Non-Government Organisations like USAID, The Red Cross and Doctors Without Borders.

All the while, fighting continued.

Unfortunately, no other long-term mission plan was ever made clear.

> *We didn't communicate the strategy well with our soldiers in Afghanistan.*
> *—Australian Battlegroup Commander.*

> *Was it all worth it? At the human level; no.*
> *—Major General John Cantwell*

Those who were listening shook their heads, in dismay, and the coalition war racket grew and grew.

---

47   There is a multitude of reasons why this training failed. Up to 90 per cent of Afghan National soldiers could neither read nor write. They couldn't count, let alone perform basic maths and didn't even know their colours.

On a deeper level, the Pentagon failed by attempting to create a facsimile of the US military, forcing Afghans to adopt American rules, customs and structures. Even simple communications failed, due to the fact that a single Afghan Army unit could comprise of Dari, Pashto and Uzbek speaking soldiers. The US instructors were reduced to hand signals and drawing in the dirt.

Welcome to the War Machine

Tarin Kowt was hot. The dust and smell from overflowing shit-pits and sewer ponds shot straight up your nose, then made itself at home.

I unloaded my bags from the C-130 Hercules cargo pallets and spied out across the airfield. There were rows of Blackhawk choppers lining the apron as an A10 Warthog taxied from a hard-stand.

An Apache Gunship banked hard right overhead and discharged its flares over the ochre colour Quoras below. Brown clouds of dust climbed high, billowed out and blanketed the blue sky.

Welcome to the war machine, boys, said Baker, slinging his body armour across his shoulders. I hope you enjoy your stay.

Real Aussies Eat Beef

The smelly Asiatic is here—in great numbers. And though, unsavoury it may be, the fact is, he's living with and marrying white women. The latter fact warrants Asiatic legislation to maintain the purity of the white race. Because anybody living with, or marrying natives of a coloured country requires imprisonment. At least until he or she forgets to like coloured men or women. What're the unionist doing; have they not approached a representative with a view to impose such a clause?

—9 November 1906 The Laverton Mercury

Australia's colours were the first thing I noticed. The deep turquoise-blue sea. The burnt orange sunsets and red sands shaded by lush green canopies.

Here's to a bright start, I thought as I marched down the gangway.

An insect the size of a small bird buzzed past my face, then landed on my arm. I slapped the gnat dead, and it left behind a blotch of blood on my arm. My skin itched for a long time after that.

Mahmout followed behind and was scratching the side of his neck.

George… what're these devilish things?

I don't know, I said, but I wish they'd go away.

Penny was the first camel hoisted off the ship. Shirtless men laughed and swore at one another from beneath their wide-brimmed hats as they led all the beasts through the loading yards.

What a strange but maniacal to-and-fro, said Mahmout.

Yes, I said, but it's hard to tell if they're all friends, if they want to kill one another, or if they're all barking mad insane.

Awwwright, said a man, the name's Stu, but yer can call me Boss. Now holster yer beasts and listen to me.

He was a thin and wiry wisp of a man with leathery skin, bronzed by an unfettered sun.

I don't care if yer black, white or yellow, he said. Everyone in my team works hard. Zero excuses. If yers not prepared for that turn yer arses about and climb back on the boat.

Nobody moved, so the man smiled and stuffed his pipe full of tobacco. He pressed down with his thumb, then struck a match.

C'mon, he said. Yer camp's right up the street.

I slung a bag over Penny's back and watched a scattering of pistachio shells fall to the ground.

Oi, you! What are those? said Stu.

Pistachios, Bossman, I said. Would you like to try one?

Looks like fucken birdseed to me.

I peeled a shell and sucked on the seed.

Yer disgusting, said Stu. Real Aussies eat meat. Prime Australian beef, and none of that fairy shit. Ye-uck!

Stu wedged his boot inside his horse's stirrups and swung his leg over the saddle.

He blew out a small puff of smoke from his pipe, then kicked his heels into the belly of his horse and shouted, LET'S RIDE! TO THE STATION YARD!

I tightened my grip on Penny's lead, then Mahmout and I followed him out from the loading yards.

The station yard was a small, red dust bowl with a rusted tin hut in the middle. There were about twenty cameleers waiting as Mahmout and I sauntered into the yard.

I tied Penny to the watering trough and peeled another pistachio.

Awww-right said Stu. Dump your shit by the shade, and we'll take you inside, so Miriam can get you all processed and ready for work.

Mahmout and I slipped into the middle of the line, which waited by a small opening to the tin hut.

Now, you bastards make sure you behave when you get inside, said Stu, as he stuffed his pipe with fresh tobacco. This here's Miriam, my daughter. She's as stubborn as a Mallee Bull, and refuses to stay at home, like a good woman should. I tell yers, what she needs is strong man to straighten her out. But if I catch any of you mongrels messing about, I swear to God I'll hang you by the short and curlies.[48]

She stood behind the counter; wearing a long yellow dress that fell to her ankles. Her hair was long and blonde and shrouded

---

48   Colloquial term for holding someone with complete power.

her golden tanned shoulder. I could smell her lavender perfume from the doorway.

That's the most beautiful thing I've ever seen, I thought. It's almost like a dream.

Name and occupation, she said, staring down at a stack of paper piled atop a bench.

Excuse me, sir? Name and occupation?

Her deep blue eyes transfixed me—shining like a wild mandala.

HEY, MISTER, she said, are you deaf? Name and occupation, please.

Mahmout pinched me on the elbow, and I snapped out of my trance.

George Sher Gul. Master Cameleer, I said, hoping that would impress her. It didn't.

Thank you, she said. Please sign this paper. Your pay's one pound, and you'll collect it every Thursday.

I took the paper with a smile, signed and passed the sheet to Miriam, but she refused to lift her head.

Thank you, and goodbye, she said.

I left through the side door. The door slammed shut and I immediately wanted to go back inside.

I don't care whose daughter that is, Mahmout, I said, stamping my heels into the red dirt. I will make her my wife.

Hayya 'alas salah,[49] chanted the Afghans, as they all knelt and bowed in a neat row.

I skulked back to the watering trough and tried to sneak a peek inside the rusty hut to the steel railing.

You'll get bitten, said Mahmout, sticking your nose where it doesn't belong.

---

49   Come to prayer.

I don't care, I said and unfastened my pants and pissed on the hitching post.

Forget about her, George, that pretty little bitch is haram to men like you and me.

Haram? Says who, Mahmout? Says who? Your Allah? Your Quran? It's all posh, my friend. Posh I left behind in Afghanistan.

I unhitched Penny and turned for the gate.

Where are you going, George?

To buggery with it all, Mahmout, I'm taking Penny for a swim.

THE MEAT OF IT

I slipped off Penny's holster and watched her goofy legs kick about as she galloped towards the ocean, then cooled once her hooves felt the slow current slapping happily against her underbelly.

She could've swum right out to the sea and died a merry girl.

I sat barefoot on the beach and squeezed the harsh sand between my toes as Penny swam.

The air was cool by the water's edge, I thought, and laid down and watched the giant grey clouds coming rolling inland.

Goldangit, said the voice from behind. The hell are you doing away from the yard?

I rolled to my side to see her blonde hair and long dress flowing in the breeze.

It's me, I said and waved. George Sher Gul, the Master Cameleer.

Christ almighty, George. I know who you are… but if you're not careful, the crocs here'll eat you alive.

Crocs?

Well, that's the meat of it, she said, and raised her arms out wide, then brought them slapping back together again. But if they don't get you, the bloody coppers will.

Storm clouds were bellowing overhead. The wind blew-up a gale, and the current coerced the waves to and fro as they crashed onto the shore.

I whistled for Penny. She stopped, dead still in the water. Come on, I called, then she waded towards the shore.

Miriam crept to the water's edge. The white water circled around her knees and swallowed the base of her dress as she gripped Penny by the holster.

She's a pretty girl, said Miriam, 'cept her breath smells like a fouled urinal.

Penny thrashed her head back in disgust. It sent Miriam tumbling into the gaping jaws of the ocean which soon had her by the scruff of it. She spluttered like a drowning rat and rolled arse over her head, as the current looked set to drag her out to sea.

MIRIAM! I dove into the ocean after her.

I rested Miriam on her back and watched the ocean water drain from her hair. Her skin was cold and grey, but her eyes still shone electric blue.

You saved me, George, she said and sat to rub the saltwater from her eyes.

I didn't say a word, and looked at Miriam and smiled at her beneath the fading sunset.

Captain Purdey

We were now smack-bang in the middle of the bad lands. And that put a huge smile on Sergeant Baker's face. It scared me—in more ways than one should admit—and the more I looked at it, the bigger it got.

I sat in my seat. It wasn't more than a plywood board laid across two milk crates. There was nothing but a rusty, corrugated panel covering our heads.

Baker sat to my left, then punched me in the arm.

You wanna durry? he said.

Don't smoke, Serge.

Baker cranked the cigarette lighter with his thumb. He sucked in a deep drag and blew out a puff of smoke. The cloud hung thick in the air, then faded away.

It's gonna be tough here, Pat … but that's just what a young cunt like you needs, said Baker as he pinched the cigarette between his lips. Fucking princess, I bet you'll be smoking by the end of this trip.

Davis carried an ammunition tin with both hands.

Dinner is served, he said, and dumped the tin on the concrete floor.

I'm going straight to hell, I said and dropped to my knees and cracked open the tin. Hey, Serge Baker… how many rounds we taking?

Baker reached inside his pouch and pulled out five Steyer magazines.

Bomb 'em up, lads. Every round should have Terry-towel-heads' names stamped down the side of it.

Davis was the first to finish loading up, and he took a final magazine and whacked it on his boot. He slid out the top round, hid it in his pocket and replaced it with a spent round.

What the hell are you doing? I said.

I don't want any accidental discharges, he said. Besides, shooting myself in the foot is the last thing I want out here.

Talk about shooting yourself in the foot alright. What happens the Taliban comes running over the next hill?

What if, what if; it's all semantics, said Davis, housing the magazine inside the receiver assembly. No Taliban soldier has ever shot at me, and until one does, I am not firing a damned thing at anybody.

I finished packing my last magazine. Whacked it on my boot and put it in my webbing pouch.

If Baker catches you, he'll cut your legs off at the neck.

Man, that old bastard won't see a damned thing. Besides, I can switch mags at the gate. It's as simple as that.

A man walked in.

He was a Captain. Tall and skinny, but with a solid chin, built like Mike Tyson's.

Sergeant Baker, said the officer.

Baker stood and crushed his cigarette into the concrete floor. CAPTAIN PURDEY, he said and shook the officer's hand. Sir, it's great seeing you again.

It's been a while, said Purdey as he scanned his eyes across me and Davis.

I thought Corporal White was joining you?

Oh, said Baker, he was. Except he had a slight hiccup on the way.

Baker and Purdey got to chin-wagging, while me and Davis wiped the dust from our rifles.

This shit gets in everywhere, I said.

Can say that again, said Davis.

I removed the rifle barrel and fed cheese cloth into the pull-through. Four Blackhawks banked across the airfield. It sounded like a thunderstorm moving overhead. It sent a large dust cloud billowing into the sky.

I rushed out—for a better sighting as they circled for landing. One Blackhawk had a Red Cross painted on its door. The other choppers flanked it as they hovered above the landing zone.

Casevac? said Baker.

Usually the Yanks, said Purdey, pointing toward the American section of the camp. That's their hospital. It's always chock-a-block, but every so often, one of our boys plucks the winning ticket.

I covered my face with my hat, to stop all the dust crawling up my nose.

Don't worry, said Purdey. After a few days, you'll get a hang of it… but wait until your first shit, that's when you'll understand— why they say—this dust gets in everywhere.

Each chopper had landed. The camp hushed as the ground crew drew a stretcher from the red crossed chopper's cargo bay.

It could be anybody, said Purdey. Someone's son. Brother. Father. Best mate. And, even if he's dead, the war just rolls on. It's business as usual.

Can only pray it isn't one of us, said Baker.

Damn straight, said Purdey, as he stretched his hat over his head. Now, who's up for some lunch? We got the best mess in Afghanistan, right in our own backyard.

Sylvia Travels

The first week in Afghanistan was a real kick in the teeth. All we did was move between briefs. There were safety briefs for every situation: what to do during rocket strikes, what to do after the rocket strikes, what to do if a rocket lands on your bed, and what to do if no rockets landed at all.

Large hesco baskets—stacked fifteen feet high—enclosed most buildings in camp.

They're thick enough to block an Abraham's tank, I thought and kicked one basket at its base. No rocket could breach these walls.

But there was a brief for that too, on the off chance one should.

The rec-hut[50] was a place to escape the monotony. Though it was always full.

I walked inside. American soldiers sat beside Australian soldiers. There were some Singaporean officers. Japanese, and Dutch as well. All jammed into this sardine tin, watching American football on a big screen.

---

50   Recreational hut. A place where soldiers can relax, watch tv, use the internet and call home.

American Football gave me the shits. Besides, it was far too hot for me, so I slinked on by to the communal phone booths.

I phoned Sylvia. Christ knows why.

That bitch no doubt considers me as good as dead.

It was early afternoon, which seemed like as good a time as any. The dial tone rang for quite a while. In fact, I'd say I let it roll on for far too long.

I bit the sides of my mouth, then licked the fronts of my teeth after tasting blood. It takes one big wuss to come out grovelling on hand and knee. But a man will do almost anything for a woman he loves. Well, almost anything. And the depths he'll sink too, at nobody's expense, bar his own.

I was ready to hang up when the phone reached her voicemail.

Sorry, I couldn't come to the phone, I'm currently travelling through Europe. If your call is important, please leave a message after the beep. Otherwise, email me at sylviastravels@hotmail.com. au. Thank you, and goodbye.

The phone beeped. I hung up quickly, worried that my awkward silence would give away the fact that it was me on the other end of the line. I wasn't born to die at the short end of a telephone wire.

I considered email as the next safest bet.

Death cannot reach us via the internet, I thought.

Or could it?

Lucky for me, I didn't know how to use a goddamn computer.

The War on Drugs

Folks knew Afghanistan for its opium production, long before it innocuously harboured world renowned terrorist, Osama Bin Laden. In fact, they were offloading anywhere up to, but not limited to, 2000 metric ton of opium each year.

Sheesh.

Yet it's a funny thing—drug trafficking in Afghanistan—as one day, the Taliban would be out destroying the poppy fields.[51] Then, the next day, farmers would sow fresh seeds. Then boom—talk about your classic game of cat and mouse—business would be blossoming once again.

The US-led coalition did little to stem the outflux of opium from Afghanistan. In fact, they did nothing short of mention it as they forced Taliban leaders to pull all their strings from East of the Durand line.

Now that we've liberated the country, it's time we attend to more pressing matters, said Bush. *Like whom we should install as chief puppet-leader of Afghanistan.*

---

51   The Taliban were widely known for destroying poppy fields, due to their ultra-conservative beliefs. However, as the war dragged on, their position changed, and the harvesting of opium became a source to fund their war-fighting efforts.

In the end, Bush handpicked a young dandy named Karzai.[52] He was quite receptive to US negotiations (and the Taliban's), had deep pockets and rocked quite the sticky handshake.

Boom. Boom. It was more business as usual, and the UNOCAL pipeline? It, once again, reared its capitalistic head.

Despite their hatred for drugs, the Taliban struggled to fund their war machine. It was a lot to inhale, and, with a fleeting sense of remorse, it'd become clear they'd have only the one place in which to return: the opium fields.

This spiked Bush's fickle attention span and likely scared the shit out of a thousand farmers. Because, in a few short years, Bush had turned from a war on terror, to weapons of mass destruction, then back to the Taliban (who had no involvement in the 9/11 attacks, nor did they harbour any aspirations for global terror—that was Al Qaeda territory; and the two were not one in the same). And with no signs of Bin Laden in Afghanistan, the Bush administration in all its Reagan-esque mind-power, was readying to hit the go-button on a new war. This time, it was a war on drugs.

---

52   In 2013, Hamid Karzai was named in the top 100 most influential people by Time magazine.
He became a shrewd politician who often played leaders and ethnic groups off against one another. At the conclusion of his presidency, he was reduced to a factional leader.

AND THE POOR FARMER GETS FUCKED

A dust storm was brewing over the camp.[53]

Ya can't even see the sky, I said to Davis, but he continued walking along silently. It seemed like all he was looking at was the ground.

This dust, he said, it gets in your ears, your nose. It's everywhere. Suffocating.

I took off my hat, and wiped my sunglasses clean. Man, I said, I can't wait to get outside the wire and meet me some Taliban.

Patterson. You'd shrivel to the size of a mouse.

We trundled into the rec-hut. It was quiet inside, and almost dust free. I took a seat on a couch and found a shiny two-dollar coin tucked beneath the cushions. I put it in my trouser pocket. Davis picked through the bookshelves and drew out a hardback copy of *Born on the Fourth of July*.

Don't tell Baker, he said, but I can't wait to get the hell out of here.

He began flicking through the book at a pace which not even a robot could pick up what was printed on the pages. I rose sharply from the couch, jaw clenched, gut roiling.

Shut your shit mouth, I hissed. I stuffed my fist beneath Davis' nose.

Get outta here, he said dismissively, and slammed the book

---

53   Tarin Kowt (in Uruzgan Province) was referred to by Australian soldiers as 'the dust bowl'.

into my chest. You know this war's a crock of shit. Hell… even if it were legit, them dumb bastards upstairs are going the wrong way about it.

The fuck you talking about? We're gonna win this war. The Afghan people will be free from this tyranny, and you'll be eating your goddamned words.

Davis turned his back on me and started to walk away.

You don't know shit, Patterson. The entire history of this country spells nothing but intrusion and wars that no one ever wins. I bet you everything I've got, right now, that the Taliban will still be here, long after we're gone. Then everything will return to ways it's always been in Afghanistan.

He opened the rec-hut door.

I tell you, this country just wants to be left the hell alone.

At half ten, we entered the briefing hut. It was a small air-conditioned demountable that could seat fifteen. An entire troop of thirty jammed in and squeezed the door shut.

Purdey lurched over a timber lectern. The air conditioner rattled, and several diggers stood beneath the oscillating fan blades. Their jaws dumped wide open to feed in as much cold air as possible.

Righto, everyone, said Purdey. Take a seat, if you can.

He switched on a projector. A PowerPoint slide covered the wall, displaying a grainy image of a mud bricked Quora.

The diggers turned from the fan blades to looked at the screen.

Take out your notepads and pens, ladies and gents, said Baker, from his position in the front corner of the hut, leaning against a wall.

Everyone unzipped their pockets. Produced a green Army notebook and turned to a blank page.

I looked around the room. There wasn't a dull eye in sight. We were about to get our feet wet, in this shit show they'd dubbed a war.

Here's the deal, said Purdey. Sale of opium in Afghanistan has been funding global terrorism. Meanwhile, the poor farmer in these Uruzgan keeps getting fucked.

The PowerPoint spun to the next slide and displayed a heroin processing compound. He walked to the back of the room.

It's a billion-dollar business, team and its reach extends across the globe: into the USA, Europe and even back home

Purdey weaved back through the troops and returned to the front of the room.

The CIA, the DEA, the FBI, ATF and even US Customs and the fucking Coast Guard are stepping in here. They want in on this fight.

Purdey adjusted his belt around his trousers. We're here to nip this fucker in the bud.

I scanned the room again. Everybody was scribbling in their notepads. Except Davis.

I punched the droopy bastard in the arm.

What the hell was that for?

Didn't you hear the captain? This is serious. Fucking, look up or something.

Purdey had paused and was staring down at me and Davis. He had a wry grin on his face and a steely coldness in his gaze.

He went on to the slide.

Our job, gentleman, he said, is to go out to the villages. There, we'll meet local Mullahs and share with them our plans to defeat the enemy.

He turned the screen off.

Gentleman. We're gonna win this, beat it, squash it. That's it. No questions. Dismissed.

The door to the hut flew open. I stepped outside to where the dust storm was still lingering.

Davis followed out and started kicking stones across the concrete path.

Mate, I said, come on. It's not every day you get to win a war.

He didn't respond.

No Bloody Boer

The yard was quiet. For most of the day, the cameleers had slept beneath the shade or sat drinking tea.

Shortly after noon, Miriam came tearing into the yard. She was barefoot and waving a telegram in her outstretched arm. Stu was bent over in a stable, clipping a horse's hoof. He whipped up his head and darted to the centre of the yard, ripping the telegram from Miriam's hand.

England's finally declared war on those Boers, he said, and now they want us to join them.

It was hard to read the look on Stu's face as he announced this.

Are you going to volunteer?[54]

Not on your life, said Stu, and he scrunched the telegram between the palms of his hands. No bloody Boer ever did nothing to me.

Stu stuffed his pipe with a fresh pinch of tobacco, then struck a match against the heel of his boot. He lit the pipe and, with the match still aflame, held it beneath the telegram. Then watched the burning ball go tumbling into the dirt.

---

54   Approximately 16,000 Australians volunteered to fight in the Boer War.

The Ghan Railway

If we're civilised folk, then we ought to know better than to speak of Afghanis as Niggers, or Savages. Yes, there's no denying it, they're of a dark complexion—as old as the chronicles will have it. But nevertheless, he's not a savage. That's a term for lower-class peoples; like the Australian Aborigine, or African Negro.

It implies a low type.

Now, no one can say he's of an inferior physical type; because, as far as mere beauty goes, he is taller. Straighter. And has finer features than the average European. But where their intellectual quality is concerned; one can examine civilisation dating back to the time when woad-painted savages inhabited the British Isles. His civilisation is in a state of arrested development. That is all; and a Savage he is not.

—*26 March 1899 The Kalgoorlie Sun*

Stu roused us out of bed and ordered all the kit be loaded on the camels.

We gotta make our move before the next monsoon hits.

He stood back and packed his pipe as we loaded boxes of survey equipment onto our beast's backs. There were tripods, theodolites, sextants, chains, and boxes of rum. The camels carried it all.

I looked at the sky. It was a dark grey and a heavy curtain of water swept its way—East to West—across the deep blue harbour.

What is in all these boxes? said Mahmout.

I squared a compass at him, landing the needle—on magnetic North—right between his eyes.

It's for the railway, I said. The Afghani have been making sure it reaches Alice Springs for several years.

A railway?

Yes, a train line that'll one day cross this country. It couldn't get built without us.

Penny dropped to her belly between two large boxes.[55] Both the boxes were the size of a bull calf and likely weighed twice as much.

I harnessed a rope around the boxes, then swung the rope across Penny's back. I hitched the boxes tight until their corners tilted off the floor. The weight was slung evenly across Penny's back; almost suspending the load in mid-air.

HOOSHTA,[56] I said, and the beast stumbled to her feet.

After dawn, the cameleers had their beasts lined up in a string along the roadside. That's when the heavens began opening.

I'd not seen a thing like it. A wall of water came bucketing down.

Stu rode up to the front of the string, where Penny had her nose up. She was ready to lead the team South.

Might have to hold up for the night, he said to me. Then he dismounted and pulled out his pipe. The raindrops crashed into the brim of his hat, hard, and folded the brim down so it kissed

---

55   The average camel, at the time, could carry loads of up to 600kg and travel 5-7 days with little food or water.
56   A command to either stand or sit.

him on the nose. There was a bit of a huffing and puffing as he tried to light the tobacco, but soon, his face became shrouded in smoke.

My girl can walk through anything, I said. This drizzle will be a walk in the park.

Stu pushed his face in close to Penny as he struggled to keep his pipe alight. He sucked in deep causing the tobacco to glow a fiery red. Then he turned with his head pointed low and looked South.

How's your navigation, Sher Gul?

I dug deep into my pocket and retrieved my compass. Its brass case had become tarnished after the trip across the sea. But its glass was clear, and the needle spun true. I held it up to Stu's eyes. He looked moderately impressed.

I took it from a British soldier, in old Maiwand.

I flipped the compass shut. He wasn't using it anymore, I said, before stuffing it back inside my pocket.

Stu kicked at the dirt. It was fast turning into mud, then he looked at sky with his eyes squinting.

Best keep that thing handy, he said and mounted his horse. You'll be my lead man for the entire trip South.

He pulled his hat down over his face. Suppose we make a start, Sher Gul? Then he kicked his horse in the gut.

Hearts and Minds

That morning, our Troop[57] prepared to head out on its first mission.

We were to meet a local Mullah and talk to him about the propagation of poppies across Uruzgan province.

Christ knows how we were gonna do it, but there was no way we'd be deflowering the countryside ourselves. No, no, no—we'd be insisting the farmers do that themselves… somehow.

And what'd be the outcome of this act in futility? Well, the local farmer would have the money reefed clean from the back pocket—all by his own hands.

Fuck *him*, was the message from upstairs. Besides, this was a matter of strategic importance, a favour, straightening out the Afghan topology by eliminating all the narcotics.

Yes, ladies and gentlemen, it was true hearts and mind stuff, delivered with a stiff boot, right up the farmer's arse, simply to spite the Taliban.

I cleaned my rifle and squeezed two drops of gun oil around the gas piston. The Bushmaster[58] drivers went through their start-up

---

57   Troop (verb) is equivalent to a platoon sized formation, or three 10–12-man sections and a headquarters element. Troops (noun) can refer to any group of soldiers, whether they're in a designated troop or not.

58   An open-wheeled and armoured troop carrier designed and manufactured in Australia.

drills. They checked their tyres by kicking their boots against the reinforced sidewalls. Cleared any mud and dust from the green-tinted and blast-proof windows. While up in the turret, a digger fed the link into .50 cal coaxial gun.

Baker walked to the head of the convoy. He wore dark sunglasses and balanced a burning cigarette on the tip of his mouth. He threw his daypack in the cabin of the lead vehicle, then sauntered toward the middle of the yard. He raised his arm and drew a big circle, with his finger pointing to the sky.

MOUNT UP, LADIES AND GENTLEMEN. WE'RE ROLLING OUT IN FIVE.

All six Bushmasters started their engines at once. As the drivers revved the engines, black soot rose into the air.

The job was on.

Baker grabbed me and Davis.

You boys are riding with me.

I finished assembling my rifle and cocked the handle, then released the working parts forward. My left hand trembled on the fore grip. I realised I might not be ready for the high-pressured fog of combat. To some (I'd soon learn), dropping bodies came instinctually. And while the act grew on others, many of us were simply shitting ourselves at the thought.

Whatever you do, don't get caught in the front or rear vehicle, said Davis, muttering to himself. Then he opened his pocket and lit a cigarette.

What the hell are you doing… you don't smoke?

It's the stress. I've tried everything to overcome it. I tried reading and meditation. I called mum; only to discover that made it worse. Hell, I even tried wanking in the dunny. With that smell… I couldn't get one up. Smoking is my last hope.

I slapped the hull of a Bushmaster. These machines can handle a rough bashing, you'll be safe in the back. If it all goes tits-up, just keep your head down.

Davis looked down and stubbed the cigarette out into the dirt.

Masturbation, I said. Could that work?

Davis shrugged. It was worth the try; he said and climbed into the vehicle.

THE SUFFRAGETTES

Towards the end of the nineteenth Australia, the word progress was on the tip of every tongue.

The days of colonial rule would soon be gone. Rich men with waxed moustaches and fine suits began drafting the Australian constitution.

White is the new black, declared Sir Edmund Barton.

Yellow can go to hell, touted Sir Samuel Griffith.

And brown be damned, stomped Charles Kingston as the country roared towards federation.

In fact, anything non-white was now inferior. And, by 1901, the White Australia Policy had prohibited all non-white immigration.

Why? Because their (the non-whites) attitudes were 'against the grain' of Australia's new way of life. Such were the common notions of the time.

The fairer sex held up no better.

Any remnants of the Victorian era faded away. Yet, in spite of this, female migrants were still made to heel to British Common Law.

Being an unwed woman was unthinkable. Even if the alternative meant you were no less than the property of your other half. Or father, if a husband didn't appear among the fray.

If you hailed from the upper classes, working was—altogether—out of the question. But even if you came from the middle class, women were scorned, and choosing to work was a matter of shame.

The girls simply could not win.

But alas, the times they were a changing. And, as the calendar ticked over, the shackles were loosening. Strong women were bucking the trend and abandoning their aprons. There was a whole wild world out there to explore. A women's trade union in formed, and the new breed of suffragettes refused to be chained to an oven.

The Only Life I Know

We hadn't even left camp because the rain continued to fall for what seemed like hours. It fell from the East, and it fell from the West, and as the floodwaters rose around the camp, it turned and fell from the North.

Unhitch 'em, said Stu. We're not going anywhere.

The cameleers didn't argue—not with the boss. I lashed Penny to a hitching point beneath the cover of an Acacia tree, then washed, ate and set up shelter before dark.

A small lamplight emerged from the darkness of the camp's tin shed, then moved from Afghani to Afghani. The light finally reached my shelter. A slim figure wearing brown leather riding boots and cream jodhpurs knelt and poked their head inside.

Would you like some tea?

Miriam?

She stumbled near a puddle. Christ, oh buggery, she said, regaining her balance and dipping her head back inside my shelter.

The smell of rain and mud and bog was strong. The scent of rose perfume soon overpowered that smell as she moved in closer and held the lamp to my face.

Oh, hello, George, said Miriam as she crawled inside and sat on the edge of my bedding mat. It was all I could do to hear her voice over the sound of the rain.

I pulled two copper cups from my travel sack and placed them on the mat. Miriam went to pour the tea but bumped her head into the shelter. It released a puddle of water that ran down the back of her neck. She drew out a purple silk handkerchief from her pocket and tried to wipe herself dry.

For crying out loud, she said. Isn't it a tad cramped in here?

I sipped at my tea. What're you doing out here, I said. This is no place for a woman!

She poured the second cup, then slid in close by my side.

Piss off, George, us Aussie girls are capable of going anywhere you fellas go.

Miriam padded her hand on a small sack I'd stuffed for a pillow.

It's all a cameleer needs to stay comfortable, I said, but someday I'd like to find a home.

Miriam dropped the handkerchief on top of a coat that I'd rolled up into a small pillow. Then she stretched her legs out and lay down on the mat.

How much longer do you want to go on living the cameleer life?

I poured another cup of tea, then held the cup to my lips.

I'm getting old now. This is the only life I know. I'd considering retiring soon, but I fear I'm too old to change and learn new things.

Oh, I don't know. Master George, the Great Cameleer … I bet there's still some adventure left in those old legs, yet, and maybe starting a family is the next frontier.

Miriam tossed out the last of her tea and blew out the lamp.

I lay down by her side, and the tops of our heads touched.

Yes, another Sher Gul. A son, an adventurer. Oh, I could only imagine.

It's a Deal

Dust bathed the Quoras as the Bushmasters circled around a desert knoll. Then—one by one—each vehicle halted, with its nose pointed outward. It created an armoured harbour, with all guns glancing out into the vast open Dasht.

I felt impenetrable as the Australian flag flitted overhead. Nothing was going to bring us down. Not from outside our secured perimeter, at least. No, the only threat in these situations discharged themselves from within. I surveyed the troops, all running about madly getting their bearings aligned amongst the blinding dust. One slip of a trigger and it could all turn to mud.

Baker marched about, calm within the harbour, and scanned into the village through his rifle scope. He waved his arms in every direction and yelled: form a defensive posture, you sons of bitches.

The diggers moved into position. The Bushmaster gun turrets panned across the dead ground, hunting.

The mission was ticking away. Baker considered the knoll, lowered his rifle, and lit a cigarette.

Purdey was the last man out of the Bushmasters and was soon at Baker's side, carrying a tan backpack.

There was a brief discussion, then Baker gave the field signal, and we moved into patrol formation.

A tall Afghan man stood by a small doorway. He wore a long blue coat that hung down below his knees and had a long, orange-dyed beard.

Purdey met the Afghan and shook his hand. The man smiled and bowed to the captain.

Both men entered the small Quora.

Baker stubbed his cigarette into the dirt, then looked back at the troops.

Eyes out! was the cry from the section commander as a small boy ushered a fat goat into a small yard.

Ten bucks says he's going to stuff that thing like a roast chook, said Baker.

I looked at Davis and laughed. Hey, I reckon that's your best chance, Davis. You can tie it up and it won't run away.

Baker coughed and lost concentration for the moment. Davis stood stiff and silent as I waited for a response. Go fuck your hat, he said, and we both followed the Serge into the Quora.

Twelve Afghan men sat on the floor, surrounding a big, round, purple, green and gold Persian rug. The men were old, had wrinkle-covered skin and fading hair, which they dyed orange and displayed proudly as it jutted out in a beard from their long crinkly faces.

Yellow rice, bread, prunes and grapes sat spread across the rug in shiny brass bowls. The men reached in, with both hands full, and shared food around the giant ring they'd created.

Ya see? said Purdey, raising both hands, open palmed into the air. Now this is the real Afghanistan.

The Afghan man who had welcomed us in smiled at Purdey, then ushered him to his seat within the circle.

For me, these were the first full blooded Afghans I'd ever seen. We shared the same blood—a small piece of history—yet it never sank in. They looked nothing like me.

Genealogy now meant two parts of fuck all.

Ancestry was a myth.

These alien men would soon be clashing with my duty as a soldier.

But killing your own was no simple thing.

Yes, it was the real Afghanistan, that's for sure.

A young boy walked, silent, around the men.

The old men wore long scarves and sat beside woven tote bags. The boy was careful not to trip over the men, or their totes, as he tiptoed his way between them. Then he leant over and topped their glasses with steaming chai tea.

The room filled with a soothing scent of cinnamon. It carried you away to anywhere but a god-forsaken war zone.

Purdey was right, I thought. How good was this? The real Afghanistan: a sight they'd never seen on the tv screens back home.

The boy topped up Purdey's glass. Thank you, he says.

Then the boy walked to Baker. Chai, mister?

Baker squeezed his fingers around the trigger guard on his rifle, then furrowed his brow. He waved the boy away.

He turned to me and Davis, with a worrisome glare.

Can't be too careful, he said. Sometimes that's code for intercourse, when they offer you that chai tea.

Bull shit, said Davis. He's a kid.

Exactly how they like 'em, said Baker. We're not in Kansas

anymore, ladies… here, it's men who keep each other warm at night.

Now, our special forces lads have been doing a bang-up job, said Purdey. He stripped off his pistol and handed it to Baker, who was now standing behind the circle.

They've gone and all but removed the Taliban command element, in Uruzgan. Cut the head clean off the snake. But I assure you, gentlemen, they'll be back.

An interpreter sat at Purdey's side and conveyed the sentiment to the men.

They smiled and nodded their heads.

Purdey continued. I heard it from President Karzai himself. The Taliban war machine isn't slowing down.

The Afghan men turned to one another and frowned. They were all muttering the Karzai name.

The interpreter turned to Purdey. They say Karzai is not their leader, because Afghanistan is not a country ruled by a single man, but many men who only answer to Allah.

Purdey and the men kept strumming along, talking; to a point where it was all white noise. I soon tuned out and watched several Afghan men entering and exiting the room.

There wasn't a woman in sight. Was Baker right?

Another fifteen, twenty passed and Baker approached me from across the room with a puzzled look on his face.

Patterson, said Baker. What the hell's wrong with Davis?

I took off my cap and wiped a slow stream of sweat from my forehead. I don't think he wants to be here, no more, Serge.

What do you mean he doesn't want to be here, no more? Where the hell else could a soldier wanna be?

It's the war, I whispered. He doesn't think we've got a right being here. Telling them what they grow in their fields, and all that.

Is that all? Baker sneered, sliding out a fresh cigarette. What about you, Patterson? Do you agree with him, being his mate and all?

I wiped some more sweat away from my face and looked out a window. It was quiet outside and the air was soft. All the dust had cleared, leaving behind a bright blue sky.

No, I wanna be here, Serge. It's just… sometimes it makes no sense at all.

That's war, he said and lit his cigarette. Sometimes it is senseless. But a good soldier still gets up each day and laces one boot after the other. That's what separates us from the civvies[59] back home.

I didn't say a word, and slipped my hat back over my head, as Baker sucked away at his cigarette.

The Afghan men broke from the circle and scattered throughout the room. One man remained with Purdey.

Purdey held up a page from the Wall Street Journal, with a headline: "The Price of Opium Soars".

Billions of dollars leave this country, each year, said Purdey.

There was an image of an Afghan opium field beneath the headline.

---

59   Colloquial term, often used in a derogatory context by soldiers to reference the civilian population.

Not a cent of it goes to the Afghan farmer, said Purdey, punching his finger into the paper.

All the Afghan men stood in silence and turned their heads towards the Captain. He unzipped his backpack and pulled out a clear, plastic, sealed satchel. It was American cash; in a pile the size of a Sydney phone book.

Now, we're willing to compensate you gentlemen, he said, waving the cash. But on the proviso that the poppy harvest stops.

The men huddled and began talking. It was in a hushed Pashto dialect that Purdey couldn't understand.

He turned to the interpreter, asking What are they all saying?

But the interpreter stood—stiffened—and shrugged his shoulders.

Then the Afghan chatter fell silent. One man approached Purdey. He had a short, well-kept orange beard and stroked his fingers through its coarse whiskers. He smiled and took the captain, by the hand, and in perfect English, said It's a deal.[60viii]

In the neighbouring valley, a viscous gunfight was kicking off.

A single A-10 Warthog zoomed overhead and sprayed the escarpment with a volley of 30mm.

I clutched my rifle clutched tight between my hands.

MOUNT UP, yelled Baker, and the Bushmaster engines cackled to life.

This was it. My baptism of fire.

A second fighter jet roared overhead. It was an F-18 Super

---

60   Billions of dollars of funding were sent to Afghanistan in order to reconstruct and regenerate the country. Due to corruption, not a lot of this money actually went to the people who needed it most.
Approximately US$8 billion (intended for Afghanistan) is currently held in escrow by the US in fear that it would all be siphoned off by the Taliban.

hornet. I watched as it sent a cloud of mountainside screaming into the atmosphere.

JDAMs,[61] said Baker. Now that's some serious shit.

Are we heading over to assist Serge?

Nah, he said, then pulled out a cigarette pack. It was empty. He scrunched it up and threw it in the back of a Bushmaster. We couldn't be so lucky, buddy.

A million and one questions barraged through my head, causing my hands to sweat.

Would I be able to pull the trigger?

Would I run and hide?

Would I crumble at the first sight of bloodshed?

I would never know. Nobody in the Troop would.

The adrenaline rush subsided once I knew we wouldn't be firing. Not today anyway.

Loud radio chatter broke out from the Command Bushmaster.

Zero-Alpha,[62] this is Zero Delta, over.

Zero Delta, what's your SITREP,[63] over.

Zero Alpha, it's raining cats and dogs out here, over.

Zero Delta. Roger that. Tell the lads to sit tight, more air support is now in-bound, over.

Roger that, Zero Alpha. Zero Delta Out.

What the fuck are we doing, standing with our dicks in our hands? I shrieked, shaking Serge by the shirtsleeve. The bastard Taliban is spraying our boys with this horseshit, and we're supposed to sit back and watch?

Calm your tits, said Purdey. I'm sure they've got it all under control.

---

61   Joint Direct Attack Munitions. A guidance kit that converts unguided bombs into all-weather, precision guided munitions.

62   A field element call-sign. Alpha is normally reserved for a command element.

63   Situation Report. A formal and tactical reporting system aimed to notify command on the relative health and fighting strength of a field element.

Davis wrapped his fingers across my left shoulder. It's not like you could make a difference anyhow.

Quit your bitching and get in the vehicle, said Baker.

Yes, Serge, said Davis, and he mounted the rear step with his rifle slung across his shoulder.

He slipped, and the weapon slung around and hit the door, causing his magazine to pop out and crash into the dirt.

Baker knelt to pick it up and spotted the empty shell.

What the fuck is this?

Davis shivered as he balanced himself on the rear step.

I'm no killer, Serge. And no Afghan ever pointed a weapon at me. There's no way I could ever squeeze the trigger on a live one.

Purdey snatched the magazine from Baker and popped out the empty shell. Do you realise what this means, soldier? You've compromised the safety of your teammates. I could lock you up for this.

Davis dropped his hips down onto the step and looked down, hot tears raining out of his eyes. I'm sorry, Sir, but I refuse to shoot another man.

Baker reached out and collared Davis, dragging him to his feet.

Squeezing the trigger doesn't make you a bad person, Private, he said. The bravest soldiers know when to show restraint; but what you've done is nothing short of cowardice.

Let him go, said Purdey, gesturing for Baker to join him on the opposite side of the vehicle.

Baker paused and waited for Davis to look him in the eye.

He let go and followed the captain. Davis remained seated on the rear of the Bushmaster. I stepped over him and took a seat.

Fark, Davis, I said. You won't be hearing the end of this.

We All Have to Eat

*Is there any habit more obnoxious than that of a camel?
While down at the government tank, I watched Afghans watering
these wretched beasts. They polluted the water in the vilest manner.
And, despite offering those blighters the use of my bucket, the
mongrels refused. I suppose the labour was far too odious for the
dusky and dirty Asiatics.
It is not enough that we should tolerate these aliens? His vile
corruption in our backyard is becoming well beyond reproach.*

—11 Aug 1893 The Inquirer

After days of torrential rain, we got the camels moving along the trek South. The train moved steadily across the soft, boggy terrain as nightfall approached.

I steered Penny to the left of the trail as we passed a bullock cart. It was carrying felled timber, and its axles had become buried in the mud. The bullocky swore black and blue that the bogging wasn't his fault. His team all frowned as they shovelled clear the mud and flung it halfway across the scrub.

The camels cleared the bog without a hitch. I halted Penny, then waited for Stu to appear.

Should we help them, Boss?

Not on your life, said Stu, sucking on his pipe. Those men don't want one of your kind handling their wood.

Stu spied an old Boab tree, nestled in a far-off clearing.

He cupped his pipe and pointed the mouthpiece at the grassiest section. It shouldered an energetic river stream.

Well, I guess we'll pull up stumps here for the night, he said, tapping the burnt remnants of tobacco from his pipe.

I circled the camels into the opening and the Afghans were fast getting to unlashing their loads.

Stu paid the team no mind and walked his horse towards the river's edge. It flowed, East to West, and its dirt-brown current lapped above the riverbank's ledge.

He stood there and I'd not seen the Bossman look so fearful as he did when his gaze focussed on the water. His eyes grew wider, and his jaw clenched. Then he turned and dumped his swag beneath the cover of the old Boab tree.

I lay on my back, counting the stars—one to infinity—as Penny rollicked through the scrub. She paused and chewed the seeds of the tall buffalo grass that speared its way across the cheerful Top-end. Then the bullock cart came rumbling down the track.

The bullocky strode his way to the front of the pack and cracked his long, razor-sharp whip. The bullocks didn't respond and dragged their mud-caked hooves low along the trail.

He cracked his whip once again for the same result. Then, as the cart rolled passed, slow, in a lackadaisical manner, the bullocky looked at the Afghans. His whip was slung low, and he glared out across the camp. Then he muttered to himself and dragged his cart onwards.

In the morning, Stu sat by the river's edge and sucked away at his pipe, watching the water lapping at the riverbank.

I walked over and said good morning, but he refused to lift his gaze.

I stared into river's wild current to see if I could see what Stu's eyes were fixated on.

We should make a move soon, Bossman? I said, hoping for a simple response.

It is not but two feet deep, he said, then cleared his throat and spat a yellow gollie downstream. One false step and we'll all be croc meat.

He stood, nibbling on the tip of his pipe, and looked at me.

The very thought of drowning scares me shitless, he said. It should scare the shit out of you too, George. You'll be the first to cross.

A kookaburra balanced on a dead tree limb. The limb jutted out from the old Boab and swayed high above the river's rapid flow. The kookaburra took flight and laughed beneath the glaze of the morning's blistering sun. Then it dove towards the river's muddy banks and clawed a tiny rodent before returning to the dead tree limb and enjoying meal.

Mahmout scoffed at the bird.

The bird raised its head, chewed and swallowed, then wiped itself clean on the tree limb.

It's disgusting, he said. One animal, eating the raw flesh of another. It's horrific and unclean.

Loosen your britches, Mahmout. We all have to eat.

The cameleers ate and cleaned up before loading up their camels.

I was the first on the path and led the team towards the river's edge. The current had calmed overnight, and the water no longer lapped over the banks. So, I hopped right in with Penny at my side.

I reached midway within a matter of strides, and the current swirled around my waist. I looked behind where the next camel held back on the riverbank.

Stu paced up and down the camel chain[64] on horseback with a coy look over his shoulder to check my progress.

The water's cold, but quite safe, Bossman.

He tugged left on the horse's reign and crept to the river's edge.

How about getting to the other side, you great Galah. Then you can tell me what the water's like.

Right-o, Bossman, I said and yanked on Penny's lead.

She stepped forward, and her load lurched to the side and dipped into the waterline.

I ran my hand down the length of her face.

Whoa, girl, I said, and she took another step forward. The load steadied then we reached the far bank.

I shook out my trousers, and a large puddle of brown river water gathered at my feet.

The Afghans clapped their hands and hooped and hollered. I waved back at the men, but Stu was turning away and I could no longer see his pipe or the smoke billowing around his face.

I sat at the base of a plump stringy-bark tree, quite chuffed with

---

64   For the purpose of organised movement, camels are tethered together, nose-to-tail in a long, extended line called a chain, or a train.

myself, and peeled a pistachio shell. A cool breeze lifted from waterline and I watched the team moving one by one across the river.

Everyone had crossed safely. Then it was time for Stu to cross.

Well, he said, with his horse's nose dipping into the water for a drink, I can't get upstaged by a bunch of Afghans, now, can I?

The horse stepped into the river, and Stu rocked and swayed in the saddle until he reached the far bank.

The Afghans clapped as he bailed muddy water from out the tops of his riding boots.

I looked at Stu. I was sure as hell that you'd fall in.

Buckley's chance, said Stu, and he pulled out his pipe and packed it with a fresh pinch of tobacco. I could do that standing on my head.

All Quiet on the Western Front

The first mission had passed and Captain Purdey hailed it as a great success.

I now nurtured my first reservations and, that night, found myself turning restlessly in my bed.

I was sweating like a killer on trial. My heart beat fast and the sound of it pumping against my chest crushed any hope of me falling asleep.

I threw back the sheets and sat up.

Davis… you awake?

No.

I swung my legs off the bed and flicked on the light. Then I got into my joggers and began tying the laces.

I can't sleep either, I said, not after that goddamn patrol and all that talk about money and heroin. And that cock up in the valley. Man … wasn't that a kick in the balls.

Davis rolled over and hugged a pillow over his face.

Ahh, Christ, you're a fun-sponge, Davis. You wanna know what your real problem is?

What, said Davis, with a muffled voice from beneath his pillow.

This war's gonna blow right by you, because you've got a thumb stuck in your arse with your mind rolling in neutral.

I stood and slipped on a t-shirt.

Hell… thinking you're so moral and shit and claiming it's nothing but a crime being here. What you should do is pack your bags and go home.

Davis turned on his back again. Are you finished?

For now.

Good. Then hit the lights.

I walked to the rec-hut, wanting to use the phones, thinking the entire camp'd be off counting sheep. The war, as I'd soon find out, stopped for nobody.

A platoon of dog-faced Marines marched by, carrying more guns and ammo than the entire Australian Infantry Battalion had ever set eyes on.

I scoffed and walked past them. Gun monkeys, I said. They'll waste every single last one of them rounds.

The Uruzgan camp ballooned to the size of a small city almost overnight. Every corner of the camp began forming its own clique.

Down at the gym, meatheads, fuelled by cheap PX-grade pharmaceutical juice pumped iron, deep into the night. And, by the camp bazaar, wannabe hopheads smoked a hookah and feigned getting high from scented tobacco. At the basketball courts, African American GIs slam-dunked and ally-oop'd as unidentifiable despots smacked golf balls over the perimeter fence.

I'll tell ya; the whole camp grew stranger every night.

I stepped into the rec-hut. It was full of American soldiers who'd all squeezed in around a hundred-inch tv screen.

It was glowing brightly and was loud. I had to stand on the tips of my toes to catch a glimpse of what they were watching. I settled back onto my heels. It was only a game of NFL, between the Patriots and the Broncos.

Peyton Manning threw over four thousand yards last year, said one soldier. At sixty-seven percent.

That doesn't mean shit, said another. Not when the Pat's have won three of the last four super bowls.

Ahhh, bullshit, man.

I'm tellin' you, bro…Brady is a future Hall of Famer!

Hall of fame, my great arse, I thought.

I turned my back and walked into the next room and picked up a phone.

Hi, you've reached Sylvia. Sorry, I'm unable to come to phone right now, as I'm now travelling through France and cannot answer.

If your call is important, please leave a message after the beep. Otherwise, email me at sylviastravels@hotmail.com.au

Thank you, and goodbye.

I hung up the phone and kicked an office chair. It knocked a mouse off the desk and woke the computer screen. I pulled out the chair and sat down. I looked at the blue screen and leaned back, clasping my hands behind my head.

I hadn't touched a computer since 1993, when a schoolteacher rapped me across the knuckles with a bamboo cane.

Mister Patterson, she said, that's not an appropriate way to operate these machines. I strongly recommend never touching it like that ever again.

Okay, I said, rubbing my knuckles. Then I swore never to touch a computer again.

I sat there, staring at the blank blue screen, for quite some time. I thought about Sylvia. I wondered if she still thought of me. Hell no. She'd be too busy drinking her way across every city in France. Bitch. I bet she'd already met somebody else.

Such was her style.

I pushed back the office chair and left the room.

A laminate bookshelf stood in a quiet corner of the rec-hut, and it wobbled as Baker drew out a book.

I walked over. Hey.

He put the book down.

What're you doing up, Patterson?

Can't sleep.

Oh, yeah.

Yeah, I said, into his silence. It's this fucking place. It's getting under my skin.

That's not uncommon, he said. The trick's finding something else to occupy your mind.

Like wanking?

Baker stepped back a pace or two and looked at me, steely eyed.

No, you sicko, he said, like reading a book.

A book?

He pulled out another book. It was a nimble little paperback, with half the front cover torn and missing.

All Quiet on The Western Front said Baker. It's a story about unfounded patriotism and disillusionment in war.

Ahh, Christ, Serge. How the hell is anyone supposed to read in a place like this?

Baker stuffed the book into my chest. It buckled as I took it from his hands.

You'll see many more things in the country, Patterson. Things you won't understand. Things that'll nest deep in your subconsciousness, and things you'll never forget. Hell, there'll even be some things you won't wanna forget, but a good book can ease that.

I know I'm a simple bastard, but I haven't got a clue what the hell you're on about.

Christ sakes, Patterson. Just read the fucken book.

Okay, okay, I said and slipped the book inside my pocket, then disappeared back to my room.

Not in Afghanistan Anymore

We had stopped by a well, north of Alice Springs to water the camels and stretch our backs. The air was dry and the ground so hot it made the hair on my toes curl up and die.

I surveyed out to the East. Then West and got hit by some mad hallucinations from staring out over the miles and miles of umber dirt for too long.

A man could wander off in any direction, out here. In *any direction* without bumping heads on another man for days. The place was so wild, and baffling. A prehistoric maze. Always ready to bury your bones beneath the layers of time. Yet, I'd never considered—not for a moment—any of that could take a life. Not the heat, and not the dry, or the endless miles of nothingness and time. No. Out here, loneliness was man's only enemy —so silent and deadly—all for the cost of his desire.

I dipped a wooden pail into the well and hoisted out the water. It was dark and choked by mud, but we'd all have to swallow it. If we wanted to survive.

I wet my lips. It tasted like water, alright, so I carried the pail to Penny, and placed it at her side.

On the far side of the track, Stu propped his left boot atop a mile-marker. It read "500 miles". He groaned and flapped his dust-filled hat against his trousers. Then blew his nose clear and deep into the crook of his shirtsleeve. That felt better than a good hot shower, he said, and ordered the Afghans drop their kit for smoko.

Mahmout gathered up deadwood and kindling and was soon stoking a small fire, with his teapot in hand.

What are you doing, Mahmout? It's too damn hot for tea.

Incorrect, said Mahmout, and he lashed in teaspoons full of old English. You may think it's too hot, cameleer, but once it gets in your belly, I bet you'll be smiling from ear to ear.

Okay, I said, only hold off on the milk.

Penny refused to drink the water, so I stuffed the pail right beneath her nose.

Drink, I said, then splashed her between the lips.

That really got her goat up, and she stomped her hooves, spat, then knocked the pail clean out from my hands. The muddy water splashed over my feet, and got absorbed by the dry, hot earth.

You demon *bitch*! I clocked her on the nose. There was enough water in there to last you two whole days.

Right then, Miriam came stomping over. She was carrying a long, whip-like stick in her hand and was swatting at the flies.

What are you doing? You can't treat an animal like that.

Penny turned her head down and kicked at the bucket. Spat again, then plodded off towards a deep green thicket.

That's no animal, I said and threw a small stone at Penny, striking her on the split of the arse. She's the beast who once guarded the gates of hell.

Sweat rolled down the sides of Miriam's face and her temples beat to the tune of irate drums.

Ugh, she said. How can you be so heartless, George Sher Gul.

She knelt and picked up the upturned pail. Stomped on my toes, then kicked me in the shin.

There, she said. Now you know how it feels.

OUCH… you mad cow, I said and dropped to my knees.

Mahmout fell about laughing.

She's got you there, Sher Gul.

Mahmout carried on laughing, not even trying to compose himself. She's got you by the prunes.

I stood over the fire. The tea pot whistled. I hoisted the pot away from the flames and poured two glasses.

Get off your arse, Mahmout, I said. You're acting like a witless baboon.

Come now, don't act so dour, said Mahmout.

He dusted himself clean and begun spinning a simple tune.

A woman has bested the Great Cameleer.
Ho-hum, ho-hum
A feat ne'er seen before.
Ho-hum, ho-hum.

I spat my tea into the dirt.

She bested no one, I said. That was a cheap shot.

Mahmout kicked dirt across the fire. Smoke condensed out from the coals, causing embers to swarm from the ashes like fireflies to light.

I poured another glass of tea and sipped at it with my back towards a now falling sun.

Penny still hovered over by the thicket, but now Miriam had joined her. She picked the greenest foliage and fed it into Penny's mouth.

That white devil bitch, I said and turned my gaze away.

Hell hath no fury like a man scorned, said Mahmout

Ahh, to hell with her; these Australian women never do what they're told.

Talk to her, you fool, and then you can apologise.

Apologise? For what?

Who cares, Sher Gul. Apologise for what you did yesterday. Today. Tomorrow, and the day after that… just in case.

In case, my arse, I said, and stormed away.

Mahmout stood up, dropping his glass of tea on the desert floor, and followed me.

Australia's a very different place, Sher Gul, you must understand.

What am I supposed to say to her? Huh?

Who cares. Say that you're sorry and move on from there.

Ahh, Christ, I said and looked over at the thicket.

Mahmout collared me by the arm, then clasped my hand. Remember, Sher Gul, he said, you're not in Afghanistan, anymore.

My breath was shaky as I approached the thicket. Neither Miriam nor the camel looked my way, so I wiped my hands across my trousers and feigned a cough.

Miriam turned. What the hell do you want?

Before, Miriam… I acted like a damned fool.

You don't say, she said, with a half smile.

I moved to her side and started plucking away at the foliage.

Would an apology help?

It'd be a good start.

Stu glared when he sighted me and Miriam talking in the outback twilight. He threw his pipe down, then reached into his side saddle and drew out a rifle.

Get away from her, you savage.

He raised the rifle to his shoulder and belted his way towards the thicket.

Christ, said Miriam, you'd better run. Daddy looks mighty ticked off.

He was, indeed.

Stu's pupils boiled, and his jaw was clenched so tight it could've gnawed through granite. The devil is his problem, I thought, turning to greet him.

You stay away from her, he said. That's my daughter you're harassing there.

I harassed her? That woman is incredulous, Bossman. The Afghani aren't used to having them around, on the job, and now she's telling me I can't strike my own camel.

Well, he said, then poked his rifle into the meat of my chest. She's a pure girl. Brought up different; that's all, and there's no keeping her on a leash.

The woman needs a good lashing, or two.

I'll do the whipping around here, Sher Gul. You so much as think about it and I'll drive a bullet-hole square through your chest.

Fine, I said and jerked Penny by the harness and led her back to Mahmout.

Well, said Mahmout. What did she say?

I kicked at the red dirt. Nothing. Only, you were right, Mahmout: we're not in Afghanistan anymore.

BRASS BALLS

The emergency speaker outside my bedroom door barked.

Incoming … Incoming … Incoming. Take cover now, said the pre-recorded announcement as it rang out continuously over the next five minutes.[65]

Taliban bastards, I said to Davis, who was laying sullen in bed. Attacking camp, at this ungodly hour.

Davis didn't bother to answer; in fact, he didn't even move beneath his blanket.

I am PISSED. Don't those animals understand fucken sleep?

I punched the bedpost with the fat-side of my fist and buried my head deep into the mattress.

Davis still hadn't made a sound.

The speaker fell silent.

Soon after, Baker tore open the door.

---

65   Incoming and Indirect Fire (IDF) could be detected by early warning systems. Through surveillance, the origin of the strike (the Taliban would often return to a known site that could reach the base with minimal set-up) could quickly be identified. In some cases, the culprits were often seen fleeing the site. The rockets (usually a 155, artillery round) were laid diagonal on a mound, the ignition was triggered, and the rocket would fly unguided towards a target.

A failed launch could be identified by a rocket spinning, comically on the mound as the culprits fled.

Right-o, get the fuck out of bed, you lazy pricks, otherwise, I'll have you both up on a charge.

I rolled out of bed and swung my feet onto the floor.

What the hell is it, Serge, I said, slipping on my thongs.

An IDF attack. Didn't you hear the siren?

Couldn't miss it, Serge. But the Taliban are always firing those rockets at us. They always seem to miss, and I figured the safest place to be is in bed.

Baker stepped inside the room, then wedged his hard fist deep into the point of my nose.

How in the hell'd you make it into my Army?

I don't know, I said, guess I was born with luck by my side.

Baker pushed me aside, danced his boots on the floor, then walked to Davis' bed.

Well, Patterson, where the hell is he then?

Buggered if I know, Serge; he was there a moment ago.

Baker's ears grew red. He danced on his feet again. If he weren't so mad, I'd say he moved like Fred Astaire. Of course, Baker never had such grace. Nor guile, and as I watched his weight bounce from one heel to the next, his head looked set to burst.

He gave out a final dancing stomp, then steadied his feet in front of mine.

I braced myself.

Patterson, he said, with his jaw clenching so tight. I'm ordering you to go out and find that punk Davis. Then, when you're back, I'm gonna box your ears. Understood?

Yes, Sergeant.

I laced-up boots, then ran out the door. I didn't know where the hell Davis had gone and I didn't appreciate being ordered as his babysitter.

My first port of call was the rec-hut, knowing Davis would not be there. Because, and in his own words, he hated that stinking joint. I just wanted to see who was playing footy that night.

I swung the front door open. The joint was near empty. Save for an old Warrant Officer watching a movie. He was fat. They all were, by that stage in their careers, but this guy's gut bellowed out over the waist of his trousers.

He sipped on a can of Diet Coke and looked friendly. So, I asked, what are you watching, Sir?

Ernest Saves Christmas, he said, diving his hand deep inside a bag of corn chips.

Good choice of movie for the deserts of Afghanistan, Sir.

Don't be a smart shit, Private.

Seen anyone else in here tonight?

Only you, me and the Padre coming by to get stuck into his Altar wine.

All right, Sir, I said. Enjoy your movie.

I strolled out the door, then jogged back to the mess, knowing full well Davis wouldn't be there, either. Because he only ate breakfast and lunch, skipping dinner.

The late Tuesday night meal at the mess was always tacos, and I wasn't missing that.

I took a seat with two shells on my plate and loaded them up with sweet cheddar and sour cream. There was more to this war than sleepless nights and IDF strikes.

I finished up, cleared my plate, and walked out the door.

I went to the gym, and the basketball courts, then down to the bazaars, but I couldn't see Davis anywhere in the whole damn camp.

Sneaky bastard, I thought, he's probably gone and done it. All that conscientious objection business, and hatred for the war. I'd had it pegged as a load of crap. But had the fella really gone and left the war? Withdrawn by own request: that took big brass balls. Not that Baker would see it that way.

I walked another loop around the camp. Then I returned to bed.

Fighting for the Taliban

Purdey flashed on the light, above Davis' bed, then peeled back the sheets. He reached down and scooped out a set of dog tags. They were black and tarnished and mould grew around the neck-chain.

Private Patterson, he said, pack up the rest of Private Davis' belongings, in a trunk, then bring them to my office.

Where's he gone, Sir?

That information's above your pay grade, Private. Just do as you're ordered.

Yessir.

I had him pegged as a communist, since day dot, said Baker, and Patterson told me himself, Davis wanted nothing to do with this war. Shit, I bet he's the type to feign trauma and hide, just to avoid facing the Taliban. A true gold-bricker,[66] Sir; feeding you a jackanory,[67] just so he can live-off a service pension back home.

No way, Purdey said. The entire military psych department's seen too many of that kind. You can't fake that sort of business. Not in this man's Army. I'll have him marched into the brig before tomorrow morning's roll call.

Baked propped a cigarette on the edge of his lips, then scrambled through his pockets for his lighter.

---

66   A swindler, or someone who shirks their duties.
67   A tall story or a nursery rhyme.

Sir, all I'm saying is that it's possible and I wouldn't put it past a kid like Davis.

Purdey snatched the cigarette from Baker's mouth, then bent and crushed it in his palm.

Listen, Sergeant, he said. We cannot have word get out that our diggers are pulling the mental health card. Before we know it, everybody will be hopping on-board; it'll be all over the news. Imagine what the Chief of Defence will say and how that's going to reflect on our performance reports. Christ, I'm due to reach Major next year.

He sprinkled the crushed cigarette onto the floor, then wiped his hands across the chest of his jacket, then stomped out of the room.

Baker looked across the bedroom.

All Quiet on the Western Front lay on my bed, with a bookmark wedged midway.

He picked up the book. Smiled. Returned the book to the bed, then walked outside and lit another cigarette.

A Sick Joke

It'd been two months since Davis left camp.

Nobody knew why, and it buggers me what they told his folks back home.

He left no notes or anything. Just an empty bed, and some hollow hope, that I would look up to find him standing there, laughing as if it was all a sick joke.

The Brass moved quick, too and struck him off the roll book—as if they'd never knew his name.

If you asked me, I was both happy he got out and sad he was gone.

As for anybody else in the Troop? It was hard to tell but the war rolled on, and we'd have all been happy to disappear, just the same.

Heaven and Hell

Baker drove a drove a rattled out, white utility around the inner perimeter of the camp. 30 days to go, he said, then wound down a window and lit up a cigarette.

Not in here, said Purdey, waving away at the cloud of smoke filling up the cabin from the front passenger seat. No way. Put it out.

Baker stubbed out the cigarette. His lips curled, then wound up the window.

The road was gravel, and speed of the ute was stunted by large dirt mounds that looked more like motocross jumps and Baker gunned it as we hit the crest. The front wheels hoisted off the ground. We came crashing back down fast, sending giant plumes of dust out from the sides of the utility.

You deadset moron, said Purdey, shaking his head.

Baker smiled and the old utility kept on rolling.

The utility reached the far side of the camp. Baker looked out the driver's side. Purdey looked out the passenger window. There were sentry towers spread along the perimeter fence. On the outside, there was just dirt. In the distance. tall sky-screaming mountains, all beautiful and capped in snow. Between the white peaks and camp stood Afghan peoples and the Taliban.

We should be out *there*, hunting them, said Purdey

Suppose we should be, said Baker. I don't believe it'll make a smack of difference. For every Taliban soldier shot, another two seem to appear.

I sat quietly in the back and looked out over the mountains.

Ghost-white clouds careened across the blue sky. They were enveloping themselves around the snow-capped peaks. Painting a surreal picture of serenity.

It was a million miles to anything resembling peace.

Somewhere, out there—between heaven and hell—sat an enemy, that we created, patiently waiting for us to go home.

Nothing Here's for Free

The camel chain passed through Alice Springs, South, where the current railroad ended, and my survey duties began.

Stu called a halt to the trek, and the Afghani unloaded their gear.

This railway line's going to make it all the way to Adelaide, he said, sucking on his pipe. For you bludgers, it's where the hard yakka begins.

The devil it does, I said, digging around the inside of my pack. I scooped out a piece of bread and a fistful of pistachios. They were wrapped in Miriam's handkerchief. The nut-oils had seeped through its satin sheen.

What are we going to do for food, Bossman?

Work for it, he said. There isn't a thing in here that comes to you free, Sher Gul—neither food, water, sleep or women.

Penny had dropped to her belly, and I was unlashing her load when a rock landed at my feet. It was the size of a grapefruit.

A second rock whizzed by my ears, then a large stick speared into the dirt right before Stu's feet.

HEADS UP! he yelled and dropped to one knee.

He cradled his rifle in both hands. Eased back the cocking

handle and raised the weapon to his shoulder and pointed it West.

More rocks flew in and rolled about his feet, then Stu squeezed the trigger.

CRACK. A bullet whizzed through a bank of trees.

The rocks stopped, but the leaves on the trees continued to murmur and bristle.

What's going on, Bossman?

Stu knelt, stiff, and stared into the trees with pipe smoke streaming out his nose.

It's the blacks, he said. They're not happy 'bout us crossing their land. CRACK. He fired off another round. Apparently, it's sacred. Bet if they ever travelled to someone else's country, they'd be singing off a different song sheet.

If it's sacred land, shouldn't we go around?

Like hell, said Stu, chambering a third round. We're not savages and don't bother with that tribal bullshit. If they don't like it, then they can jam it up their arse.

That doesn't sound too fair, Bossman.

Nup, said Stu, but I guess that's the cost of progress, so stuff the Aborigines.

I draped my arm over Mahmout's shoulders and looked out to the horizon. A hazy mirage floated close to the Earth's edge, beckoning a warm welcome to anybody wishing to wander her way to the sure and profound promise of a slow, Outback death.

Isn't she beautiful, Mahmout?

Sure, he said, then brushed my hand away from his shoulder.

What's the devil's gotten into you?

Mahmout flared his nostrils and sniffed, then turned from the horizon.

We're no better than slaves, out here. Paid a pittance by an uncouth infidel and unwanted by the bushmen who claim this land.

I removed Penny's harness and fed her a handful of sun-dried grains. She groaned and chomped away at her meal, then swung her head west and roamed towards the wild unknown.

Wait until we get to Adelaide, I said. Miriam tells me the hills roll across the Earth like jolly green giants, down to the ocean's edge where they're covered and caressed by juicy vineyards that harvest the finest wine in the land.

That, said Mahmout, is of no use to me. He rolled his eyes towards the sky. Besides, we've come halfway across this country and haven't seen one man drinking wine.

I turned to the stockpile and cracked open a timber box with an iron lever. Inside the box were hoops of rope, rusted iron chains, survey pegs and some tins of bully beef and fruit. I hoisted out a bundle of survey pegs and a rusty tin of fruit. I sat with my back to the box and pierced the tin with the sharp point of a stone. Then slurped out the juice.

Stu spread the legs on a hefty wooden tripod. He set the head level and mounted the theodolite. Then, he spun it South and placed his right eye to the scope.

When this railroad is done, said Mahmout, it'll stretch from one end of the country to the next. Then, there won't be any use for us anymore. Or the camels. We'll be useless.

I peeled back the tin lid, then scooped out a cube of plump, moist pear. I placed it, delicate on the crest of my tongue and tasted the syrupy juices roll down to the rear of my throat.

There'll always be work here, I said and sucked out another cube of pear.

Mahmout shrugged and smiled with an indifferent smile. Then he grabbed his mat and turned to the West.

The Afghani hoisted up a small canvas tent and rolled their mats out in tight, neat rows. Outside, in the direct sunlight, Miriam was rustling through her bags. Except she wasn't unpacking. Instead, she shifted her belongings from one camel to the next—like her work here was done.

I finished the last pear cube. Crushed the tin and dumped it inside the box.

Would you like me to help?

Her eyes shifted, sharp and searching for the Bossman.

Stu spun his theodolite and was swinging bearings far off into the distance. He had no interest at all in what was occurring behind his back.

Miriam's eyes softened and her face relaxed. Oh cheers, George. I'm in a mad rush.

Where are going?

Back to Darwin.

I picked up a bag. It clinked and rattled as all her possessions shifted inside.

Darwin? I said. What the devil for?

Oh, it's Daddy, she said. He's finally cracked the shits and no longer wants his darling daughter cavorting across the countryside in the company of savages. I refused to adhere, of course, but now he's cut off my pay.

And?

I told him to go stuff-it in his tobacco pouch, there's better work back home.

Miriam took the bag from my hand.

I'm coming with you, I said.

Her eyes squinted as she looked up at me.

Absolutely not, she said. The Bossman will string you by the balls.

The devil he will, I muttered and scuffed my hells into the dirt.

Don't be a boofhead, George… stay with the men. Until Adelaide, at least.

I didn't answer but played with her handkerchief. I rubbed it between fingers, while looking at the ground, then raised it to my face breathing in all my nose could manage.

Poor, poor George, she said, laughing. I'm not dying.

No, I said, but it's the next worst thing.

We looked at Stu, still with his back turned and still naïve to the skulduggery occurring behind him.

I hugged her—in full view of the Afghani, with their mutters and groan—then said goodbye.

Ducks in a Row

Each day without Davis was much the same. Yet, each day in Afghanistan told a completely different tale.

It felt like yesterday he'd jumped aboard the freedom bird; only to be found guilty before an Australian military court of law.

Prejudicial conduct was the charge. Whatever that meant. It cost him 30 days in Holsworthy cells, and Baker was not happy. No. He thought the punishment was too soft, but yonks had passed, and Davis was somewhere else now. It was time the Troop moved on.

Don't forget what you came here for, Baker would say. Our job's only half done.

Me, I'd lace my boots the same way. Trousers still went over my underpants. I cleaned my rifle. Ate my three square a day, then went to bed each night knowing we'd barely put a dent in the Taliban.

Sometimes I could not sleep and often wondered what the hell we all came here for.

Orders were after lunch and I was the last man to enter the briefing hut.

Leave the door open, said Baker. The air-con is on the blink.

I latched the door open. Looked for an empty spot, then took a seat.

My entire face was sweating. So were my hands. I hadn't noticed it before, some diggers had longer hair. Longer than regulations allowed. Others had beards, or stubbled faces, and we all looked years older than the day we'd arrived.

Baker stood at the back of the room. He removed the batteries from the air-con remote. Blew out the dust, then banged the remote against the wall. Fucken machine's sending me mental, he said.

Purdey rolled his eyes. Looked at the ceiling, then switched on a PowerPoint presentation.

For most of you, the initials MK won't mean a thing, but he's been helping us fight the Taliban. Therefore, he's an ally, and now he needs our assistance.

Baker dragged a plastic chair beneath the air-conditioner. Stood on top, then pulled out the air-con filter. Whole thing's caked in mud, he said.

Purdey held a fist to his mouth and coughed. For most of you, this'll be your last trip outside the wire. So, let's all remain switched on. Keep our ducks in a row and come home in one piece.

He clicked on the PowerPoint. An image of a stone fortress on the screen.

This one's big, lads, he said. Next slide.

An Afghan man's face appeared. He was a tall, bald, bearded, ugly, and powerful man with a row of medals stretched across the breast of his green coat.

That's Provincial Police Chief Matiullah Khan,[68] the most powerful man in Uruzgan.

What's that got to do with us? Said Baker.

He's a Pashtun millionaire. Some people even call him 'The King of Uruzgan', and say that he often holds dinner parties with movie stars and presidents.

Baker took out a cigarette and rest it between his lips. Doesn't sound like he needs our help, Sir.

Yeah? Too bad the Taliban want him dead.

Purdey turned his attention back to the Troop.

Our mission is to drive out to his compound and discuss personal security.

He advanced the slides. A route map, from our camp to Matiullah's compound appeared on the screen.

Bushmaster drivers, take notes.

The air-con compressor rumbled, then the fan blades moved to the left—then right—as cold air blew throughout the room. The diggers turned from the briefing and gasped in the air-conditioned breeze.

We roll out at 0-600, gents. That's the end of orders, are there any questions… no?

Purdey switched off the PowerPoint.

Troops dismissed.

I left the briefing hut; the sun was high. My face and hands continued to sweat.

---

68 A powerful figurehead in the Uruzgan region, Matiullah Khan (MK) and his Police Force were vital to securing the province and reducing the number of Taliban in the areas surrounding Tarin Kowt.

He was a complex character who made his millions from Australian taxpayer dollars and, as reported by the Australian Broadcasting Commission (ABC), he often gifted ADF commanders with gold watches, in return for undisclosed favours.

MK was also known for his dealings with the Taliban, through bribes and blackmailing, and often ensured that associated Taliban members were released from prison, irrespective of their crimes.

In 2015, he was killed in a suicide bombing. The Taliban claimed credit for the assassination.

VISA-VIS

I carried my book everywhere, along with a notepad and biro. I read in bed each night to get myself to sleep. I read it the dunny. At the dinner table and even in the gym, jotting down notes between my sets.

When I neared the end, I slowed, reluctant to put down the book. *All Quiet on the Western Front* started making sense. I didn't want to see it end, because in the fishbowl of this camp, the book was my only friend.

I never wanted to let that feeling go.

What goes on after a chapter ends? A new one begins, of course, until you reach the last page. Then it's time to close that book.

It was the night before the last patrol. I carried the book into the rec-hut. The room was empty, except for Baker, hunched over by the bookshelf.

I ignored him and stretched out on the couch, as if it were only me and my book in that room.

I read slow. Hung on every word. Analysed every line, and every page; so small, so brown and so old.

Then came the time I'd been dreading: the last page.

I licked my thumb, then dabbed it on the top corner of the second last. The paper was hard, textured, and stiff. I slid my thumb down to roll the paper, but it was all a big mess. Something had glued together the last pages.

I threw the book on the couch. What the hell am I supposed to do now?

I looked across to Baker. He had an unlit cigarette jutting from his mouth and was sucking on it like it was burning down the house.

The man is not human. Or he's God damned insane.

Hell… we all were by that stage in this sick war experiment—mere rats in a cage. The whole screaming-lot of us. All scratching our knuckles, hard against the desert floor. All burning to get out. All—as a matter of preference—while our brains were still intact.

I considered, once again, to leave Baker to his own devices. Free to go diving off into the deep end. Into books, and his own madness and matter of nowness. And free to go, wherever he chose. Way down to the darkening basements of his mind. Forever looking back at that man in the mirror. It was his life—after all—and it was mine. Visa-vis, and to each their own.

Then I walked into the phone booths and dialled a familiar number

Sorry I can't come to the pho—

SHIT, I said, and hung up.

I walked to the bookshelves and drew out a fresh title: Wait Until Spring, Bandini, by John Fante. I'd never heard of him, and guessed nobody had. It was a wretched looking book. Well-travelled and had lost its jacket and front cover. Not that I cared.

I flicked to the opening page, then sank deep into the corner of the couch.

Three Pips and a King's Commission

We had worked our way south to Port Augusta where an airless tin hut sat by the side of the road.

Stu dismounted his horse and let it to meander to a shallow watering trough. The trough was lined with thick green sludge, and the horse licked at it with the fat side of its tongue as Stu disappeared inside the hut. He reemerged with a small tin can, which he cracked open and took a short sip.

Reckon we'll camp here the night, he said, and whisked his fingers inside his tobacco pouch.

The Afghans didn't bat an eyelid, and soon the camel string was ready to count stars by a campfire.

Hey, Bossman, I said, is that an outback pub?

Stu laughed then sipped at his new tin can.

Christ, Sher Gul. No. Ain't no sane piss pot would ever travel out this far for a tipple.

The Afghani tents went up, mats rolled out, and the sun was winding down. Stu laid with his back rested on a swag and blew smoke into the cooling night air.

None of us looked up when we saw a cloud of dust rising from the North-South trail.

It was a team of six men, travelling from the South. When they arrived, the dust quickly settled. Then they dismounted by the hut.,

What the hell do these bludgers want? Stu muttered, softly raising his head from the swag.

Three of them wore military khakis—dress of the day— with long golden silk lanyards hanging from their left shoulders. The other three wore denim jeans and old bushman hats.

That's a mighty fine stead, you have there, said a man in khaki.

He had three brass pips pinned in a row on each shoulder. A long sword hung, sheathed at his hip.

That she is, said Stu, puffing out fat white clouds of smoke that billowed about his face.

How's the turn o' foot?

Louder than thunder, and quicker than lightning, said Stu.

You don't say, said the man, arching over to inspect the horse's hooves.

The Mother country[69] is preparing a force to clean out the Boer, he said. And, well, we're on our way to Darwin, to set sail for Africa, and we could use a young man like you.

Well, I don't know the King, said Stu, and I sure as shit haven't met no Boer before in my life. So, I can't tell what business I have, clearing some stranger out from a far-off land.

Stu whacked his pipe against the heel of his boot. Black sediment sprinkled on to the dirt.

Sure sounds like it'll be a ripper of a trip, he said, then laid

69   Prior to federation, and as part of the British Empire, the six Australian colonies volunteered troops for service in South Africa.

Even post-federation, in 1901, Australian soldiers would have to wait several years into WW1 before they could form ranks beneath an unencumbered Australian command structure fronted by Generals Birdwood and Monash.

Journalist Keith Murdoch, in his correspondence with the Australian Prime Minister, was a vocal in the shift.

Australian officers still receive a Kings commission upon graduation from military college. This commission is personally signed off by the Australian Governor General, on behalf of King Charles III.

down and pulled his hat over his face. But if it's all the same, h, I think I'll sit this one out.

The man kicked Stu's swag.

Every Australian has his role to play, he said.

But Stu didn't budge. Not a single bit.

The three men in khaki walked inside the hut.

They all turned and came straight back out, shaking their heads.

That place isn't fit for a leper, said one man.

Too right, said a second.

Seen worse, said the third. Then all three laughed.

The tree men in denim watered the horses. Inspected their hooves. Adjusted the saddles. Topped up all the canteens. Set up an eating area, then began propping up three tents. One each for the men in Khaki.

I walked to Stu.

Why didn't that man ask the Afghani?[70]

Stu rolled his face to one side, and peered out from beneath his cap, showing me the whites of his left eye. Those men in there, George? Those men with gold pips lined across their shoulders? They're all serving on a King's commission. Silver spooned mongrels, and the only the coloured men they've known are viewed as peasants.

---

70   Australian Forces heavily employed camels, in South Africa and throughout WW1, including Beersheba.
The Royal Australian Corps of Transport's 26 Transport Squadron mascots are the camels Penny and Vernon. This is a testament to their significance within Australian military history.

So, he's *royalty*?

Well, he might think he is, and at the very least, he'll consider himself a class above me and you, said Stu. Then he rolled to his side, and drifted off to sleep.

The Afghani kept the campfire burning, until morning.

When the sun rose, Stu was on his back, snoring with six empties spread around his swag.

The men in Khaki bypassed him. Boiled a pot of water. Shaved, then mounted their horses.

Care if any of the Afghani join you? I asked.

Sorry, Australian's only, said one man.

He wedged his feet into the stirrups. Took a sip from his canteen. Surveilled the Northern horizon, then steered the horse's reigns in the same direction.

I would have gone, I said to Mahmout.

What in the hell for? There's nothing for us in Darwin. And I've got no beef with the Boer.

I held Miriam's handkerchief to my nose but did not answer.

Dirty Afghanistan Dust

At 0500, my alarm clock hit me like a brick to the face. I scrambled out of bed and into my pluggers. A giant dust storm swirled outside. I slipped my towel from the drying rack. Scooped up some soap and a razor and I took a quick shit. A shower, a shave, and was in the mess hall by half-five.

The Bain-Marie was empty and cold, so I grabbed Coco Pops with milk instead.

Baker walked in. He was unshaven and had a cigarette hanging from his lip.

Don't forget, Patterson, he said, we're out the gates at six, and you're riding up front with me.

Got it, I said and lifted the breakfast bowl to my mouth and slurped at the cocoa flavoured milk.

The Troop was en route to Matiullah Khan's fortress as the Bushmasters travelled North, and the sun climbed over the mountain's peaks.

Baker peered through the scope of his rifle, then wiped the glass with a strip of cheesecloth.

We're not looking for trouble, he said, but we are always *primed* if trouble finds us.

We rolled fast as we approached the next village, and Baker nudged the gunner who sent the guns panning through their left and right arcs. The radio was continuously squawking, and the Signaller began relaying critical titbits back to camp.

Stay vigilant, said the Convoy Commander.

I looked out through the green tinted Bushmaster windows at the archaic Quoras abutting the route. Each had their own set of war-burnt eyes, peering out from windows, doors and barren courtyards. All those dead-soul villagers dressed in their sky-blue burqas and tight-wrapped shemaghs.

How about those A-Rabs, yelled the driver. They're all shitting bricks!

Wrong. They are not frightened, said Baker, they've seen too much blood. And they won't lose no sleep if they see a little more.

Hell, said the driver, reaching across the cabin for a bottle of water. They ought to nuke the whole damn joint, Serge. Grind it all to dust. The only way to win this fucken war.

The Bushmaster swung westward and rolled uphill.

Matiullah Khan's fortress stood at the peak of the rise.

Fucking no *way* said Baker. We're here to stop the Taliban; not play God.

God wouldn't piss on this joint, said the driver.

Then the cabin fell silent.

DEFENCE HAS A ZERO DRUGS AND ALCOHOL POLICY

Matiullah Khan's fortress stood towering over the village with its imposing walls. A band of armed guards patrolled the perimeter. Sharpshooters mounted themselves in sentry boxes at each corner, their high-powered rifles trained on anything that moved.

We stopped at the entrance, where four Afghan soldiers strained to push the gates open. The Bushmasters rolled in, and the soldiers strained as they pushed the gates closed.

The lead Bushmaster rolled across the wide, cobbled driveway. Past the lush green lawns. Past the marbled steps and past the pink roses, lining the gardens like rows of soldiers on parade.

Fuck me. Isn't this the most beautiful thing I've ever seen. And wouldn't this place be better if we'd pulled out all those bastard poppy seeds ourselves. Then replaced them with roses. Then every soldier, Taliban or otherwise, could stuff their faces with the pink smell of flower.

Nobody would have time left for fighting.

Matiullah Khan stood, poised at the top of the stairs, smiling a wide, shit-eating grin.

The first person out was Captain Purdey. He bound up the stairs to greet the Khan with a meaty handshake.

Damn, said Baker. Isn't *that* a match made in heaven.

He slung his rifle over his right shoulder and lit a cigarette. The troops sat idle, watching the two men tossing niceties about atop the stairs.

What a beautiful home you have, said Purdey.

Thank you. It's been in my family for over two centuries and let's pray, two hundred more.

Matiullah then hugged his arm around Purdey's shoulder and ushered him inside.

Patterson, you're with me, said Baker, as he jogged up the stairs and through the slowly closing front doors.

I followed quickly inside to a foyer that was wide and long and sparkling like an Olympic size pool. Persian rugs covered the length of the polished floors. Millennia old oil paintings and portraits spotted the walls. It all caused my eyes to swell. My heart tore, right in two. Outside, the Afghan world was so dirt riddled, war torn and poor; here, in Khan's halls—it was another land.

Usual drill, said Baker. He opened his shirt pocket and reached inside for his cigarettes. He surveyed the room. There were two main openings, and a window which overlooked a secluded poppy patch.

For private use only, said Mutullah Khan, smiling.

Baker smiled back, closed his pocket, then turned to me.

I'll be behind the boss. You're over by that entrance.

Roger that, Serge.

I walked to the entrance. Two white and blue vases sat on either side of the doorway. The vases reached hip height, with several long, blue-green peacock feathers jutting out from the centre. I moved from the entrance and stood with my back to the wall beneath a gold-framed painting.

Hell, I thought. Does this Khan have more money than the entire country, or what?

Push in closer, said Baker. He pointed two fingers inside the next room, then pointed them at my eyes. I need you watching both entrances, Patterson. Like you've got eyes out the back of your head.

Roger that, Serge, I said, then pointed at the paintings. Serge, these must be worth millions.

Fuck the art, said Baker. He pointed to each of the entrances, then at his eyes. Both rooms, motherfucker. I want you watching both rooms.

Matiullah Khan laughed and rubbed his belly, then gnashed the end of a fresh cigar with his yellowy teeth.

Come, sit, he beckoned to Purdey, pointing at a long and mirror-polished oak table. Bowls of Challow, Bolani, spreads, dips, grapes and melon sat, spread out across the table.

A servant carried in a pot of tea and moved to place it at the head of the table.

NO, said Khan. Hooshta, boy, and bring out some of my finest whiskey.

Sorry, said Purdey, but Defence has a zero drugs and alcohol policy while on duty.

Ahh, your Defence has a zero policy on every fucking thing, but right now, you're a guest in my home. It would be a grave insult if you said no.

Matiullah pulled out a chair, then leant his weight back.

Now, *Mister* Purdey, I wish to ask you a favour.

Sure.

Your Army has many soldiers, including some of the finest?

Of course.

The servant returned carrying a whiskey decanter and a white box. He placed the white box to Matiullah's side, then poured two even glasses.

The room filled with a scent of burnt peat, and Matiullah pushed the white box towards Captain Purdey.

The Taliban do not fear my guards, so it's unsafe for me here.

Purdey didn't respond but sat back into his seat.

Open the box, said Matiullah, with a wave of his hand.

Purdey lifted the small lid. It was a gold Rolex.

A gift for you, *Mister* Purdey.

Baker shifted on his feet, then arched tall on the tips of his toes, trying to get a look inside the box. His lips pursed and his eyebrows frowned. Don't fucken do it, Purdey, he said with a muted whisper. Don't do it.

Baker shot a stare my way.

Move your arse to the next room, Patterson, and pretend you didn't see a thing.

Roger that, Serge, I said, then clicked my heels and marched into the next room.

Two Afghan men, wearing white shirts with black vests and Pakol hats, froze at the sight of me. They had Ak-47s slung across their shoulders and their gazes became locked with mine.

I went to move backwards, but my feet, knees and heartbeat all protested and refused to move.

I was fucking frozen.

The Afghans grinned, removed their rifles and leant them against the wall. Then they unfurled a long Persian rug along the white marble floor.

The men smiled again and left the room.

I didn't get a moment to catch my breath before they returned pushing a wooden barrow. It was full of blackish-brown mud cakes all wrapped in a clear plastic, which they laid on the mat.

Fuck me, I said, private use, my arse. I raced back into the next room and waved down Baker.

Serge, you gotta check this out.

Give me a tic, he said, never taking his eyes off Purdey and Matiullah.

No, Serge… you gotta come *now*. There's enough midnight oil in here to power New York City.

What the hell are you talking about, Patterson?

FUCK, Serge, you gotta come and see it for yourself.

The Afghan men were down on hand and knee. Each with a spool of wiry hemp twine and were fastening off the bags.

FUCK ME, said Baker. What is *THAT*?

Some of Afghan's finest, said the men, in perfect English.

I'll be the judge of that, said Baker, prying into one of the open bags with the sharp end of his bayonet.

He pulled out a biscuit-sized chunk of opium.[71] It looked like cool, dry tar, scooped up from the roadside, and he held it to his nose.

Yep, this here's some mighty potent gear. But it's quite the shame, gentlemen, that we're gonna have to take this off your hands.

The Afghan men stood back and laughed and for the moment, I thought they were going to reach for their guns.

Serge, I said, we oughta get the hell out of here. This does not feel right.

Baker lifted a bag in each of hands and dumped them into the barrow.

Shut your mouth, Patterson, and come give a god damn hand.

Hell no, Serge, these guys are gonna put holes straight into the backs of our heads.

Move, or I'm gonna shoot you myself.

Roger that, Serge, I said and picked up a bag.

---

71   Although many tribal elders, Mullahs and farmers agreed to the cessation of opium harvests, processing of the poppies continued behind closed doors.

Purdey entered.

Sergeant Baker, drop the dope and stand down.

HELL, Sir, isn't that what we came here for?

Affirmative, Sergeant, but there's only one man giving the orders around here. Now step back from those bags.

Sir, said Baker, the questions and fury obvious in his eyes.

Baker held up the chunk of opium on the end of his bayonet and waved it in the air.

The world's at war on drugs, Sir, and now we've found some, we have to seize it?

Stand down, Sergeant. That's an order!

Roger that, Sir, said Baker. Then he left the room.

Matiullah and Purdey shook hands and said goodbye.

Now, I can't promise you any personal security, said Purdey, but I'm going to guarantee you I'll do the best I can.

Matiullah smiled, then slipped a fresh cigar into the Captain's breast pocket.

That's all I ask of you, my friend, he said. Then he led Purdey to the front door.

Purdey rolled down his sleeves and walked down the stairs. He looked high at the wide blue sky. Then down at his watch, glistening gold in afternoon sunlight.

Right-o, team, he said as he smiled. Mount up; it's time to roll.

Black to White

Before daylight, the local constabulary had raided the Afghani camp. And it was there they discovered five native women sleeping with the camel drivers.
Police arrested the Gins and seized a quantity of apparel, bush tucker, beads and whatnot.
Four Afghani pleaded guilty to harbouring the women and received fines of up to $5 each.

—4 April 1908 The Hedland Advocate

The dry umber desert gave way to rolling hills covered in lush green Australiana. Vineyards. Plantations. Farm life and long clear rivers flowing in between.

The team called a halt in an open field, where they could eat and drink and lull for the night.

Mahmout pointed out a lodge, on the bend of a winding road. It stood in the shadows of a sandstone church. There was a spire jutting out from the roof. It culminated in a Holy Cross that cast a fat, dark shadow over the neighbouring lodge.

Ahh, what I'd give for a fresh cook meal and a bath, said Mahmout.

I walked into a small vineyard and strolled along the alleyways, probing at the green bunches of grapes. Squeezing at the fattest ones until fresh juice came bursting out.

A bath for the Philistine, I said, then chuckled, still squeezing at the grapes. I want to taste some great Australian wine.

Mahmout looked up at the sky. It was clear and blue. Wine, for the cameleer, yet he calls me the Philistine.

Mahmout hobbled down to the lodge.

I followed him, dumb, thick, and naïve inside.

A woman stood at the reception, behind a guest book, that lay open wide on a polished cedar bench. She wore a long emerald-green dress that covered her down to her wrists and wrapped tight around her neck.

Deliveries to the back, gentlemen, she said.

We're looking for a bath and cooked meal, said Mahmout. He pointed to himself, then me. But we'll settle for a meal, Ma'am, if that isn't too much trouble.

Your best bet is to cook your own, gentlemen, she said, and slapped the guest book closed. And, if you want a bed, the nearest Gin camp is two miles West of town.

Mahmout reached into his vest pocket and pulled out a thick roll of paper pound. We have money, he said, unfurling the notes.

I don't care if you're J.D. Rockefeller with pockets full of oil and gold, said the woman. She removed the guest book from the bench and tucked it inside an open draw. We're closed, gentlemen. I must leave now… have a good day.[72]

The woman turned and left the room.

---

72   For the Afghani, social integration was prohibited whilst they worked in Australia.
Nearly all were forced to camp outside of the local town limits, often establishing their camps adjacent to First Nations camps where integration was mostly welcomed.

Cow, said Mahmout, rolling back his stack of notes. Now where are we supposed to go?

We returned to the camels. Stu was flat out on his back, with a pipe in hand, fast asleep.

All the Afghani were nowhere in sight.

Where do you think they all went?

I couldn't say, I said and traipsed back into the vineyard. I probed at the grapes and began squeezing out their juices.

I bet they're at the camp.

It makes sense, I said, dropping a fat green grape into my mouth.

The grape burst, and juice went shooting into the roof of my mouth and coating the breadth of my tongue. It was a fresh taste, but sour, and made my gums water and my eyes squirm. I spit out the seeds and plucked another grape.

Don't you wanna go find out? said Mahmout.

It can't hurt, I said, then picked a handful of grapes.

The Afghani were resting snug on the sand of a dry creek bed, side by side with three Aboriginal men.

A bottlebrush tree shrouded over the creek, providing dappled shade. Its bright red flowers fed a flock of parrots that came zooming down from above.

A short Aboriginal woman rose from the sand. She stretched out high on the tips of her toes and plucked at several flowers. The woman muttered words in her native tongue. Sat. Then sucked at the nectar.

Mahmout threw his mat into the sand. All I'd like is a hearty meal; is that too much to ask?

I cleared a patch of the river's dry, soft sand and took a seat.

Why don't you relax, Mahmout? We're only here for a night.

One night or two? What does is it matter? You heard how that woman spoke. How she treated us, and the sheer scorn she had for us, living out here.

Mahmout began rolling out his mat. One night, he said, yet out here It feels like a life in purgatory.

Two women came walking along the creek bed. One carried a handful of wild rooted vegetable. The other, a dead goanna. It swung, limp in her hands, with bright blood rolling down the length of its lifeless body. It's tongue hanging long, dry and blue from its lazy, dead mouth.

Look at this, Mahmout! I chuckled at the frown drooping heavily across his face. There's your fresh meal. It's arrived after all.

That's disgusting. All riddled with maggots, disease, and germs. It's unclean.

My friend. We all have to eat.

The women walked through the camp and dumped their bounty into a scalloped-out hole, in the sand. It was steaming with hot coal and tiny, red-hot embers burst into the air. The goanna's hardened, leathery skin singed and burned as smoked billowed out from the hole.

Oh, the smell, said Mahmout, retching. Tell me they're not eating that thing.

A tall, skinny Aboriginal man emerged from the bush. He wore nothing but blue jeans and walked barefoot. His skin appeared darker than the others—it glowed mahogany red. And his eyes boomed out, like white pearls, peering straight through me.

Something smells *good*, he said and hovered over the goanna, barbecuing on the red-hot coals.

Hey, Charlie, said another Aboriginal man. Why you always showing up empty-handed when it's time to eat?

Charlie sat beside the fire pit and brushed sand from the palms of his hands.

Ah, you fellas always complaining about something.

Then he spun on his sit bones and faced the Afghani.

And who's this mob, then?

This them Mohamed fellows we always talking about. They come to build the railway line.

Railway line? White fellas do anything to escape walking.

A woman reached into the fire pit and clutched the goanna by the tail. She hoisted it above the coals. Its belly was charcoal black, and the woman smiled, flashing her broad, white teeth. Then she spun the goanna and lowered it onto its back.

You fellas wanna come and join us? Us fellas out here, don't own nothing, but we've always got plenty of tucker to eat.

Mahmout covered his eyes with a shemagh and turned face away.

Hey, what's his problem? said Charlie.

It's the goanna, I said. It's scared the old boy off his tea.

Charlie laughed. Well, if he stays out here long enough, it'll change the colour of his grin.

The woman dragged the goanna off the coals. Then laid it on a flat cluster of leaves. She took a short blade and sliced along the gristle of the belly. Jerked out the guts. And with the flat side of the blade, fed a small fleshy organ into the side of her mouth.

The devil with this lot, said Mahmout. I can't take it no more.

He climbed to his knees. Dusted the sand from his shemagh then hobbled off into the scrub.

Charlie stood then moved and sat by my side.

You got a name?

George. George Sher Gul. Cameleer.

Charlie smiled. He peeled back the black roasted skin on a length of goanna limb, revealing a white sinewy flesh. You're a long way from home, Mister Sher Gul.

Someday I wish to call Australia home.

Yeah, said Charlie. That's what all the bloody white mob says—

Charlie gnawed away at his meal, peeling back the cooked flesh, almost strand by strand. Then chewing slow, with a soft glow of enjoyment, spread from one cheekbone to the other, he held the limb in front of me.

No thanks, I said.

The glow on Charlie's face spread brighter.

You've got them camels, right?

Are they good eating?

I've never tried.

He tore off the last morsel of flesh, revealing a clean white bone. He threw it onto the coals.

Yeah, he said, I bet they're bloody gamey. God ugly and a smell that'll make a dog run for its life.

Charlie removed a small pouch out from his pocket. Then, with a pinch of tobacco, he rolled a cigarette.

I heard all that mob are heading off to some faraway country. Say they're gonna fight some war. Gonna hunt some fellas they've never met. They go calling it their duty all because some English fella, in a funny hat, says it's his time to go.

Charlie stood and leant over the fire pit and lit his cigarette on the coals.

They never ask us black fellas, though.

Charlie moved away from the fire pit and headed for the river bend.

I followed.

That's a good thing, I said, pointing back at the Afghani. My friends have seen nothing but war, our whole lives. We want to get far away and never look back.

True? Our mob knows about that, too. All us fellas want is a job and fair go.

A fair go?

Yes, said Charlie. A fair go's all white fellas talk about... depending on which way the wind blows.

What's that mean?

I dunno, but it all changes when the brothers put on that soldier garb, and his skin fades to white.[73]

And when he takes it off?

Buggered if I know, said Charlie. Spose it turns black again.

He knelt and peered into a pinhole on the rising edge of the riverbank, then snapped a stick in half and dug into the hole.

It opened wide, showing the brown, scaly skin of a wild-looking creature.

What the devil is it? I said, creeping my way over.

Food.

It doesn't look like food. Why not try some thing that crawls above the dirt?

Charlie heaved the reptile by the writhing end of its tail. It stretched and pulled away. Charlie dropped to his knees and adjusted his flailing grip.

You fellas couldn't feed yourself if your life depended on it.

---

73   According to the Australian War Memorial, enlisting into the Australian military was a life-altering experience for First Nation's soldiers, and for the better part of their service, they were treated as equals, without prejudice, and received equal pay.
First Nations soldiers continue to provide exceptional service within the Australian Defence Force.

THWOP. The head popped out. Its jaw spread wider than a barn door and flashed its long, curved and teeth. HISS.

YOU'RE MAD, I said.

Then, with a slick whip, the reptile flickered through the air.

THUD. Its body slammed into the face of a smooth river rock and fell limp.

If you want to eat, said Charlie, then you're gonna have to go get it your bloody self.

He turned and walked back to the fire pit.

I followed; some distance behind.

The Afghani were all sitting back and sipping on hot bush tea.

Charlie dumped the limp reptile flat onto the still red-hot coals. It sent fat, white smoke booming into the air, and a wide smile beamed across Charlie's face.

If you go, I said, would you trust the white man by your side? To England, or wherever?

He arranged the coals with the pointed end of a stick. Wrapping them around the burning reptile, before falling into his seat.

No, he said. But would I have the choice?

I didn't answer, and rolled onto my back to watch the smoke drift by. I thought about that war. Far away. No, I wouldn't trust them either.

Star Crossed

Stu rode camp, unbathed, unshaved and smelling like a dead cat. He was without his old bush hat, and there was no smoking pipe over his stubbled chin.

What he did hold was a bottle of sherry.

I lifted my head off the mat and rubbed my eyes.

Stu? My eyes stung as they hit the morning sun.

Georgie boy! I'm gonna need to round up the men… pronto.

He leant forward, moved to dismount, but his boot slipped from the stirrups, and he crashed into the sand.

We've got a job on Bossman?

No, he said, rolling onto his back. One of you savages has gone and upset the town publican. We gotta move or else someone's gonna get hung.

I climbed up off my mat and stared out into the scrub, thinking Mahmout had gone on the run.

Listen, Bossman, the team's settled here, so, if there isn't a job on, I don't think we should move. The animals need rest.

Stu stumbled back to his horse and reached for his rifle.

While you work for me, you'll do as I say, slurred Stu, cushioning the rifle butt into the crook of his shoulder.

Or what? *You white devil.*

Or you'll be out of a job.

And so will you.

Awoken by the fracas, Charlie sat up in his scalloped-out bed of sand and turned towards the fire pit.

The coals had long gone cold, but Charlie picked up a stick and went probing deep into the pit. It stirred up a cloud of warm, grey smoke. Then faint glimmers of red-hot heat grew into smouldering coals.

He looked around the pit.

Bugger me, he said softly to himself, why's there never any food around here. The whole mob must have worms or something.

Stu tipped the bottle back against his lips, hissed, then squinted before lowering the bottle and wiping his face along a shirt sleeve.

Where the bloody hell've I seen you before?

Not too sure, boss, said Charlie, digging about in the sand

and uncovering a raw yam. You ever been to the Wanna Munna[74] before? Plenty'o white fellas go digging about up there.

Stu turned away from Charlie. He had a puzzled look on his face.

Gawd-blimey, he said, then took another drink.

Stu continued working on the bottle and when he'd taken his last swig, he turned and tossed it into the bush.

Hoy! came the shrewd voice. I'm sleeping out here.

Who's that?

I chuckled.

That's Mahmout.

Stu sat down empty handed at the base of a dead tree.

What the hell's he doing sleeping out there?

It's the food, said Mahmout, hustling his way out through the scrub. It smells like filth and is unholy and unclean.

Unclean? How clean does he need it to be?

Halal clean. Us Muslims must repent if we eat non-halal.[75] The thought of it turns Mahmout's face purple.

Well, wah bloody wah, said Stu. With all the bastardy you lot get up to, the last thing I thought you'd bother about is fucken halal meat.

I began rolling my mat.

What are you doing? said Mahmout.

Bossman says we're out of here.

Stu?

That's right. I want you mongrels out on the road before morning tea.

Then he lowered his head and fell asleep.

---

74   Located in the Pilbara region, Wanna Munna is home to the ancient Wanna Munna rock carvings which depict spiritual symbols relevant to First Nations culture.
75   Halal meaning lawful or permitted. Non-halal meaning prohibited, or haram.

My thoughts spun to Miriam. I held out her handkerchief and draped it across my hand. Her scent held strong.

We were two star-crossed lovers, with a million miles wedged between us.

Fortunate Sons

I boarded a 737[76] in Dubai, with three hundred other faceless soldiers.

It was a direct flight home without an empty seat board, and I'd gotten myself sandwiched between two fat Warrant Officers whose bellies cascaded over their seatbelts. Plus, they smelt like cheap prison cigarettes that oozed out from between their yellowy tar-stained teeth.

I stretched and kicked out my legs. Then I rolled my ankles in big, neat circles. Three times clockwise, then three times counter.

The Warrant Officer to my left (who was in deep sleep) chortled through his dribble-soaked lips. Farted, then kicked his heels out front of my seat, striking me on the shin.

Fuck, I said and winced and tucked my feet beneath the seat.

Good evening, ladies and gentlemen, said the pilot, over the cabin PA. *On behalf of myself, and the flight crew, we'd all like to welcome you, our proud Sons of ANZAC home. It's also my honour to inform you we'll soon be landing in Australia. I trust you've enjoyed the trip.*

The seatbelt light flashed on.

---

76   ADF members travelled between the UAE and Afghanistan via RAAF Hercules and Globe masters; however, for flights to and from Australia, they travelled via chartered civilian airlines.

Thank God. I clipped on my seat buckle. Then I turned to the window. The Warrant Officer to my right was out cold, with his lips pressed against the windowpane.

Please return your seats to the upright position, and fasten your seatbelts, said a female flight attendant.

She was tall, with sun-bleached skin, and wavy blonde hair, and smiled with her eyes as glanced across the seat row.

Yes, Ma'am, said the Warrant Officer, sitting up tall and clearing the window.

Outside, the night air was cold, blank and dark.

The 737 banked, starboard, and hard. All the soldiers moved in sync as its now warped speed fuselage pitched, then rolled out of the turn.

Grab yer ankles and kiss yer arse goodbye, said a voice.

It came from the row directly behind me and launched across the cabin with a high-octave squeal, sending the entire flight into a fit of laughter.

The flight attendant pushed her trolley. A bright smile plastered on her face as she wheeled past row after row, carrying an expression that hinted she knew how damn well she looked.

She halted the trolley at the row directly behind me.

If you could please fasten your seatbelts, gentlemen. Then return your seats to their upright position.

Excuse me, Ma'am, but can a thirsty Digger bother you for a drink? Rum and coke's preferred, but anything we will do, said the voice.

This is a dry flight, Sir, you'll have to wait, like the rest of the passengers, she said, then swished her hips, pressing the trolley forward. Besides, we'll be landing in Darwin, at any moment now.

DARWIN said the soldier. Christ almighty. Spin this airliner around and return me to Afghanistan at once.

The soldier slunk back in his seat. I looked out the window to see the glow of the orange runway lights beaming below. Breathed out, then shut my eyes as the plane moved into land.

The cabin lights flickered on and I rubbed my eyes open. I still didn't recognise anyone on board. I didn't care. All I wanted was to get off the plane, except no one was moving. I opened my carry bag and burrowed my mind deep inside to my book.

The 737 taxied slowly to the terminal where I could see a thousand faces gleaming back at us through the tall glass airport windows.

Cabin crew, prepare the plane for disembarking.

I closed the book and turned my attention back the window. The ground crew zipped around the plane, all on their tiny boxcar wheels preparing to refuel, refresh and unload the plane.

The plane stopped, and all the soldiers stood in unison. As if they were all standing to attention and waiting on parade.

Once again, welcome home, said the captain.

Hoo-RAH, said the soldier from the row behind, pounding the sides of his fists into the top of my seat.

Hey, quit that, motherfucker, I said, or else you're gonna really tick me off.

Go wrestle a Siamese cat, he said.

That put some serious heat underneath my collar, so I turned around.

Quit your wriggling, said the Warrant Officer to my right. He yawned and stretched his shoulders out wide. I can hardly move in here, with you hopping around, he continued.

Sorry, Sir, I said and fell back into my seat.

The cabin door opened. The soldiers all filtered out like sheep through a farm gate. I smiled at the flight attendant. She smiled back, blushing pink through her thin, high cheekbones.

Goodbye, I said, then stepped on to bridge.

A sliding glass door separated us from the families waiting in the arrivals lounge. A small girl held up a cardboard sign. She'd scrawled writing over it in red crayon. *Welcome Home Dad,* with the lettering enclosed inside a cute red love heart. Beside the girl, a mother stood and cried.

The glass door opened and the first soldier walked through. He dropped to his knees, and the girl came rushing forward, diving into her father's arms.

A woman pushed through the crowd. She wore a high-cut, blue dress. Layers of makeup smothered her face and razor-thin lips. A young, pimple-faced cameraman towed in close, behind her. She lurched forward and stuffed a microphone in the soldier's face.[77]

How does it feel to be home?

The soldier squeezed his arms tighter around his daughter. Turned his eyes up towards the reporter and smiled.

It's amazing, he said, beaming at her and the camera. I haven't seen my wife and baby girl for a whole eight months.

What do you think about the war? Do you think it'll end soon?

DADDY, said the soldier's daughter. I WANT TO GO HOME.

Of course, he said, then lifted her to his shoulder and walked to his wife.

Make sure you're getting this all on camera, hissed the reporter to the cameraman.

---

77   One thing a soldier can often look forward to upon repatriation is the media circus taking up space within the arrivals lounge.

She flicked her hair, clearing it from her forehead, then she walked to the next soldier.

Welcome home, she said.

Thank you.

Can you tell the people at home your thoughts on the Hussein regime? Is he really harbouring WMDs?[78]

WMDs? Ma'am, we've been in Afghanistan.

Isn't it all the same war?

With all due respect, Ma'am, NO, said the soldier as he lunged past her.

I threw my hat onto the floor and rocked back into the hard plastic lounge.

WMDs, I said, what a horse's arse.

An arse is an arse, is an arse, said a soldier. I recognised him as the soldier from the row behind me on the plane.

He stuck out his hand. Ben Day's the name, but every bastard around here calls me Daisy.

Like the flower?

Can't stand it, myself. Yet, the more you rail against it, the more it sticks around.

Daisy sat beside me and slapped me on the back.

I didn't move.

If he didn't get the FUCK away from me…

What stop are you hopping off at?

Brisbane.

Now how about that! So am I.

Wonderful, I said, and bent and peeled my hat off the floor.

---

78   Weapons of Mass Destruction. It was reported that Saddam Hussein harboured chemical agents, including Sarin gas, 25,000 rockets and 15 000 artillery bombs. George Bush used this information as his justification to invade Iraq.
No WMDs were ever located or accounted for.

The flight attendant stood at the entrance of the bridge.

Ladies and gentlemen, the captain and crew are ready to welcome you back on board.

Yo, said Daisy, isn't that sweet music to my ears.

He grabbed his backpack and slung it across his shoulder. Then walked towards the attendant.

So, sweetheart. What're the next stops? I've gotta get home pronto because I've got a lotta catching up to do.

Melbourne, Sydney then Brisbane. And, Sir, please don't call me that.

Ahh, shit, I'm sorry, said Daisy, it's just my good-loving and charming nature.

If you say so, Sir.

Are you sure there're no drinks on board?

The attendant smiled. Positive, she said, then waved Daisy onto the bridge.

I took my seat in the back row. Daisy took the opposite aisle.

Half the plane's seats are empty, I said. So why the hell do you have to sit near me?

Well, maybe I like you.

What a load of crap.

I unfolded a blanket and laid it over my lap and the two seats on my right.

Soon, the runway lights were disappearing beneath us. Then the plane levelled out. The seat belt release light came on. I closed the window shade and buried the side of my face deep into the headrest, searching for some sleep.

So, said Daisy. Any plans for when you get home?

What?

He got out of his seat. Crossed the aisle, then sat in the seat beside me, right on top of the blanket.

Would you like some bubble gum?

No.

It's Hubba Bubba, Bubba. Strawberry. Couldn't buy it in Tarin Kowt and Christ knows how I ever lived without it.

Oh yeah? I said and leant forward. Unzipped my bag and took out my book.

You know? That Afghanistan gig was one crooked affair. I almost got clipped three times. Can you believe it? Once from RPG frag, and twice by some gung-ho 'Merican. Hell, I was more frightened by them Yanks—and our own brass—more than any Mufti or Taliban,

Yeah?

Fuck yeah.

Well, aren't we glad she's over then, I said, and turned to my book.

Daisy swiped the book from out of my hands.

Well? What are you gonna do when you get home?

Christ, man! I don't know. I'll probably sleep for a week.

Sleep?

YES. I haven't had one good night in the past eight months.

I hear ya, he said and gazed towards the ceiling, chewing on his Hubba Bubba. Then he rolled his jaw from side to side and stuck out his tongue and blew a pink, juicy bubble.

The bubble burst and the gum fell and glued to his chin. He licked out his tongue. Cleared his face and returned to his chewing.

You got a girl?

No.

Man, the first thing I'm gonna do is buy myself an ice-cold coke and rum, then find me a skimpy.

A what?

Yeah, you know, something to squeeze up next to and keep my arse warm in winter.

That rum oughta get you across the line, I said, smirking and snatching my book back.

The flight attendant pushed her trolley along the aisle.

Coffee or tea? she said.

I opened my eyes. My right ear was pressing against the window corner and felt numb and senseless. I straightened, relieving the pressure. The lobe itched and tickled as fresh oxygen flushed in until my hearing had returned.

Coffee or tea, Sir?

No, thank you.

The attendant looked across at Daisy. He'd returned to his side of the aisle and had stretched himself out across the adjacent seats. His head was resting, crooked against the armrest closest to the aisle. The attendant stared at his lulled face and shut eyes.

He doesn't want any coffee or tea, Ma'am. Best to let him sleep.

Good idea, she said, and smiled between her pink, high-boned cheeks. Then wheeled the trolley back to the front of the plane.

I awoke to the sun shining through the window and the plane touching down on the tarmac.

Welcome to Sydney, announced Daisy, when he saw that I had opened my eyes.

Sydney. Aww, shit. What happened to Melbourne?

You slept all the way through it, you dumb sonofabitch.

I threw off my blanket and unbuckled my seatbelt, then grabbed my bag from between my feet.

Why the hell didn't anybody wake me?

I don't know, said Daisy, and he stuck out his hand. But I got us some more Hubba Bubba, Bubba. Would you like some?

NO, I said and climbed out from my seat. I'm not a child. Get out of my way. I wanna get the hell off this plane.

Well, someone is a *grumpy*, he sang, clearing the aisle with his jaw bumping up and down on his bubble gum.

The pilot repeated his speech.

I couldn't give a shit. I bustled my way to the cabin door. The attendant stood beside the open door, smiling as she said goodbye.

All I could manage was a forced smile.

Excuse me, I said and strode passed her and stepped onto the bridge.

Daisy followed behind.

See you in sixty, said Daisy through a cunning grin.

I can't wait, said the attendant. Then she stretched out for the handle and quickly shut the door.

We were in the arrivals lounge again. This time, the crowd was much thinner.

The first soldier stepped through a tinted glass door, and the crowd cheered and clapped as a young woman ran into his arms.

Now THAT's what I'm talking about, said Daisy.

Christ, what the hell is wrong with you?

What's wrong with me? Hell, Patterson, what's wrong with YOU? It's not right if you're not frothing over a tight bit of ass.

I rolled my eyes, then threw my hat onto the floor.

Another reporter pushed through the crowd. She held a

microphone in her outstretched arm and turned back to the cameraman.

Are we live?

Sure, said the cameraman, we're rolling.

The young woman's face was burrowed deep into the soldier's chest. Tears rolled down his cheek.

Welcome home, said the reporter.

Her arm flung out, and she rested the microphone on the young woman's shoulder.

What can you tell us about the Taliban? Are they as vicious as they make out to be? And can we expect to see them, in Australia, anytime soon?

The soldier pushed the microphone aside. I haven't laid eyes on my wife in eight months, he said. Now… we want to be alone.

Sheesh, she said through gritted teeth. Then she reeled in her microphone cable and moved onto the next soldier.

The tinted door closed, and Daisy laid himself out across the waiting room lounge.

You have a missus, back home?

I'm not too sure.

What do you mean you're not sure? You've either got one, or you don't.

It's complicated.

Bullshit, fella. BullSHIT.

I sat on the lounge and unfolded a ruffled-up newspaper. It was two days old but updated me on the home front.

Well? Daisy prompted.

Listen. She didn't agree with the war. That's all there is to it.

Christ, said Daisy, reefing the newspaper from my hands. You're better off without a bird like that.

Yeah, I said. But she was alright.

The flight attendant walked into the arrivals lounge.

Okay gentleman, the Pilot is ready, and we've only got one more leg to go to Brisbane.

ALRIGHT, said Daisy. He tossed the newspaper onto the floor and whipped his legs off the lounge.

I picked up my hat and followed him to the bridge.

Daisy stopped. Listen, he said to the attendant, when your shift is over, let's say me and you grab a drink?

Sorry, said the attendant. I think I've already got plans.

She looked away and Daisy smirked.

Can't hurt to ask, he said.

The plane was near empty, save for the front row where two senior officers sat. They were eating prawn sandwiches and drinking Earl Grey from fine, white china cups.

Yo … would you look at those fat, pompous pricks, said Daisy. I bet they've never set foot outside the wire or seen a bullet fired but are gonna go home to draft up their own commendations.

I laughed but didn't say a word. Finally, we had landed on common ground.

Ahh, who gives a shit anyhow, said Daisy. So, what if they drink their wine and eat caviar, while us Diggers up the back get served microwaved meals and sit on top of each other.[79] It's Army 101: a straight-up class divide, Patterson. Us versus them. That's where the real wars in history have been hard fought and won, right?

I guess.

Yo … it's all semantics anyway, you know. Hardly ever worth fighting about.

I suppose not.

Prawns, Daisy scoffed. He looked around at the empty plane.

Shit, Patterson, where'd yer wanna sit?

---

79   Despite Australia's egalitarian roots and cultural bedrock, the Australian Defence can be readily defined as structure built upon a class divide.

We sat midway, in line with the emergency exits.

Daisy leant his face against the glass and was asleep before the plane had taxied to the runway.

Me? It would have taken a slap to the side of the chops with some old English willow to put me out so close to home.

The plane's engines roared. The nose lifted, then the landing gear folded in. I looked out the window, down over the current and waves rolling into the bay and drank a sip of water.

At the front of the plane, one officer clicked his fingers and held his teacup in the air.

The attendant sprang out from her seat. Stirred a chrome steel tea pot and topped up the officer's cup.

The cabin lights returned with a warm buzzing glow.

I grabbed my bag and stepped into the aisle. Daisy was still asleep. I crossed over and kicked his feet.

What?

We're home, I said.

Daisy sat and looked towards the front of the plane.

Wait… where's the attendant?

Gone, I guess.

Shit, he said and stormed into the aisle. Why the hell didn't you wake me?

I didn't say a word but chuckled beneath my breath and we both walked to the exit.

We stepped off the bridge, and the arrivals lounge was barren.

The officers had departed, along with the attendant. Best of all, there was no media around.

Shit, said Daisy, I'll never see her again.

Forget about her. Let's get the hell outta here. I'm dying to get home.

The sun was high outside, but the air was cold. We made our way to the taxi ranks and shook hands.

Nice meeting yer, said Daisy.

Same, I said, and I opened the cab door.

Patterson. Make sure you go straight home and get yourself a good night's sleep. Hell, an entire week's worth, if you need to. Just don't go locking yourself away for good. Go out sometime. Get piss-rotten drunk. Find a girl. It doesn't matter how she looks. Anything will do. And, if you can't find a girl, pay for one instead. It doesn't matter, so long as you blow off some steam. It's how to survive. Then, if you can't remember anything at all, well... the less you remember the better. Get even drunker the next day. Go piss in some dark alleyways and pass out in the gutter. Punch a copper— if you're able—and get yourself arrested, then go on the run and travel to Mexico or Spain. Hell, even Istanbul or Gaza. Just don't go locking yourself away or else you might not wake up. It's all a one-way ticket to going insane, because once you go hopping over that cuckoo's nest, that's when they'll really lock you away.

Alright, I said, grinning wryly. See you later mate.

I shut the taxi door and threw my head back against the rests.

Where are you headed, Soldier?

Gallipoli Barracks, I said, and don't spare the horses.

The driver held one eye to the road. The other eye interrogated me through the rear-view mirror.

Back home from Afghanistan?

No.

Half your luck. I heard it was hell on earth and reckon those Yanks oughta blow the whole place up.

Yep. Well, they're trying, I said, and wound down the window.

The taxi was moving fast and the cold Queensland air bit hard against my face. I closed my eyes, and squeezed them tight, then opened my mouth and tasted its dampness on the bridge of my tongue. It tasted like home. Hot meat pies drowning in fat red tomato sauce. Ice cold XXXX Gold and fish and chips. That piping hot Queensland sun.

It tasted like home.

The taxi hooked a left, south along Sandgate Road. The traffic lights were blank. A long, smouldering eucalyptus lay limp across the southbound Lane. The driver slowed, then veered around it.

A massive storm came through here only about an hour ago. Christ, you shoulda SEEN it! Damn near taking out half the city.

I didn't answer, and kept looking out the window, staring at the blank traffic lights and fallen power lines.

Do you need to make any stops on the way? A bottlo, or something?

Sure. A bottlo will go down fine.

Consider it done, fella, said the driver. He pressed down hard on the accelerator. Reached across for the radio and switched on 4KQ.

Creedence Clearwater was playing. It was Fortunate Son.

Ahh, now here's a song, said the driver. I bet all the soldiers dig it.

It's an anti-war song, I said.

Sure, it is, said the driver, but don't you fellas all just dig it?

We arrived at the Barracks gate.

$32.50 said the driver.

I gave him $35.

Keep the change, I said and closed the door.

Geez, thanks, fella, he said, leaning out the window. The white reverse lights lit the tail end of the cab, and the car began reversing away from the gate.

The taxi stopped. Hey, fella, called the driver. If you ever go over, be sure to slay one of those towel heads for me.

I waved goodbye, and the taxi soon disappeared into the dark of the night. I picked up my bags and two bottles of Bundaberg Rum and walked the rest of the way home.

Dreaming of Miriam

It'd been five months since the chain first left Darwin. The country was all talking about wars in far-off countries. About Federation and what was going to become of the new Ghan railroad.

Old Bossman wasn't buying into any of it.

Blast it all to hell, he'd shout, swaying drunken, obscene and absurd on the back of his horse, with a bottle, swinging, in one hand and his pipe in the other.

The whole damned country will never remember who built it, anyway.

I'd no idea what'd gotten into him.

The camel chain continued North, not saying a word while Bossman got rolling drunk, and kept their eyes and noses to the ground.

Every night, when the camel chain stopped, and the stars shone bright, I'd sit beneath them and stare at the deep infinity that reached out to nowhere. Then fall asleep, dreaming of Miriam.

It's Going to be Alright

There's an unlawful iniquity in those wretched Afghani marrying Australian wives. Why? It's because he can enslave and degrade them—which's a fact beyond description. A fact that which affects West Australian women. These women should heed warning—in the strongest of language—and sidestep the brutes. Lest they become damned into following them back to their native lairs. And, lest they become social pariahs of the worst, and most degrading class.

—15 Jan 1901 The West Australian

It was late in the afternoon, and the camel chain was back in Port Augusta. The sun buzzed hot, kissing itself against the rolling horizon and sending a low kaleidoscopic shimmer across the Outback's sunburnt backside. It wound around us from the North, all the way through East and West. Then down to the South, calling to us like thirsty gentry to a watery mirage.

Come in, come in, it whispered.

I waved a halt to Mahmout.

We'll stop for the night, I said, pointing to a familiar tin hut. I signalled to the rest of the train by holding an open right palm to my chomping mouth.

Stu rolled by on his tired old horse. He stopped and fiddled around inside his tobacco pouch (which was now empty).

Why are we stopping here, he grunted, and threw the pouch to the ground.

His face was tired, dry, and wrinkled. His once clean-shaven chin was now over-growing with thick grey stubble. His lips flaked dry, pasty and white, and his breath rasped like a donkey.

You're in the grip of the grape, Bossman, I said. Go get yourself some sleep, or another drink, and let me take care of things.

God-damn you, Afghanee, said Stu, slurring and lurching forward for his rifle. No savage tells me what to do.

He jerked on the rifle butt, but the trigger guard snagged on a saddle strap.

If I ever get this damned thing out of here—

He wrenched the rifle against the saddle strap.

I'm gonna put a giant hole right through you and your big bloody mouth, Sher Gul.

Mahmout and I didn't move.

Then Stu removed his right boot from the stirrups. Lurched forward and slithered in his saddle. Yanked hard on the rifle, then toppled to the ground.

You think he's dead? said Mahmout.

No, I said, placing my hand on the rise and fall of his chest. But when he wakes up, he might wish he was.

I followed Mahmout inside the tin hut.

A young man lay sleeping on a canvas stretcher with a thin newspaper strewn across his face.

I rapped on the tin walls with my knuckles and the young man leapt from his bed.

Crikey, fellas! Shit! Whadda ya want?

The young man stood and rubbed his eyes.

We want food and drink, said Mahmout, reaching to the canvas stretcher and taking the newspaper.

Ha, said the man. None of that stuff here. This here's just a listening post. Kinda like a grapevine for the Outback, so word can travel around, and all I've got is some dry crackers and some homemade grog to drink.

Grog?

Yer. Booze. I bring it out here for passers-by. Tis the kinda stuff my old man says will put hair on yer balls.

Mahmout's face faded.

No thank you, he said and scuttled out of the hut, shaking his head.

Heck, said the young man, who yanked his chain?

He's Muslim. Alcohol is against his religion.

Christ! Bugger that for a joke. Most fellas wouldn't survive a day out here, if it weren't for the grog.

The young man reached inside his pocket, pulling out a small, leather tobacco pouch and some thin white papers.

Where are you fellas from, anyway? Yers don't look much like Australians. Yers Indian or what?

Ahh, no, I said and turned for the exit. We're Aussies…just like you.

Hey, wait up fella… now I recognise ya. Youse those savage camel-herding fellas out here fixing to finish that railroad.

We're cameleers, I said, and some of the finest.

Huh, he said. A telegram came through here, must have been about a month ago. Says it's for some fella named Sher Gul. That you?

He rifled through a small stack of paper near the canvas stretcher.

I took the telegram from the young man's hand.

I'll see you later.

The paper was thin and soft and folded along the short edge to conceal the contents, but the ink bled through. I held it to my nose. It smelt of rosemary.

Mahmout looked over, eyebrows raised.

What's that you're holding?

I folded the paper doubling it over itself and slid it into my pocket.

A telegram.

Well, aren't you going to read it? said Mahmout, trying to worm his sticky fingertips into my pockets.

I pushed him away.

It's from that Miriam, isn't it?

No.

That cow, hissed Mahmout. She's no good for you, George. Or me. Or any other of the Afghani. You mark my words, or you'll find your neck inside a noose.

I kicked the dirt, then spat into a sprawling salt bush. They can lock me up now. It won't matter. I held Miriam's handkerchief to my face and took a deep inhale.

I cannot breathe when she isn't near, Mahmout. It ain't right their laws should keep us apart.

Mahmout screwed up his face. His eyebrows merged into one and he turned toward the Afghani, who were all sitting around a small fire, boiling their pots.

And the men; it's their necks too?

Sure, I said, but I don't see any of them standing in my way.

Then I kicked the dirt, again. This time it stubbed my big toe, sending it folding underneath itself.

WHAT THE DEVIL, I said startling Penny. She groaned and kicked her head back, yanking the lead clean from my hands.

Quiet you, bitch. It was my toe, not yours.

I walked away then sat with my back to the tin hut. Its sun-soaked corrugated edges pressed into my spine. My toe throbbed.

I unfolded the telegram.

To George Sher Gul
Here is some good news, and bad.
You're going to be a Dad.
Unfortunately, this is something my father will never allow.
I'm going to a home for unwed mothers until the baby is born.
Stay safe, George. We'll meet again someday soon.
Yours always
M.L

I didn't even know her surname.

I slept with the telegram pressed tight to my chest. In the morning, the cameleers lined the trail, heading North. I unfolded the paper and read one more time.

Bossman clawed himself up from the ground. Burped, scratched his bum, and walked inside the tin hut.

Should we go? said Mahmout. Take the drunken fool's rifle and leave him for dust?

No, I said and fed two pistachios into my mouth. That old fool's got our pay.

Ahh, hell.

He punched the hut wall, splitting his middle knuckle. Dark red blood dripped onto the dirt and his left foot.

Mahmout snatched up a camel lead. Fed the leather strap into his mouth and chomped down with gritted teeth.

It hurts, he said through his bite on the strap.

Blood continued trickling out.

I know, I said and laughed, then slapped his camel on the shoulder.

The camel lowered its head and gnawed away at a salt bush. It ripped and teared until the entire shrub became uprooted, leaving a foot-sized hole in the dirt.

I'm going to be a father, I said.

We sat down on the dirt. Then Mahmout smiled and wiped his hand with a white cloth.

It's going to be alright, he said.

READY TO BURST ALIGHT

The air grew thicker, and the heat and humidity glued to my skin. Deep grey clouds bloomed overhead, and the Top-End readied to shed its monsoonal load.

Stu had tossed his last empty bottle to the side of the trail weeks ago.

His skin grew pale grey, almost transparent, as his muscles shrunk and withered. He constantly swore and cursed the cameleers. His horse. Himself. Even the sky.

The Bossman took a long time drying out.

Tiny, speckled raindrops pitted their way into bull dust. Then the thunder rolled and roared, always followed by a flash. Or a strike of lightning somewhere up ahead.

Count the seconds between the thunder and the flash, said Mahmout, then you'll know the distance to the lightning.

And if the flash does not arrive?

Mahmout smiled, then looked my way. You always see the flash, he said, counting down the fingers on his right hand. Unless of course you find yourself dead.

I unfolded the telegram, clutched it to my chest, then held it to my nose. Sniffed at the dry ink, then smiled.

I recalled the day we left, Darwin, I said to Penny. How the earth was soft and wet underfoot and how the mud clung to your fat hooves. And how you trudged on through, showing the other camels the way, and how I couldn't be here without you.

Penny walked on, without so much as a groan. Then the rain thickened and I tucked the telegram away.

No Fun at All

When US forces first entered Afghanistan, they did so with almost unanimous support from the public. Bi-partisan support in Congress soon followed, and half the globe jumped on board. Australia, Canada, Britain, New Zealand. Hell, even Japan, Germany, the Dutch and Singapore reached out to lend a helping hand.

I guess they'd all signed up thinking it'd be a cakewalk.

What they received was a bloody and lengthy affair. By 2008, the Global War on Terror risked growing long in the tooth. As did President Bush.

Bush is a natural-born loser with a filthy-rich daddy who pimped his son out to rich oil-mongers. He hates music, football and sex, in no particular order, and he is no fun at all.
—*H. S Thompson*

The impending President-to-be, Barack Obama, was chief among the many who vowed to 'Bring the Troops Home'. Yet, by the third year of his first term, US troop numbers had more than tripled in Afghanistan (>100000 by 2011).[ix]

More troops weren't the only things he delivered to Afghanistan. Drones were also buzzing all over the Middle Eastern Area of Operations and Obama poised to drop more munitions than any other US President had ever done before—all to significant effect.[80] Or, 'too significant' it may seem.[x] Because let's not mince our words here: bombs do not discriminate, and women and children stand little chance, once the button is pushed. HUA.[81] But that's a tale for another book.

> *Obama is worse than Bush and Blair and would be subject to the Nuremberg Principles if they applied today.*
> —*Noam Chomsky.*

In 2011, we finally captured Osama. His bloodied and bullet ridden body found its way, unceremoniously, to the bottom of the ocean.

He sank straight to the bottom, like a good beer turd, said a member of the fabled Seal Team Six.

Despite the notorious terrorist's magnanimous disposal and newfound purpose in life—*as shark food*—The War on Terror continued for ten more years.

In 2016, when Obama left the Oval Office, Trump[xi] gripped the infidel reigns with all the gusto his forty-fifth could muster. Because God knows what the American Government would do without war.

---

80   During his eight-year tenure, President Obama ordered 540 drone strikes, killing 3797 people, including 324 civilians. (The recording of Trump's drone data ceased in the latter half of his sole term as President. He was, however, responsible for over 240 strikes in his first two years, killing approximately 150 civilians).
81   Heard. Understood. Acknowledged.

THROWNNESS

I peeled back the curtains.

I hadn't slept in weeks.

I pressed my face against the warm windowpane and watched as troops jogged by, yelling: left, right, left.

It was too much—as if the sun beamed too hot and the Sergeants barked too loud. I had to rip the curtains shut until the room was dark and blank again. Until it was only me sitting there, hugging my own ambivalence and ignorant of life's thrownness.

Of course, many experience some of that doom in their lifetime. With a sense of existential dread, no doubt. Some swim ashore; others drown. Me, I dove in blind, and headfirst.

No parachute, and no fucking life raft required. That's what I told myself. It was 'go all the way, or go nowhere at all—Army greens, or death'. Although, it beats me why, but people aren't thinking too deeply by this point.

Anyway, what the hell did I know?

I never stopped to consider the thought of climbing out.

The bare necessities—I swore it's all I'd need. Yet, I found a myriad of ways to wear all that out.

First, it was beer. The ale only built my tolerance until I'd reached a point where it all went through me like lolly-water. I grew fatter around the waist then I pissed it all away. I tried whiskey too, but then the room went all gloomy, opening many doorways for my demons to come trampling on out. Then, one by one, I sat them down on my knee and said, Let's play a little game.

They were more than happy to oblige. They always are.

I lived on two-minute noodles and tins of tuna. It made my stomach throb and my butthole itch. My brain atrophied. Then my porn cache was the next to shrink. And believe me—brain or no brain—you can only stare at the same cheeks for so long before it all fades to grey. The smut had to go.

I had money, of course—too much if we're telling the truth. Money wasn't my problem.

I tried sweeping my actual problems underneath the rug or burying them beneath the mattress. That only caused them to multiply like fire-breathing dragons. Christ, how much strife those little bastards would get up to every night. Flapping their wings. Spitting fire, then plopping their shit in every corner of the room.

No, money wasn't the problem. Not this time. Because this time was sheer purgatory. I couldn't get outdoors. Not even if I tried.

Army friends, family and everyone in between grew concerned. They'd all ring me, morning, noon, and night. Venting their frustrations and voicing their fears.

C'mon, Patterson, they'd say, shed those bloody nightmares. The war is over it's time to go outside.

Okay, I'd say. One day.

Then, at the end of the call, each and every one of those bastards would ask for coin.

I'd crack the shits and it grew old, so I tore the phone from the wall, then drowned the headset in the loo.

Fuck them, I thought. I was better off alone.

At half past midnight, my drunken brain dragged me out of bed and went digging through the trash.

And SHIT, did I have some trash. It was all piled a quarter mile high, right there in the corner of my room for all my demons to play in, and to go to sleep in at night.

Ha, sleep, what the hell is that, anyway—besides some fabled bedtime story. Any soldier, and his rat pack team of demons can get by without it—if they're willing. And, believe me, my demons were some of the most willing bastards alive.

I flipped aside a half empty pizza box, then dived into the hubbub and the rubble; laughing to myself, and at myself, then reached out for a bottle and fell onto my back to take a swill.

The night is young, I said, and I'm still alive.

Did I mention I hadn't slept in weeks?

The clock strikes one.

My bottle is empty and I'm itching for more and as the curtains are going flap, flap, flap, a cool breeze blows the world wide open and lets the moonlight creep in.

A cockroach scuttles into the room.

A foolish mistake. It should have run for the hills, but I hear him all the time, chewing away at my rubbish and gnawing into the walls.

There's a war going on halfway across the globe and he couldn't give a damn.

I drop my heel to the floor and feel his guts squish into the carpet. His antennae continue to wave about, and I can imagine hearing the sounds of him screaming, but all there is is silence.

It's cold in here, and I'm alone again now, and life feels feeble.

Fleeting even, like a final breath. I go back to my bed and try to get some sleep.[82]

---

82   For many soldiers, deploying on operations marks the highlight of their career. Yet, operational service can be more than austere, confronting soldiers with a pantomime of emotions. This can be a euphoric experience for some, and traumatic for others. In a lot of cases, neither emotion truly catches up with a soldier until they've returned home. PTSD is a life-changing injury that's now only beginning to shed its stigma, but a lot remains to be said for the post-deployment blues. It too is very real.

RUNNING OF THE BULLS

In the morning, I turn on the radio and listen to the news.

A roadside blast has detonated, South of Kabul, announced a female news reader. *Four US Marines lost their lives during the incident. It's believed the Taliban's responsible for the attack. No Australian soldiers were involved.*

She moved onto the sports. Then, with some brightening inflection, exclaimed that Tom Brady had thrown a season high 385 yards.

The season high resulted in three touchdowns against Kansas City, she said. *American sports reporters' adamant the Patriots look set to secure consecutive Super Bowls.*

Wouldn't that be wonderful, said a male DJ.

Ha, I'd be happy just to play, said the newsreader.

I turned off the radio and opened my email.

There was a message from Sylvia.

>From 'Sylvia M' <sylviatravels@hotmail.com>
>To 'B Patterson' <beepatterson@hotmail.com>
>Sent Wednesday, 04 October 2002
>Subject RE:

I deleted the email, then walked into the bathroom and splashed my face beneath the basin tap. The water flowed down the bowl and into the drain. Where did it go after that? There was no reversing the flow; and once it was gone, there was no bringing it back. I towelled my face dry then went back to bed.

A Soldier Knows No Other Way

It's now noon.

I switch on the television and sprawl out on the floor.

A man in black leather jack boots marches across the screen. Halts with a great, stoking thud and salutes the flag.

Behind him, an Apache helicopter touches down on the tarmac, followed by a Blackhawk. Then another Blackhawk floats in and above the tarmac with its nose beaming towards the sky.

They all land. Simultaneous, and with enough military precision to make even the most ardent of pacifist rise hard.

Tens—if not more—pairs of black leather jack boots dash out to greet the state-of-the-art craft. All with their turbines still grinding with the sound of metal on metal. It's a helluva sound that'll tear out your eardrums if you're not prepared.

The camera zooms in.

The chopper's cargo bays are bubbling like a bloodbath. The tourniquets twists are coiled-on white-knuckle tight. That only creates more pain as nasopharyngeal tubes leak brain snot, blood, phlegm and fragments of broken skull out onto the floor. A real vomit inducing sight.

There's blood and guts and loose body parts and casualties screaming everywhere.

They're laid out on stretchers.

Morphine needles pierce the skin. A well-trained medic will have little trouble finding a vein—or two—so the painkilling injections can sneak in through an IV drip. The noise and the pain soon disappear.

I roll onto my belly and yawn, a big guffawing yawn. I've seen it all before.

Then, the plot twist arrives and hits like a cold chisel to my two front teeth.

A young GI asked, What the hell's going on?

He leant over the cargo bay with his hand wrist deep in blood. The tens—if not more—men in black leather jack boots march by.

The cargo bays are empty, save for the blood—enough to fill an Olympic size pool.

Where am I? says the GI. And why isn't nobody listening to me?

A pilot flicks some switches and courses through the shut-down manual. Then, the chopper turbines fall silent, but the rotor blades still HOOFT overhead.

The GI yells out again and throws his hands in the air. Deep red, viscous blood drips down his limbs.

Nobody answers him. Nobody is even listening, and he drops to his knees and claws at his hair.

How in hell can anyone operate in these conditions? he says.

I laugh at the television screen. Then flutter my feet into the air—kicking them back and forth—like a happy little schoolgirl.

Still plump on my belly, I yawned and laughed. Only a soldier would try.

The scene ends without closure—

SHIT, I say out loud and peg the television remote at the wall. It splits, sending the two triple-As sprawling onto the floor.

Hey, yells an outside voice. Shut up! Some of us are trying to sleep.

Go shit in a hole, I said, then crawled to the power socket and unplugged the television.

Outside, the sky was cold, dark, damp, and grey. My demons were hard at play.

It was a Monday. Or Friday?

Hard to tell without a television. I pulled out my work uniform and started ironing.

The soldier's life, that's how it goes. Sometimes, it was a blur. Many times, nobody's listening. A soldier knows no other way.

Bugger Him

The Afghani temperament is often violent. Likewise, the Asiatic hold no fear of the consequences of their actions. So, it's without a doubt, their temper flies uncurbed.

There's no questioning the result of any conflict between Australians and Asiatic.

For all it's worth, this should cause people to be more thoughtful.

—4 Sep 1897 The Coolgardie Pioneer

It was only a short while after tea, and the camel chain moved slowly through the Top End's big wet and stifling heat.

I'd whipped Penny and pushed her hard over the last two miles.

Come on, I cried with my feet dragging across the trail's harsh and razor-edged facade. HOOSHTA, YOU BITCH.

No, no, no, said Stu. Pull em up, over by that fat Boab, Georgie boy.

He turned on his horse and swayed in his day-drunken haze, then trotted to the point of the chain where he threw his swag to ground and dismounted.

Christ, Bossman, I said, if we push on now, we'll make Katherine by nightfall. All before the big wet arrives.

Stu just shook his head.

Roger that, Bossman.

I whistled to the Afghani, then pointed to the lone Boab.

It sat tall but looked upside down, with its roots were jutting into the air, while its leaves burrowed underground.

West of the tree stood countless rows of termite mounds. Some big, and some small. All propping up from the earth like menhirs left behind by some mad-forgotten civilisation that had learned to survive out in the desert.

Stu reached inside his saddlebag and pulled out a tobacco pouch and a stainless-steel hip flask. A red leather sheath wrapped around the flask, and he stuffed it in his breast pocket then took out his rifle.

What are we stopping here for? said Mahmout. This ground is too hard and rocky, and there's all these green ants crawling around. I'll never get a good night's rest, sleeping out here.

It's the Bossman… he sure looks set to crack.

We'll move on without him.

No, Mahmout… think about that. Who're they going to blame when they find his body picked apart by the vultures and the crows?

They'll have no proof.

Ha… do they need any? We're aliens to them, and it'll be a sporting event for a whole town to see us hang.

Mahmout released his camel to wander.

I'd rather forget we ever came here, and sooner I get home, to the high snow-capped peaks, spiced chai tea and honest Persian women, the better I'll be.

I didn't speak.

Mahmout headed for the shade of the Boab, with its upside-down roots sprucing in the air.

Stu swore, kicked the dirt, spat at a fly, then pissed on a termite mound.

God have mercy on me, he cried, then sat with his tobacco, his rifle and red leather sheathed hip flask and faced his back to the Afghani.

The Afghani had a small campfire burning bright, and Mahmout stabbed the steel ends of a trivet into the ground around the fire so his billy could boil.

He's going to kill us all, said one Afghani.

Nonsense, said Mahmout. He hasn't got enough lead in his pocket, or meat left in his brains to get us all.

The Afghani stoked the fire and dropped in a small lump of deadwood.

What if we split up? Some go North. Some go South, and the rest head West to the Kalgoorlie mines.

The mines? said Mahmout. No bloody way am I going to no mines. I'd be better off dead.

Mahmout slung his billy can over the fire. Looked at the darkening sky, then smiled.

I say we let him kill himself, then bury him in the desert. Not even a maggot will find him out here.

Nightfall came and stars spotted the sky.

Stu remained out by the termite mounds. He was still drunk and waved his rifle as he sang at the moon.

Come, all my hearties,
we'll roam the mountains high,
Together we will plunder,
together we will die.
We'll wander over valleys, and gallop over plains,

And we'll scorn to live in slavery, bound down with iron chains.[83]

He burped, and he hiccupped, then he fired his rifle at a colony of bats.

The Afghani huddled around the fire.

Ahh, let him go, said Mahmout. He'll pass out soon, then we can enjoy the night.

I thought about Miriam and my unborn child. Then hoped and feared and prayed that I could see him, or her, and that one day we could sit together beneath a moonlit sky. Then I could tell them all about the Greatest Cameleer who ever walked the earth. The Great Sher Gul who feared no man, and there was no mountain, desert or river he couldn't cross and that all the Afghani revered him and how he made the Great Southern Outback his home.

It was blistering cold in the Outback tonight.[84][xii] I sat back from the campfire while the Afghani laughed and drank tea. Bossman was still out by the termite mounds, struck by his own delirium, and he rocked and sang with mad and drunken glee.

Then I looked to the horizon where the sun's rays still glowed, and I thought about making a run for it. Running until I found Miriam's arms.

If only the dark of the desert, the cold, chilling wind, and the howls of the wild, undiscovered Outback didn't render me so frightened.

---

83   The Wild Colonial Boy. A. B (Banjo) Patterson
84   Australian deserts are often associated with extreme heat, dryness and a lack of food; however, the temperatures in outback and remote regions (as far north as Katherine, in the NT) do fall into the minuses during the winter months.

Not On My Watch

Father McCullough adjusted his clerical collar and slapped his hand on the table. The impact rattled its timber panels and tipped over a pot of tea. Hot black tea rolled across the tabletop and soaked Miriam's best tablecloth.

This is an insult to God, he said and picked up the teapot and slammed it into the wall. You'll be lucky if the church lets you stay at my home. You'll be lucky if they don't put you in a home for unwed whores, and you'll be lucky if the Lord himself doesn't strike you down. God damn it.

Miriam cried, slumped into her seat, and brought the tablecloth to her eyes and wiped at the tears. My baby will be born, right here in this home, she said.

Whore. Never. Not on the good Lord's watch.

Oh, Father McCullough, don't! Don't say such a thing, said Miriam, distraught, and she stood and collected the fragments of the tea pot from the floor. Then removed the tea-soaked tablecloth and wrung it out in the kitchen basin.

Father McCullough ripped the tablecloth from her hands and tossed it onto the dusty floor. He then stomped on it with both feet.

It's too late for cleaning, he said. You are moving out of here, so go pack your bags this instant, then pray for your soul and the soul of your bastard child.

And Miriam did as he asked. She left the kitchen. Packed her bags, then got on her knees and prayed.[85][xiii]

A Blister and the Sun

We were fighting a war many Australians didn't understand. The longer it lasted, the less they cared.[86] It was as simple as that, unless you were a soldier. We pushed on; there was no other way.

That's all bullshit, of course. There was no medal for showing up to work on Monday morning. A soldier is not a General, after all. Nor would he ever want to be. Not me especially. Too many pips and crowns left you prone to head swellings.

Truth is, the Army was having a helluva time keeping its soldiers. Because veteran of war or not, the Brass were treating us like nothing but numbers. Then, they still had the temerity to ask why so anybody would wanna quit.

Perhaps they did not care.

Either way, my contract was up. The decision was simple. Get out now or march on in the green.

In the end, I was too late. I'd already bashed[87] my slouch hat, flat, and hung a freshly ironed uniform by the door.

The fuel was on the fire.

*

---

86   Just like in the Vietnam War, the ADF and its soldiers were now feeling the effects of a long, drawn-out war. However, it was still strange being in uniform. While some members of the community went out of their way to thank you, many remained indifferent to Australia's commitment in Afghanistan.

87   The shaping and the formation of the slouch hats crown into a military specified shape.

It'd been two months—and then some—since I got home from Afghanistan. Two months of sitting, drinking and wallowing in pure filth, but it felt like much less. And that stank. I stank, and my skin and breath stank. My PT shirt stretched tight around my burgeoning stomach, revealing a gaping cotton dimple where my bellybutton sat.

Allow me to put it this way: I was looking nothing like a soldier. Nor did I feel like one. I wasn't ready to go back. Not yet.

At half-seven, I marched onto the parade ground.

The Regiments soldiers stood around, out of formation. I passed through the middle, trying to remain unseen.

I stood out, of course, and was bigger and fatter than any other soldier.

I sucked my gut in and moved to the back of the ranks.

It was mid-January, and peak summer, just to add to the hurt. Sweat poured out from every hole, then slipped down every crack, causing my arse cheeks to squawk like rubber soles on polished tiles, whenever I walked.

Every soldier noticed too. Diggers never miss-sight the fat kid when he stumbles in.

ATTENTION, said the Commanding Officer and the troops stamped their feet and clicked their heels.

Listen up, team, we've got a big year ahead. Although I can excuse it now, you're all looking like bags of shit, and I can tell you all it stinks out here.

He stepped off from his parade mark, then marched past the front rank of troops from The Left to The Right.

Afghanistan is far from being over, gents. We keep knocking the Taliban over and they keep worming their way back again.

He stopped. Performed an About Turn then prodded his finger into the air, like Benito Mussolini.

We're very much going to win the war, but we've got to remain professional. We have to be fitter. Olympian fit, and smarter, and I promise you all I'll be building yous cunts into hard-dick war-fighting machines.[88] Understood?

YESSIR!

Good. I'm going to be riding you all the way. Duty NCO.

SIR!

Take over.

The Duty NCO marched to the top of the parade square.

This morning's PT will be a sharp run up Enogerra Hill. After I've fallen you out, wait the by the front gate where we'll conduct a warm-up, then head up the hill. Understood?

Yes Corporal.

Good. Troop. FALL OUT.

The Troop moved to a Bali-style hut near the gate to prepare for the run.

The Duty NCO leant on a picnic table beneath the hut and rolled a Winfield Red.

You got a light?

Don't smoke.

Hey, you're that Patterson kid who got stuck with Baker in Afghan?

Yeah.

Ha… you poor bastard.

---

88   Although the Australian Army has set (minimum) standards for fitness, Commanding Officers may impress it upon his or her soldiers to attain a higher-than-average standard.

He was alright.

Maybe, said the Duty NCO. Still, it's a shame what happened to him.

I didn't answer.

What? You didn't hear?

I sat at the picnic table and noticed a crack in the concrete below. A row of ants poured out from the crevice. It was a chain and they carried between them stale crumbs which they hauled to a small nest. Each ant also carried its own weight and the string of mutual support stretched its way along the concrete. From one end to the next, blindly following the lead ants. No questions asked.

I've been off the map, Corporal. I haven't heard a goddamned thing.

Well, get this, said the Duty NCO. That old dog got caught up in one of those roadside blasts. Protocol is to stay inside your wagon, right? Not that Baker, hey. Mad bastard leapt straight out. Crawled on his guts for say ten… nah, twenty meters, then got whacked by a secondary blast. Dumb prick had to spend two months in a German ICU. My doc says that blast would have killed anyone else, but not that Baker. Not that day.

I watched the ants as they squeezed their stale crumbs through an ant-size hole.

We got on the road.

The younger soldiers bounced out the gate like wild gazelles and were soon a blur. Me, I took my time. My bones creaked. My knees grated, and my back screamed in sheer horror.

I felt my chest for a heartbeat—

C'mon, Patterson. Move it, said a voice out front.

Alright, I said. Alright. Let me get out this god-damn gate first.

Have some grease spread across my axles and allow a good dose of oil onto my chain. Then we'll see how I'm flying, you bastards.

Quit your moaning, fat boy, said the voice.

My breaths shortened; I didn't respond, I couldn't. A stream of sweat rolled down my back, and before I knew it, I'd stopped sweating. And that's when I began chaffing.

You pacing yourself, Patterson? said the CO. He slapped me on the shoulder.

A little rust in the wheel bearings, Sir… that's all it is.

Oh yeah, he smirked. And you enjoyed your break?

He looked down at my gut.

It bounced and jiggled as I loped along the road.

My inner thighs were on fire, so I widened my stride. Slowed, then glanced up at the peak of Enogerra Hill. It looked higher than I remembered.

I'd grown soft.

Sir, I gasped between breaths. Might've… put my feet up… once or twice… but I'm here now.

Ha, said the CO. And he smiled. He hit the go juice, and then he was gone.

I reached the first climb with nobody behind me, the sun on my arse, and a throbbing blister on the ball of my right foot. I had to stop so I sat on a flat rock and peeled off my shoes and socks.

The blister was about the size of a fingernail—perhaps bullet hole.

I pierced it between the sharp edges of my thumb and fore fingernails and watched its clear fluid drizzle onto the dirt.

The throbbing stopped. I laced up and ran for the top of the hill.

The troop had formed a circle at the peak of the hill. They were down on their guts—flat on the hot bitumen—and the CO stood in the middle.

His hands were on his hips.

PUSH-UP POSITION READY.

The troops straightened their arms and legs and tensed themselves into a plank hold.

DOWN.

The troops lowered, their chests inches from the ground.

HOLD.

The CO turned.

Private Patterson. So glad you could join us.

Yessir.

HOLD. C'mon, Patterson, we're waiting for you.

I got on my guts, then pressed myself off the bitumen.

UP.

Thanks, arsehole, muttered a young Digger.

He spat at his front, then glared at me from the corner of his eye.

Not a problem, I said, then spat.

On yer feet… UP, said the CO.

The troops bustled off the bitumen. Their faces glowed like ripe tomatoes, and they shook the lactic acid from their arms.

RIGHTIO, GENTLEMEN. See you back at the Regiment.

The CO led us back down the hill, and as we took off the young Digger bumped my shoulder.

Linger,[89] he said, and spat again then glided past the CO.

Soon, it was just me again, with only a blister and the sun.

---

89   Malingerer.

Promotion

After showering, I towelled my face, then took a handful of talcum powder and fluffed it between my thighs.

I shook the bottle and let more talc spill out into my hands. Spreads my knees, and in a half squat, I powdered behind the sack, then bent forward, to inspect the chaffing rash.

The skin was red-raw, and clear plasma glazed over the inside of my thighs. I powdered over that too.

You survived then, Patterson? said a voice from behind.

I turned to see the CO.

Sir, I guess so, Sir.

Well, Patterson. You'll do better next time, won't you?

Yessir.

Otherwise, you'll need more than talcum powder on your balls. Understood?

Yessir.

At half nine, I parked myself in the breezeway.

Bored diggers sat around. Some played cards. Others cleaned

and swept the concrete corridor. The rest sat, speaking shit about what they did last weekend while we waited for the day's orders.[90]

It was the Army in a nutshell.

Hurry-up and wait.

A young soldier sat to my right. Said his name was Lawrence.

Lawrence was fit and wiry and could have only been eighteen, nineteen. And, though I wasn't much older, he made me feel aged.

You're just back from the Ghan, he asked.

It's been a few months now, but sure.

The soldier's eyes widened and brightened, and his cheeks glowed.

What's it like?

Like making a football grand final after a year's worth of hard work—the build-up and the pantomime—then the loss.

His eyes sharpened and creases deepened across his forehead.

Loss? I thought we were carving up over there.

Yeah, a loss, I said. That's how I'll remember it.

Lawrence stood and picked up a broom, then began sweeping. He swept at the dust which had gathered in the breezeway and he swept at the leaves. A small mound of dust and leaves gathered at his feet. He stopped.

I reckon I'd still want to go. Only to see it for myself.

That's the only way.

I grabbed a dustpan and knelt.

Private Patterson, said a voice from behind.

I turned. It was the young soldier from PT.

He had two chevrons stitched to his shirtsleeves.

Yes, Corporal.

---

90   An unhealthy and unproductive proportion of the average soldier's career is spent waiting for senior ranks and officers to deliver orders.

Get upstairs. The LT wants to see you.

I collected the dust and leaves into the pan, then scanned through the pile. There were ants in the mix. Some remained alive, but most were dead. They were loyal to the end.

I turned to the Corporal.

What's the LT want?

How the fuck am I supposed to know, *Cunt.* Just get upstairs.

I walked up the steps and banged on the LT's[91] door.

Who is it?

Sir, Private Patterson. You wanted to see me?

There was a hurried shuffling of paper. The wheels of his office chair skated across the floor. Then I heard a soft drink can pop.

Give us five, Private.

The door opened.

A man with thick glasses stood on the other side. His forehead shone blood red—spotted with pimples—and a long cowlick hung over his eyes.

He sipped at a can of Coke.

I saluted.

Come in and sit down, he said after throwing up a lazy boxer. I'm Lieutenant Jack.

He sat behind his desk, and I stood at the opposite side.

Are you ready for a big year?

Yessir.

Good, the boss has big plans for you.

For me, Sir?

Yes, he said. Your experience will be invaluable to the younger troops.

---

91   Lieutenant. Lt, abbreviated, and indirectly referred to as El-Tee.

LT Jack leant back in his chair. Sipped at his Coke and glanced out the window.

How's promotion sound to you, Patterson?

Promotion, Sir?

Yes, he said. You'll start with one stripe, then climb the chain.

I'm not interested.

LT Jack began punching his fingers onto the keyboard. The blue hue of the computer screen reflecting in his glasses. He tapped one final key, then rocked back in his chair.

The boss has recommended your name.

What if I say no, Sir?

This is the Army, Private. Nobody says no. It's against Standing Orders.[92]

He pushed the office chair back from his desk. The wheels squealed, then screeched to a halt. He stood and blew the cowlick away from his eyes.

The next promotion course begins in one week. And your name is already on the list.

He smiled, then pointed me to the door.

---

92   Official orders relevant to a single military Unit/Regiment that is published and formally acknowledged by a Unit's/Regiment's soldiers. Failure to comply will attract a formal punishment.

Without the Muslim Cameleers, Where Would Australia Be?

At the dawn of Federation, Australia was changing, for better and for worst.

Racial intolerance gripped the nation.

The Chinese, Japanese and Pacific Islanders were in the thick of it, and for the thousands of Afghanis work was drying up. Faster than a desert lake in summer.

Decades earlier, Afghanis had arrived with their invaluable desert craft and camels (20,000 between 1860–1940).

Dost Mahomet assisted with the ill-fated Burke and Wills Expedition (1860–61). He was bitten by a bull-camel and died on the trail, but the Afghani worth was plain to see.

His fellow countrymen opened the Outback, carting daily tonnages of cargo into the guts of Australia's arid interior. Then grafted the Overland Telegraph Line. Queensland's border fence. A Rabbit-Proof Fence. Western Australia's Canning Stock Route, and the Transcontinental Railroad (now The Ghan Railway), becoming the unsung heroes of the Outback.

But the White Australia Policy (the *Immigration Restriction Act* 1901–1958) arrived like a kick in the s for the Asiatic camel handlers.

A kick like that causes a long-lasting bruise. To the Afghani men, repeatedly labelled as Aliens, this bruise left them alienated in the country they one day hoped to call home.

Such a policy soon seared away at their desire to become Australians and impeded day-to-day business affairs. Work conditions grew boorish, and interaction with civilians brutish and often punishable by law.

The combustion engine followed; it was another painful kick that all-but rendered the cameleers obsolete.

Along with the thousands of now useless camels.[93]

To manage this conundrum, the South Australia Camel Destruction Mandate[94] passed through the government. However, most Afghani refused to kill what they considered family. The men defiantly released the camels into the wild.

By the mid 1940s, the great majority of Afghani were gone—leaving few remnants of the brief Afghan legacy behind. Save for some mosques, a train, and the camels that now plague the Australian Outback.

---

93   Australia is home to the world's largest population (approx 300 000) of feral camels. The Department of Agriculture and Food.
94   *Camels Destruction* Act (No 1704 of 1925).

Shut Your Stinker

Giant great storm clouds rumbled overhead. It was like hard granite boulders clashing in a fight to the death. The thunder let out its loud, prehistoric growl, and Mahmout counted the seconds: one, two and three.

Thunder struck on the horizon and the old Afghan sighed with relief. Death would not arrive today.

The chain moved slow through the thickening mud. It collected around the camels' shin bones and squished between the men's toes. Mahmout bitched and moaned.

Shut your stinker, I said. Let's finish this job.

And he did, without complaint.

Stu was the next to warble.

His horse sank deep into the mud. He grunted and burped, spreading his grog-soaked breath down the chain.

That's it. I flaming well quit, he said stuffing his pipe full with stale tobacco. The closer we get to Darwin, the worse this country gets and I can't stand another day of it.

Penny remained out front and kept the chain straight and narrow as the mud and sludge piled around her knees. She felt the strain, but the bitch forged on.

I looked into her eyes: they were wide open and motivated. I pat her shoulder, said good job.

The gesture was long overdue. No other animal could do what she'd done.

How much further you reckoning, Boss?

Stu lowered his pipe.

We'll make camp by the Katherine River, he said, then looked towards the rainswept sky. Then, if we don't get washed away, we'll head for Darwin tomorrow morning.

The skies cleared that evening for the first time in days. Then the sun's bright burning face tucked itself beneath the horizon.

The Afghani made camp and Stu disappeared before the last light.

Mahmout gathered rain-soaked sticks, kindling and branches, then made a fire.

I sat alone on a red rock and counted the stars. They were quite different to the stars back home. The same colour, the same shape and brightness but laid out in different arrangements.

I found the biggest one and decided on a name.

What'll happen with the camels? Mahmout interrupted my thoughts.

He knelt over a small stack of branches and blew at a tiny spark.

What the devil do you mean?

A tuft of rolled grass ignited and flames.

Mahmout's face shone. He sat back to watch the fire grow.

Well, now that the Bossman has quit, it means we're out of a job.

I sat quiet on my rock. I hadn't thought about the camels. Not for a moment.

Then my mind turned to Penny.

HE'LL KILL HER, I said, and stood then stomped my feet. The bastard wouldn't dream of it.

Don't think he won't try, Sher Gul… don't think he won't.

Stu sprang out from the scrub. He was stumbling and smelt like toxic fumes. He threw his pipe into the fire.

Red embers trickled into the sky, then Stu kicked at a branch. The fire spread, and the Afghani scattered.

Nahhh, he snarled, stomping on a smouldering fire log. We can't go setting off a bunch of wild camels into the wild. He thumbed through his tobacco pouch, then looked at Mahmout. One between their eyes is the only answer.

Mahmout and I sat silent, not wanting to confront him. Then the Bossman walked off. Kicked his horse's feed bag, then tripped over his swag. He landed face down in a prickly bush, and that was the last we heard of Stu that night.

You Haven't Got Buckley's

Sunrise. Cold desert air blew across the camp. Stu lay sprawled out on his stomach with his face in the dirt.

I must get away from that madman, Mahmout.

Mahmout stood, skulking over the fire, and turned his head.

And what about the Afghanis?

What about them? If I go, who the devil's the Bossman going to follow. Them or me?

Mahmout grimaced and stared into the fire. He didn't say another word.

Stu awoke. Scrambled to his hands and knees, then went scrounging through his swag.

Where the blazers is my pipe? He unsheathed his rifle.

Which of you Mufti buggers stole my pipe?

You threw it in the fire last night, you drunken fool, I said.

Stu jabbed the rifle barrel up beneath my nostrils.

It peeled back my top lip.

What's happening with our camels? I spoke through gritted teeth.

I don't care, Sher Gul. All I want is a fucking smoke.

I pushed the rifle away.

If we're going to cull them, then let me do it.

Why, Georgie Boy? Why should I trust *you*? Spit was flying from the corners of his mouth.

I turned to the Afghani. They stood spaced in an even row beside the fire.

Camels are the only family these men have, Stu. Not one of them will pull the trigger.

The corner of Miriam's telegram had become visible from my vest pocket after Stu had shoved his rifle into my face. He reached out and snatched it. Unfolded it then read it.

Christ, look at that, he said, laughing. Georgie Boy's gonna be a dad.

He tore the telegram in half. Took a pinch of tobacco from his pouch, then spread it across the telegram paper and rolled a cigarette.

A father? he sneered, lighting a match. I had my suspicions, Sher Gul.

He took a puff of the cigarette and blew grey smoke into the air.

Nearly laughed when I learned my Miriam was up the duff. It got to thinking, who the poor prick might be.

He knelt down, close to my face.

But then I caught wind; it might be the great Sher Gul.

I didn't say a word.

Stu handed me the rifle. Start with your own beast, Cameleer.

I carried it back to the fire.

The Afghani were still standing there, but now they had their backs turned to me and had formed a tight huddle.

I pushed through to the centre.

Listen, I said. Don't worry about the camels; Stu ain't fair dinkum, and I've never shot a thing in my life.

The Afghani looked at me, with Stu's rifle in my hands.

Bugger Stu, said one. What about us?

I stepped through to the fire. It had shrunk, and I knelt and held my open palms over a glowing coal.

It's two days to Darwin, I said. Unless you have other plans, go there and board the first boat. There's no life for us here.

The Afghani muttered amongst themselves.

Mahmout tossed half a cup of tea across the fire. It fizzled and sent up thick grey smoke.

And what about the Great Sher Gul, he said. What will he do?

I stood and smiled.

Don't worry about a thing, my friend, I said.

Dante's Hell

The day started like any other day.

I paraded, the usual Left, Right, Lefts, salutes, orders, and all that other AJ crap.

The Duty NCO dismissed the troop for morning PT.

I stretched my hamstrings, through a forward fold and smiled. I can still touch my toes.

What the hell are you doing, Patterson?

Stretches, Corporal.

Quit that shit, right now. The boss wants to see you upstairs.

Roger that, I said and pulled my socks up, then walked into HQ.

The orderly clerk was sitting at his desk, nose deep in a bag of Smith's crisps.

Breakfast of champions, I said.

What the fuck you want, Patterson?

The boss said he wants to see me, Corporal.

The orderly clerk stood and walked to a small bar fridge. He opened it and took out a can of Coke. Cracked it open, then skulled back half the can.

He burped, then sat behind his desk again. His gut pushed hard against the table's edge, and he sucked in his breath as he attempted to reach for the Smith's.

I don't think the boss is in, he said. Go, see for yourself.

Okay.

I knocked. The boss was in.

Patterson. Come on in.

I walked in. Slammed my right boot onto the floor. Braced-up, then threw up a boxer.[95]

The CO slapped a pair of hooks[96] on my sleeve.

Congratulations, he said, then dismissed me with a limp boxer, to the front.

There was no parade. No celebration. No fanfare or good lucks. A slap on my sleeve, then my first set of orders and a flight to Adelaide.

I passed the orderly clerk on the way out.

I forgot to ask, I said. Was there any mail today?

He stood. Looked at my shirtsleeves, then grunted.

They'll promote anyone nowadays, he said.

I looked across his desk, noticed his trousers button had gone missing and his belly hairs hanging out over his underwear. They were Astro-Boy undies, and he must have been pushing forty. He was an overweight man-child.

Yes, I said. Anyone.

I asked about the mail, again.

Just some shitty car magazine.

The next afternoon, I touched down in the City of Churches, then boarded a chartered bus. It was an old Greyhound, with vinyl seats

---

95   Braced Up is a form of salute, typically conducted indoors, or when seated and where the arm is not raised. Bracing-up will also take place where the soldier is not wearing a hat. Unlike a standard salute, it is not referred to as a boxer.
96   Colloquial term for rank insignia, ie, Chevrons.

and chrome trimmings that burnt your fingers on behalf of the sun.

Not recognising any other soldier on the bus, I sat to the front near the driver.

Some call Adelaide a city, he called to me over his shoulder, but she's really just a big town.

This is wine country, right?

Wine country? said the driver. All yuppie wank, if you ask me.

We drove through the city's arterial streets and head on into the sun.

The driver flipped his visor down. He sprayed the windscreen, then gave it two swipes with the blades. It smeared bug guts and road grime across the glass and somehow diffused the sun's rays.

I sat back in my seat. Unlaced my boots, then opened my carry-on bag. I took out a Street Machine magazine and flipped to the centrefold. The feature was a '69 Monaro. Midnight blue with a chrome blower stretching through the bonnet. It was worth more than an Adelaide home. I put the magazine away and gazed out the side window.

The engine hummed. It sent a slow vibration through the bus. The windows were the frame with which I watched the sandstone cottages on outskirts of town disappear from my view.

I almost wept, saying goodbye to civilisation. Again. That's something only a soldier can comprehend, because it's not only goodbye. It's farewell free world, and bend over, because here it comes. Plenty of raw sunshine, rain and bright yellow pineapples— served sideways and whole—on a platter of dust and mud with a dose of Army immorality.

The sun hung low, glowing a deathly red over what was now my new home. The fucking desert. I could feel the hurt coming already.

The bus halted at a railway crossing. A slow, red passenger train rolled through the intersection. There was a large black camel painted on its side, next the words 'The Ghan'.

It was a cold reminder of where I would soon be heading. Back to Afghanistan. It also reminded me of my family, and where we'd come from.

Mostly we were German and Irish, but fourth generation Australian. Then, somewhere inside of me was a sprinkling of Central Asia.[97]

That's the wild side in you, my father would say, back when I was a boy. Savage men who couldn't be tamed. All from your mother's side, of course.

No one in my family looked Afghani though. Save for my mother who had that dark Arab skin and a pointed Persian nose.

But, after 9/11, no one ever spoke about that.

I was the only one who'd actually been to Afghanistan. I'd seen those men, and they didn't look savage to me. Some did, but a lifetime of war had burned that out the rest of them, and when I looked into the mirror, there was no other connection I could see.

On the return trip, I'd hoped that would change. There were many questions, of course. Where that Persian bloodline came from. Who was my great, great grandmother, or grandfather, and how in the hell did my family become Afghans, and where did that heritage all go? And, why the hell were we now at war?

Those were all questions which no living relative had an answer for.

I closed my eyes, and when I reopened them, the train had passed.

---

97   Although it's commonly referred to as the Middle East, Afghanistan is located in Central Asia.

We arrived in Woomera, with a thud and a clunk, as the bus driver nosed the Greyhound into a steel gate.

The troops at the back jeered him.

You're a pack of mongrels, he said, and crunched the gears into reverse. Who puts a giant steel gate up in the middle of the desert?

The Australian Government, I replied and pressed my face to the windowpane.

Here was our camp. An abandoned detention centre[98] surrounded by a fifteen-foot-tall fence, topped with rows of concertina wiring. The fence was old, tiring. Rusted in many places, and brittle in others, but enough to keep any occupants locked inside. It was perfect for soldiers, and I could see why they dragged us all the way into the guts of Australia. The training conditions were as near as one could get without stepping foot in Afghanistan.

LT Jack ordered us off the bus. He stood silhouetted against the bus headlights, which glowed through dead moths and other highway debris.

Grab your shit, he said. Mess hall is to your left. Accommodation is to your right, and the showers and dunnies are somewhere in the middle. Your name and room numbers posted on the Mess wall, and morning parades at zero-six hundred. Questions—no? Good. I'll see you all tomorrow.

I walked into my room. It was Cellblock E-West, room 12. I switched on the light. It flickered with electrical static, but was white and

---

98 The Woomera Detention Centre was opened in 1999 and held up to 1500 detainees, but due to capacity issues and human rights controversies, the centre closed in 2003.

The Australian Defence Force began using the centre for its accommodation, amenities and vicinity to the nearby desert training area.

Greater Woomera is a prohibited area, used mostly by the RAAF from 1947 and most commonly noted for its historical testing of war materials and 'Space Activity'.

bright. The floor was concrete, painted green and stained by umber dirt. The walls were a bare grey Besser brick job covered in hand carved graffiti, written in languages I'd never read before.

I unfurled a slim mattress onto a rusty spring bed and sat down.

There was a window to my left. All its glass removed and replaced with steel bars.

I lay back and looked at the graffiti. Above the bedhead, there was a small drawing of a hang-man's noose with Arabic text scrawled beneath the loop and the hang-man's frame.

I pretended it was a poem, or haiku.

Hail to Dante's Hell
It's some wonderful place
Ya can never leave

I rolled over to switch off the light when my dog tags slung out. I kissed the discs, then tucked them away.

Prisoner 1814636. Goodnight.

Then it was dark.

With a Dose of Salts

I ate breakfast at five. Baked beans on toast and a bowl of cornflakes. I bathed the flakes in sugar, then washed it down with a tropical juice box.

At six, the Troop split into three sections.

Jack ordered each section onto separate Hi-Ace buses.

Welcome aboard, said the driver.

He had a familiar voice.

First stop's the Outback, then we're express all the way to Afghanistan.

I sat in the back. The driver started the engine and pumped up the radio. He tuned into the BBC. The broadcast relayed world news from Afghanistan: another four US Marines dropped by a roadside blast.

The roads were straight and barren. There was dirt to the left, the right, and the next thousand miles.

The Hi-Ace hit top gear, then swerved to miss a pothole.

Hold on to your hats, ladies and gentlemen, said the driver. We're expecting some turbulence out here.

Who the hell is this madman? I looked.

Daisy? Who the fuck let him drive?

The road felt smooth again, and I reached inside my day bag and took out my Street Machine Magazine and held it to my face.

HOLY FUCK, said Daisy, slamming down hard on the brakes.

There were two camels grazing on the centre of the road. They were tall, and their long necks jutted out high as they stared at the bus as Daisy clutched the wheel.

Christ, Corporal Daisy, slow the hell down, said Jack, you're going to get us all killed.

Corporal? I said.

Killed, Sir? Said Daisy. I don't know how anything could survive out here, let alone those two ugly things. Should I just drive straight into them? The bus'd take it?

Shut it. Just drive safely, Daisy. Slow the fuck down.

Roger that, Sir, said Daisy, and he let out the clutch.

Daisy hit top gear again as we neared the training site on the crest of a barren hill. It was a mock Afghani village with tiny mud bricked Quoras all abutted in two even rows.

Pull up here, Corporal Daisy, said Jack. The road gets too rough for a white fleet bus. We'll have to yomp the rest of the way.

Roger that, said Daisy. He stopped and looked at the camp. Helluva place for a holiday, Sir.

Yes, said Jack, the Army sure can pick 'em.

The troops entered a compound surrounded by high-set mud-brick walls.

A Sergeant walked in. He was tall. Fit and had a jawline you could bust steel on, but walked with a jagged limp and failed to introduce himself.

Come in. Sit down, he said. Welcome to Woomera. It's hot as hell here and I haven't seen a bird in two weeks. I'm pissed off, my back hurts, and my dog refuses to talk to me. He grinned. But isn't that why we get a service allowance? Besides, who else would do this fucking job?

He snorted to himself.

The troops sat with their backs to the wall. They all looked at the Sergeant. Nobody smiled and nobody said a word.

Huh, tough crowd, said the Sergeant.

He took out a cigarette. Lit it, then exhaled smoke from his nose.

If you've got 'em, light 'em, gentleman. We know what we're here for and it ain't to fuck spiders.

Again, nobody moved and nobody said a word.

The Sergeant paced the dirt floor. He held one hand to his lower back. The other pinched the cigarette between his ring and middle finger.

Afghanistan. What a shithole, hey? Nobody wants it, except for those backwards and bearded bastards. FUCK THEM. Still, Western democracy has fought hard to keep the Russians out for a hundred years. Why? Well, God knows. The soldiers' job is not to ask. Diggers take orders with a dose of salts. We're good at it; we get the job done. No excuses, no failures. Shit, a soldier shouldn't even know how to spell that word and should erase it from their vocabulary. We aim to succeed… with extreme prejudice, gentleman. That's the purpose of the next three weeks. Training and preparing you to succeed on all future missions. Understood?

The troops sat tall.

YES, SERGEANT.

Good. Break into your three sections. That's how you'll deploy. Now let's get to work.

The troops moved into their respective sections. Corporals dished out orders to set up comms. Secured the perimeter. Establish an around the clock picket.

It was a two hour double staggered picket, and after dinner, I took the first shift. The picket was inside a small wooden tower, reinforced by a double wall of sandbags.

I leant against a corner post. Took out my issued compass and held its prism to my eye, then shot a bearing to a knoll, North of the tower.

The needle landed on 325 degrees; North-Nor-West.

I placed the compass in my pocket. Took out a range card where someone had already marked the bearing. It read 327.

Christ. That's a long way out here, I thought. Not quite the difference between Darwin and Cape York, but enough to find you lost.

The second picket entered. It was Daisy.

He rests his rifle against the tower wall, then looked out across the darkening horizon. The view hadn't changed since arriving; dirt and dust were all there was to see.

Daisy sighed, then turned my way.

How's it hanging, Knackers?

Low and slow, I said and set down the range card.

Two digs; one tower and the desert, he said. This'll be my most challenging wank to date.

It'll be a difficult picket, too, I thought.

I took a sip of water. Smiled at Daisy. Laughed, then started writing in my journal.

Fuzzy Logic

LT Jack climbed into the sentry tower.

God damn these fucking flies, and this heat, he said. There's just no escaping it. It's fucking *impossible*.

Don't worry, Sir, you'll get used to it, said Daisy. We'll stink so bad in a week even flies won't come near us.

I don't know about you, Corporal, but I like to keep my fire engine clean.

Suit yourself, Sir. Come week two, there'll be no flies on me.

LT Jack snarled.

Either of you have a driver's license?

Yes, Sir, I said.

Good, said Jack. Wait here until I find some dog's body to relieve you. I need someone to get me to the heavy munitions range. Pronto.

Roger that, Sir, I said, then watched Jack exit the tower.

A swarm of flies wafted about his head. He removed his hat and swat at them, but they wouldn't go away.

Can't teach those young subalterns a damn thing, said Daisy, staring out from the tower. Yet, for every two-pipped Bob that comes along, they try re-inventing the wheel. But it's all common dog-fuck business out here, Bubba. We keep it simple... if you understand what I mean?

The relief arrived.

I stepped down from the tower. Turned to Daisy and smiled.
We've already got wheels, so enjoy the wank, I said, then left.

Jack sat in the passenger side of a white Land Cruiser. A textbook sat closed on his lap. *Fuzzy Logic: An Introductory Course for Engineering Students.*

You don't have a license, Sir?

I don't like driving, he said, and laid the book on the floor.

Dog ears, coloured flags and pink and yellow highlighter perverted the pages.

Then how do you get around, Sir?

Jack sighed, rolled his eyes, then glanced out the passenger window.

I walk and I cycle. Sometimes, when it rains, I catch the train or bus.

Public transport, isn't that filthy?

It's better for the environment, Corporal, and one less car on the road.

The road to the range was gun-barrel straight. It rose gradually, but the going was slow because of the road's corrugated surface. I hit the accelerator. The Land Cruiser skated across the bumps and Jack white knuckled the arm rest. I slowed. Turned on the radio, then wound down the window, and heard a great KARUMPING. It was a bomb blast from the far side of the rise.

Windows up, said Jack. I prefer the air-con on.

Sure, I said, peering through the windshield. A mushroom cloud billowed towards the sky.

I wound up the window.

Yes, Sir. I could see how one less car would help.

We arrived at the munitions range.

Jack pointed at two officers standing beneath a mobile floodlight.

Moths infested the cool white glow of the light and danced beneath the hot bulbs. They flew low, then zipped up high and their wings burnt on the glass sending them crashing down to earth.

Jesus. If it isn't the flies, there's always something else out here.

I drove towards the light. Fascinated, I turned to Jack.

You know they're attracted to light, bananas and beer. Without that, they'd zoom away, Sir.

Who gives a crap. Pull over beneath the light.

A small dust cloud breezed over the two officers. One turned, looking angry, and wrapped his knuckles against my window.

I wound it down.

YOU HORSE'S ARSE, he said, then slammed the ball of his palm into the door and walked away.

The dust was climbing into the cabin. I wound the window up.

Stay in the damn car, said Jack. He opened his door and climbed out.

I reached across and picked up Jack's textbook then started reading about Fuzzy Logic; and, occasionally, I looked outside.

Several moths flew too close to the floodlight. Then, one by one, they each hit the dirt.

As Good as Gone

It was bright and early in the morning. The sun shone through a long break from the wet season clouds.

Stu shit the bed and was up early. He bounced about, dangling a cup of hot tea in one hand and an unlit cigarette in the other. His face was clean shaven for the first time in weeks, and he had on a fresh shirt.

I've been saving it for the home stretch. Can't ride into town looking like a dog's breakfast, can I, he said pronouncing his joy with a smile. It was clear his joy was the relief of having the cameleers, and me, out of his hair.

I hadn't slept at all. I'd sat beneath a rotted eucalypt with Stu's rifle crested on my lap.

Mahmout stood over a fire pit. Much of the timber was soaked through by the endless torrential rain.

He split several branches to expose the dry inner core, then ignited them with fist size balls of paper.

Yahoo, he said, bopping gleefully up and down on his heels. It worked; it worked. I told you it would work!

Once the fire was roaring, the Afghani sat around sifting through their billy tea. The smell of hot cinnamon and cardamom engulfed the campsite. It placed smiles on many faces. Not mine.

I swept a scarf around my neck, then wrapped it around a second time, covering my nose and mouth, then walked over to the camels.

I want them gone before the men have finished breakfast, said Stu.

We're on our way, I said.

I whistled for Penny. The bitch didn't move.

Alright, you hag… we'll play this your way.

I walked to the next camel, slung a holster over its long furry face. Then I fed it some damp kibble. The snack sparked the eye of several other camels, and they all sauntered over, searching for a feed.

Not my Penny.

She wandered into the scrub, knowing just what she was doing. Knowing it would trigger my switch and spark my temper. It almost did.

I harnessed the remaining camels.

Penny, I said. You'll be last.

She kept her head low and ignored me, gnawing away at the scant desert floor.

At last, I'd tethered the camels together. The Afghani had turned their backs on me and refused to help. They already had their visions of home.

I holstered Penny.

She was slow in joining the chain because, like me, she preferred working alone.

HOOSHTA, I said and whipped her across the rump.

Soon the chain was lined up on the trail.

I walked over to Mahmout. He was entertaining the cameleers around the fire. The men laughed and drank tea while he told jokes but went quiet when I came closer.

Boss wants us on the road soon as breakfast is over.

Mahmout looked at me with a raised chin.

Sure thing, Sher Gul, he said. Right after breakfast.

His eyes left mine and returned to the Afghani.

I thought about leaving. Heading out alone, me and leading the chain of camels. The Afghani—I was sure—would not mind.

I've survived in the desert before. Australia would be the same.

I dropped my strides and pissed on the base of a dead tree stump.

A line of green ants marched out from the desert soil which shrouded the tree stump's withering roots. They climbed upwards. Followed the lines of the harsh timber grain until they reached the leaf of a sprouting weed. Corralled the width of the stump, then scurried back into their home.

I plucked the leaf. One green ant had remained, and as I pinched the stem, the ant crawled onto my forearm.

It bit me on the knuckle.

BUGGER ME, I said, then slapped the ant, squishing its body flat, then flicked it to the dirt.

Several ants moved to the dead body. They lifted it and carried the corpse on their back, then returned to the hole.

Well, I'll be.

I always fed Penny long before I fed myself. Even on the trail, where we'd both often last days without food and drink. Then, and only then, I'd make sure she was far away before anything went between my lips.

I placed a dry cob of corn beneath her nose. She furled her lips, snorted, then licked out her long pink tongue. The cob disappeared.

Good girl, I said and pet the crest of her long face.

I peeled a handful of pistachios then tightened Penny's harness and moved out the trail.

The Afghani were still seated. Some were laughing at Mahmout's jokes others chatted amongst themselves. Some were quiet. But they all had their backs to me. Except for Mahmout. He stood tall, shrouding the fire and glaring out at the camel chain.

To hell with them.

Penny grunted as I yanked on her lead.

The chain was moving slowly, one step at a time.

I looked around for Stu. He was nowhere in sight. I waved to Mahmout.

He waved back, then turned away.

The camels and I were as good as gone.

EMU WARS

Our training in Woomera ended prematurely when the Troop Sergeant leapt from the roof of a mock Quora. He was in pursuit of an errant emu. The fall fractured his leg in three places and caused Jack to hurl his Earl Grey at a nearby wall in fury.

Fuck it. Let's get these boys out of here and onto the next plane to Afghanistan before one of these sweethearts breaks another leg in some fucking emu war.

The CO agreed and two weeks later the Troop touched down in the UAE for a brief staging camp.

It was there we drove for mile on a bus through the desert towards Al Minhad Air Base.

To the North, the Burj Khalifa rose, like a steel Godzilla trampling on the Mid-Eastern terrain.

I heard it costs thousands a night, just to sleep there, said Daisy.

Twenty K if you want the honeymoon suite, said Jack

I turned my gaze away from the reptile like monstrosity.

I shook my head and as the bus rolled on I tried to sleep.

Tomorrow, we'd be arriving in TK.

Helter Skelter

The Hercules banked starboard, down and over the snow-capped peaks of the Great Hindu Kush.

It was a remarkable view. All pitched against the dichotomous, arid and war-torn deserts of Afghanistan below.

The plane banked again lurching slowly through the air until the mountains disappeared, leaving us with a view of nothing but bright blue sky.

It was the last we would see of anything so remarkable for a while, and I couldn't count a single face onboard who took that for granted.

We levelled out, the flaps went down, and the engines roared beneath the increasing load placed on them.

I sat back in my seat. An LT General sat across from me. He was old—like most of the brass—and unfit and his hands did not look like they'd ever seen the desert, let alone one in the midst of this generation's Vietnam.

He held up his arm and pulled on his shirtsleeve to check the time.

He wore a gold Rolex.

Where in hell have I seen one of those before. I sat stunned, just thinking of it.

First time in a Herc, Corporal? said an Army Lieutenant General.

No, Sir, the last time I flew across here, I never got the chance to witness such a view.

He unclipped his Kevlar helmet then sat it on the deck of the plane.

It's a thing of beauty, isn't it, he said, before reaching across the aisle and unclipping my chinstrap. There's no need to wear these things mid-air, Corporal.

I didn't argue. Up here, or down on the ground, and anywhere else, a military General was the law. And his law trumped God's and everybody else's.

Yes, it is beautiful, Sir, but, all the same, it's quite the shame, Sir.

What do you mean?

The war, Sir. I can't help but think how beautiful it could be.

Well, he said, adjusting himself in his seat, thanks to soldiers like you, Afghanistan has a brighter future.

And after we leave, Sir?

Well, that'll be for the people of Afghanistan to decide.

I rubbed the clip of my helmet, between my thumbs and fingers and stared out the window.

Let the people of Afghanistan decide? I'd never heard that before.[99]

LT Jack sat farther along the aisles. His feet were on the seat, and he hugged his knees tight into his chest. He'd buried his face between his shoulders, but lifted his gaze and turned my way.

Why aren't you wearing your helmet, Patterson?

---

99   We brought war to their country, under questionable pretences. We trained their military, via Western cultural practices. Advised on their educational systems and built their schools. We oversaw their elections, with leaders we'd selected, just so the country could build to a position where it was able to defend itself post coalition departure. But, throughout the entire campaign, we as Westerners remained mostly ignorant to Central Asian culture.

I turned to look at the LT General, whose eyes were now shut tight.

I reached for my helmet and slipped it onto my head.

The plane pitch downward, and the landing gear extended out with a rusted groan. The LT General's helmet rocked, then rolled, then tumbled down the aisle. It came to rest beneath Jack's seat. We'd banked again[100] hard, and the LT General's sleeping body lunged to one side. He opened one eye. Sat tall, then scanned beneath his feet, looking for his helmet.

Lieutenant, said the General, with an indignant grin spoiling across his face. Be a sport and hand me my helmet.

LT Jack sat shaking in his seat. He peered down at the helmet, then across to the General.

The General looked at me.

What the hell's wrong with your Troop Commander?

He doesn't even like driving. He doesn't own a car and prefers to ride the bus, I said. Then I laughed.

The LT General slapped his thighs, then let out a giant belly laugh.

Well, fuck me, he said. I have never met an Army Officer afraid of flying.

He stood. The Herc tipped its wing. The LT General stumbled but caught his balance by putting one hand on the cargo wall. He walked to Jack and picked his helmet off the floor.

How're you going to manage in Afghanistan if a plane flight scares the shit out of you, Lieutenant?

I'll be fine, Sir, said Jack.

---

100   Known as tactical flying, a military pilot will manoeuvre their craft, through a series of sharp banking turns in order to avoid becoming an easy target for Surface to Air Missiles (SAMs) or rockets, and gunfire.
For the uninitiated, this can be an adventurous ride.

He looked so anxious; and the LT General could smell it seeping through Jack's paper-thin skin.

Ha, he said. We'll see. We will see.

We hit the tarmac in Kabul.

The LT General kicked Jack in the shin. You can open your eyes now, Mister Jack , he said, laughing.

The Hercules taxied in, and the ramp booms eased their way down. LT Jack unfastened his seatbelt, then bustled his way to the rear of the plane.

TAKE IT EASY, said the loadmaster—an Airforce Sergeant. No one's getting off this plane until I say so.

Jack stamped his foot on the cargo deck.

That's Lieutenant to you, he said, trying to muster some authority through his obvious misery. Now, I order you, *Sergeant*, let me off. Now.

Sit down, Sir, said the Loadmaster. I act on behalf of the Flight Captain's orders, and no one gets off this plane until I say it's safe to. Understand?

Jack screwed his face. Returned to his seat where he folded his arms across his chest and sat in surly silence.

Outside the Hercules, it was busy as hell. Forklifts shifted cargo pallets about, on and off the planes. Soldiers marched to the transit bays. They carried their field packs. Dive bags, weapons, acoustic guitars, pillows and even a coffee machine full of beans.

Afghanistan was always hot. So fucking hot. Hell, in some parts, winter didn't drop below twenty degrees.

Forty-three was the day's predicted temperature. It hit forty-six by afternoon tea and would have been cooking out on the tarmac, but as the wind blew down from the snow-capped peaks of the Hindu Kush, the plane filled with a chilling breeze.

The ramp closed, not one of us had stepped off the plane. Not that we cared, because Kabul was a top-heavy city. Full of brass, politicians, dignitaries and suicide bombers.

It was a relief to be back in the air.

Next stop was Kandahar, a Taliban Mecca and the fighting heartland of the long-gone Mujahideen.

Our seatbelts remained fastened even on the ground.

Then it was on to Tarin Kowt and Camp Holland, where we melted outside a briefing hut. It was a long hop back to the Hindu Kush.

It was smaller than a shoebox, but the air conditioning worked. Somehow, everyone fit inside. The door closed.

I need to piss, said Jack. He fastened his Kevlar, burst out the door and ran towards the bathroom.

The briefing lasted for three hours before the brass dismissed the troops and ordered we all wait out in the yard.

I sat on a small plywood bench and wrote in my journal.

First day back and it's as hot as I remembered. The war doesn't seem half as bad this second time around, but I can't see my boss making through the second week …

Holy fuck. Bubba! said a familiar voice.

I turned to see Daisy who'd flown in with an advanced team. He was walking into the yard, bouncing a football with his hands.

I closed my journal.

When did you arrive, Patterson?

I haven't even got a room yet.

No shit, he said, then kicked the football into a chain-link fence on the far side of the yard. It's gone completely balls-up out here. Karzai has stamped his foot, and now wants only Afghan nationals holding the fort.

Hell, I said, it's their country. Why not let 'em have it?

Let 'em have it? Crap, Patterson, don't you know their soldiers aren't worth a horse's shit?

I picked the football off the ground. Bounced it, then kicked it at the fence.

Well, I shrugged. This country hasn't been conquered in a thousand years. They must be doing something right.

Yeah, said Daisy, but those old wars didn't include the Taliban, tearing the place apart from the inside.

Put that fucken ball away, said Jack. He was glaring at us from across the yard. If I see that football out in work hours, I will confiscate it, then put you all on double guard duty.

Yes, Sir, we chorused, then Daisy took the ball and stuffed it inside a storage bin.

Jack snarled, then disappeared back inside the briefing hut.

What crawled up his arse? said Daisy. Jack? He's been shitting himself since we boarded the plane.

He'll do well here then, said Daisy.

We both sat down, and I returned to my journal.

Daisy and I moved up the accommodation blocks.

The rooms were long, abutted rows of converted shipping containers. They stood two storeys high. Hesco baskets full of rock encased the bottom floor to shield from indirect fire. The second floor was soft-skinned and only the steel shipping container walls stood between their occupants and a 155 rocket.

That should've been enough to scare the crap out of me, but it beat sleeping in a tent.

I'll see you at dinner, Bubba, said Daisy and he walked through an opening in the Hesco barrier.

There's something not right with him, I thought. Was he mad? In an Army sense of the word: yes, no, and maybe. We were all destined to go insane at some point. The dumb diggers fought back against the yo-yo ride that military service set a young man's psyche on. It caused many men to suffer. The smart ones hit the eject button long before their brains painted the ceiling, and the Brass swept their remains beneath the rug. But then there were people like Daisy who leant into such insanity and embraced it. I guess that made him certifiable, yet he seemed to like it. His cavalier attitude kept him level and grounded. And the uniform? Well, it was the only thing moving him forward. Wilfully and or blindly, one foot after the other.

I shook my head at the notion: what a wonderful and freeing thing it would be to trudge that path of such welcomed insanity.

Atop of the stairs was a motorised sliding door. I pushed a green button. Stepped over across a small ledge and got slapped in the face by a wall of frosted air. Shoe stands, clothes racks, bookshelves, weights, and cheap Persian rugs lined the hallway. It smelt like green apple scented hookah pipe.

I looked inside all the bookshelves as I walked to my room: B 316. Outside the door was a timber draw crammed full of smutty magazines and molested books, including an auto biography on Charles Manson. I flicked through the pages until I'd reached the section of the book with glossy images and there he was. All that long, bedraggled hair, blood crazed eyes, and a hand carved 'X' marking his forehead.

Yep, I thought, that's Helter Skelter alright, and I tucked the book (plus one magazine) beneath my arm and entered room B 316.

A young soldier poked his head inside the room.

Said his name was Gabriel, from a sister troop.

Like the archangel, I said.

I don't know who that is, but, yep, sure.

Gabriel was tall and skinny, and had a goofball face plagued with acne. He stood shirtless, and the acne flecked across his shoulders. I could see the indents of his spine poking through his hollow diaphragm. I thought of Monty Burns yet that would be lost on him; Gabriel could've only been on the high side of eighteen.

You're Corporal Patterson?

Yes, I said.

You've been here before?

I'm trying hard to forget.

I bet it hasn't changed a single bit?

Gabriel asked a lot of questions.

Why would it? I said, then sat on an empty bed and pulled open the magazine.

Gabriel leaned against the door opening. He held a dirty grin on his face and glanced at the magazine cover.

The centrefold is a ten, he said.

An Australian ten, or an Afghan deployment ten?

She's a ten, no matter what country she's in, Corporal, and my entire troop agrees.

Okay, I said, then flicked through to the middle of the magazine.

The pages were stuck together.

I threw the magazine on the floor.

She's a zero now.

Gabriel blushed. Lowered his head, then vanished from my sight. He was hopping on that yo-yo ride.

Paper Thin

It was on my fourth night in the country when the IED siren sounded. It was five past midnight and I lay in bed with the glow of a Maglite, reading about Manson and a Yellow Submarine.

Gabriel came rushing into my room. He switched the light on, causing my eyes to automatically squint from the glare.

You bastard! I said. What gives?

He had long feet, and they clapped on the floor as he strode to my bedside.

Corporal Patterson. Are you awake?

Well, I'm not sleeping.

The IDF alarm's going bat-shit. What do we do?

I hugged a pillow to my face and pressed it in—tight and silently screamed—until I struggled for breath.

Go back to bed!

The alarm went silent.

What do we do now?

Shit, man. Go back to sleep?

There might be another strike—

Safest place to be is yer bed.

Nope, said Gabriel. I heard a 155 tore straight through the roof of one of these shelters. Only last year. It landed right on some poor bastard's bed, and if he wasn't at the gym, he'd have become burnt toast.

So what? Go sleep in the hallway.

No way. I'm staying in here with you.

Whatever…just turn off the damn light.

The motorised door rolled open.

I switched off my torch and rolled over, dragging a pillow over my head.

The sound of combat boots came down the hallway. They stopped outside my door.

Corporal Patterson. Are you in there?

I didn't answer.

The light flicked on and LT Jack stormed into the room.

What the fuck are you doing, Patterson. Didn't you hear the alarm?

I lifted my head. Jack was standing over my bed. He was wearing his Kevlar helmet and vest.

Yes, Sir, the damn alarm speakers are right outside my door.

Jack unclipped his chinstrap and put his hands on his hips. Then why are you still in bed. And why's Private Gabriel on the floor?

Gabriel sat up. It's the safest place in the camp, Sir.

The roof on this shelter is paper thin, Patterson. It was only last year a bomb tore through the roof on one of these and blew the jaw clean off a Marine. He was fortunate to survive; you might not be so lucky. That was an actual bomb out there, tonight.

Yes, Sir, I said. And there'll be plenty more.

Jack clipped the buckle on his chinstrap and walked out the door.

Gabriel stood and switched off the light and returned to his position on my floor; and me, with the soft glow of my Maglite, carried on reading about Manson. It was a good end to an eventful night.

It's Coming

The journey was to be a short one: from the heart of Darwin to a small hostel for unwed mothers on the outskirts of town.

Miriam rode side-saddle on an ageing, grey mare.

She wore a brown dress that flowed down past her knees. It stretched around her waist and stomach, causing her to look more like a water buffalo than a woman.

She put one hand on her back while the other wiped her forehead and sighed; she felt like a water buffalo, too.

Next patch of shade, we'll stop for a break, said Father McCullough.

Father McCullough was the patriarch to the hostel for unwed mothers. He was old and had seven children of his own. Four boys and two girls whom he was proud to declare had all left home before their sixteenth birthdays.

A magpie always kicks her hatchlings from the nest the moment they can spread their wings, he said. It's the fastest way they learn to survive, and humans should endeavour to do the same.

He lifted the floppy roo-skin Akubra from his head and took a drink from his canvas canteen. It sure is hot, he said. I don't know how any man could survive out there.

The two stopped by a brown billabong where the water levels were receding.

Father McCullough was the first to dismount. He fastened his horse's lead to a fallen tree limb. The limb was grey, flimsy and infested by white ants. Father McCullough took another sip from his canteen.

Miriam remained in the saddle. Her skin was cold and damp, and her face flushed with a pink shine. She looked worried.

A quick drink, and we'll be on our way, said Father McCullough, and handed her the canteen.

Miriam declined.

No thanks, she said. One drop of water inside me and I'm afraid I'll burst at the sides.

Opposite the billabong, an Indigenous man watched.

The priest splashed his face with water. Stood. Unbuttoned his trousers, then pissed into the billabong.

The Indigenous man scurried out from beneath his shelter. Pinned his fingers to his lips. Let out a sharp whistle, then shouted *OI*.

Father McCullough stumbled and fell back. He caught himself before his bum kissed the crust of the billabong's banks but not before he wet his trousers.

The man stood still.

I drink that bloody water, ya know.

Father McCullough squinted, then removed his spectacles.

I'm sorry, he said, but I can't hear a word you're saying.

Wait one minute, fella. I'll come around, said the man, holding out a single finger.

The priest squinted then turned to Miriam.

What did he say?

I can't tell, but I believe he's trying to send you some sort of signal.

McCullough turned to see the Indigenous man still holding out his finger. The priest then made a fist and shook it in the air.

Well, up yours too, he said, then buttoned up his soaked trousers.

Miriam hunched forward. Her face lost colour, and she turned it to one side, causing her hair to fall across her eyes.

Father McCullough held the canteen to his lips again.

What is it? he said.

I think my water's broke, Father.

Nonsense. You're not due for another two weeks. I'm sure it's nothing but a false alarm and besides, you can't give birth out here. I've never delivered a baby in my life.

Miriam's skin was pale. She looked down at her soaked dress, grit her teeth, then scrunched her face and moaned.

It's fucking coming, she hissed. Whether you're ready or not—

Ahh, Christ, Mother Mary, Jesus and Jehoshaphat, said Father McCullough. At least wait until I'm back on my horse.

He slipped his foot inside the stirrups. Hoisted himself up. Slipped then fell onto the dirt.

Don't think this is the Lord's way of saying you get to keep that child, he said.

Miriam squirmed then bit down on the reins and groaned as another wave of pain roiled through her.

What's that? said Father McCullough, finally awkwardly mounting his horse and glancing across to Miriam.

She didn't answer, so he kicked his heels into the horse's side.

They were on their way and so was the baby.

For the Birds

Week two, and the tour was rolling on. The monotony was torture. Eat. Shit. Sleep. Repeat.

Are you coming to dinner? said Daisy.

No, I said, been thinking I'll give it a miss. My pants are getting tight from sitting on my arse all day.

You know the gym's open, twenty-four-seven?

Screw that, I said. Have you seen inside those places?

Daisy smiled.

I'll see you in the morning, Bubba.

It was hot outside. It always was. The rec-hut was the only quiet place. Or your accommodation. I'd spent too much time in the rec-hut on my last trip, so I climbed the stairs, grabbed my journal and laid in bed.

The air conditioning sat at eighteen degrees. Medical tape covered the dial. It had a message scribbled across it, in biro: Touch this and die.

I wrapped my chest, my shoulders, my feet and my neck in my sleeping bag. Then I tucked my fingers between my thighs and tried to sleep, thinking about that dial.

Tomorrow, we'll do it all over again.

In the morning, I met Daisy at the coffee hut.

Above the hut was a sign: Welcome to Green Beans. The Freshest Coffee in Afghanistan.

Outside the hut, there was a line, ten Officers long. All ranking from Major and only travelling higher.

Three more Officers stood inside.

I checked my watch. It was ten past seven.

I squirmed. We've gotta be at work in five.

Calm yer tits, Bubba. Old Jacky can wait.

One Officer left the hut. He was carrying five jumbo cups on a tray and couldn't hold the door. The next Officer took the door handle and stepped inside.

I checked my watch again. It was eleven past, and the line was down to nine.

You know, Bubba… for every enlisted soldier in Afghanistan, there's at least three Staff Officers to order that soldier about.

Three? What's it they do all day?

Hell, he said. I don't know, Bubba… I guess they drink coffee and scratch each other's back. The rest is all bling for their post-Defence CV.

That'll grind your gears, I said.

Yes, said Daisy. It does.

We drank our coffee. I had a tall latte. Daisy, a Frappuccino with fresh cream. It looked prissy but the boy was chuffed. The war seemed like nothing but Hubba-Bubba and cream to him.

Although, I thought. I'd love a sip of what he's drinking—

We reached the work yard at twenty-nine past; an entire minute before the start of play.

Outside, it was a beautiful morning, for Afghanistan. A gentle breeze drifted through the camp. It lifted the dust and haze, and

I could see clearly for the first time in days, but the breeze just pushed the heat around.

It was already forty-two degrees.

Where the hell've you two been, said Jack.

Getting coffee, Sir, I said. Only the cafe was full of Staff Officers. All we could do was wait.

What?

This entire camp runs on coffee beans, Sir, said Daisy. Without it, we'd all be packing up our PowerPoint and going home… Sir.

Jack ushered the pair of us towards a shipping container. A fat Chubb padlock secured its doors, and a tin AQIS Customs tag dangled from the pressed steel door handles.

I don't drink coffee, said Jack. It's bad for my guts and it gives me the shits. I only drink tea.

You're a true Officer *and* a Gentleman, said Daisy, sucking the cream from the top of his cup and yanking hard on the tin tag.

We've got important work to do, fellas. This container needs a good clean out and nobody can find the stupid key.

Daisy left the tag to play with the fat Chubb padlock.

Leave it to us, Sir. We'll get the job done.

Good, said Jack. I want it completed by lunch.

He left the yard. Daisy and I sat in a shady corner of the yard and drank.

How do you plan to open it?

Daisy licked the cream from the top of his cup. I haven't got the faintest idea, he said, then leaned back and smiled at the sky.

Overhead, three Blackhawks banked hard right across the airfield. Two Apaches flanked the slick—one left, the other right—then hovered as the Blackhawks landed.

Casevac? I said.

Hmm, Americans, I guess, said Daisy.

He stood, wielding an iron crowbar, and wedged it into the padlock.

Gabriel, he said, come give me a hand.

Gabriel lifted his hat. Opened his eyes. Stood, then brushed the dust from his long, gangly legs.

There was a deadpan look on his face, and his eyes and jaw drooped.

Daisy looked at the kid and raised one brow.

If a picture can say a thousand words, he said, then there'd be a million more for you, Gabriel.

Gabriel's eyes and posture did not change. It was like there was nothing working inside, except for a peanut. Or a pea. A little green pea, shrivelled up, and substituting for a brain.

But then his eyes sparkled, and a grin pearled across his face.

Daisy shook his head.

Gabe, he said, what would do if a bomb was coming down over you?

Gabriel scratched at his groin. He kept eye contact with Daisy.

I don't know, Corporal he said. I'd duck for cover, I guess.

HUH, said Daisy, you wouldn't need to. The bomb would miss every time, then they'd say it was just dumb luck.

Gabriel didn't respond so Daisy handed him the crowbar.

Just stick the pointed end in the hole, Gabe. Then wedge down hard.

Gabriel poked the crowbar into the eye of the padlock, then wiggled it until it jammed in tight. He clasped his fingers and knuckles around the far end. Brought his elbows in together. Took a deep breath. Held it, then dropped his hips real fast.

CRACK. The padlock opened.

Daisy knelt and gathered the busted brass chunk. He looked up at me.

Well, I'll be, Bubba. I never thought that'd work but that bastard is *strong*.

Gabriele smiled and his face glowed as he crossed the crowbar over his arms. He didn't say a word—didn't need to. He'd already said enough.

The shipping container was packed with green Army trunks, cardboard boxes, a small diesel generator, and a Weber barbecue.

We had it emptied, swept clean and ready to repackage before morning tea.

Gabriel sat on the generator and lit a cigarette.

Is it true, he said, that the Afghan Government has blocked all coalition-led patrols into Uruzgan?

Not quite, I said, our SF gunslingers are still out there taking names.

Yeah, said Daisy. Where'd you hear that crap anyhow?

Gabriel sucked hard on his cigarette. Coughed. Turned pale, then punched himself in the chest. It cleared his lungs and throat.

It's in the news, fellas. They're saying the Taliban are gearing for a takeover.

Bullshit, said Daisy, ripping the cigarette out of Gabriel's mouth. That won't happen until we leave.

Yep, I said, they're just waiting for us to get back on that plane.

He took a drag, then handed back the cigarette. Daisy pulled the football from out a nearby bin, bounced it on the concrete path, then kicked it into the fence.

The fence rattled, and the ball crashed into the dirt.

All yer gotta do is look to the Soviet occupation, Bubba. A whole other war, I'll grant you that, but the results will be much the same.

I pulled aside a green Army trunk and sat on top, with a clear view West to the Sar-e Tangi Mountain. It towered over the valley, with its brown, demonic and razor-sharp craggy edges. We were sitting in the middle of hell on earth, but those mountains were the most beautiful thing I'd ever seen.

Gabriel pushed a broom along the concrete footpath, then stopped before the open shipping container. He looked inside.

Do you suppose, with all this cleaning-up, they'll be sending us home early?

No way, I said—at first—then stewed on it for a moment, while staring out at the mountains thinking, *Christ*, that's gotta be the most profound thing that stupid bastard's ever said.

I walked over to the fence. Poked my fingers through the chain-linked mesh, then pressed my face against it.

The feeling of the steel pressed upon my skin was cold and hollow. I sucked in my breath as I looked at the mountains before returning to the trunk.

I sat and dropped my hat on the path, then turned to Daisy.

Media says we earn all this money, tax free and all that shit, but all we do is sit around all day, then go to the gym. They say we're practically bumming off tax-payer's money and that this war's a waste of time.

Ahh, bullshit, said Daisy, snatching up the football. Media will say anything, just to sell a rag.

He bounced the footy once on the concrete, then kicked it in the air before catching it. The problem is, Bubba, nowadays all the journos want to do is play Judge, Jury and Executioner. The truth, to them, well, that's for the birds.

He kicked the football one last time before returning it to the bin, while Gabriel went on pushing the broom. And then it was lunch.

A Drink to Forget

At half-two, a controlled detonation announcement came over the camp PA.

Attention, attention, said the pre-recorded message, *the following is a controlled detonation. The following is a controlled detonation.*

Daisy was asleep, his bush hat pulled down over his eyes.

A loud, crumping sound shook the camp. The ground trembled and Gabrielle curled himself into a foetal ball. His hands covered his ears.

The earth settled then a thin shower of dust came down. It covered the concrete path, turning it from a cool grey to a warm light brown.

Shit, said Gabrielle, unfurling himself and reaching for the broom. I just finished sweeping that.

Forget about it, Gabe, I said, we're in a desert. You'd have more luck pushing shit uphill with that broom than keeping these footpaths clean.

Gabrielle rested the broom handle against the container wall. He sat down, head in hands.

That's better, Gabe.

He smiled, then looked at the ground. A line of ants marched along the edge of the path—past Gabrielle's feet—following their leader.

If Daisy and I aren't moving, I said, then it's a smart idea you don't either. I took up a pebble and tossed it at the ants. It bounced once, then twice, rolling past the ants. They didn't move.

Hey, Pat?

Yeah.

Do you hate Afghanistan?

I sat tall and looked at Gabe. His mouth drooped and his eyes were glum. No, I said, but I don't enjoy being here. Why do you ask?

No reason, he said, then sat on the pavement.

LT Jack came storming into the yard. His boots were thumping on the concrete path, kicking up small clouds of dust around his bootstraps.

Daisy heard the footsteps and sat tall. The football he was using as a pillow squeezed out from beneath his neck lay and rolled along the path.

What the fuck?

Jack stood in the centre of the footpath and kicked the football, launching it over the fence.

OI, that's my only ball, said Daisy.

It's now the property of the Taliban warlords. You lot will be too, if you don't tell me why the hell you're all not cleaning.

Job's done, Sir, I said.

Jack stepped in close until we were almost nose to nose.

The yard looks like a dog's breakfast, Corporal Patterson… there's dust everywhere.

We're living in the desert, Sir… ninety-five percent of this camp is dust. And if Gabe keeps pushing that god damned broom around, I swear he'll wear the bristles out.

Jack didn't answer, but I could see into his eyes. His mind was turning over.

What will the Base Commander say if he sees this mess?

Ha, said Daisy. That man won't come down, even if they chained him to a donkey then whipped its ass.

Jack snarled. You've got a big mouth, Corporal Daisy, and one of these days I'm going to put you on a charge. You hear me?

Roger that, replied Daisy before heading to the fence to locate his football.

Listen, Sir, I said, we did what you ordered us to, but this war has turned into a snooze fest. Allow the boys to see beyond the wire sometime.

Jack straightened his hat, then adjusted his collar.

No chance, he said. Karzai has halted all kinetic patrols indefinitely. The brass are even ordering field commanders to pull back their defences. Outposts like Camp Hadrian will soon go. Then the Afghan National Army will take over. The Australian Defence Minister will be here to announce it tomorrow. Our work here's as good as done. It's high time the Afghans took care of their own bloody country for a change.

So, we're going home.

Negative, Corporal. The camp requires packing up. Security needs maintaining, and we all must keep our ducks in a row… if you know what I mean. Discipline. The war depends on it.

Well, Sir, what do you want us doing in the meantime?

Jack walked to the empty shipping container, where he looked inside. It was clean and hollow and sent out an echo when he stepped inside.

I don't care; he said. Put these boxes away or something. Show some initiative, for Chrissakes, I'll even help. Just don't let me catch you lazing around.

Roger that, Sir.

He hopped back onto the concrete path and stepped towards a green Army box, then looked at his watch.

Well, I've got to get back to HQ. It's the boss's birthday

today. They're serving chocolate mud cake… got fresh cream and everything… you fellas oughta see it—

Then he pulled on his cap and marched out the gate.

Ha, said Daisy, then he kicked a box.

It tumbled onto its side. The latches sprang loose, and the lid flopped open.

Chocolate cake, and initiative my arse, Bubba. I'll give him all the chocolate cake he God damn wants. Then I'll shit in his boot for kicking my damn football over the wire.

Daisy knelt to close the box. He looked inside, then his face glowed brighter than the North Star.

Bubba, look-ee what we have here.

What?

Daisy reached inside the box, then came back out with a litre bottle of Jack Daniels and camphor cigar box.

They're Russian cigars, fuck. Too strong for even the most battle-hardened fighter but we'll enjoy this whiskey, Bubba. A pittance for our efforts.

Don't let Jack catch you, said Gabrielle.

Fuck him, said Daisy… and fuck the Defence Minister too. That's who I'll drink to forget.

ENOUGH ROPE

The Afghani burned everything they couldn't carry. The camel saddles were the first to go. They lumped them onto the fire—one by one—until the flames reached double the height of the tallest man. Then went on the harness. The stirrups. The reins and even the canvas feed bags.

The men prepared to travel light.

The fire looked out of control, but when the last bit of kit got tossed onto the flames, the Afghani turned their backs and headed North for Darwin.

It was midday. I'd been on the trail for hours and was headed for a gorge, West of the main track.

Dispose of the stinking camels there, Stu had said. One bullet between the eyes that's all they'll need. Then push 'em over the edge before joining the team back on the trail.

Okay, I'd said.

Stu knew I couldn't do it. Not like that, anyhow. He knew I didn't have the stomach for killing. So, he leant me enough rope, then bitterly awaited the outcome.

I took that rope—of course—like a gullible hungry fish, swimming in a big desert sea and arrived at the gorge two hours ahead of time and planned to shoot the camels, right there and then. Or at least fire off the shots.

I must have been ten miles West of the track. The wind blew that way, and the smell of me and twenty-odd head of camel would, no-doubt, carry across the flat desert landscape.

Bugger it, Sher Gul, you've got the time, I thought and sat in the shade. Chewed on some pistachios, then fell asleep.

When I awoke, the sun was shifting down towards the horizon.

Penny chewed on a twisted root as the other camels ambled back towards the trail.

I got to my feet and charged out after them.

Penny blew her nostrils, then followed me. I stopped.

The devil you do, I said and threw a rock at her feet. Go back, you bitch—

She continued.

I threw a second rock.

She continued.

The other camels continued.

I slumped back into the ground. We were all heading the wrong way and there was nothing I could do.

There's No Escaping It

The sun was shrinking, but it was still hot. The days were always hot here in the North. The heat got in close and crawled beneath your skin. There was no escaping it.

I pulled out Miriam's handkerchief and wiped it across my brow.

The handkerchief became soaked after a single wipe.

Ah, bugger this. Bugger it all to hell.

I shouldered Stu's rifle. Pointed it at a tree. Slid the bolt back (a round was already chambered), then forward and fired the shot.

The shot was loud and scared the hell out of the camels. They scattered. Some ran East. Some continued West, while Penny and the rest vanished into the bush.

I chambered another round, then fired another twenty-two shots.

Then, I ran.

What Day Is It

Jack would disappear most afternoons. Then he'd reappear, long after the sun had faded and the Central Asian Summer swelter settled.

It was a welcome break, and we took our respite all the way to the bank.

Daisy and Gabe threw their watches in the bin. The pair laughed and joked about it.

Hey, Daisy, what time is it?

Damned if I know… I don't own a watch. Hey, Bubba … what day is it?

Monday—

Thank you, good Sir. I didn't know… on account of not having a watch.

Daisy waited for me to laugh.

I didn't but the joke didn't go over my head. Then Daisy slapped Gabe on the back, and they both chuckled off to the mess.

I headed for the rec-hut.

Two soldiers sat on the couch. One was American. The other, a female Aussie.

Burke's Backyard was on the TV.

I can't stand that creep, said the Aussie.

Aww, heck, said the American, forget about that.

He took her hand. A tight gold wedding band wrapped around his left ring finger. She squeezed his hand tight, and then rubbed her fingers along the gold ring.

I don't know if this is a good idea, she said.

Don't worry, the wife won't hear about a single thing. He squeezed her fingers. Besides, she knows how tough it is, being away.

A US Marine walked in. He sat on the couch and lifted the remote.

Are you watching this crap?

No, said the Aussie.

Good. The football is on.

He switched the channel. The game was at the break. The Patriots were leading the Broncos, 12 to 0. A blonde-haired commentator followed the Patriots into the locker room. She took Tom Brady by the arm and began her interview.

Tom Brady isn't shit, said the Marine. He turned off the TV, then left the room.

The Aussie girl and the American man moved closer together. They didn't bother searching for the remote.

There was still much of the night left, with little to do.

I ignored the TV and the Aussie girl with the American man and walked to the kiosk to check my mail.

The Defence Minister

The days and the nights flip-flopped, side by side in their own haphazard way, until it was morning again. The mornings argued with nobody—only you argued with them.

Lt Jack came bouncing through the compound gate. It was a short while after breakfast, and he was all hopped up on caffeine and sugar-soaked Fruit Loops.

His rifle was slung over the right shoulder. He stamped his boots on the concrete path. Shook out all that wild Afghan dust that collected anywhere it could.

He looked at Daisy and me to see if he had captured our attention.

Daisy and I looked back.

Jack smiled. It had worked.

The Defence Minister will be here in fifteen minutes, said Jack. He unslung his rifle and rested it against the rack. I want this place in inspection order before he arrives.

Okay, said Daisy as he levered the shipping container door shut, then kicked a pebble clear from the path. Done. Now what?

Well, said Jack, standing there, thinking to himself. Order Private Gabriel stand by the door and wait… in case the Minister wants to look inside.

Roger that, Sir, said Daisy. He snapped his fingers at Gabe, then pointed to the door.

Gabe huffed. Stood. Gathered his rifle and sat by the door.

I want you standing, Soldier. Standing, said Jack. We don't want the Minister thinking we're a bunch of lazy arses, do we?

No, Sir, said Gabe, as he stood.

Jack picked up his rifle, slung it back across his right shoulder. His eyes glistened beneath the hard sunlight, and he bounced towards the gate.

I'll be back in fifteen, he said. Don't mess up the joint.

Roger that, said Daisy.

We all watched him leave through the gates.

Who the hell is the Defence Minister, anyway? said Gabe.

Buggered if I know, I said. I held my Charles Manson book in one hand, then sat beside Gabe.

Hey, Pat?

Yeah.

You think the Afghanistan people like us being here?

I opened up the book and removed the book marker. I dunno, Gabe. I've never asked them.

I don't think the people of Afghanistan want me here.

I put down the book. Well, I'm an Afghan descendent, and I say it's alright.

Gabe's eyes widened.

Really, he said. You don't look like one of them.

No. But somewhere back along the line, my ancestors met an Afghan man visiting Australia. Now here I am.

Gabe laughed, then shook his head. Must have been one of those Afghani cameleers, Pat.

A what?

The old camel herders. They're responsible for all the wild camels running around my old man's cattle station. It's a hundred miles west of Longreach. Dad swears he can't get rid of them.

Is that right? I said, smiling. Then I returned to my book.

All Out of Beans

We cherished every moment without the LT around. I guessed the feeling was mutual.

Such moments felt quiet and the tepid silence allowed the boys time to think and the space to process the war dragging on and on outside—and inside—our heads. Only we couldn't escape the war going on inside, and were prohibited from getting closer to the war outside. It was an embargo of mind, soul and body and we were chained to the fence posts of our camp like rabid dogs, unfit to be let off our leash.

Gabe sat leaning against the container door; he was too afraid to step away, knowing Jack would have his balls if he ever abandoned his post. Still, he found some way to drift off to sleep, while Daisy played with the cats and kittens which had recently inhabited the camp.

He'd laid down the lid of a green ration pack bin and poured in a dollop of long-life milk, trying to coax the famished and wild felines in. I'd discovered that Daisy was hard as granite on the outside—nothing could crack him—but occasionally you could spot a glimmer of warmth pulsing out from his eyes when he cradled a feral kitten.

I questioned that, of course. I'd been wrong before. Maybe Daisy had much darker thoughts for those cats.

Don't touch those damn cats, Daisy, they've all got rabies.

I know that Bubba, but they're still cats all the same.

I ignored Daisy, after that and turned to my book on Manson. There were glossy pictures of Helter Skelter, in the middle pages, and his eyes were wild and punctuated by that mad X centred on his forehead. It was easy to see how such a human could so lavishly harm and maim another living being.

Thou shall not kill. That was the difference, I thought, between a warrior and killer. I closed the book.

I'd began watching a line of ants marching their way towards Daisy's bowl of milk. The cats had wanted in, but Daisy had kept the bowl too close to his feet. The cats were afraid—as hungry and starved as they were—but the ants had no such angst.

Footsteps were clomping their way towards the gate and we all sat tall.

Gabe hopped to his feet and stood by the container door. Daisy kicked the milk aside and the cats scattered. I fastened my shirt buttons. Slipped on my hat, then looked towards the gate.

Sergeant Baker walked into the compound.

Here we go, I thought, but did not smile. I haven't seen that bastard in years.

It was all too soon.

He moved with a limp, and a wry grimace strained across his face. There was a small, white pill bottle in his left hand. He twisted off the cap and poured in a mouthful of pills, then swallowed.

Patterson, you cunt, he said and let out a dry smile. Who the fuck let you back into country? He put out his hand. How are you, lad?

Alive, I said.

Ha! I see you got promoted, but you all look bored as hell, sitting around with your thumbs up your arses. Why don't ya's come up to HQ, sometime? I'll show ya's to the heartbeat of this fucking war.

They have fresh milk and coffee up there, Serg? said Daisy.

More than you can drink in one day, son.

Baker turned and looked at Gabe.

What the hell are you doing?

LT Jack wants me standing here in case the Minister arrives.

What a load of bullshit… that God damn bureaucrat isn't coming down here. It's too close to the wire and his tight-ass sphincter would explode.

Damned skippy it would, said Daisy who was down on hand and knee searching for the cats and kittens. They'd all gone into hiding beneath the shipping container.

Baker watched Daisy, crawling about, but wasn't aware of the cats or their kittens, and he shook his head then looked away.

Tell your cockeyed boss he's a damn fool for thinking otherwise.

Gabe laughed. Kicked his boots at some rocks, until a small, round rock scuttled across the path and into Daisy's tin milk lid. Then he sat down, with his back to the shipping container.

Quiet, you bastard, said Daisy, you're going to scare the cats.

Baker looked bemused.

Well, he said, scratching at his temple. I heard you were down here, and I only came to say hello… if not for anything else, but I gotta go now. This war stops for no one, not even me, haha.

What war? said Daisy. We've been trapped inside this bullshit compound with a nitwit for a boss and nothing but stick-mags for entertainment. I'll die from atrophy, or blisters long before the Taliban gets hold of me.

Well, you can come up to HQ… anytime. I'll show ya's what the wars all about. We've got all the gear ya only see in the movies and then some. It'll blow your fucken minds.

Daisy did not answer. He kept on searching for the cats, and their kittens.

Baker smiled. Raised both brows. Waved, then turned and marched straight back out the gate, shaking his white pill bottle in his hands.

Who the hell was that? said Daisy.

No one important, I said, just a ghost from the past.

Jack returned, twenty minutes after fifteen minutes had passed. His hands were shaking, face was red, and sweat was trickling down his neck.

He removed his bush hat, then crumpled it between his hands before swiping it across his forehead.

Bad news, gentlemen, he said, staring at the concrete path, failing to notice that Gabe was now sitting down, with his eyes half closed and battling not to fall asleep. Nor the fact that Daisy had buried himself halfway beneath the shipping container—chasing rabies infested cats, and their kittens—and all that could be seen was his feet kicking mad up into the air.

What is, Sir?

The Minister won't be coming down.

Oh, shit, said Daisy, trying wildly to claw himself backwards out from beneath the container, realising the boss was now back in town. He resurfaced. His hair was caked in brown and grey dust that had gelled with sweat, spittle and fluid from his eyes, forming an ugly coat of mud. Just sweeping beneath the containers, Sir.

We all looked at him; knowing now that he was actually insane.

What is it? he said, with his eyes wide like dinner plates and this mad grin slapped across his face.

I looked at my watch; it was half twelve and already forty-six degrees outside. A wild sandstorm was building its way across the long, wide dust bowl of Tarin Kowt. Soon it'd be bearing itself down on the camp.

Sir, I said, it's cooking up something mighty hairy out there. We should duck inside before it blows us all away.

Not a chance, said Jack, we've been ordered up for a group

huddle. The Commander says it's compulsory. The entire camp will be there… for the Minister. You don't want to miss out.

What about the security? I said. The Taliban are still out there—

Jack turned away, then massaged his hat and flopped it back over his head.

Just grab your gats. The Minister will address the camp in fifteen minutes.

Fifteen, I thought. Fifteen before the fifteen, then it'll be a big hurry up and wait.

Gabe and I grabbed our hats and gats. Daisy walked around to the far side of the container—to see if any cats or kittens had emerged.

C'mon out, we heard him say, as he kicked rock after rock into the side of the container, making a hollow KERPHUNK sound each time a rock clashed with metal. Then, after one whole minute, the KERPHUNKs stopped. Daisy had given up.

Jack watched in silence.

On second thoughts, he said, one of you boys'd better remain behind. Someone's pilfered the padlock. Daisy… do you know anything about that?

Daisy smirked. Then he slapped Gabe on the back.

Boys, you gotta go. You don't want to be late!

Jack threw his hands in the air, then turned to Gabe.

Daisy's not staying. You are. I don't believe it's safe leaving that maniac here… not unattended. Bad things happen when he's left to his own devices… and I'm the one who'll, no doubt, bear the brunt.

There was another KERPHUNK. It was big and loud. Daisy was not happy, but he slapped on his hat then grabbed his rifle, just the same.

Aw shit, Sir, said Gabe. I need to get out of here for a bit. It's my mum's birthday today and I promised her I'd call.

Relax, said Jack, Australia's hours behind. Your old lady would still be in bed.

Huh? said Gabe.

Never mind. You can spend all the time you like calling you mum when we get back. I'm sure the Minister will not mind.

Ho! That he won't, said Daisy, as he slung his rifle over his right shoulder.

I slung mine, and, side by side, we followed Jack out the gate.

There were two, maybe three, hundred soldiers crammed beneath the hut. The afternoon was growing long, and the sun burned down overhead. The temperature passed fifty.

I'm sweating my arse off in here!

Tell me about it, Bubba. My balls are melting to the inside of my leg, but… if ever there was a time for a Taliban attack, then it would be now.

I thought about that for a moment, then looked at Daisy, and all the soldiers cramped inside the hut. His face was calm and tranquil. It always was. Life was simple for him. He knew it. I knew it. And he was rarely ever wrong.

Ten, fifteen, then twenty minutes passed. The soldiers grew restless.

Where the fuck is this bastard? one Digger yelled.

Shut the hell up, replied a Senior Officer, or else I'll have you up on a charge.

Bite me, said the Digger, and all the soldiers hollered and laughed.

Then the soldiers parted, creating an open channel through the centre of the hut. Two special forces soldiers plotted their way towards a lectern. They wore dark sunglasses, and their sleeves were rolled midway up their forearms. They carried M4 rifles. All the soldiers stared with jealousy and awe. We'd been stuck with the green, plastic Austeyer that melted in harsh gunfights. The M4 was superior, and every soldier knew that was *the* rifle to get the job done.

The Australian flag hung limply on a wall behind the lectern. A short man walked through. His hair was sharp and groomed, and he wore a pressed white shirt and a blue ballistic vest. The letters V.I.P, in white, eight-inch font, covered the vest's front and back.

He stepped behind the lectern. Cleared the sweat from his face, then adjusted his vest and grabbed the microphone.

Daisy stretched on tippy toe to get a better look.

That him, Bubba?

I didn't bother looking and stared at the boot heels of the soldier in front of me.

Guess so, I said.

An attaché unscrewed the blue cap off a disposable water bottle and placed it before the Minister.

The Minister took the bottle. Sipped. Wiped his mouth, then pushed his attaché away.

A camera flashed.

Delete that… right now, he barked, then the soldiers laughed.

The Minister sipped again at his water.

Ladies and gentlemen, he said. I have a busy schedule but would like to thank you for coming out to see me this afternoon—

Well… the boss fucken *ordered* us… all while I was busy too, whispered Daisy.

The Minister paused. The hut was silent. He gripped the

lectern. Another camera flashed and the Minister's knuckles glowed white until his attaché put his own hands together and began clapping.

The entire hut joined in with a sharp round of applause. More and more, the cameras began to flash.

What the hell are they all clapping for? I've never clapped for a politician in my life … fuck him, let's get out of here… I've got better things to do.

I didn't say a word and continued staring at the boot heels in front of me.

Daisy did not move.

Now, said the Minister, we've got an upcoming election at home. It's a very important election that will influence the outcome of this long, enduring war. Therefore, I say it's imperative that the Australian Defence Force doesn't take its foot off the Taliban's throat.

He paused again. Stared down the barrel of a nearby camera lens. It flashed and stunned his eyes. He blinked, then continued.

We all must play our part: every soldier, sailor, airman, and white-collar staff to elect the right candidate who can bring this terrible war to a close. Australia must plot its way back home, and the prime opportunity is standing right in front of you!

Daisy kicked at the concrete floor with the tips of his boots. His face burned red and his temples were thumping. While outside the camp, the sandstorm was boiling.

The Minister looked worried, too. He kept glancing at the doorway, then took up his water bottle and rushed it to his mouth.

Before I jet, he said, I'd like to invite Major General Steele to the lectern.

The General from the Herc-flight into the country stepped up to the lectern. He'd rolled his shirtsleeves too, exposing a fat, gold wristwatch.

Shit, Daisy, I recognise that bastard from the flight over.

He sure is a long way from the Burj, hey, Bubba.

Tell me about it, I said. They don't call those bastards five-star for nothing.

The Minister continued.

For those of you unaware, General Steele has been a driving force behind Australia's efforts, here in Afghanistan. So, it's my honour to award him with the Distinguished Service Medal.[101]

The attaché handed the Minister a small, black vinyl case, wrapped in a white cardboard sheath.

He removed the sheath, then opened the box and removed the medal. It was silver, with a red and white ribbon, and the Minister pinned it to the Major General's chest.

The PR cameras flashed. The medal sparkled, as did the gold watch, and everybody clapped.

The Major General raised his hand in the air to hush the crowd.

The hut fell silent, and the General spoke.

What the hell's he saying, Bubba?

Fucked if I know, I said, looking out over the dust clouds. They were now burgeoning over the camp's perimeter fence.

Are there any questions, said the Major General, for me or for the Minister?

The Minister shook his head and waved his arms as the dust storm sprawled closer. No questions, he muttered, then turned

---

101   The DSM is awarded to ADF members for distinguished leadership in war-like operations.

to the SF soldiers. I need to get out of here, fast, he said. These conditions are not safe.

The two SF soldiers jumped to it, and escorted the Minister from the hut, then ushered him to the VIP accommodation.

The Major General wished us all well for the rest of our deployments. Then dismissed us… right as the storm got too close.

Every soldier dispersed, all two to three hundred of them.

Jack was nowhere in sight.

What do we do now, Bubba?

I don't know, I said. Probably should go and find Gabe?

Screw him, said Daisy, that boy's too dumb to get into any trouble. He's probably asleep and if he had his way, he'd sleep through this whole fucking war if he didn't have to eat his three square a day.

I laughed.

Let's go sit this one out in the rec-hut.

Daisy smiled, so the rec-hut is where we went next.

The storm's cleared, Daisy said, poking his head out the rec-hut door. Wanna grab a cuppa, Bubba?

I could slay one, I said, then we walked to the coffee hut.

The dust was still settling. It coated everywhere, and everything and climbed up my nose when I tried to breathe.

When we reached Green Beans there was a line-up a hundred meters long. On account of the storm, the dust and the great line-up, I couldn't see the coffee hut front door.

Bubba, when you're old you'll be able to tell your grandkids how the Mid-East was hard fought and won.

Hell, I said, looking at my watch, it was nearing tea. On second thoughts, I'll skip the beans or else I won't sleep tonight.

Really? said Daisy. I hardly ever have trouble sleeping… even here. And, if I get a little edgy, I take melatonin…it's way better than codeine. Have you tried it?

Codeine?

No, Bubba, melatonin. It helps with sleep.

We joined the coffee line.

The only thing that works better is a quick pull. I tell you, Bubba, nothing eases the stress of a hard day's war faster than a quick pull.

So, I've heard. I just don't believe it.

A little hard in shared accommodation, though.

I can imagine.

Well, that's why I take melatonin.

I laughed.

Hey, Bubba… look at that.

What?

Daisy cocked his head to the side.

I turned. Major General and the Defence Minister were walking down the line, towards the coffee hut. They were talking out loud.

I can't stand this place, said the Minister, I don't know how you do it.

Ahh, said the Major General. We do what we have to do. We'll be back in Dubai tomorrow.

Have you thought more about shrinking the base defences and scaling back the troops? The coalition government needs the budget space—it's very important?

It's on the cards, Steve, but that call will have to wait. I don't want to be in-country when the troops find out.

They'll jack-up, no doubt.

Yes, said Major General Steele, that they will.

Well, said the Minister. Fuck them.

At half-four, the line to the coffee hut hadn't moved.

The Minister and the Major General had slunk back to their accommodation.

At a quarter to five, the doors closed and the barista posted a sign: *All out of beans; will return next week.*

The Officers in the line jacked up. They were all less than impressed and vocally displayed their displeasure; in ways that only the Commissioned ranks can.

What'll we do now? said an Air Force Flight Lieutenant. One fucking WEEK? I can't work under these conditions. Let's go speak with the union rep.

God damn Air Force, said an Army Captain, spitting at the ground.

The line dispersed.

Daisy and I turned and headed back to the compound. Our day was over. Or so we thought.

At ten to five, the sirens sounded.

Incoming, incoming, incoming. Take cover now.

We rushed to a nearby concrete barrier and hit the deck.

The skies were quiet. I couldn't see a damn thing through the dust still hovering over the camp. After a storm, the dust took days to settle.

What a time for an attack.

It's the perfect time, said Daisy.

Then the rockets hit.

GABE.

HO! BUBBA!

We both ran—

I Thought You Were Quitting

No one saw a lot of Jack, not after he thought Gabe got hit.

Gabe was fine—of course—and they moved him back to Al Minhad, where he'd spend the last days of the war, recuperating, before going home a hero. Yes, Veteran's Affairs were going to give him a handsome payday.

His face was even printed on the cover of the *Courier Mail.*

The real fact of the matter is the bomb landed some one-hundred and fifty feet away. It startled Gabe, that's all.

The kid stumbled and broke his wrist.

It was far from a firefight. Not that it mattered anything, it was still a mighty blast.

Mum's the word, said Daisy. And we kept Gabe's mishap hush-hush.

Jack, who never learnt the real truth, blamed himself for ordering Gabe to guard that container, alone.

He carried the guilt of it everywhere he went, and it pained him to show his face.

Shouldn't we tell him, Daisy?

No way, he said and laughed. That's a Digger's prerogative.

Our jobs didn't change after that. We simply carried on maintaining the compound, and the same war rolled on and Daisy would challenge me to see if I knew what day it was.

Friday, I'd say.

Well, of course it's Friday, Bubba, but what date is it?

Christ, I don't know, I'm not a damned calendar.

Then Daisy would grumble and start pushing the tired old broom through the never-ending dust which coated the paths.

The dust storms continued, for days on end. The choppers still flew of course, and the Afghan dust always found some path in and up your nose.

Fuck this, said Daisy one day. Let's go see Baker and see what that bastard is talking about.

I snatched the broom handle from his hands, then threw it against the wall.

No way, fella, I said. That Baker's not some lid[102] you can jerk around. You won't like him one single bit!

Ho, Bubba. We'll have to see about that.

We slung our rifles. Slipped on our hats. And as two green Apache banked hard overhead, Daisy and I trundled off to Headquarters.

A locked steel gate secured the HQ compound.

I pressed the buzzer.

Who is it? said a voice through a speaker.

Corporals Patterson and Daisy, Sir.

What do you want?

Here to see Serg Baker, Sir.

There was a pause.

Sergeant Baker? What the hell do you wanna see him for?

---

102   Colloquial term for a soldier with better than no experience, but not yet considered a senior soldier. He may or may not still be susceptible to peer-to-peer skulduggery.

God only knows, Sir, he invited us up.

The gate unlocked.

Come in, said the voice, but don't make too much noise.

Baker stood behind three horizontal rows of plasma screens. They were displaying live drone footage of Tarin Kowt and some outlying villages.

It was dark throughout the building, and Baker held an unlit cigarette between his lips.

A small, white bottle of pills sat on a table right by his side.

Welcome boys, he said, what took you so damn long?

Daisy looked up at the screens, and all that he could see was dirt, motor cars, a dry riverbed and a stray donkey.

Is this it, Bubba? This is what you were talking about?

Baker pinched the cigarette between his fingers and smiled.

You should have been here last night… the entire town was alive, and we've got these drones up everywhere. It's like a live episode of Deadwood out there, boys, and we never miss a scene.

An Officer walked out from a back room. He was wearing a pair of dark sunglasses, despite, or even in-spite of, the darkness that blanketed the room.

Sergeant Baker, who are these gentlemen, and why are they in my HQ?

Oh, said Baker, these are some old digs of mine. I'm just showing them around.

So long as they're quiet, said the Officer, before pausing. Sergeant Baker… I thought you were quitting? He jerked his head towards Baker's hands.

I am, Sir said Baker, then he put the unlit cigarette back in his mouth and turned to the plasma screens.

A drone camera zoomed in on an alleyway. It switched to white-hot infra-red.

A woman ran out from a Quora. She was wearing a burqa. The long flowing gown showed up black on the plasma screens.

Other parts of her body glowed white, like her chest, midriff, and shoulders. White-hot air blew from mouth as she ran along the alleyway. Four men were in pursuit.

Ha, said Baker, this sheila's gonna get wrecked.

The men caught her right outside an open Quora.

One man punched her in the face; she refused to fall.

Daisy winced. I don't know if I want to see this, Bubba—

A second tore off her veil, then kicked her to the ground, where they ripped her gown apart.

They're going to *fucking* rape her. Daisy looked around, *crazy*.

No shit, said Baker. They'll fuck anything that moves over here. They'll fuck goats. They'll fuck donkeys and horses. They'll fuck small boys, if the mood's right, they'll even fuck each other. But this? This here is punishment. Straight-up sharia law. It happens all the time. It's their way of *justice and order*.

And we just sit here and *watch*?!

Yep, said Baker. Social intervention is not part of our mission… besides, it's their laws. We don't have a say on the matter.

I couldn't stop looking at the screen. There were people in the back of the room laughing. A clock on the wall struck five and the screens went blank.

That's enough fun, everybody, said the Officer. Why don't you all go outside and get some fresh air.

I stepped outside. The air was full of heat and dust. I rubbed my eyes closed, then opened them.

I was still in Afghanistan.

RABIES

It was too hot for dinner, and I was too hungry to sleep, so I skipped the mess hall. Skipped the accommodation. The rec-hut and the gym held no appeal, so I slinked to the work compound.

Nobody would ever find me there.

I was wrong.

Daisy was sitting in the yard. He had the tin lid down and covered it with a layer of fresh milk. Three kittens lapped at the bowl's edge, while the mother cat sat back and preened her inner thigh.

Where'd you get that milk?

Stole it from HQ, Bubba, what's it to you?

I picked up the one litre of Paul's full cream from Daisy's side. It was half empty.

The entire camp's living on long life milk and you're feeding fresh full cream to some stray cats?

We've all gotta eat, said Daisy. He stood and walked to the chain-link fence. Pressed his face against the steel, chain link wire and stared at his football, resting on the dirt outside the fence.

It was losing air, and its colour, tarnished by the wind, the dust and the sun.

Why'd you join the Army, Bubba?

Why?

Yeah? We all got our reason, right?

Hell, Daisy. I've long forgotten why, but I guess it must've felt like a good idea at the time.

Daisy left the fence and returned to the kittens.

The bowl was empty.

He picked up the milk, sipped from the bottle, then topped up the bowl. The kittens turned away. Then, with their bellies bloated, rolled onto their backs and stretched out their legs.

A good idea, huh? Daisy took another sip from the bottle. Well, I guess that makes us about the same.

Would you have changed your mind… in hindsight?

Ha! Nah. It never pays to look behind. The past is dead, Bubba. We've made our beds and the only thing from here is to see it through. Live to fight another day, right?

What the hell are you two doing? said Jack, charging into the yard with a scowl upon his face. I've been looking for you everywhere.

Haven't left this compound for the past two hours, said Daisy, sipping at his milk blatantly. I don't know where else we're supposed to be?

What the… where'd you get that milk?

It was a gift.

Bullshit. From who?

Patterson's friend… Serg Baker.

What the fuck was he doing down here?

Beats me, said Daisy, then he emptied the last of the bottle.

Jack plotted his way around the yard. He inspected the concrete path for dust. Checked the container for security, then walked to the fence to see if Daisy's ball was still outside the yard.

He kicked the milk bowl. The tin lid scuttled, spilling out the milk across the path.

What the hell's that out here for?

The kittens, said Daisy, pointing to the shipping container.

One kitten and the mother cat crawled from beneath the container and moved towards the bowl.

Ahh, said Jack, raising his rifle. Those things all have rabies.

It isn't a problem if they don't bite and they only bite if they're scared.

Bullshit. I want them gone from my yard.

And how do you suppose we do that, Sir?

I DON'T KNOW. Chase them out with the broom or something.

Daisy looked at the kittens. They were back hiding beneath the container while ants scrounged through the milk.

The mother cat sat and watched Jack through its one good eye, then meowed and licked its paws.

Jacked kicked his boot on the path towards the cat and sent a small cloud of dust in the air. The mother cat did not move.

Stop fucking *feeding* it, said Jack, picking up the empty bowl.

Daisy didn't answer, and Jack slapped the bowl against his thigh. It made a 'tinging' sound, then Jack turned for the gate.

The mother cat followed, running by Jack's side, meowing and looking at the tin bowl.

Go on, GET! said Jack. He kicked the cat's side. The cat hissed, then begun clawing for the bowl.

FARKING RABIES, screamed Jack, suddenly frightened. He raised his rifle with his right finger curled over the trigger, like an eagle's claw. Then he squeezed. *Bang.*

Daisy lifted the cat's limp carcass by the tail. Its jaw dropped open, and its tongue hang out one side as blood dripped onto the path.

He threw it in the bin and closed the lid. All the kittens watched from beneath the container. Daisy wiped his hands on a sheet of paper towel. Grabbed another tin lid, put it on the ground, then looked at me.

I hate that bastard, Bubba.

I nodded, and we both sat and watched the kittens come crawling into the open once again.

FEE-FI-FO-FUM

The rifle shot was heard across the entire camp. Jack couldn't explain his way out of it. Couldn't blame it on the Taliban, either. For fuck's sake… he killed a cat.

The Base Commander wouldn't buy any excuses—not for a minute—and the next morning he had the young Subaltern standing at attention.[103]

This is flagrant disregard for weapons discipline, said the Commander. Plus, I knew you were skiving off the moment one of your own team was knocked by that blast.

SIR. That was a blatant misunderstanding.

Semantics.

The Commander stood. Placed on his hat then opened the office door.

The next flight outs in two days, he said, and I've got no choice but to send your entire team home. I suggest using that time getting your team in order.

YES, SIR.

---

103   Standing at, or to attention is a fundamental drill position; however, the term may be used, in military jargon, to describe someone who is confronted, by a superior, for disciplinary reasons.

Daisy and I were in the accommodation, where I was pretending to read.

The truth? I was thinking of Sylvia. Where she was. What she'd be doing. Whether she'd be thinking of me.

Bubba. I've got an idea that'll wash away those end of deployment blues.

What? I said.

Daisy flipped the lid on his green Army trunk. Dove to the bottom then came back out holding a bottle of whiskey in his hands.

Whiskey? It's two in the afternoon.

Yeah, so? It's always midnight somewhere in the world.

He cracked the cap.

Besides, what are they gonna do? Send us home?

It was thirty minutes from dinner, and the bottle was half empty when I took it from Daisy's hands and held it up to the light. Tilted it to one side. Rotated the bottle then watched the small bubbles inside rise to the top of the amber spirits.

You gonna fuck that bottle, or you gonna drink it?

I wiped the lip of the bottle, then took a sip.

You wanna know what the best thing about it is, Daisy?

What?

In this heat, we'll sweat the booze out by morning.

Then I guess you best be handing back that bottle, Bubba.

I did, then we moved outside and sat on the accommodation balcony.

It was a steel cage more than anything, prison-like in appearance, with shrapnel holes in the roof and floor. A hard mesh wrapped around it, with holes in it only big enough to poke your eyeballs through.

The balcony looked Nor-East towards the long, sharp mountain ranges. Its ragged ascents shimmering a golden pale that only a mountain goat or a mad sherpa could endure.

It was beautiful, calm and peaceful, save for tired sounds of war.

Daisy had soon fallen asleep, his arms folded across his chest. The bottle rested in the crook of his elbow.

I took the bottle and left him there, happy, content, sleepful and wild.

My head long ejected any further thoughts of war, and my soul was halfway home. The bottle was almost empty and my eyes were seeing double. Then these boot steps came up the stairs. I giggled to myself, thinking they matched the rhythm of fee-fi-fo-fum. A fucking giant coming into this shithole tin.

They stopped at the top of the stairs.

You're a goddamned embarrassment to the uniform.

The voice hit heavy clatter, but I didn't move. An arm reached out and gripped me by the collar.

Get off your ass and explain yourself.

I stood. I staggered and swayed with the whisky bottle dangling by my side. I opened my eyes and saw Jack standing there with fire in his eyes.

Well?

What?

Well, why are you drinking my whiskey?

I dropped the bottle. It bounced across the steel floor but did not break.

What's it matter? I laughed. This fucking trip is useless… it was from the start. Gabe is gone… and Davis too. So—

Jack's grip tightened on my collar. He pulled me in close until we were touching, nose to nose.

I don't need this crap, Patterson. I've got enough heat purring up my arse, because of Daisy and those fucking cats. You'll both be on a charge.

Ha! Charge us, it'll never stick. You're the laughingstock anyway.

Yeah? said Jack and shook me with both arms, his spit flying into my face.

I pushed him back.

He stumbled. Steadied, then raised his fist.

I raised mine too. Stepped forward and swung. Missed. Fell, then landed on my arse.

An embarrassment, sneered Jack, and he walked back down the stairs.

Daisy and I never saw him again.

Don't Look Back

It was a Friday afternoon, and the sky was clear and beaming out its brightest blue.

Sylvia parked her car outside the Gallipoli Barracks' gate. She sat on the edge of the car fender and watched as a stream of cars trickled in through the gate. They were full of families, all arriving to welcome a squadron of soldiers' home.

For Sylvia, the families were far from her mind. She'd come to see one person only and turned her back on the traffic, then punched a number into her phone.

The phone rang out. Its dull green micro-bit screen went blank. Sylvia closed the phone and walked to a nearby telephone pole.

Activists had stapled it, top to bottom, with throwaway flyers. She read them all, then tore the biggest flyer off for a closer look.

NO MORE WAR
Bring our
Soldiers
Home.

She scrunched the flyer into a ball and tossed it in the gutter. Those activists are selling their message in the wrong place, she said, looking back at the gate.

She dialled the number, one last time. It rang out, then she climbed back into her car and turned the key.

The phone sat blank, on the passenger seat. She shifted the car into reverse, then drive. The car rolled forward.

Sylvia did not look back.

Praying for Rain

Rain hadn't fallen in days. My mouth was dry. The sun's rays were vile, and the heat had me dreaming of desert waterfalls.

I held my compass up to the northern horizon. Adjusted the dial to a modest three hundred and fifty-five degrees. Then plugged my way on that bearing, through the wild, Outback scrub.

There wasn't a camel in sight.

I whistled and called for Penny: Whoo-up, come here, girl. But she never came, that bitch.

The short, bushy growth groped around my shinbones. Its foliage looked lush from afar, but cut like shattered glass as I dragged my bones through its undergrowth.

My trousers were all tor, and blood seeped out of the lacerations that lashed my legs.

The Outback had devoured me; I was down to skin and bone. It had almost taken my mind too.

I opened my drying mouth into a silent scream. The sky, the bush, the bull dust, Penny and the rest of those damn camels. It was all part of a plot against me. *What a laugh... the Great Sher Gul... finest cameleer of the Outback. He's a monkey's arse.*

They were right, of course. I had nowhere to turn, nowhere to go, and all I held was Miriam's handkerchief and a compass that no longer worked. I was lost. Led by my own intrepid delusions and hopes that I could make it through this burning country on my own.

What a foolish notion that was. The Great Sher Gul, king of the frontier, in a place where the desert is his home. Now begging, crying out loud, scratching at his arms and legs in desperation. No woman. No camel. No home and no bloody hope.

I sat in the shade and sucked on a pistachio nut, staring across the desert's hot plains beyond the Outback horizon. It was wild and pink and cared for no one.

Still, it wasn't the Outback, or the heat, the snakes, spiders, or crocodiles that killed a man. It was the quiet desperation, that race not to die out here alone.

I dropped another pistachio nut on the tip of my tongue. Then prayed for rain.

An Abusive Lover

Back in Australia, nothing had changed. It never changed, and the further and longer I was away, the only thing that did change was perspective. My single viewpoint transmogrified. People seemed impatient and less interested with anything but themselves. Yet, they always appeared to be heading somewhere, to meet with someone else.

I felt like a stranger, on friendly soil. Like I never truly came *home*. Not to the same place, at least.

The Commanding Officer gave me the option of visiting the Padre or the psychiatrist.

It's only protocol, he said. Gotta tick the boxes for the medical board.[104] He wrapped his knuckles on the desk. Can't boot out an

---

104   Upon repatriation, soldiers will pass through a period of decompression. Designed to re-acclimatise them home life, and in order to prevent them 'wigging out' on a family member, the soldier will go through medical and psychological screening, all while confined to the barracks environment.

Although the psychological screening is a valuable process, a more stoic, or macho soldier might avoid treating these sessions with sincerity, all in order to avoid having that psych mark against their name. On the other hand, the ADF will not medically discharge a soldier until all rehabilitation measures are exhausted. This might be in stark contrast to what the commanding officer believes is best for the soldier. After all, there's nothing a call to 'Soldier On' cannot fix.

unfit soldier—wanna make sure mothers can still recognise their babies—now that the war's over.[105]

I went for the Padre, he seemed, to me, the least insane but even that was a stretch.

I knocked on the Padre's door.

Come in, he said.

I walked in. Hesitated, then saluted.

Ah, cut out that AJ crap, he said, stepping out from behind an old timber desk. Come. Come in, shut the fucken door behind you. Too many God damned ears out prowling those hallways.

Roger that, Padre.

I took off my slouch hat and rest edit on the Padre's timber desk.

Whiskey?

It's ten in the morning?

Yeah, well, it'll help you get a head start on the rest of your day.

Padre walked past an open window towards a locked cabinet. The sun was shining through a dark tinted glass pane. It highlighted his red rum nose. His hands were shaking, but they steadied as he turned the cabinet door handle.

He took out a half empty bottle of Laphraoig Twenty-Five and two crystal glasses.

---

105   For the purposes of Health and Safety, Commanding Officers (a CEO equivalent) are subject to Commonwealth Law; however, in war-like conditions, such as Afghanistan, Commonwealth Health and Safety regulations can be wavered—for obvious reasons. Therefor, an order that leads to a soldier's death is an unfortunate consequence of war. If there is any apparent negligence, leading to death or casualty, the Inspector General of the ADF would carry out an internal investigation that could lead to formal disciplinary action; eg, a court marshal, or dismissal.
Duty of care is a whole separate matter and, as it's the duty of a Commanding Officer to adequately train, prepare and provide provisions for the soldiers to carry out their duties, any such responsibility generally ceases once the final siren sounds. Then, upon a soldier's separation, from the ADF, a Commanding Officer will wipe his/her hands clean and the soldier may, or may not become familiar with the Department of Veterans Affairs.

How've they been treating you, anyhow, son?

Alright, I guess.

Anything you want to talk about.

I sniffed the Laphraoig. The alcohol burnt my nose hairs. The scent of vanilla, smoke and apple soon replaced the smell of alcohol.

I'd never drank expensive whiskey before and was cautious with the first sip.

It tasted much the same as it smelt, and I put the glass down on Padre's desk.

No, Padre. I can't think of anything.

Okay then, he said. How about Afghanistan?

What about it?

I understand you had some kinda altercation? he read off a piece of paper. With your Lieutenant?

So, the story goes, I said and sipped my whiskey.

The Padre finished his in a single mouthful. He lifted the bottle, then refilled his glass to the brim.

Tell me more, he said.

A wall clock ticked loudly, almost comically. The hand seemed to move counter clockwise, and thumped like a killer migraine, chiselling through the top of my skull.

I finished my glass.

The Padre sat across from me, waiting for a response.

What's there to tell?

Well, he said, you know they're talking of booting you out. Why don't you start there?

I didn't speak, and just sat looking into the bottom of my whiskey glass, thinking how hard it was to quit the Army. How hard it was to let go. And how for all those years I spent rolling in the green, madly showing up like an abused lover scared to bail on the relationship and kept coming back for more.

Deep in my heart, I still loved it though.

But now, it was my brain telling me, *it was time to patch-out.*[106] *You don't belong here anymore. They don't want you. You've outgrown this job.*

Go. NOW. Leave everything behind. Identity. Rank. All your sacrifices and friendships. The lot. Just go!

None of that mattered anymore. Not in my own naïve state of ignorance, and knowing that I could have left, of course—at any time—but not without dragging all that baggage behind me.

That was a soldier's cross to bear, of course. It was never 'just a job'.[107]

Padre topped up my glass, then his own.

Well, he said, I can understand why you don't wanna talk. You boys never seem to wanna. Not to anyone outside your tight bubbles, at least. But you know, Patterson, my door's always open… at least until they toss you out.

Appreciate that, Padre, I said, and finished my glass. I put my hat on. Stood and then turned to leave.

One last question, said the Padre. What're you planning on doing after the Army?

I don't know. Guess there's some family I'd better catch up with. People I haven't seen in years.

The Padre poured himself one more glass.

He smiled.

---

106   Slang. To pack up and leave.

107   It's often quipped that it's harder to get out of the Army than it is to get in. This is, of course, dependant on the individual; however, separation from a job that is bound by indoctrination, rites of passage, camaraderie and honour so much of a soldier's identity can become defined by the uniform. For better, or worse, the individual has been forever transformed. Yet, when they separate from the military much of this is torn away from them, and the individual will struggle to move on with their lives.

Yurlunggur

It wasn't the cold which woke me during the night, but the sudden down-pouring of rain. And God, it fell like an avalanche, thicker than a tidal wave, crushing the Outback to life.

I rolled myself over in the dark corner of an earthen hole and dragged a sheet of torn canvas over my eyes.

The rain finally abated by daybreak. Across the soaked desert landscape, the flood waters spread to the East, and to the West and well beyond the horizon, leaving me stranded on a lonely desert island.

It was still some several days walk until I'd reach Darwin and find Miriam. I'd either have to swim or wait until the waters receded. I opened my knapsack and peeled a pistachio shell. Chewed on it, then went back to sleep.

The sun peaked overhead, turning my telluric abode into a cranky little steam pot. It was enough to make me swell up like a clam.

I watched the waters slowly shrinking, then held my compass to my left eye. Squinted through its, now cracked quartz prism and adjusted my bearing for Darwin.

The needle spun wild, meaning it couldn't tell North from South. I banged the hard brass casing against a rock until it stopped and landed at 360 degrees.

Maybe we'll make it after all, Sher Gul, I said, talking to the blue opening in the sky. I was seeing double from the heat. The starvation. And the great hopelessness of prayer.

I had abandoned hope of ever hearing the voice from any God, Buddha, Allah or whoever the hell was up there, not bothering to listen to me. Whoever or whatever they were, they are cruel masters of the imagination. Fictional forces, alas. Man had to find his own forsaken way. He's free to navigate his own way through and, if he could not, then he should be left to his own demise. And so goes the holy way… meaning the ignorant among us have some case to answer for; we're just too stupid to know it.

I rubbed my eyes to focus them. Nope, there was a man, dark-skinned, walking across the water. He'd painted his body, head to toe in white clay and carried a long spear in his right hand.

I studied him, reassuring myself this wasn't some apparition sent to test my blasphemous thoughts. But who else could walk upon water? Only gods and the deceased wield that kind of power.

STOP, I said, and held out a foot-long branch. I have a gun!

George, said the dark-skinned man. I knew that was you. Only a mad Afghani would be stupid enough to walk out here alone.

Who are you? What-you talkin' about? I'll shoot!

The man laughed before stopping and putting his hands in the air. It's me, George. Charlie, from back in Adelaide.

I dropped the branch. It tumbled and rolled down the rock ledge.

What are you doing up here?

Charlie got closer. I could see his eyes, clear through all the white clay spread across his face. He smiled and his teeth glowed a miraculous pearly white.

This is my home, he said and pointed the head of his spear West, then South, East and to the North.

All this is yours?

Yep. What's left of it, anyway. My country. But the bloody white fella and the Gub makin' sure it gets smaller every day.

At sundown, Charlie had a small fire burning with dry branches we'd collected. The sky was clear, dark, with bright stars glowing way out beyond a point where any man could imagine.

It's so beautiful, I said.

Yep, said Charlie, dumping a dead, fat goanna across the fire.

You're going to eat that?

Yep, said Charlie. You gotta be crazier than them white fellas if yer thinking of surviving out here with no food.

Charlie cooked the goanna until it was charcoal black. It smelt like oily chicken and he tore off the hind legs, exposing chicken-white meat.

He gnashed the leg down to the bone, then tossed it on to the fire.

Where's your camel?

Penny?

Yeah… and the other fellas?

Oh, I said, pointing out in front of me. Penny is somewhere out there and the men are headed for Darwin.

Charlie laughed. Hope they all got a better sense of direction than you. North is bloody that way.

The night grew chilly.

Charlie sat at the fire's edge. His eyes glowed, and he watched silently as the small embers floated away into nothingness.

How do your people survive out here? I said. I see no food, but you're always eating. Sometimes, I see no water, but you're never thirsty. And you have no compass, but you're never lost.

Charlie lifted his gaze and looked my way.

Back in the beginning, he said, what my people call the Dreaming, this land was flat and sleeping. Then Yurlunggur… the rainbow serpent… came down from the sky and gave birth to all the rivers and the lakes.[108] She gave life to all the trees. The plants. The animals. All that obeyed Yurlunggur took human form.

Charlie shifted from his seat, then with a long branch, stoked the fire.

My people have lived here for a very long time. We cared for the land, and she cared for us.[109] She's our teacher, and we listen.[xiv] There's much to learn. But one day, that learning will all disappear. Or maybe it won't. I don't know.

I didn't say a word; my belief in a god held no comparison to that. Then Charlie laid down on one side of the fire. And the flames continued to flicker and crackle until we both fell asleep.

---

108   A potent deity in Aboriginal religion.
109   Land is very important to the Aboriginal people, with the common belief of "we don't own the land, the land owns us". They hold a deep connection with the land, and because of this, many will not leave their land.

BY MY SIDE

In the morning, Charlie was up like a jackrabbit and delivered me a firm kick in the guts.

The sun was big and bright, and the sky was back to her peaceful blue self, but the heat remained. The heat sucked up the previous day's rain, leaving behind nothing but a dry, crackling desert bed.

C'mon, George, Charlie said with a smile and pointed North. Darwin's thatter-way.

I rolled up my mat, then went digging head-first through my bag searching for some tea.

Sure you don't want a hot brew first, Charlie? It'll keep you cool?

Charlie mounted the crooked rock ledge. Raised his nostrils to soak in the clear desert air, then glanced towards the South.

Nah, he said. Don't need tea. I travel Black-fella way.[110][xv]

He winked at me, then climbed off the ledge, with one eye locked on the South.

I was curious and had to take a peek, but as I turned South, all I could see was umber dirt and a rustling in the trees.

What is it?

Charlie did not answer, but there was a look of calm upon his face.

Is there someone out there, Charlie?

---

110   An ideology and practice in the Aboriginal community.

He turned his attention North. Looked up at the sky and down at the dry desert bed and at the trees blowing in the wind, and winked at me. Then nodded.

Your mob will be up here soon, he said, but not before the next big rain.

He picked up his spear and began walking, North.

I stowed my tea back in my bag, then followed.

It was still a long way to go, and I'd tucked Miriam's handkerchief beneath my collar.

No matter how far away, I thought, she'll always be by my side.

DADIRRI

Charlie walked light footed across the blistering desert floor. He'd stop only on occasions, where he'd start smelling through the trees and listening to the sounds in the air.

There were birds singing. They swooped from tree to tree, hunting for shade. Or some kind of tiny desert morsel to eat, all while avoiding the sun's rays.

Moments of stillness and pure silence followed.

Charlie would stop, and turn his ears to the ground, and then his nose to the sky as vast waves of nothing carried over us. Here, I suspect, is where he'd heard the most.

What is the Black-fella way? I said.

I'll show you, said Charlie. Then he continued North.

Charlie knew his way through the bush. Although I was only plucking at straws, I suspected this was the Black-fella way. But there were times I'd stopped and questioned his methods.

Like in the early afternoon, when the sun peaked, I looked to the East. Then the West. Then stopped and looked at Charlie.

Wait a minute, I said, pointing to what I knew was North. Isn't Darwin that way?

Charlie paid me no mind and continued walking. But then he stopped. Cocked his leg, then farted.

You smell that? he said with a wide smile perched across his face.

Yes, I said, it smells like last night's dinner. Why'd you do that?

You are standing downwind just like them other mob. They can smell us from miles away. So… we go West… then North and lose the trail. That's the Black-fella way.

I stood behind him and shook my head. It was genius and I never questioned him again.

Charlie knelt by a small shrub. He was holding a pointed branch in one hand and dug into the dirt.

Hey, George, come over here, he said.

And I did.

He dropped the branch, then started scraping away at the soil with the stubs of his fingers. It left behind a small hole and revealed long, white, fleshy shrub roots.

With a small rock's jagged edge, he began carving away at the roots, until the plant broke away. He held it to the sunlight.

It was moist.

Watery juices trickled down Charlie's forearm and then he fed it into his mouth.

Djubac,[111][xvi] he said, chomping away at the moist, flowers. Tastes better cooked but out here if ya hungry, taste don't matter.

I agreed and sucked and chewed on a bud that was yet to bloom.

It left my mouth wet and refreshed, then I ate some more.

---

111   Prasophyllum Sargentti, known as Djubac to the First Nation Noongar peoples of South-Western Australia. It is a tall orchid with a single smooth, tubular leaf and up to thirty or more purplish and white or golden brown and white flowers with a frilled labellum.

Charlie pushed the soil and back filled the hole, then sat and looked towards the sky.

I looked at Charlie. He was calm and happy, as though he wanted for nothing.

How did you know there would be food down there?

Dadirri.[112][xvii] If you look. And if you listen, he said, and scanned the horizon, then closed his eyes. This land will tell you most things.

I closed my eyes and held my breath so I could hear better. Then I lifted my nose and smelt the air.

You smell that, George?

SMOKE!

True, said Charlie, pointing his finger, South. Your mob got a small camp over there to spend the night.

Then we should move, I said. I want to be far away from them. Not safe for me.

A breeze swirled and lifted over our heads, blowing wisps of sand across the plains. Birds sang out loud, cackling tones, and small creases formed across Charlie's forehead. Then they burst out from the trees and spread their wings, flapping across the desert sky.

Charlie stood. He listened for the wind. Watched the birds flocking South, then pointed his arm signalling our direction.

He took up his spear. Me, my bag, and we both continued West.

---

112   Inner deep listening and quiet, still awareness and waiting.

THE ARMY WAY

It was a Monday morning, and I was back in the breezeway again, fresh from getting busted back to Private.

Not that the demotion mattered. It was a knuckle-wrap more than anything, and, in the soldierly sense, I knew I was knocking on death's door. Demotion only made the death slow and painful. The Army intended to make every last day hurt.

The breezeway was alive with the sounds of brooms pushing along the concrete floor. Tools clanged. Young diggers swore. A Corporal ordered them all about, using language so foul it would make a sailor blush.

That much I was going to miss, I thought as I bent to tighten my right boot laces.

An ant crawled along the bridge of my left boot, and I flicked it away.

A young Sergeant stood over me, before I could finish the last knot.

Private, he said, why is your boot lace undone?

I don't know, Serge… sometimes they do that.

Not if you fasten them to correct Military Protocol, as per the Army Standing Orders for Dress.[113]

---

113   A formal document that intensively details the standards of dress which apply to the entire Australian Regular Army. Set punishments are applied for failure to comply with these orders.

I looked down at my bootlaces. I'd fastened the left bootlaces with a double bow. I'd intended to do the same with the right.

I can see my mistake, Sergeant.

Good, then FIX IT, he said, then walked off.

I tied off the right bootlace.

Some parts I would not miss.

After the morning parade, I picked up the broom and started sweeping. I began at one end, moving along until the piles of dust grew too big for the broom to move. There were leaves in the pile. Dirt. Dust. A frayed shoelace. A dead mouse and a five-cent piece.

I stepped around the pile. Then, with a single push of the broom handle, I began a new pile.

The Troop Sergeant poked his head out into the breezeway.

He looked down at my boots, but I had my trousers—as per standing orders—bloused over the double bows I'd tied.

Private Patterson, when you're done, the Troop Commander wants to see you.

Me, Serg?

Yes. You. Fuckwit.

Did they say what for?

No one gives a crap what for, Private… just hurry the hell up.

I sat in the hallway, outside the Troop Commander's office. It used to be Jack's office, but he was now gone because of the Army's revolving door culture.[114] Leadership and Development were

---

114   The average posting cycle for a soldier and officer is 2-3 years, therefore it's not uncommon for a soldier to have multiple commanders in a short period of time.

passing buzzwords that relegated everybody to just another number in the queue. Some left their mark, while others attempted to play God. But most just did their job and kept the seats warm for the next man in the queue. The rest were just arseholes. Egomaniacs, control freaks, and all hell bent on revenge for a lifetime's worth of bullying. Or for always being the last picked on the football team. They were the fastest at promotion and I'd met them all.

The hallway space was narrow, and the floor was a dark blue linoleum. A janitor mopped from one end to the next, and I lifted my boots as he slowly moved past.

The janitor didn't lift his gaze, he didn't smile, and the mop went gliding past.

The hallway became quiet, so I knocked on the Troop Commander's door.

WAIT, said the voice, and I sat back in my chair.

Five minutes passed, then the door swung open.

A young soldier walked out, carrying in his hand a sheet of A4 paper. He scrunched it into a ball and threw it at the wall.

The door closed behind him, and he walked up close to my ear and whispered.

Been back from leave for barely a minute, already the LT wants to chuck me on a promotion course. Fuck.

No shit, I said. You'd think that'd be a good thing.

Yeah, well, we know better, right?

Right, I said, and the young soldier walked away.

Private Patterson. Come in.

I pushed open the door. A young subaltern sat and leant back in his chair. His arms folded across his narrow chest as he hid behind a computer screen.

I stopped at attention. Saluted with my right arm.

Don't bother sitting, he said, then rested his elbows on the desk. This'll only take a minute.

Ok, sir, I said. Then I looked around the room.

The walls were flat, boring and white. A lone brass plaque hung on the wall behind him that read:

AUSTRALIAN DEFENCE FORCE ACADEMY
For Leadership
Awarded to —

I didn't get to reading the name. I didn't care. And, for the moment, it didn't seem to matter. I adjusted my hat, tilting the brim downwards, until the plaque disappeared.

You know, it's both an honour and a privilege to wear that hat, said the LT.

My days in the uniform were running out, yet the hat gave me comfort. I'd keep it for as long as it would last. It was my identity but it represented so much more, and I clung tight to it, fearing such things were about to change.

I looked at the Subaltern and smiled.

Of course, not everyone deserves it, I thought. Almost nobody does, but we still thrust that weight of an ANZAC legacy upon our heads. Through our own volition, too, only to get told by some clown-child behind a desk that we hadn't earned it.

Of course, we fucking hadn't. Only the dead have the skin to claim such valour. Yet, here we all stand, beneath a Rising Sun[115] and glowing Southern Cross.

The Subaltern stacked several sheets of A4 on the centre of his desk. They were official military forms. Red tape. All with designated file numbers and military formatting, neat and rigid and aligned before him. It was sharp and pristine enough to

---

115   The Rising Sun is a highly valued insignia, worn by all ranks of Army, dating back to the Army's inception on 1ˢᵗ March 1901.

make a Sergeant Major crumble beneath the sheer size of his own throbbing hard-on.

The Subaltern measured twenty-five millimetres from the left edge of the sheet. Twice, then signed his name with a black biro and slid it across the desk.

Sign it, Private.

What is, Sir.

A notice to show cause. You're on your way out the door.

I knew the drill. I'd now been around long enough and seen it all before and signed without hesitation.

CO says you have six weeks left, Patterson. Use your time with smart intentions.

Roger that, Sir, I said, then threw out the perfect boxer. Turned, then walked out the door.

Shut the Knocker's Up

Friday morning was Regiment Battle PT.

Thursday afternoon was a compulsory boozer parade.

Only an Australian Soldier could find solace in that masochistic irony.

Some soldiers tried to refuse a drink.

What are you, a faggot? the Corporal would say.

No way, the soldier would reply.

Then get yourself a fucken beer. I don't trust nobody who doesn't enjoy a beer. And I won't tolerate anybody in my team who can't scull a beer.

Yes, Corporal, the soldier would say and off he'd trot and buy himself a beer. This is where it all started.

Come the morning parade, and the entire regiment would somehow be alive. Still half cut, but alive. Ready for the forthcoming hell where they'd sweat it out.

Daisy sat in the shade and smoked a cigarette, while he waited.

I'd never seen him smoke in all our time together. He was un-shaven, too, and he smelt like day-old beer.

Big night?

Fight with the missus.

I didn't know you had one—

Been dating for two weeks.

And already you're fighting?

Says she doesn't like me drinking… says she wants me to make a healthy start.

Say no more—

I took a seat beside him and watched all the young diggers warming themselves up for PT.

A soldier with shaved blonde hair got down and started doing push up. His shirt stretched tight across his chest. There was a Rising Sun and Corp emblem tattooed on his right arm. He stood, then stretched out his pecs, and great fat veins bulged across his forehead.

Bubba, I bet his turds have more muscle than I've in my entire body.

I laughed.

I'll never doing another push-up, again, after I discharge.

Daisy smiled, then sucked hard on his cigarette.

There was a violent heat and draining humidity which rose out from the footy fields of long green grass. I was sweating at the sight of it.

Daisy had stopped sweating and his face looked pale and clammy. He was dangerously dehydrated and looked ready to double over. The Troop Sergeant stood at the halfway line. There was a scent of slow death coursing through the ranks.

Stacks of truck tyres sat to the Sergeant's left. Copper logs, fifteen feet long, and fat hemp ropes sat to his right. And behind him were several green Land Rover trailers, each covered in a canvas tarp.

What the hell's inside those things, Bubba?

I don't know, I said. I felt sick.

The Sergeant blew a silver whistle and the entire regiment froze. SPLIT YOURSELVES INTO FOUR EVEN TEAMS. One team grabs the rope. One, the tyres, the logs, and the final on the trailers. We're going up the hill.

That's not a hill. That's a fucking mountain.

I laughed. Not because Daisy was funny but because he was right. There was no way the trailers, the logs and the tyres were going up that *hill*. The rope, yes, but the rest was a sick joke.

C'mon, I said, let's grab a rope.

We stood in even ranks. The rope draped across our right shoulders. It felt light, but the fun hadn't yet begun. The logs, the trailers, and the tyres weren't looking so confident.

The Sergeant blew his whistle.

PREPARE TO LIFT.

The logs, the trailers and tyres knelt on the grass and wrapped their hands around the load.

The ropes watched on.

We need one more, over here on the trailers, said an Officer.

The Sergeant looked at Daisy and grinned.

Daisy lowered his eyes.

C'mon, Private. Get your arse on that trailer.

Daisy dropped the rope, and went over to the trailers.

You'll be right, I said. Don't let 'em beat you.

Shut your mouth, said the Sergeant. Or you'll be next.

He blew his whistle a second time.

PREPARE TO LIFT… AND LIFT.

The trailers tilted on their axles. The tyres stood vertical, ready to roll, and the logs dug into shoulders and the soldiers grunted.

The life of a soldier, huh. We volunteered for this, don't forget get paid so *well* for it, too, said a voice in the ranks.

I laughed. A murderer would get less.

The whistle blew a third time.

PREPARE TO MOVE… AND MOVE.

We began marching. Left, right, then left a gain. The pace was slow. Every few steps I'd look at the hill getting closer and closer.

The more I looked, and the closer we got, the heavier the rope became.

OKAY. LET'S GET SERIOUS, said the Sergeant, blew the whistle and we broke into a double-time shuffle. My resolve crumbled.

I was facing discharge and didn't need this crap… I didn't need to be going out and chasing no ghosts, up and down a mountain— for whatever it was worth. The Army could shove the mountain up their regimented arse.

The pace was quick but once the incline sharpened, we slowed. The bitumen gave way to gravel. The logs. The trailers. The tyres and even the rope were getting heavier, and the regiment started bunching up. It got hotter in that tightening space and was harder to breathe.

C'MON, said the Sergeant. MAINTAIN THE SPACINGS… MAINTAIN THE PACE. And, for fuck's sake, KEEP IN STEP!

The regiment slowed. A soldier tripped, and the Sergeant snarled.

Fix your shit up, he said. If you can't handle it, then go join the Air Force.

It was Daisy that stumbled.

The trailer he was pushing skewed. The left wheel rolled backwards, downhill and over the Regimental 2IC's[116] toes.

Oh, you piece of *shit*, he said.

Sorry, Sir, said Daisy and bent over with his hands on his knees, then puked on the road.

---

116   Second in Command. Within a Regiments Order of Battle (ORBAT), the Commanding Officer (a Lieutenant Colonel) sits at the top of the tree. Directly subordinate to the Commanding Officer sits the Officer Commanding (a Major) who is in command of a Squadron, Company or Battery (Artillery). A Second in Command has a wider variety of applications. At a section level, a Lance Corporal will be subordinate to a Section Commander (Corporal). At the Company, Squadron, Battery level a Captain will be subordinate to an Officer Commanding. At a Regiment Headquarters level, a Second in Command may also be assigned to a CO, along with an Adjutant (Adj.) and an Executive Officer (XO.) All carry the rank of Major.

Get up, Private, said the 2IC. A real soldier knows how to hold his booze.

Daisy didn't answer. He wiped his mouth, regained the trailer and continued pushing uphill.

I passed him, with the rope hanging across my right shoulder. We rounded a bend in the road and the incline kicked up, steep. The heat was so intense that we were all drenched. Except for Daisy; he was bone dry but had a sickly gleam spread over his face.

The tough soldiers knew how to cope. All it took was a hard bite down. An imagination and a trip to another place.

The Regiment reached halfway, and the trailers had slowed to a slow crawl.

The Sergeant blew the whistle.

We'll halt here, he said, and the trailers completely stopped. The logs stopped. The ropes stopped, and the tyres toppled to the ground.

The Regiment[117] looked exhausted. The Sergeant had carried nothing but a whistle up the hill. He was fresh and bobbed up and down, whistling between the soldiers, singing:

The first Staff Officer jumped over the second Staff Officer's back.
The second Staff Officer jumped right over the first Staff Officer's back.
They were only playing leapfrog—

The whistle burst to life.
ON THE GROUND, DOWN.
The Regiment dropped.
PUSH-UP POSITION, READY.
I was slow to the ground.

---

117   A Regiment is comprised of several Squadrons (or Companies). A Squadron is comprised of several Troops. A Regiment will operate within a Brigade that is comprised of several Regiments of key, specific roles. Multiple Brigades form a Division to form a hierarchical Order of Battle (ORBAT).

A young soldier knelt beside me, then got on his hand and knees.

You're a wash-up, Patterson, he said, with his lip curling in a sneer.

The whistle blast again.

PREPARE TO LOWER AND… LOWER. RAISE. LOWER and… RAISE. Off the ground, UP.

I dusted off my hands, down the side of my trousers. They were wet with sweat.

Right, said the Sergeant. He stood on the hillside, whistle in mouth and hands on hips. There wasn't a lick of sweat or redness on his entire body. We're going to do a teams change. If you were on the ropes, witch with the trailer. Tyres and logs—swap.

The teams swapped.

Daisy left the trailer with some look of relief, but with no energy to raise the rope.

I stepped behind the trailer, with the young soldier to the front of me. He looked young, fit and fat veins pulsed out of his forearms. He looked back at me over his shoulder.

Don't fuck this up… you wash out.

RIGHT. LET'S GO, said the Sergeant.

We all lurched forward and pushed. The trailer's steel body was hot from the sun and began cooking the skin of my palms. There was a tear in its tarpaulin, wide enough for me to peek inside.

It was full of rocks.

FARK.

Shut up and push, old man, said the young soldier.

We tended towards a sharp bend in the road, then onto a nimble, downhill reprieve. The trailer rolled under its own stream. I took my hands away and ran behind, then jumped back on when the road kicked back into an incline.

There was still another four even five hundred meters to the peak.

PUSH, said the young soldier.

I am pushing. *You* push.

And he did. As did the rest of the team, except for me, I fell back and lost contact.

Weak as piss, said the young soldier.

He got down lower, then pushed the trailer harder and soon they were running uphill.

The tyres, the ropes, and even the logs were streaking away up the hill.

I looked downhill, and all I saw was Daisy, sucking in deep with his hands on knees.

I wondered what the hell's the matter with Daisy. Didn't he know, no matter what, you never come last in PT. Especially in Battle PT.

I *can't* keep up, Bubba.

The young soldier turned his head.

C'mon, princess, he said. We're almost at the top—

I put my right hand on Daisy's shoulder. His skin was boiling and in the direct sun had no chance of cooling down.

Listen, I said, jump back on the trailer to finish. That'll shut the knockers up.

We joined on at the back of the trailer, and I got down low and dug my shoulder into the trailer's side. My right cheek kissed, firm up against the green tarp. I could hear the rocks rolling around, crunching against each other, the trailer's steel sides sounding like a thunderstorm.

It was burning my skin, but I dug in my heels in on every stride up that hill eager to reach the top.

PUSH HARDER!

Fuck off, I said to the young soldier. This shit is NOT worth breaking your back over.

He growled, gutturally. Louder. He stamped his feet into the bitumen, straining against the trailer. The veins on his forearms were pulsing, and the veins on his forehead bulged. Blood trickled from his nose. He took a deep breath in, then pushed again, opening the bleeding, right up, until it gushed like a waterfall.

Hey, kid, are you alright?

Shut up, old man, he said and gnashed his teeth together and fresh blood spilt across his lips and soaked his gums.

Let him go, Bubba. These young ones don't wanna learn.

That pissed him off. He pushed harder, but the trailer jinked, causing his hands to slip. He fell and crashed face-first and unconscious into the road.

What happened here? said the Sergeant.

The young digger lay flat on his face with his body moving through a slow rise and fall.

The Sergeant rolled him onto his side.

Well? Isn't anybody gonna tell me what the hell happened?

Daisy found some shade and sat with his back against the trailer tyre. He took out a cigarette. Lit it, then looked at the Sergeant through the corner of his eye. Smoke drifted up and over the trailer.

Well?

Daisy smiled.

He pushed it too hard, Sergeant. Redlined… that's all.

The soldier came too. He rolled and panicked, then cried, and the Sergeant rubbed his back.

Calm down, he said. You took a tumble, that's all. You're going to be alright.

I sat beside Daisy and shared his cigarette. We were hurting but we were happy and, in a far-off land, a bearded man sat too, sharpening his knife beneath a cold candlelight—smiling too— while melting wax drips into the desert sands.

Just Another Day

Living in the Outback became easier with Charlie leading the way.

He taught me where to find water, when all the land was dry. Food, when the land was barren. What not to eat, when to walk, and when to sleep. Navigation without a compass. It was movement by the stars and the spirits that inhabit the land.

Charlie and I had so much to say, and plenty of time to say it. Most evenings, I sat still and listened. Charlie sat and listened too, to things I could never understand, nor hear. Things beneath the earth, above it, in the sky, and he'd move his eyes around and hear it all and know what it meant. Then, he'd sing a song in his own tongue and I'd hear that, but *this* morning it was quiet because Charlie was gone.

I stepped across the soft sand and climbed up on a red rock. Its hot, slate-like surface crackled and burned beneath my feet.

Stop and listen, Sher Gul.

It was one foot after the other, all the way North to Darwin. To Miriam and becoming an Australian Afghan, and a father. That's all I wanted. I strode across a narrow water crossing where the water trickled by, dark and brown.

I cupped my hands, shallow, in the soft flow of water. It was cool and soothing on the skin, and if it were any deeper, I may have dived in.

I took only short sips and swallowed in a rush. Sitting. Looking. Listening.

We're only visitors here—that's what Charlie would say— burdened with a sense that we did not belong. That was the Earth's quiet reminder that everywhere, in fact was a sacred place.

Sacred, hmmm.

A sharp wind blew as I stepped through the warm grey trunks of the paperbark trees. The wind carried a telling whistle as the leaves rustled, and the branches swayed, bent and groaned.

I turned my face towards the sky and peered through their canopy and up to the clear blue sheets of eternity. *Oh heaven.* There was nothing in this world that kept me grounded like those wild blue fields.

It left me feeling small. I was George Sher Gul, the Great Cameleer, incomparable to anything else except for that, which hung above.

The wind remained, but the calm blue weather turned itself on a dime. It could happen so fast in the Northern interior and, often it did. *So beautiful; so violent.*

Charlie taught me to chase the grey clouds. *There will always be food and endless water, George* he'd say, *so long as there's a rainbow.*

I tended North-Nor-West and traced the biggest, greyest cloud I could find.

The skies rumbled. Darkness was on the horizon, then the entire sky swung again. The thunder roared, and the heavens grumbled and the blue sky turned maleficent and black.

The trees grunted. It was beast-like, mad and wild.

I pinned my ears to the ground, listening for the sounds of danger or hint of footsteps through the trees.

The grunting continued, followed by deep guffawing yawns.

What the devil? I thought. That's a goddamn camel?

I bustled my way through the scrub and ran clear of the trees to where the thin canopy gave way to the long and irked spear grass. There she was.

Penny. *You bitch*, I cried, then fell at her feet and wrapped my arms around her long furry legs.

She groaned then reached down with her long neck and yellow teeth and chomped on my vest. I fell to the ground and laughed.

I sat with Penny, masked by the spear grass, and grazed on pistachio seeds. I fed some to Penny too until there were only ten seeds left. I tucked them away and laid down to rest.

I awoke at dusk. The wind had quietened, and the air was cold. Fat happy mosquitos buzzed about, landing on my face and on my arms, digging in with their tiny mouths and sucking out my blood.

I slapped at them all—one, two, three and then a fourth—spreading blotches of blood and dead insect across my arm.

It itched and I spat a glob of spit onto my arm and rubbed it in as the trees rustled and soft, wet twigs cracked.

I reached for Stu's rifle and opened the chamber. There was only one round left, and I slid the bolt forward, silent and slow.

My arm continued to itch, but both my hands gripped so tight it was impossible to scratch. *Hell.*

Then came that wild bushy laugh, careening through the bush.

You thought you could do it, Sher Gul, said the voice.

I didn't say a word. He laughed.

You really thought you could take me for a fool.

I lowered the rifle.

How'd you find me?

Finding you was easy, catching you napping was the hard part, but I got you because I know this bush better than any man.

Oh?

Plus, all I had to do was follow that dopey camel of yours. She led me right to you.

I turned to Penny. She was chewing on a spear of grass, then lifted head and groaned.

You *bitch*, I said, then slapped her on the mouth.

We made camp for the night; me, Stu and Penny beneath the cover of a drooping Boab tree.

Stu got a small fire going and I prepared some billy tea.

I could shoot you right now, I said.

Stu laughed.

Well, he said, I could shoot you too. Only difference is, they'd come looking for me—but you? Out here, you're no better than a coon.

I lowered my eyes and worried about the tea.

The skies grumbled, and the storm clouds roared with treats of lightning and rain that did not come. Then the moon arrived and blew all those mad storm clouds away.

Tomorrow would be just another day.

No Other Way

I led Penny out through the scrub and to the North where the spear grass, Boab and paperbarks gave way to the stock paths and bullock-backed cut roads.

Stu followed on horseback. He smiled and sung, sober like a clown, going:

Too-ra-lie, oo-ra-lie, addity, singing Too-ra-lie, oo-ra-lie, ai.

All with his freshly stuffed pipe hanging limp from the tip of his lips.

Neither of us said a word to one another. I could have shot him, of course. Between the eyes. In the back; even in the gut. Yet, for some reason, I handed the Bossman's rifle back to him.

He sat back in his saddle and stuffed that rifle back in its sheath.

He didn't even say thank you, but it was his rifle, after all.

The sky hung unsettled, interchanging between blue and grey, from grey to green, and often even black.

There were no rainbows in sight.

Better get a move on, said Stu. He removed his hat, and swatted at the buzzards of flies, trying to feast on his sweaty brow. He wiped his face with his shirtsleeve then looked at the dark, rolling clouds and drank from his hip flask as tiny rain droplets softly pelted down.

Where?

North, still, but where the path won't turn to bog.

We looked around. It was the same umber dirt and sunburnt thickets of grass for miles and miles.

This rain, and whatever mud we pass, won't stop Penny, Bossman.

I'm not worried about your damn Penny, he said, then spurred his heels into his horse's rump and rode ahead.

Daylight was fading beneath the tired grumbling of the ever-growing storm clouds.

We stopped at the edge of a tall riverbank. There was a cutting where man and horse could each traverse to the far banks of the river.

Stu dropped his swag on a cleared patch of brown dirt.

We'll camp here, he said, looking at the skies. It's getting too dark, and I can't see a damned thing.

Then he climbed down from his horse and, like clockwork, packed his pipe.

We oughta cross, now, I said, tasting the freshly squeezed raindrops as they touched down on the end of my tongue. When that rain comes down, it's going to come down hard then we'll never get across.

Rubbish, he said, there is no river I cannot cross. Hell, I bet I've had more river crossings than you've had hot mugs of tea, Georgie Boy.

Stu struck a match and stuck it in his pipe.

I thought that pipe was burnt in a campfire.

I good Bushman always carries a spare, he said, then blew out a long puff of smoke.

I let Penny wander for the evening.

She went meandering along the banks of the winding river's edge. I sat back and watched her sweeping her long nose across the ground, both ignorant and happy. She was tearing at bits of green growth and kicking at the dirt. Then lifting her head high and chomping away with her ragged yellow teeth. It made me laugh, and it made me hungry.

I took a long branch and snapped it over my thigh. Then I started grating the tip across a flat river rock, sharpening it to a point.

What are you doing? said Stu.

I'm sharpening this branch, so that I can dig and so that I can eat.

Eat? There's nothing out here to eat except that crap the natives eat.

Exactly, I said and dabbed my finger on the pointed end of the branch.

Crikey, said Stu, and laid in his swag, pulling the canvas cover over his face and hiding it from the rain.

The skies were opening wide. To the East, a great wall of rain came rolling across the Outback terrain. It sounded like an avalanche and brought the river came to life.

I crawled down into the riverbed with my stick and dug into the mud.

First, I clawed out a fat, white grub. It was long and pale, but fleshy. I opened my mouth and swallowed it whole.

Are you sure you're not hungry, Bossman?

Let me know if you find any mullet, or bream. Otherwise, I don't bloody well want to know what it is you're trying to eat.

Suit yourself, I said and continued digging away.

At some stage, he would have to eat… hell, we all had to eat.

River Deep

The rain moved in, thick and fast, and fell harder than a granite slab. It spooked the hell out of Penny. She grunted and groaned then stomped and kicked her hooves high into the air.

Calm that thing down, before she tramples the camp and gets one of us killed.

I didn't say a word and watched the Bossman run for cover beneath the canopy of a wilting acacia tree.

I didn't bother moving. I was already wet. Plus, Penny had bolted again.

Get in from the rain, else you might catch the sickness.

The sickness? What? No, I've got to find her.

Let that mad camel bleeding well run. She's too stupid to get very far.

I thought about that for a moment and stepped towards the river's edge. The banks were soft, and the once dusty river dirt clumped around my ankles into a muddy mess.

I tell you what, Bossman, I said, looking down at the rising rapid churning over the river's once gentle bed. We shoulda crossed when we had the chance.

Bollocks, said Stu.

He'd bunkered down beneath the thin cover of the acacia, but now had a canvas blanket draped over his shoulders as the rain fell hard.

He kicked the tree's stump. Its branches bowed then rattled. The water drooped and dripped through the paper-thin canopy and landed on his head. He hunched over and sucked on his pipe, in the faint hope of bringing it back to life.

This water is rising, Bossman. What do you want do?

Nothing. It's a river, he said puffing hard on his half-lit pipe. That's what rivers do—they rise or fall, but it'll be gone by morning.

And what if it doesn't?

Then it doesn't. We'll find a way across.

The rain abated, and Stu left his useless shelter and trudged through the mud right up to the river's edge.

Crikey, he said, and looked down at the wild rapids slapping over the river bank.

His pipe was cold, and he pressed the tobacco down, firm with the butt of his thumb, then struck a match.

I walked away and whistled, again, for Penny.

I wandered out towards the edge of the scrub.

PENNY.

Ahh, forget about her, said Stu, snapping off a long, dead tree branch. She'll come back, I'll tell yer, but in the meantime… I need your help to find some way across here.

Hell no, I said, moving as far back from the river as I could. I'm not going anywhere near that water.

Why, he said. You scared?

No, I'm not scared of anything; it's just that… well… I can't swim.

Ahhh horseshit. That's not stopped anyone before, and it won't stop anyone now.

I followed Stu to a spot where the river turned and the water swirled, mad like the ocean.

This looks like a good place to cross. What do yer reckon?

I stayed silent.

He prodded the branch deep in the water and it bent and flexed beneath the pressure of the current. Then he removed the stick. A clump of grey, brown mud stuck to the end and Stu waved it before my eyes.

See, he said, it isn't even that deep.

After you, then, I said and stood and watched as Stu put one boot in the water. And then the next.

He reached a point where the water was only knee deep. He leant forward with his long and muddied stick and reached further out into the current.

I had to turn away; I couldn't watch.

Stu kept moving, and soon the water washed around his armpits.

He stood tall and slapped at the rapid with his hands until the water splashed across his face.

You're much braver than you are smart, I said and knelt and reached into the current and cupped it with my hands.

Just step in, George.

He prodded with the branch again, further out into the stream, then took another step.

His shoulders were the first to go under. He stopped and turned and tried to retreat, but it was all too late, and the whites of his eyes were the last thing I saw.

I froze at the river's edge and looked for the Bossman's head to re-emerge. The current continued to roar, and chunks of tree-trunk and deadwood washed its way downstream. The deadwood made it look all so easy.

Stu didn't put up a fight either, now… he was as good as dead.

I turned and whistled again for Penny… she returned as Stu predicted, so I took her by the reign and led her to the Bossman's horse.

She grunted and groaned, and the horse pinned its ears back tight. Then it dragged its front hooves across the dirt and swished its tail.

I ignored the pair of them and tethered the horse's lead to Penny's saddle, then I slapped the camel on the rump. The two, I hoped, would get along.

The river flowed West, and somewhere down along the river's grumbling bends lay Stu's body. I faced the East and yanked on Penny's lead.

Penny did not move, and lulled her furry neck and flapped her long, luscious eyelids.

HOOSHTA, you bitch, I said and slapped her on the mouth.

She didn't move. Stu's horse dug her heels in and lowered her sullen head then wobbled her gums before peering West.

No, no, no, I said, tugging on Penny's lead. We're going East.

Penny and the horse would not move.

I'm not going that way, I said. There's nothing out West but sand and death.

We headed West and traversed along the river's edge. Penny and the horse happily followed, and we moved slowly past a dead stringy bark. Past a bullock cart (it had no wheels), and past a dead eucalypt. It was grey, hollow at the base, and its grain was sinewy and harsh. It was also home to a hawk that sat high in the tree, preening its wings and waiting for something to eat.

I ignored the bird and continued West.

We were still a long way from home.

A Glimmer of Life

The river quietened as it neared its end.

Stu's horse stopped when she saw his body lying limp and lifeless in the crooked riverbank.

I knelt and looked down at his pale, cold skin. His lips were blue.

There was a length of deadwood pinning his body against the muddy riverbank. I thought he was dead. In fact, I thought he was definitely dead, and I'd never seen a body look more dead outside of a timber box. But his left fingers fumbled and there was a wisp of air that passed through his lips.

God damn it, I said, he's trying to claw his way up the bank.

I climbed down the bank and looped a length of hemp rope around his chest. I'd tied the far end to Penny, and when I clapped my hands, she dragged him out.

He lay flat, and still on his back, and there was a soft rise, followed by a shallow fall of his chest.

No man can survive these wild rivers like that.

I hoisted his body onto his horse and across the saddle. Then I slapped the horse on her rump, and we all continued West.

Two Fat Majors

It was my last Monday in the Army, and man, didn't it come with a blast.

Before first parade, the Troop Sergeant ordered me up to HQ.

Aww hell, I thought, that place was always swarming with Officers, and since the war began their numbers only swelled.

Most of these Officers loiter around the boss's front door and fight over who'd be the next to carry in a hot brew, drive him to the mess, or even pick up his daughters after school. Complete brown-nosing to get their name on that illustrious next big gig to Afghanistan, Timor, Sudan and or anywhere that could bump up their next pay day. The harsh truth? Many never got to leave the Barracks, they stayed safe at home, but that also made them happy, because they could keep the boss happy, and their names front of mind.

Two fat Majors leant over the orderly room photocopier. They sipped their coffee and joked about what subaltern they were planning to fuck over next.

That's a marvellous idea, Bill, said one Major to the next, but won't that create a trail which leads right back to us?

No-ho-ho-ho, laughed the other. We're Majors, remember.

Nothing sticks to us—it's the *Lieuy's* who'll get caked in shit. Which… may I add… is a problem not belonging to us.

Both Majors smiled and continued sipping at their coffee. And the orderly room clerk? Well, he hid behind his desk, pretending not to hear a word.

I ignored the two fat Majors and continued through HQ until I'd reached the boss's door.

I knocked three times.

I've already had two fucking coffees this morning, and… if I have another, I'm going to shit my pants, and I'm too busy for that, so… FUCK OFF and leave me alone.

It's Private Patterson, Sir. You requested to see me?

Who?

Formerly Corporal Patterson, Sir.

Oh, you. Hurry it up and get in here.

I walked in and came to a stomping halt, then threw up a stiff boxer.

The boss stood, then turned his back and looked out the window.

Outside, an entire infantry Battalion formed up on the football oval. They'd turned the whole thing into a giant parade ground and were marching up and down.

FIX UP THE DRESSING, ordered the 6th Battalion Regiment Sergeant Major[118] with a bark so loud the HQ windows rattled and threatened to shatter.

---

118   Technically a Regiment, all main Australian Infantry Units are referred to as Battalions, and although they effectively fall under their own Command structures, they all belong to the Royal Australian Regiment. In total, there are 7 Battalions—each carrying out various roles.

The Regimental Sergeant Major (RSM) maintains the discipline and welfare of the Regiment's soldiers. Traditionally, he or she will carry with them an aura of authority, which in military terms translates to fear.

Damn grunts, said the boss, and pulled the shades down.

Private Patterson. Do you know why you're in here?

I haven't got the foggiest, Sir.

Have you thought about what you might do now that your career here is over?

I've thought about joining the circus, Sir. I've already got experience.

The boss didn't answer, and simply tapped his knuckles across the office desk.

BY THE RIGHT… RIGHT TURN, ordered the Sergeant Major. COME ON, FIX UP THE DRESS. QUICK MARCH… DON'T ANTICIPATE MY WORDS OF COMMAND, AND… HALT.

The boss's shoulders shuddered.

I don't won't you around my troops anymore. I'm afraid of the influence you're having on the new guys, and that's a risk I can't afford.

Should I just go home?

No *bloody* way. The Regiment is still paying you, and I intend to squeeze every single last bleeding drop out of you.

What'll I do then, Sir?

The Troop Sergeant has work for you. After you're dismissed, go see him. Understand?

Yes, Sir.

Good, now get the hell out of my office… this morning's coffee is running through me like a harsh dose of salts, and I'm afraid I won't make it through to lunch.

Roger that, Sir, I said and threw up another boxer, then turned and left the room.

The two fat Majors were still talking over the photocopier. Their coffees were still hot, and the clerk still hid behind his desk. He was still pretending not to hear a word.

It was all just another day in the Army.

THE LAST LEG

All that stood between me, Darwin and Miriam was the mud, the bog and the rain.

That rain. It never stopped. It never slowed, and it damn well never took a break.

Penny and Stu's horse moved slow. Slower than the mud could swallow the rains. The constant wet was eating me alive.

I held my compass prism to the horizon but failed to take a reading.

My mind was fading: I could pack it all in now. Leave Stu. Again. Leave the horse. And leave Penny. She was tough and would survive. But one look into Stu's eyes told me he would not last a single minute alone. Not in his state.

His skin was a deathly grey with eyes sunken deep and a pulse that beat slower than an earthworm. There was no way I could leave him alone out here to die—that wasn't the Pashtun Wali way. Miriam would scorn me and my soul would rot away.

I looked deep into Stu's eyes, one more time, searching for a faint glimmer, or a sparkle.

Nothing. I touched his hand.

All I wanted was to be a father.

It was coming on dusk, and I found shelter beneath the cover of a bustling Boab tree. Its leaves and limbs were alive with the heavy pattering of rain. And the soil at its base was the driest I'd seen in days.

I lowered Stu onto the ground, then laid him on his back.

His breath was weak and his heartbeat weaker.

He tried to speak, so I put my ear to his lips.

Kill me, George… just roll me over and pull the bloody trigger.

I'll do no such thing, I said, then reached inside my pocket and pulled out my last three pistachio seeds.

It's not much, Bossman. But it's all I've got to eat.

I peeled the seeds, then crushed them between a rock and the base of a billy tin.

I'd ground the seeds into tiny crumbs. It looked no better than paltry feed and collected bites of charcoal from the base of the billy tin.

Stu would hardly notice; besides… it was all we had to eat, and he was dying fast and would have to down it either way.

I fed it into his mouth, on the tip of the spoon.

Just swallow, Stu… you'll feel better in no time.

Stu closed his mouth and chewed.

His eyes screwed up, and his lips pursed, and then he spat the pistachio out.

You trying to poison me, or what?

That was perfectly good food!

I uncapped the canteen and poured a sip of water into Stu's mouth.

He swallowed then his face softened.

You're going to be alright, Stu… you're going to be alright.

A line of green ants circled out from a hole between the Boab tree roots and scuttled towards the pistachio. Several ants hoisted the crushed seeds onto their backs and crawled back into their hole.

All the pistachio was gone. The rain continued to fall, and Stu and I both fell asleep.

I was up at first light and whistled for Penny.

She slowly came loping in from the rain, and I fastened her harness tight as she pined for food.

Where am I? said Stu.

It surprised me to see him up, almost finding some strength from deep inside to drag himself off the canvas. He was a tough mongrel.

You're still in the bush, Bossman. Another day's walk and we'll be back in Darwin again.

Okay, he said and rested his eyes, almost in resignation that he would—in fact—make it home.

For me, Penny and the horse, it wouldn't be so easy. The rain continued to pour. The mud continued to bog and clump up thicker than wet cement and leeched onto my tired limbs. Only to dry out, hard, and seize what little mobility I had left.

I'd stashed a pile of firewood beneath the shelter of the Boab tree, hoping it'd dry out overnight. It did not, and my tea leaves remained inside my billy tin and I sat and watched the rain pour, pour and pour.

Where's my pipe? said Stu.

I opened Stu's saddle bag and removed his tobacco pouch. I pinched out a thumb-sized clump of the stringy fibres. Then I pressed them inside his pipe before placing the tip of the pipe between my lips. It was cold and sticky and smelt like an old drover's boot. I struck a match and lit the tobacco—like I'd seen Stu do so many times before and inhaled a small puff of smoke. It tasted worse than it smelt. I coughed and wheezed, then jammed the pipe into Stu's mouth.

Why would anyone wish to taste such a thing?

I could think of worse things to put in my mouth, said Stu.

Stu grimaced as I slung his near lifeless body across the saddle.

I fastened the stirrups around his cold and feeble hands. He grabbed me by the wrist and squeezed. The grip was faint, but he still found the strength to roll his head left and glance my way.

I know I've been a miserable old bastard, but you saved my life. Thank you, George Sher Gul.

Think nothing of it, I said and took Penny by her lead.

George.

Yes, Bossman.

You really are a great cameleer.

I know… I really know.

Then Penny took her first steps, out into the mud, and the bog and the rain—without faltering. Stu's horse followed too. We were on the last leg home.

Sylvia Speaking

Daisy became a ghost after vanishing overnight. One minute he was there, and the next he was not. The last I'd heard of him was a crazed story about him living in the back of a van along the coast of Mexico: Daisy, a dark-skinned girl and a surfboard; or so the story goes.

No one believed that much of it. But I knew Daisy better than anyone and unwrapped a cube of Hubba Bubba as a quiet salute to a genuine mad man. There were few too many of his kind left in this world, and to him I say see you around the bend, old friend.

The Troop Sergeant assigned me some mundane tasks to get me out of the way.

I was happy to go along and made my way up to the abandoned transport yard.

The task was to clear out all the weeds, and to see if I couldn't get any of the unserviceable Land Rovers started.

Why, I didn't care to ask, but when I approached the yard, I saw that it was far too great a task. Weeds and vines overgrew the fence, and the padlock to the gate had rusted shut.

I squeezed through the gate. There were two Land Rovers

parked inside. One had no wheels, while the other had fallen completely apart.

To the far side of the yard was another fence. It separated the yard from the footy oval. There, the Infantry Battalion continued with their drill.

HOW MANY FUCKING TIMES DO I HAVE TO SAY IT. FIX UP THE FUCKING DRESSING, YOU USELESS PACK OF CUNTS, said their Sergeant Major. THE NEXT BLOKE THAT MUCKS THIS UP, I'M GOING TO STAB THEM WITH MY PACE STICK. UNDERSTAND?

YES, SIR.

GOOD, THEN LET'S GET THIS SHIT SQUARED AWAY. WE'LL STAY OUT HERE ALL WEEKEND, IF WE HAVE TO. UNDERSTAND?

YES, SIR.

GOOD. BY THE LEFT. OH, FOR FUCKS SAKE.

I climbed into the rear tray of a Land Rover. I wasn't going to miss this, that's for sure. Inside was an old newspaper and a magazine with the centrefold page spread wide open.

I unlocked my phone to read the news.

The first headline read:

Labor Government Announces Australia's Withdrawal from Afghanistan.

I opened the article.

The Defence Minister, Stephen Smith today announced the withdraw of Australian troops from Afghanistan.
Australia has been in that war-torn country, far too long, said Minister Smith—

I closed the article.

Far too long?

I found Sylvia's number.

Fuck it, I thought, and dialled.

The phone rang out. I dialled again.

First, I heard a baby crying in the background, then a voice.

Hello, this is Sylvia's phone; this is Sylvia speaking. Hello… hello… who is this?

Suddenly, I didn't have the guts, nor the heart to speak and I hung up. Put the phone away then picked up the magazine.

The centrefold had long wavy blonde hair and nipples like raspberries.

I unzipped my pants, stroked it for a moment, and five minutes later… I was asleep.

You Are Sher Gul?

We arrived in Darwin moments before nightfall. The town was quiet, and the streets wrung wet from the endless rain. Stu's bruised body clung on, his breathing rattling.

Hang on just a little longer, Bossman, I said and opened the canteen and dripped water into his mouth.

He didn't have the strength to swallow, and the water dribbled out, down the side of his chin, then dripped onto the ground.

A man stood hunched on his front lawn, his skin wrinkled by time and toned bronze by the mad Australian sun. He strode, slow towards a row of blooming red poppies with a rusted pair of secateurs in one hand and moved to prune the wilting canes.

I approached the garden fence.

Hello. The town's so quiet, I said. Where is everybody?

The man raised his head with jaw wide open, and for a moment, he didn't say a word. Then he looked at Penny, the horse, and finally up at Stu.

The war, he said finally. The war. Everyone, and anyone who isn't going, is down at the harbour saying goodbye.

Oh, I said, and the man turned and hurriedly walked inside his home, and locked the door behind him.

I headed for the old homestead, the place where I'd first met Stu. Someone there could help him.

I lowered his body onto the front porch and knocked on the door.

A house maid answered.

Mister Stu, she said and dropped to her knees. What happened?

He fell into a flooded river, two days South of here, Miss. I told him not to cross, but he would not listen, and now he's barely spoken a word since. I sure hope he survives—

The maid pinched the tips of Stu's fingers. They turned white, then back to red.

It doesn't look good, she said, but let's see what I can do.

I carried Stu inside and the maid led me to a room where she pulled back the covers on a tired-looking bed.

Put him down here, she said, and I'll fetch some blankets and water.

Did the Afghani come through here? I asked.

Oh, yes, said the maid, but they've all gone home now. And those who haven't… well, they're trying to enlist. A slim chance, might I add.

And Miriam?

The maid froze.

What's your name?

George, Miss. George Sher Gul.

Oh, she said, looking down at the floorboards. You're Sher Gul?

Yes, Miss.

The maid turned my way. Her cheeks were blushing bright poppy red.

I'm under strict instructions from Father McCullough, not to utter a word but Miriam was sure you'd come by this way.

I put my head in my hands and tears streamed from my eyes.

Come with me, said the maid and we walked back out onto the porch. You see that road over there?

Yes.

Follow it… for a day or two… all the way to the end. There's another homestead there.

Thank you, I said and stepped off the porch.

And George—

Yes?

Don't mention meeting me.

I smiled at the maid, then took Penny by the lead and left the homestead.

A House of God

I walked through the night and long into the morning where the sun rose, red hot and blazing over a small rundown homestead.

I banged on the door, then waited.

No one answered. I walked around the yard, through the overgrown fireweed which plagued the property. Then into a flourishing vegetable garden. It must've stretched for fifty yards.

A habit-wearing nun crouched over a garden bed. She was humming cheerfully. She was lost in the sound as she pulled weeds from between the carrots, the broccoli and the squash and wiped her brow as the weeds piled high.

I coughed; she turned.

Shoo! Go! Get away… scram, you dirty old man, she said and threw down her trowel. This is a house of *God*.

I'm looking for a woman please.

Sweet Mother Mary, she said, this is neither the time nor the place.

Then she picked up a steel garden rake. You'd better leave before Father McCullough awakens. He's a violent one in the morning and does not fool about.

Miriam is her name. I heard she is here?

The nun raised the spade above her head and waved it about.

There's no one here who goes by that name. Now LEAVE.

I left, via the side of the homestead and down an overgrown footpath. Above me, wooden-panel window boards hinged open. A blood-stained bedsheet hung over the sill and the sound of a newborn wailed from inside.

I poked my head through the window. A nun sat in a wooden chair. She was feeding the newborn through the teat of a glass bottle. No other women were in sight.

I moved to the next room. There were rows of beds lining each side. The beds were empty, except two; one smelt of rosemary.

Miriam, I said and climbed through the window.

She stood, barefoot, at the end of her bed, wearing nothing but a brown dress.

Christ… you scared the shit out of me.

She turned her back and started stuffing clothing and baby items into a canvas sack. There was a pair of red baby bottoms. Slippers. Glass bottles. A wooden rattle and a white, silk muslin.

What are you are doing here?

There was scornful tone in her voice.

I had to see you. I just *had* to, don't you understand?

George. They're going to take my baby away. If I don't get out of here tonight, I'll never see her again.

I have a daughter?

The loud sound of boots came marching down the hall.

Quick, George. That's the Father… you have to go… NOW.

I climbed through the window. Hung my legs over the ledge, then turned to Miriam.

Where will you take her?

She pulled the sack chord tight and pushed it beneath the bed.

Somewhere not even God will find her.

Miriam smiled then came to the window.

I handed her my compass. It had meant so little to me, when arriving, but now it meant the world.

That's so you'll always be able to find me—

Miriam tucked the compass inside her dress pocket.

I kissed her on the forehead, then jumped down onto the footpath.

Off to Fight the Boer

I left the homestead, happy that I'd seen my Miriam again and reached the Darwin wharves the following morning.

A small Naval ship docked in the harbour, and a young soldier rode around on horseback. The horse was tall and red, and it snarled through its nostrils and swished its tail.

Australians to the front of the boat… everyone else to the rear, he barked.

The Australian soldiers lined up before the gangway.[119] They were dressed neatly in their khakis with feathered plumes jutting out from their fur-felt hats.

To the rear, a group of Aboriginal men huddled around a pile of military uniforms. They burrowed through the pile, hunting for any uniform which fit.

Three Afghani sat in the far corner of the docks. They had no uniforms at all, but prepared to board—with, or without a uniform.

I searched around for Mahmout, but he was nowhere in sight.

Two ladies passed by me. They were each wearing bright pastel sundresses and held umbrella shades above their heads.

---

119   The author notes that it may not be historically correct that Australian soldiers ever departed from Darwin en route to South Africa.

Where is this ship heading? I asked.

It's off to fight the Boer, said one lady. I think it's so brave, what those men are doing.

I think it's horrible what's happening to the Boer, said the second. No human deserves that kind of treatment.

The ladies continued walking. I looked up at the sky. It was bright and blue, but to the North, across the harbour, those grey rain clouds were building again.

I looked at the soldiers. They were happy and proud, and they were ready for duty, come rain, hail or shine.

I tied Penny to a water trough, inside the loading pen, patted her nose, then walked to the Afghani alone and prepared to board the ship.

A Family Heirloom

It was a Monday, or a Tuesday. I can't remember, but I was at a family funeral.

I didn't know the passed relative that well, nor many in attendance. Still, a man came up to me and introduced himself to me as an uncle. He'd heard about my service and exclaimed that the family was somewhat proud before handing me a small leather pouch.

Perhaps you'll appreciate this, more than anybody else.

Thank you.

I smiled and took the pouch.

It was an old brass compass. The prism was cracked, and impossible to view through and the casing looked like it'd been buried beneath a century's worth of clay.

That was your Great, Great Grandfathers, the late George Sher Gul. At one stage… I believe… it was the only thing that kept him alive.

Really?

I then raised the open compass, levelling it in my left palm. The needle spun wild and refused to settle on any cardinal.

I looked at my uncle, who simply shrugged, then smiled.

Later in the afternoon. I crashed on the lounge and flicked on the news.

Tom Brady was being interviewed after a game.

So, Tom, how does the body feel?

The body feels good. I'm definitely fit, and I'm definitely healthy.

No immediate plans for retirement?

Right now, it's the furthest thing from my mind.

I changed the channel.

A man was falling from the wing of a soaring C-17 as it launched from an Afghan airfield. The man let go and his body crashed into the tarmac. It must have been a two, three-hundred-meter fall.

This news just in, said the anchor. Correspondents in Kabul have reported the Taliban captured the city overnight. Plans to evacuate all foreign nationals are now underway.

After twenty years of occupation, and with the click of a remote, the world's largest terrorist organisation was pillaging through Kabul city. It now belonged to the Taliban—just like that.

I turned off the television. Outside, the world had gone insane. Everybody was Einstein and everybody was dumb.

We were all ready to tear one another apart as the world sat on the precipice of whatever war would happen next. But it was clear, to me, that the time was almost near—

War is a Racket

War is just a racket. A racket is best described, I believe, as something that is not what it seems to the majority of people. Only a small inside group knows what it is about. It is conducted for the benefit of the very few at the expense of the masses.

—General Smedley D. Butler

11 September 2001 is a date that'll remain etched into our psyche's forever.

The world's retaliation to that incident was at an unprecedented and almost unobstructed scale. But was it justified or legal? Who's to question or determine that?

For Australia, 9/11 was the catalyst to our longest war ever. One in which Prime Minister Howard had zero qualms in signing up for. After all, he and his cronies did not have to go and physically do anything. The country lost forty-one sons, brothers, fathers, uncles and best friends. Yet, the losses did not end there, because it's impossible not to bring a war, like the Afghan War, home.

Estimates have ranged around eighty plus suicides from returned soldiers per year since 2007.[xviii] And those names of the men and women whose lives we lost back on the home front will never appear—individually—on any official memorial. And that's a shame. They did their job and they've earned their place. May they Rest In Peace.

The US and coalition forces, like the UK, lost many thousands more, and their numbers continue to rise. War is a serious game that does not stop when the full-time whistle's blown.

Fiscally, the publicised cost of fighting 'terror' trends north of $14 trillion dollars.[xix] Yes, freedom is NOT free, but what often gets overlooked is where that $14 trillion went.

It isn't ironic—not to me—that at least fifty percent of that $14 trillion found its way back home to American corporation warring coffers, aka, the Military Industrial Complex. What is ironic is that members of the US Congress also benefited from personal and financial investments into these corporations.

I'll ask it again: was the war on terror justified? Is any war justified?

It's a question that hangs on the lips of anyone that has the courage to ask it. To wonder what really happens when the cameras aren't watching.

And we could do worse than tying our nation's leaders to the railroad tracks until they hand over a definitive answer. Why? Because they view war as nothing more than a racket. The rest is in our hands, and on our heads.

ACKNOWLEDGEMENTS

In total, I spent fifteen years in the Australian Army. Throughout that time, for ill, or goodwill, I was shaped and influenced by many personalities. Without their impact on my life, this book would have never been written.

I would like to thank, Max Bondi and Davery for their input and guidance in crafting this novel. And, it would not be fitting if I ignored the time my editor, EG dedicated to steering *Afghani* into the story that sits before you.

And finally, to my Great Great Grandfather, the late george Sher Gul. A pioneer of the Australian Outback, and the man behind this story.

As with many novels based in historical fiction, many sources are relied upon, for both accuracy and context. The following sources were used in *Afghani*:

Endnotes

i   Obsession With Sykes-Picot Says More About What We Think of Arabs Than History. The Australian Institute of International Affairs.

ii   Robert Fisk: The Great War for Civilisation

iii   Secret Files: US Officials aided Gaddafi. Aljazeera.

iv   Reuters

v   Razing the Truth About Sanctions Against Iraq. Geneva International Centre for Justice.

vi   Costs of War. Watson.Brown.edu

vii   Craig Whitlock. The Afghanistan Papers.

viii   The Atlantic Council

ix   The Afghanistan Papers: The Grand Illusion. Craig Whitlock

x   The Council on Foreign Relation: Obama's Final Drone Strike Data.

xi   The Afghanistan Papers: Trump's Turn. Craig Whitlock.

xii   Geoscience Australia.

xiii   The Australian Institute of Family Studies.

xiv   The Importance of Land. Sharingculture.info

xv   Australian National University.

xvi   The University of Western Australia.

xvii   Dadirri.org.au

xviii   The Royal Commission into Veteran Suicide.

xix   Corporate Power and Profiteering. Costs of War. Watson.brown.edu

About the Author

Brendon Patrick is an emerging voice in the world of historical fiction. In writing, he skilfully crafts narratives that bridge cultural divides and the often-overlooked histories in Australian communities.

His debut novel, *Afghani*, draws upon his experiences as a soldier and a descendant of Afghan Cameleers. Throughout the novel, he weaves together personal stories with rich historical context.

Through his compelling storytelling, Brendon offers a unique perspective. He intertwines his personal heritage with broader historical narratives, allows readers to connect with the past in profound ways, and offers a fresh perspective on history. He's quickly gaining recognition as an Australian Historical Fiction Author.

His words promise to inspire and engage audiences who seek to explore the complexities of identity and history.

www.ingramcontent.com/pod-product-compliance
Lightning Source LLC
Chambersburg PA
CBHW050958180726
48291CB00006B/1889